A TWIST OF FATE

Joanna Rees

WINDSOR

PARAGON

First published 2012
by Pan Books
This Large Print edition published 2013
by AudioGO Ltd
by arrangement with
Pan Macmillan Ltd

Hardcover ISBN: 978 1 4713 2032 3
Softcover ISBN: 978 1 4713 2033 0

British Library Cataloguing in Publication Data available

GW 2920238 8

Printed and bound in Great Britain by
MPG Books Group Limited

For my sister, Catherine

ACKNOWLEDGEMENTS

This has been such a fun project to work on from the very start. Many thanks go to the team at Macmillan, but most especially to my brilliant publisher, Wayne Brookes, whose faith in me made this book happen. Thanks also to my wonderful agents at Curtis Brown, Vivienne Schuster, Felicity Blunt and Katie McGowan. Also, my thanks to Katy Whelan for all her help, and to Toni Savage and Sara Sims. A huge thank you to my three amazing girls and my ever-supportive husband, Emlyn Rees—I couldn't have finished without you. And lastly, my heartfelt thanks go to you, my readers.

EAST GERMANY, 1971

The grubby white Trabant pulled to a stop in the forest, the shuddering brakes sending a flurry of birds screeching into the night sky. When the noisy engine cut, a cloak of inky silence descended once again.

Inside the car, Sebastian Trost kept the lights on, illuminating the frozen track ahead, which disappeared deeper into the forest. There was no moon tonight and a light snow had started to fall.

Sebastian had hunted here with his father as a boy and knew this seldom-used route to the outskirts of Schwedt on the Polish border well, but in the dark the familiar woods felt hostile and he wished again that he was back home in his apartment.

He cupped his hands and blew on them, trying to get some warmth into them after the long drive, then stole another glance in the rear-view mirror.

Volkmar, his boss, sat behind him with his hat pulled down low. Sebastian had heard whispered stories at the steel factory where he worked about how Volkmar's family had been imprisoned and tortured by the Stasi, and that Volkmar himself had been born in jail. His face was thin and rat-like. The face of a man who would do whatever it took to get by.

Sebastian had only been Volkmar's driver for two weeks—recruited against his will after he'd witnessed Volkmar stabbing a man in the loading dock at the steel works. Sebastian, fearing for his own life, had looked the other way. He knew the

1

score only too well. If he kept his mouth shut, then his family would live.

Sebastian sparked up a cigarette, trying to cover up his shaking hands. He glanced in the rear-view mirror again, this time looking down towards Volkmar's right.

On the back seat next to Volkmar was a bread crate containing two sleeping babies, each one bundled up in a crudely knitted blanket. With a stab of guilt, Sebastian wondered how long it would take his wife, Martina, to notice that those precious blankets had gone. He remembered his own sons and how they'd been wrapped in those very blankets as babies.

'Where the hell is Solya's man? He should have been here,' Volkmar said, checking his watch, before taking a pistol from inside his coat pocket and weighing it in his hand.

Solya.

The most feared man around. Even to know his name would mean a brutal execution for Sebastian and his family at the hands of the Stasi.

Sebastian forced the thought away. Instead, he thought of Martina at home and the rabbit stew she had prepared for him. He tried to imagine sleeping beneath the fur throw on their hard bunk later on, his hand cupped around her ample breast. How he'd match his breathing to hers. How he'd never tell her that he'd come here tonight. Or why.

But try as he might to think of other things, the same questions kept queuing up in Sebastian's head, as he stared out into the tunnel of snow. Where were the babies from? Who were their mothers? How had Volkmar come to be in possession of the two of them?

2

One of the babies snuffled and stirred. A soft mewling sound that wrenched Sebastian's heart.

'What?' Volkmar growled impatiently, as if sensing his unease.

'I was . . . I was thinking . . . Where will they go?' Sebastian asked, trying to make it sound as if he was interested, and not terrified at being complicit in all of this.

'What does it matter? I get a thousand marks for each one,' Volkmar said. 'But it is rumoured one child is destined for America.'

Sebastian heard a flash of pride in his tone. 'Don't they have enough babies of their own in America?'

'Not anonymous ones. Not ones that look small like these, with no paperwork and no past,' Volkmar said.

'And the other one?'

Volkmar shrugged and, in his dark look in the mirror, Sebastian understood the fate of the other child. He'd heard that Solya's underground network was linked to Bolkav, the orphanage in the hills, a place shrouded in secrecy, where many children went in, but few ever came out. Sebastian had heard talk in the clocking-out room at the steel works of some of the orphans ending up in films. Horrible, sick and violent films that would haunt a man forever.

If that was one of the children's fate, then tonight would probably be the only taste of freedom she would ever know.

*　　　*　　　*

Lights appeared through the trees ahead.

3

Sebastian blinked, blinded by them as they drew up closer and an old Mercedes ground to a halt on the track ahead. Only then did the headlights cut.

Sebastian felt Volkmar's pistol barrel jabbing into the back of his seat.

'Get out and help me with the crate,' he said.

Sebastian hurried to do what he was told. The quicker this was over, the better.

Outside it was no colder than inside the car, but the conspiratorial silence of the forest made Sebastian shudder. Compared to the town in which he lived, where the air was always acrid with industrial smog, here the air was penetratingly clear and he felt all his senses on alert. Peering into the darkness of the stationary Mercedes, he could make out the silhouettes of two men.

He dropped his cigarette on the ground, where it hissed in the fresh dusting of snow, and quickly opened the back door of the Trabant and lifted out the crate, instinctively holding the babies close to protect them.

Then he heard the slam of car doors. Turning, he saw two men walking towards them. One was huge—a great bear of a man with a black beard. The other was wearing a long leather coat. Sebastian saw that he was young, in his early thirties at most, and was broad-shouldered and athletic-looking, with cropped blond hair. He might have been called handsome, had it not been for his pale-blue eyes. They were predator's eyes, as if, given half a chance, he'd strip the meat from your bones and leave them to bleach in the sun.

'Solya,' Volkmar said, stepping up beside Sebastian. 'I wasn't expecting you.'

Sebastian felt his throat constrict with fear.

4

'Volkmar, old friend,' the smaller man—Solya—said, spreading his arm out wide and stepping forward to hug Volkmar. His teeth, Sebastian noticed, were perfectly white. 'You have them for me?' he asked, pulling back and altering the cuff of his coat to reveal a thick gold bracelet.

'Yes. They are both here. As you requested,' Volkmar said, nodding to Sebastian, who stepped forward, holding the crate as if he was proffering bread rolls to be inspected.

Solya's pale eyes glinted as he looked down at the babies. 'Good.' He smiled. From inside his coat he produced a clean white envelope. He pressed it to Volkmar's chest. Sebastian saw the edges of a stack of crisp bank notes inside its open flap.

Then Solya raised one gloved hand to his minder behind him. 'The vodka, Udo,' he said, waggling two fingers in command. 'For our friend.'

Solya handed Volkmar the bottle that Udo passed him. A black glove against a silver label.

'As a gesture of goodwill,' he said.

'Thank you. Thank you, sir,' Volkmar told the younger man, taking it and curtly bowing his head.

Solya clicked his lips and then turned towards Sebastian. Two dewy rosebud noses poked out from the top of the green and yellow blankets that Martina had made all those years ago.

'So which one shall it be?' Solya said in his Berlin accent. The lightness of his tone made it seem as if this were all a joke. 'Because, in fact, I think both are adequately small for the purpose. You choose,' he said, his eyes locking on Sebastian's. He took a coin from his pocket and flipped it up in the air, catching it and slapping it onto the back of his hand. 'Which one of these

5

sisters should have the good life? And which the bad?'

Sisters? Nobody had told Sebastian anything about the babies being sisters. Somehow that very fact made this all so much worse. Sisters born so close together in age—no mother could bear such a loss.

Sebastian felt his heart begin to hammer. Solya cocked his head to one side as if he could almost hear the noise. His ice-blue eyes seemed to pierce Sebastian's soul and he knew with absolute certainty then that this man was a devil and that he, Sebastian, was damned.

He stared down at the two innocent girls. He wished he could grab them both and run away, deep into the forest and never come back.

'I . . . I can't,' he said, his voice cracking. At first he thought Solya would be angry, but then he saw that he was smiling.

'Yes,' Solya said, finally inspecting the coin, 'you're right. If anyone should play God, it should be me.' He reached inside the crate and scooped up the babies, holding one in each arm. The crate felt desperately empty in Sebastian's hands.

It was only now that Sebastian noticed that one of the babies was awake. The bigger sister.

She made no sound. Just stared up at Solya, her eyes shining like black pebbles.

'I like this one,' Solya said. 'Yes, this one I'll keep for myself. Now say goodbye to your little sister.' He turned the babies momentarily towards one another, as if it was all a game. 'And this other one, the lucky one, we'll give to Walchez. He'll know what to do,' he told Udo, the guard, handing over the younger sister in the yellow blanket.

6

The baby looked impossibly small and vulnerable in the big man's arm. She didn't wake.

'It is done,' Solya said, nodding, before turning away and walking back to his car, with Udo trudging heavily behind him.

Sebastian looked towards Volkmar. He was examining the label on the vodka bottle, approvingly.

Could it really be that simple? That this terrible thing they had done here was now to be forgotten and mentioned no more?

No, Sebastian thought. *He would never forget.*

He held the empty crate in his hands, watching the men get into the Mercedes. Then the engine started and the car reversed back up the track, and the babies were gone.

Volkmar slipped the bottle into his coat pocket and rubbed his hands together. 'What are you waiting for?' he asked. 'We have celebrating to do.'

PART ONE

CHAPTER ONE

OCTOBER 1979

Unlike the name suggested, there was nothing diminutive about Little Elms. In fact, the 125-hectare estate with its grey turreted castle and ornamental lakes was famed for its majestic elm trees, which now, in mid-October, were the pride of New England.

At the front of the house, at the centre of a vast gravel turn ing circle, Theadora Maddox was up early for her riding lesson. Dressed in an immaculate red riding jacket with cream jodhpurs and black riding hat, she sat with her back ramrod-straight on Flight, a grey Welsh cob. She breathed in the fresh morning air, looking at how the sun was melting the frost on the lawn and turning it into a field of diamonds. She loved it here and she already knew that today was going to be another perfect day.

In the distance, past the avenue of gleaming gold and copper trees, was the block of stables where her father, Griffin Maddox, had once housed Showbiz, the three-times Kentucky Derby champion. And Starburst too, the show jumper that Thea's mother, Alyssa, had ridden to gold in the 1960 Rome summer Olympics.

But Maddox—renowned newspaper editor, businessman and now CEO of Maddox Inc., the rapidly expanding global media group—was a betting man of a different sort these days. He rarely rode his thoroughbred horses, or drove the

11

customized Lotus or vintage Aston Martins in the estate's garages, preferring instead to stay in Manhattan in the week, from where he could control his burgeoning empire more efficiently.

And Alyssa Maddox? Well, she was the reason Thea was up so early. Thea was determined to learn to jump before Mama came home from the hospital. She knew it was her mother's heart's desire to get back on a horse and ride with her only daughter, and Thea was going to make it happen. No matter what.

Mama had grown up in England, but had moved here when she'd inherited Little Elms from her grandparents, the McAdams, who had made their fortune in Manhattan real estate. They'd built this estate as an embellished replica of their ancestral home in Scotland. Her inheritance had coincided with Alyssa falling for Griffin Maddox, and she'd left England behind and had moved her heart and home here to Little Elms.

Thea never forgot how lucky she was to live here and, like her mother before her, felt that this place was her soul-home. A place where everything was right with the world.

Yes, everything would soon be back to normal, Thea was sure of it. Just as soon as this stupid cancer thing that her mama had got was over and she came home. Then Alyssa and Griffin Maddox would be the toast of New England once more. There'd be the gymkhana in the spring and then, in the summer, all of Mama and Daddy's glamorous friends would flock to the annual Maddox ball.

Below her, Johnny, the head groomsman, slipped her polished boot into the stirrup and then patted her leg.

'All done,' he said, in his English accent, smiling at her. He was wearing his usual uniform of a mud-splattered Barbour jacket and riding boots, and when he looked up at her, she saw that his tanned cheeks were flushed from the effort of readying her horse and bringing it up this early to the house.

Johnny and her mama had grown up together in England, and it had been Johnny who'd brought over the McAdams' horses and had somehow never left to go back home.

'Where's Michael?' Thea asked.

'Probably finishing his chores,' Johnny said, rubbing Flight's flank and moving round to take the reins.

'But you will show me *exactly* the jumps you taught him, won't you, Johnny?' Michael Pryor might be twenty months and five days older than she was, but he was a boy, and Thea was determined that anything he could do, she could do better.

Johnny Faraday rubbed his eyebrows and smiled to himself. He might have known that as well as wanting to put a smile on her poor mother's face, beating Michael was Thea's motivation for insisting on this extra lesson. He'd never met a child so tenacious or competitive as Thea. She was nearly eight years old, but she had the determination of an eighteen-year-old.

Johnny often wondered, like the other staff did, where her relationship with Michael would eventually lead. The Maddoxes had decided to home-educate Thea at Little Elms since Alyssa had been diagnosed. But in this rarefied environment Michael Pryor was the only child her age and, at Thea's insistence, they shared their

13

lessons, as well as all their recreation time together.

Johnny couldn't see it ending happily. Bright as Michael might be, he was still just the housekeeper's son, and Thea Maddox was . . . well, just that, Theadora Maddox, an heiress with a glittering future ahead of her. And the sky was the limit for a girl like Thea, with her ingrained belief that she was just as strong as any boy. Hell, Johnny thought, maybe she was right. After all, if they could elect Margaret Thatcher as prime minister back home in England, who knew where Thea might land up one day, with all the opportunities she had here in the States.

The sad thing was that, personality-wise, she and Michael made a perfect match, despite coming from opposite ends of the social scale. God only knew what would happen once they hit puberty in a few years' time.

But that was the future, Johnny reminded himself, and for now Thea was just a little girl. So what if sparks flew when she and Michael rubbed each other up the wrong way? Johnny knew his job could be a whole lot duller if Thea didn't have the personality she did. She took after her mother, Johnny thought affectionately. The two of them were as tough as teak.

'I sincerely hope you're not encouraging Thea to attempt jumping anything too high,' Mrs Douglas said, stepping out from the open back door.

Johnny put his hands on his wiry hips and smiled. Thea's governess always looked as if she were dressed for church and chewing a sour lemon, and today was no different.

'Now don't work yourself up, Mrs D,' Johnny

14

replied, knowing how much this abbreviation of her name annoyed Mrs Douglas, who thought she was owed extra respect for having been Alyssa Maddox's governess back in England, as well as being her daughter's now. 'I've told you before, I'm perfectly capable of supervising Thea's riding lessons.'

Thea smiled, grateful as ever to anyone who would stick it to Mrs Douglas. Seeing the adult staff squabbling over how best to educate her was a common amusement.

'Do be careful,' Mrs Douglas called out, as Johnny led Flight across the gravel driveway towards the paddock.

'We will,' Johnny called back, saluting without turning around. 'Now listen up,' he told Thea, 'don't you let me down, or give her the satisfaction of proving me wrong by getting hurt or anything.'

But Thea didn't think for a second she would. Mama had been a famous show-jumper, so it only stood to reason that Thea should take after her.

*   *   *

Half an hour later Thea was out of breath, having cajoled Flight into jumping over the small bar ten times, without clipping it once.

'Can Michael do it like that?' Thea asked Johnny, circling round towards him.

'Oh yes, Michael can do it just like that,' a voice said, impersonating her.

Thea turned to see her best friend and rival, Michael Pryor, riding into the paddock on Buster, the scruffy and stubborn brown pony that was the joke of the riding stables, but which Michael

15

always managed to ride like a dream.

Unlike Thea, Michael didn't have any correct riding attire. He was wearing tatty old jeans and a checked shirt under a denim jacket, and his honey-blond hair curled down across his brow from beneath his green woolly hat.

'He can do it just like that, but faster,' he goaded, riding up beside her with a twinkle in his eyes.

'Oh, really?' she said, her cheeks burning. 'You mean faster than *this*?'

She kicked her heels into Flight and took a run up at the jump, willing her horse to make it over without a mistake. He did it and she felt a flush of satisfaction as she turned and saw Michael sitting back on his saddle, applauding her.

'Too easy. She can go higher, right, Johnny?' Michael called. 'I'll help you raise the bar.'

Johnny nodded. In spite of Mrs Douglas's earlier warning, he knew that Thea was more than ready to take on the bigger jumps. Plus he knew there was no way in hell that she'd shirk from Michael's challenge now.

'You OK?' Johnny asked, seeing the dark circles under Michael's eyes, as he helped him with the jump.

'I did Guido's shift,' Michael said in explanation.

Guido the gardener had a bad back, so Michael had covered for him, but Johnny knew he'd never let on to Thea that he was exhausted. It just wasn't in the boy's nature to complain.

From the other end of the paddock, Thea watched Michael and Johnny stand back. The bar seemed at least two feet higher than before.

'We can do it,' she said, patting the soft neck of her horse, before circling once more, then setting Flight off cantering straight towards the jump.

This time, though, she got it all wrong. Instead of sailing majestically over the jump, before rounding on Michael and grinning in triumph, as she'd planned, Flight missed his stride coming into the fence and, worse, landed awkwardly, throwing Thea clean out of her saddle and hard onto the ground.

Michael was the first to reach her. 'Thea, Thea,' he gasped, sliding to a halt on his knees by her side. 'Oh God. It's all my fault.'

Thea took a breath, determined not to cry in front of Michael. So she'd messed up. So what? That didn't mean she'd give him the satisfaction of seeing her be a baby about it. But then she saw that he wasn't laughing at her at all.

'I'm so sorry,' he said, staring into her eyes.

She'd never noticed how lovely the golden specks in his hazel eyes were.

'It's not *your* fault.' She managed to sit up. 'Don't they say: pride before a fall?'

Johnny arrived just as she was saying this and smiled with relief that she was clearly OK. He reached down and ruffled her blonde hair. It broke his heart that she sometimes said such grown-up things when she was still only a little girl. He helped her to her feet.

'Nothing broken, I hope?' he said, picking up her riding hat and handing it back.

'Not this time,' Michael said, putting his arm around Thea's shoulder and giving her a hug.

'Ow,' she winced, knowing her shoulder was almost certainly going to bruise. But she knew

17

Michael hadn't meant to hurt her, so she said more gently, 'Get off, or I'll get boy fever.'

'Yeah. Well, just don't tell Mrs D or your father what happened, or he'll probably fire me,' Johnny said. He was smiling as he said it, but he meant it. Griffin Maddox could be a tough bastard to work for, and this little girl was the apple of her father's eye.

Thea laughed. 'Of course not.' The thought of ever getting any of the staff in trouble appalled her. She'd always thought of them being almost like family too.

But just as they were both about to help her back onto Flight, something snagged Thea's attention. She shielded her eyes against the bright sun, with her now-muddy white riding glove.

A sleek black limo flashed between the avenue of trees. 'Look! It's Daddy.'

'I'd better go warn Mom,' Michael said, flashing a look at Johnny. 'She wasn't expecting them back till the weekend.'

But Thea wasn't listening, she was already running away from him, diagonally across the paddock, her hat toppling from her head, as she waved her arms, with a wide happy smile on her face.

*   *   *

She arrived, breathless, at the paddock gate as the black limousine drew up parallel with her on the gravel drive. She stood up on the wooden rung of the gate, her heart beating with anticipation. She hadn't seen her parents for the best part of a month, but surely, them being here could only

18

mean one thing: her mother was better.

Mama was home.

But her hope fluttered and faded as Anthony, her father's chauffeur, got out. He usually had a wink for her, or a smile, but today he wouldn't meet her eyes. He walked quickly around the car and opened the far passenger door.

Griffin Maddox stepped out, blinking into the morning light, and placed his black trilby on his head with a weary sigh. When she thought of her father, Thea always remembered him dressed in a cowboy shirt—throwing her up in the air and laughing. How he always told her that she was the light of his life. How he'd one day teach her everything he knew. How everything that was his would one day be hers.

But today the shadow of dark hair on his cheeks made his usually handsome face look haggard and worn.

'Daddy,' Thea called, but all he did by way of response was weightily lift his forefinger to his lips to signal her to be quiet. He was a tall, powerfully built man, who'd rowed for Harvard in his youth. He was dressed in a fine camel coat, opened to reveal an immaculately tailored suit, but he moved stiffly as he walked around the car.

As she climbed quickly over the gate, Anthony opened the nearside passenger door and that's when Thea saw her mother's familiar leg stretch from the car down to the ground.

Thea stumbled and stopped, still five yards from the car. She felt her breath catch in her throat, as Anthony and her father helped her mother to stand.

Her mother looked so different. So desperately

frail. She was wearing a brightly coloured swirly silk scarf wrapped around her head, but it only served to emphasize how much paler and more gaunt she was.

Thea ran up to her mama and threw her arms around her, pressing herself against her fur coat. Her mother felt terrifyingly thin beneath it.

'You're home,' Thea said, finally stepping back and forcing a brave smile onto her face.

'Oh, Thea, my Theadora,' her mother said softly. 'My beautiful gift from God.'

She took Thea's head in her hands and gently kissed her brow. Thea's nose wrinkled. Despite her familiar perfume, her mama smelt strange—of chemicals and something else Thea couldn't put her finger on.

Her voice sounded different too. A scratchy, difficult whisper. She reached out her hand to Thea's face. Her touch was so cold that Thea couldn't help recoiling as she stared into her mother's sunken eyes.

'Didn't they make you better, Mama?' Thea asked. She couldn't stop herself. Everything she'd dreaded, everything she'd prayed for each night not to happen, was coming true.

Her mother didn't answer. She didn't need to. As Thea looked into her eyes, she saw something terrible there, magnified by the pools of tears. Something she had no name for yet, but which she'd one day come to recognize as sorrow of the deepest kind. The sorrow of saying goodbye.

Thea felt anger swell up inside her. Her father was Griffin Maddox. He had all the money in the world. As well as Dr Myerson, their family doctor, he'd paid for the best physicians. Grown-ups like

20

her father were meant to be able to fix everything. So why hadn't they fixed her mama?

Thea felt her chest shudder, that familiar prelude to tears, but knew instinctively that she had to be strong. That this was the only way to make her mama happy. And being happy could fix a person, right? Thea was certain it could.

She reached inside her pocket, remembering the present she'd made. She'd been carrying it around for weeks now, hoping and praying that Mama would be home, or that at the very least her father would let her go to the hospital to visit her there.

She'd cut the red silk herself and had embroidered it with careful stitches as Michael's mom, Mrs Pryor, had taught her. It was covered in fluff now from the inside of her pocket, but it didn't matter, she supposed. She pressed the small heart into her mother's hand.

'I made it for you, Mama. I knew you'd come home,' she said.

Alyssa Maddox gripped the heart in her hand and held it to her chest, then closed her eyes. Thea's father held her shoulders as she started to shake.

'Getting you was the best thing that ever happened to me,' Alyssa Maddox whispered, her eyes now glistening with tears. 'Whatever happens, I want you to know that, Thea.'

Why was Mama talking like this? Like she'd run out of hope. They'd just have to get her new doctors. Better doctors, who could make her well.

'Come, Lis,' Thea's father said, gently. 'You mustn't be out in the cold.'

He tried to turn her back towards the car, but

she stood her ground.

'No. I want to see Thea ride,' Alyssa Maddox said, with a hint of her old defiance. 'Just . . . just once,' she said, her voice turning paper-thin again.

'OK, watch,' Thea said, her eyes shining brightly, determined to lift her mother's spirits again.

She turned and, knowing she had to go fast, she half-climbed, half-vaulted the paddock fence, landing with bent knees, knowing that she had to perform—that this somehow was the most important thing she would ever do for her mother.

She took off, running, back towards Johnny.

Mrs Douglas was waiting for her in the paddock, holding Thea's riding hat ready for her. The old woman looked strange, standing in the middle of the mud in her sensible black coat. Why was she in the way, *again*? But Mrs Douglas wasn't taking any notice of Thea for once. She was looking behind her towards her parents.

Thea pulled the hat down on her head.

'I gotta show Mama how well I can jump,' she called to Johnny.

He nodded, helping her up onto Flight's saddle, securing her feet into the stirrups.

'Give me a moment to lower the bar,' he said.

'No, I can do it,' Thea told him sternly, yanking on the reins to force Flight to raise his head from where he'd been cropping the grass.

They circled around and Thea stared at the jump. Then, digging in her heels, she raced Flight right at it. Her heart soared as they sailed over.

She couldn't have done it better. A broad grin broke across her face.

A second jump was blocking her view of the

limousine. As she brought Flight around it, she looked at Johnny for approval, but saw that he too now was staring towards the driveway.

Thea's smile died then. Her mother hadn't seen her jump. She'd collapsed and was lying stretched out on the ground. Thea's father and Anthony were kneeling on the gravel beside her. Together, they raised Alyssa Maddox up and quickly bundled her into the back of the car.

Thea galloped the horse to the paddock fence, just in time to see the limousine completing its turn and setting off at speed away from her and the house, towards the road that led back into town.

And that's when Thea saw it: the red heart she'd made for her mother, lying forgotten on the gravel, abandoned, crumpled and torn.

CHAPTER TWO

MAY 1980

It was lunchtime, and after the long morning shift in the industrial laundry attached to the Bolkav State Orphanage, 183 children barged and jostled their way into the draughty canteen to take their places on the filthy benches beneath the buzzing strip lights.

All together like this, they were a sorry sight. Ranging from toddlers to teenagers, they had many things in common, including headlice, worms and bedbug bites. Despite laundering clean bed-linen and uniforms for powerful State officials, they were dressed in ill-fitting and worn beige boiler suits—all of which had an ingrained stench of urine and sweat that was generations old.

In the lunch queue, holding her dented metal tray, impatiently waiting her turn at the counter for her allocated bowl of cabbage stew, nine-year-old Gerte Neumann, known to her closest friends as Romy, stood out from the crowd. Even beneath the grubby stains on her face, her violet-blue eyes and high cheekbones set her apart as a thing of beauty, and her happy demeanour and wide smile made the younger children orbit her like planets around the sun.

But today something far more tangible marked her out as someone special too. She was wearing a sparkly clip in her roughly cropped dark hair—a hard-won treasure in a game of dice. But she might as well have had a neon sign pointing down at her head, such was the level of provocation the clip was bound to cause.

Any pretty item was rare in the orphanage. The few broken toys, torn books and trinkets that were stolen from the pockets of the uniforms sent into the laundry swiftly became currency used to curry favour, or purchase food, medicine or cigarettes.

'Take it off, Romy,' her best friend, Claudia, whispered in her ear, looking up the queue towards Fox, one of the meanest of the elder boys, who was nearly at the serving hatch, where the cook was mechanically handing out ladlefuls of stew.

It had been Claudia who'd given Romy her nickname years ago, declaring Gerte too ugly a name for someone so pretty. Now Romy looked to where Claudia was staring and pulled a face.

Everyone was frightened of Fox, especially

Claudia. He had a shaven head and his face and scalp were dappled with scar tissue, where his mother had sprayed boiling water on him as a baby so that she could use him to beg. He was thin, with sharp coppery-brown eyes, and that, along with his reputation of getting away with everything, had earned him his nickname.

'Stop worrying so much,' Romy said to her friend. 'Nothing bad is going to happen.' She looked at Fox again and then up to the far end of the canteen.

There, walking in between the rows of chipped wooden benches, Ulrich Hubner, the youngest of the orphanage guards, smacked his cane into his hand and surveyed his charges, muttering to himself at the din.

Ulrich himself had grown up here. A vicious bully as a child, he'd developed into an even more unpleasant man, and Professor Lemcke, the Orphanage Director, spotting his potential for instilling fear in others early on, had given him a job the moment he'd turned sixteen.

Ulrich hated and loved this place in equal measure. He loved how easy his job was, particularly considering that his only alternative would be to work back-breaking shifts in the nearby steel works. But he hated the children here. Not just for what they were—nobodies, who could and did disappear—but also because they reminded him on a daily basis that he had come from nothing too.

But it wasn't all bad. Oh no, not now that he'd infiltrated his way into Professor Lemcke's lucrative side-business. In fact recently a whole new world had opened up. Beneath his guard's uniform, Ulrich felt his fat member twitch. Those photographs of those little sluts . . . they'd excited him beyond his wildest dreams.

Just as his mind began spinning off into another deliciously depraved fantasy, an explosion of noise jerked his attention to the queue at the opposite end of the hall. Already the other children had bunched up into a tight, frantic circle around Fox and Romy, clattering their metal trays as the gleeful cry of 'Fight' went up.

'Give it back,' Romy hissed, but it was too late. With a sneer, Fox chucked her hair-clip upwards and back over the crowd. A hand shot up and snatched it out of the air. No doubt one of his stupid friends, Romy thought.

Romy grabbed Fox's arm, bending his right forefinger back to breaking point.

'Bitch!' he shouted, breaking free as he slammed a tray hard against her, sending her flailing backwards into the crowd of screaming children.

Fox was almost twice her height, but he didn't frighten Romy. She leapt right back at him and swung her fist hard, aiming straight for his nose.

But he was too good a fighter. He ducked and she missed. He seized her, spinning her round by the hair, as the other children continued clattering their spoons on their trays.

Ulrich muscled in, blowing his whistle, violently elbowing the children aside. He snatched up Romy, as if she weighed no more than a doll. He marched her out of the canteen, bellowing at the screaming children behind him to shut up. Romy made a show of kicking and screaming under his arm, stealthily plucking the packet of cigarettes

26

that Ulrich had recently taken to openly displaying sticking out of his back pocket, no doubt as a reminder to all the other kids of his recent and rapid social rise. She slipped them into the secret inside pocket that she'd sewn into her boiler suit.

*   *   *

Professor Lemcke, the Orphanage Director, stared out of his office window towards the billowing steam coming from the laundry's chimneys, then swivelled in his chair to face the door, as Ulrich banged it open and deposited the panting, red-faced girl on the patterned linoleum in front of the professor's large metal desk.

The office was austere. Photographs of government officials dominated one wall, a patch of black mould crept down the other. The orphanage buildings should have been condemned long ago.

Professor Lemcke had a condemned look about him too. He was forty-nine and extremely tall and gaunt, his cheeks sunken beneath his wire-framed glasses.

'You again,' he said, as Ulrich left.

'It wasn't my fault,' Romy protested. 'Fox started it—'

Professor Lemcke held up his hand. *Yes*, he thought . . . *Neumann*. That was this one's name. A troublemaker. Popular with the other children too, which was even worse. But she was an attractive child and in a few short years she would, of course, prove useful to him, so he didn't want to damage her permanently just yet.

And of course she was an investment of Solya's.

27

The Professor would be unwise to forget that.

'Child,' he said. 'Am I correct in thinking that this is the fifth time in the last two months that you have caused a disturbance in the canteen? If you are not careful, you won't be getting any meals at all. Is that what you want? To starve? Is that what you're going to force me to do?'

Romy stared at the Professor. He had abnormally long arms and legs and, sitting there now, his sharp elbows on his desk as he rested his pointed chin on his thin fingers, Romy thought he looked like nothing so much as a spider waiting to pounce.

Romy made her eyes well up with tears. 'Please, sir, it wasn't my fault, I swear it.'

'I'm not a cruel man,' Professor Lemcke said, creaking out of his chair. His knees cracked loudly. His eyes met Romy's and his tone changed. 'Haven't I treated you as my own? Haven't I looked after you since you were a baby here?'

Romy tried to hide from her eyes the hatred she felt for this man. He was clever, she knew, even more clever than Fox. She knew how much he liked to inflict pain on the other children, particularly the boys. But something had always made him hold back with her. Perhaps he really did have a soft spot for her after all.

'Please don't punish me,' Romy said, with a plaintive sob, edging towards his desk.

The stainless-steel letter opener was by his blotter, just where she'd known it would be. She'd been planning this all week, since last week's visit, when she'd stolen the book—a novel about fishing—that she was still working her way through with Klaus, the elderly laundry supervisor. Romy

28

was determined to learn how to read. How to read and escape. To escape and then, somehow, win through to a better life than this.

'Everyone else thinks my heart is hard, but it's not, Gerte,' the Professor was saying. The use of her real name shocked Romy. He never referred to any of the children by their Christian names. She hadn't even realized he knew hers. 'It's not. I do an impossible job here. You must understand. Now please don't cry,' he continued, coming around the desk.

He put his arms around her and pressed her face tight against his long legs, the way he'd done once before. She could hear him breathing deeply.

'There, there,' he told her, not letting go.

This was her moment. This was going exactly to plan.

As he ran his hand through her hair and trailed his fingers down her spine, sending a shuddering tremble through his whole body, Romy reached behind him and grabbed the letter opener, sliding it up her sleeve.

Footsteps sounded on the other side of the office door. With an agonized sigh, the Professor released her and quickly stepped back.

She looked up at him, her eyes round with obedience. 'I'll do an extra shift at the laundry. I'll do it right now. I'll be good.'

He was about to answer when there was a knock on the door.

'Come,' Lemcke called.

One of the older boys, Drum, barged into the room.

'Bit young, isn't she, Prof?' Drum said, looking between Romy and the Professor, a thin smile

29

playing on his fleshy lips. 'You should feed these ones up, Professor,' he sneered. 'The faster they grow, the better for us all, eh?'

'What do you want?' Professor Lemcke walked back around his desk, his composure ruffled.

'You know what,' Drum said. 'Come on, I've already got the basement ready.'

The Professor nodded, opening his desk drawer with a tiny gold key that he took from his inside jacket pocket. Both he and Drum had clearly both forgotten that Romy was even there.

She edged nearer the desk, trying to see what was inside the drawer, already mentally clocking where the Professor kept the key. Somewhere in this office, or in the filing room next door, would be her birth certificate and perhaps documentation relating to who her parents were. She was determined that one day she would make that information hers.

'What are you doing?' Drum snapped, looking over his shoulder at her. He hissed at Romy, making her recoil. 'Get out of here, pipsqueak. Shoo. Before I give you nightmares to last you for the rest of your life. Or I'll tell Solya about you.'

He was grinning when he said it, his eyes widening, but it didn't sound like a joke. It sounded like a promise. Solya was the orphanage's bogey-man. Romy had no idea who he was, or if he even existed, but rumours about this shadowy figure crackled around the dormitories at night. It was said that Solya was so mean that he'd make even Lemcke wet his pants.

Romy ran. She knew when her luck was up.

* * *

Three hours later, hungry but triumphant, Romy had finished her extra punishment shift in the boiler room of the laundry.

At precisely three-thirteen the two men who supervised the afternoon shift took their break, which gave Romy a clear seven minutes on her own before the next shift began.

As everyone filed out past the hissing boilers and clanking pipes, she joined the back of the queue. But as the others marched on into the main laundry area, Romy peeled off and hid in the giant drum of the end dryer and counted to a hundred.

Then, looking both ways, she sneaked out of its doorway and slipped into the service shaft next to the dryer, quickly climbing up the hot metal rungs of its ladder and heaving with all her might against the ventilation hatch at the top, before crawling out onto the cracked asphalt roof.

Smiling, she lay back, relishing this delicious moment of solitude. She spread her limbs out and closed her eyes, feeling the sun on her skin and listening to the birdsong drifting to her from the nearby woods. A blue sky stretched out above her.

If only she could get out of here. No, not *if,* she told herself, *when*.

She rolled onto her stomach and crawled on her elbows to the edge of the roof to survey the perimeter of the orphanage, a high fence fortified with rolls of barbed wire.

She knew it was electrified, supposedly to keep thieves out, but in reality to keep her and the other children in. It was also patrolled by dogs. The worst two, both Alsatians, belonged to Ulrich. It was rumoured he fed them live rats.

31

But there must be a way out, Romy thought. There must be a way that she could be free. In the distance she heard a church bell clang from the nearby town of Schwedt.

From inside the breast pocket of her boiler suit, she took out the old postcard that she'd found in a colonel's uniform three years ago. The image on it was almost obliterated, it had been folded so many times. It showed a balustrade on a terrace, the fine wall of a beautiful building stretching up one side. But beyond the fancy balustrade was a view of the vast, twinkling ocean, with a yacht in the background. The faded words said 'Hotel Amal . . .' something. The letters were worn away. But as she looked at it, Romy felt a surety creep into her. Someday, no matter what, she was going to go there and stand in the picture and feast her eyes on that view.

The ocean. What would it feel like to dip her toes in it? Maybe even walk in right up to her waist? What would the other people on the beach be like? Would they talk to her? Would they want to be her friends?

Her reverie was interrupted by the harsh bell that signified the start of the next shift. She rolled across the roof and looked down into the yard below, where the children were already starting to gather for roll call. She shimmied down the drainpipe behind the old pine tree and blended in with the others.

As the children lined up, she slipped the cigarettes along to Fox.

He leaned forward and looked back along the line to Romy and she saw respect flash in his eyes. The two of them had planned the petty robbery of

32

that fool Ulrich just a few minutes before lunch. She was gratified now as her hair-clip was passed back along the line in exchange.

But more importantly, thanks to Fox's growing influence amongst the elder boys and the guards, tonight the dormitory arrangements would change as a result of this transaction. She'd get the big bed all to herself. She'd let little Magda sneak in beside her, as she always did. And Tara, too. But when the littlies were asleep, she'd be able to move the box that she kept hidden under the floorboard in the corner of the room to a safer hiding place beneath her new bed.

Then she'd add the stainless-steel letter opener to her other treasures, and she'd sleep happily, safe in the knowledge that she had a weapon. A good one.

One that she was sure would prove useful one day.

CHAPTER THREE

DECEMBER 1982

From the back sun-deck Thea stared over the side of *Alyssa*, her father's sleek blue racing yacht, as it sliced through the Caribbean water. She sighed sadly to herself as the compilation tape Michael had made her for her new Sony Walkman finished, the last bars of 'Ebony and Ivory' fading out to a static hiss. She pressed the button to stop it, before it reversed back to the A-side where Michael had recorded Chicago's 'Hard to Say I'm Sorry' for her, but had deliberately cut it off before the end with the start of Jackson's 'Thriller'. Michael's mixing definitely needed some improvement, but Thea was so touched that he'd made the tape of all their favourite music, with a couple of 'soppy ones', as he put it, thrown in for her. But here in the sunshine the music just made her feel more homesick.

Now, as she took the headphones off, she listened to the wind and the waves slapping against the hull, gazing up at the white sails billowing against the cloudless blue sky. Then she looked to where her father stood at the ship's wheel, taking instructions from Rupert, the captain, who seemed only too happy to indulge his boss in sailing lessons. Their laughter carried towards her on the breeze.

In his yellow shorts, his white shirt flapping, Griffin Maddox looked deeply tanned and healthy, and it seemed to Thea that, despite how hard he still worked in the swanky new Maddox Inc. headquarters in Manhattan, he'd become the happiest she'd known him in these last eighteen months. In fact Thea often wondered whether he missed her mother at all.

He certainly seemed determined to live life to the full. His latest purchase was Crofters, an old banana plantation on Mustique, which he'd assured Thea she was going to love too. This was where they were heading right now.

But even though she knew she should be excited, Thea couldn't help thinking that this recent distraction was a mistake. Daddy spent so little time at Little Elms, as it was. Wouldn't this new home just keep him away even more? And even if he did bring her out with him every holiday, it was still so far away from everyone Thea knew and loved. The whole thing jarred, in fact. It rocked her sense of well-being, just as surely as the waves had rocked this boat last night in Petit St Vincent.

It just felt too weird being here, when the snow was falling back in New England. It was the first time she and her father had ever spent Christmas away from Little Elms, and Thea wondered whether all the staff and Michael would be sharing Christmas dinner at the long table in the kitchen, or whether they'd have bothered to go to the trouble of chopping down an alpine spruce from the estate and heaving it into the hall for decorating, knowing that Thea and her father would be away until well into the new year.

She hoped that Mrs Pryor would find all the presents she'd left for them in the pantry, the labels of which she'd decorated by hand. She'd sent off for an English riding hat for Michael. She wished she could see his face when he opened it.

Why, oh why, couldn't they just have Christmas back home instead? This holiday would never have happened if her mother were still alive. Thea tried to imagine Alyssa Maddox here aboard her namesake. But the second she did, she pictured the way she'd last seen her, three long years ago, lying there on that bed in the private hospital, slipping in and out of consciousness, pressing that little plastic button on the tube going into her arm.

And as soon as Thea thought of that, she remembered the horrible funeral. The people and the platitudes. That cold stone grave. Would there be anything left of her mama now? Anything left

35

there but bones?

'Not far now. Just around that headland,' her father shouted out over his shoulder to her.

He looked so excited that, straight away, Thea hated herself for being so selfish and so maudlin. Not many people ever got to go on a trip like this in their lifetime. She was the luckiest kid in the world—wasn't that what Daddy always told her? *Well*, she told herself, *isn't it about time you start behaving like it, and start making him feel lucky too?*

She looked over the top of her sunglasses to where he was pointing. There, less than half a mile away, was the palm-fringed coast of Mustique. The bluest of waters lapped up against its pure-white sands. Densely forested green hills stretched up into a clear blue sky. It reminded Thea of the pictures in her mother's treasured first edition of *Robinson Crusoe* in the Little Elms library, and she scrambled up from the cushions now to join her father.

Thea felt her excitement mounting as she helped the crew furl in the sails, sweating and laughing as they let her turn the handle on the winch. As they rounded the headland she saw a wooden landing jetty jutting out from the beach. Behind it, she could make out a red-tiled roof with a high turret nestled in the trees.

'Welcome to Crofters, my darling,' Griffin Maddox said, as he lowered the passerail to the jetty and held out his hand gallantly for Thea to step past. He'd done up his white shirt now and waved a straw trilby in salute, before putting it on his head.

She giggled at his playful mood, hoping it was a good omen for the days ahead. The water was breathtakingly clear, shoals of blue and silver fish darting beneath the jetty's worn wooden planks. On first impressions, this place really was as much of a Caribbean paradise as he'd promised.

As she sat together with her father in the small golf buggy and he set off along a path leading into the trees, she strained to look between the dense foliage on each side of the track. But she could sense him looking at her for a reaction.

And OK, she had to admit it, she could see immediately why her father had fallen for this place. It was like something out of *The Jungle Book*. All around were trees and giant green plants and bushes, bursting with orange and yellow flowers, and the dense, damp air was filled with the sound of buzzing insects and trilling birds.

Who was she kidding? She was going to have a great time here. She grinned at her father and, seeing the sparkle of pleasure in his eyes when she did, found herself finally letting go.

She really had him all to herself for two weeks. Here. In this tropical hideaway. With time stretching ahead of them and no work commitments that he had to rush off to, she knew this was finally her chance to show him what she was really like. Not just the smartly dressed, demure little girl he liked to talk to politely over supper on the rare times they were alone. But the real Thea Maddox. The girl who liked the Rolling Stones and poetry. The girl who liked to stay up late and go swimming and climb trees. The girl who'd watched *E.T.* three times already at the cinema, and *Cats* on Broadway and knew all the words to 'Rio' by Duran Duran.

In fact there were so many things she wanted to

talk to him about that she now didn't know where to start. How about by telling him how cool it had been to go to New York with Mrs Douglas and Michael on her eleventh birthday? And how they'd given the old governess the slip in the Guggenheim and taken pictures on her camera of all the crazy exhibits behind the guards' backs. Or how about how Michael's mom had taught her how to make pancakes? There was already so much of her life that her father knew nothing about.

But just as her mind was jamming with all the anecdotes she wanted to share, the house came into view and Thea gasped, momentarily forgetting everything.

'You like it?' Griffin Maddox laughed.

'Daddy, it's incredible,' she said, staring wide-eyed at the elegant teak and stone structure, with its series of sloping terracotta-tiled roofs and its window-studded turret poking up above the trees. She couldn't wait to go and explore up there.

'I've got a special surprise for you inside,' Griffin Maddox said, his eyes dancing.

His excitement was contagious. What had he got her? An early Christmas present? *Oh God, please let it be a puppy*, she thought. But then, just as quickly, she started to worry about how they'd get it home. Maybe he meant there was just something really cool, like some kind of amazing forest pool. *Oh yes*, she hoped, *please let it be that*. Then she could show him how well she'd learnt to dive.

She squeezed his hand and skipped beside him up the steps to the large wooden front door.

'Ready?' he asked, grinning down at her.

*　　　*　　　*

38

He opened the carved teak door. Together they stepped into the hall, a giant circular fan beating the humid air above their heads. A grand piano filled the space below the swooping staircase. Enormous terracotta pots stood filled with fluffy cream pampas grass against a wall filled with a massive painting of a fat naked woman. Her strange breasts made Thea want to giggle, but she just managed to stop herself in time, in case Daddy had bought it and liked it himself.

He winked at Thea and then led her through an open-plan living area, with low sofas and shaggy rugs, and on into the back of the house. Pulling back a tinted glass sliding door, he stepped with her out onto a wide wooden veranda.

'Hello?' he called. 'Anyone home?'

Is there supposed to be anyone home? Thea thought, following him past a bamboo bar area with bohemian swing-seats and a view of the twinkling sea. Wasn't this *their* home? He must mean the staff, she realized. A cook, or a housekeeper. She hoped they wouldn't be actually living here, that it would just be her father and her.

But then she saw someone.

A woman, with extremely long legs, was stretched out on a wicker sun-lounger, next to a sparkling circular swimming pool. Her face was hidden almost entirely from view by a giant black straw hat.

'Hey, honey,' Thea's father said.

Honey?

'Oh my God! You're here!' The woman's voice, a southern drawl, with long, dramatic vowels, was as mesmerizing as the way she looked.

39

Thea watched, slack-jawed, as the woman swung her legs off the sun-bed and stood up. She was topless, her large, perfectly tanned breasts tipped with soft pink nipples. A long pearl and diamond necklace stretched down to her black bikini bottom, and gold and silver bangles jangled on her wrists as she flung her hat dramatically aside, revealing a tumble of rich auburn hair. She strode over to Thea's father's and kissed him fully on the lips.

'I've missed you, I've missed you so much,' the woman said, finally coming up for air, but keeping her body pressed firmly against his.

Thea's eyes widened. She'd never seen anyone greet her father like that. Not even her mother. Certainly not her mother. Not *that* way. In front of Thea. Never in a million years.

Perhaps sensing Thea's confusion, Griffin finally pulled away. 'This is Thea,' he said to the woman, bashfully scratching his ear. He was blushing.

'Oh my God, oh my God,' the woman said, noticing Thea only now and clapping her bejewelled hands together in delight. She snatched a black paisley kimono from the back of a chair and shimmied her slender curves into it.

Thea exhaled for the first time since seeing her. At least she wasn't half-naked any more.

'Come here, you pretty little thing,' the woman said, now focusing her full attention on Thea. 'Let me look at you.'

She took hold of Thea's shoulders and leaned down. Now that she was dressed, she wasn't so intimidating. In fact, Thea had to admit, her face seemed kind and she smelt of exotic, expensive perfume. Thea couldn't help but stare at her

40

flawless skin and her green almond-shaped eyes, thickly lined in kohl.

'Yes, your daddy's certainly right about one thing. You're clearly going to turn into a fine young lady.'

I am?

Thea only just managed to stop herself from saying the words out loud.

Being described as 'a fine young lady' didn't sound so offensive, the way this lady said it, so Thea didn't tell her that she didn't actually want to be a fine young lady at all, and that she actually wanted to go into business instead. Like her father.

'It's nice to meet you . . .?' she said instead, remembering her manners and holding out her hand.

'I'm Storm,' the lady said, splaying her large bejewelled hand across her chest and looking from Thea to her father. 'Griff, you didn't tell her?' she said.

Griff. Only Thea's mama had ever called her father *that*.

'Tell me *what*?' Thea asked.

'Storm's your special surprise, darling,' Griffin Maddox said. 'She's your . . . well, she's my—'

'Fiancée,' Storm announced, enunciating each syllable. 'Your father's quite the romantic, sweetie,' she said, smiling warmly across at Griffin Maddox.

And in a rush of clarity Thea realized that it had been Storm who had put the colour back in his cheeks, and Storm who had kept him away 'on business' for all these months. Storm who was so clearly behind this new Caribbean home. It wasn't for Thea and Daddy to hide out in at all. It was for Griffin and Storm.

What an idiot she'd been to think that Griffin Maddox was going to spend the whole of Christmas alone with just her.

Or, for that matter, the future.

'You're . . . you're getting married?' Thea was staring up at her father, but it was Storm who replied.

'Aww, don't look so shocked, honey,' she said. 'I don't bite. Do I, Griff?'

Her eyes flashed at Thea's father again, and Thea saw something then—a connection, something private—that she knew had somehow already locked her out.

'Trust me, sweetheart,' Storm said, 'I intend to be more of a fairy godmother than an evil stepmother. Girl-stuff is my absolute forte,' she added. 'You wait until you see your room. I always wanted a daughter of my own, you see. But up until now I've never been given the chance.' She bit her lip, her eyes sparkling. 'But do you know what the best thing of all is?'

'What?' Thea said. It came out as more of a grunt than a word.

'I have got a wonderful son. He's called Brett.'

Thea noticed the enormous diamond engagement ring on Storm's finger as she chucked Thea under the chin. Her green eyes shone. 'I just can't wait to start playing happy families,' she said.

* * *

Later that night Thea sat hunched on the pink frilly cushions of the windowseat in her turret room. Storm hadn't been kidding when she'd said that girl-stuff was her forte. The room was a vision

42

of pink frills, like one giant candy floss. But Thea already knew she could never be the little girl Storm so clearly yearned for.

She looked out again at the water sparkling in the moonlight, the palm trees silhouetted against the shore, the lights in the trees swaying in the breeze and the yacht moored against the jetty.

Downstairs on the terrace the night air was filled with the pop of champagne corks, along with the chink of glasses and the tinkle of laughter and music too, from the guitarist who played in the bar, singing a gentle reggae love-song into a microphone, his slim black fingers slapping the wood of his guitar with a beat.

All day guests had been arriving, a succession of glamorous Brits and Americans who seemed to know Griffin and Storm so well that Thea had constantly been reminded that her father had been leading a life she'd known nothing about. She'd watched him being the perfect host—and the perfect couple—with Griffin's arm never far away from Storm's waist. And Storm herself dazzling everyone, bestowing hugs and kisses, her head rocking back as her trill of raucous laughter filled the night, until everyone was smiling.

And as Griffin Maddox had introduced Thea, his happiness had been there for all to see, and it had been obvious to Thea just how much he'd wanted her to be happy too.

But up here alone in the dark, she couldn't help feeling lost and confused. When had all this happened? How had she never suspected that her father was involved with someone else? She'd been such an idiot. It had been three whole years since her mother had died. Griffin Maddox was a

43

wealthy, good-looking widower in the prime of his life. Of course he was going to get snapped up by a gorgeous woman. One who wanted to take that sad look away from his eyes. Thea might be his adoring daughter, but Griffin Maddox was a grown-up. Shouldn't she have known that with a heart as big as his . . . well, she was never going to be enough, just on her own.

But why had everyone at Little Elms kept her in the dark? Had Michael known anything about all of this? And if he had, why hadn't he warned her? She racked her brains, trying to recall whispers that she'd missed, or hints that she might have picked up, but nothing came to mind.

She couldn't begin to imagine what Mrs Douglas and Mrs Pryor would make of Storm. Was Storm really going to come and live at Little Elms? Would she sit in Thea's mother's place at the dinner table? Would she sleep in her mother's bed? Wear her mother's antique jewellery? Read her books?

Sighing, Thea closed the treasured copy of *Huckleberry Finn* she'd been reading, his own adventure suddenly seeming tame in comparison to this new and strange direction that her life had taken. She pulled back the coverlet on the pink bed and climbed into the soft pink Egyptian-cotton sheets.

She had almost fallen asleep when she heard a quiet knock on the door and her heart leapt. It must be her father. He hadn't forgotten. He'd come up to kiss her goodnight, after all. She sat up in bed, smiling with anticipation, as the door opened.

But it wasn't Griffin Maddox. It was a boy. Well,

44

not a boy exactly, Thea thought. He must have been about sixteen or so. He was wearing shorts and a striped shirt with the collar turned up, and he had very suntanned legs and bare feet.

'Hello,' he said. 'I thought I'd come and introduce myself. I'm Brett.'

Storm's son.

He stumbled slightly on the pink-painted floorboards as he made his way over towards her bed, where he sat down right next to her.

'Lie down, lie down,' he told her. 'I didn't mean to wake you.'

'I wasn't asleep,' she said, wanting to get up, but he was sitting so close to her that she had no choice but to do as she was told.

He smiled as she cautiously lay on her side, her hands under her pillow. She was amazed that Storm had a son who was so grown-up. She felt a sudden sharp stab of demotion to little sister. He was so good-looking and athletic—just the kind of son that any father would want. Was that what he was already to Griffin Maddox? she wondered. A son?

'I'm sorry I wasn't here earlier when you arrived,' he said. 'I was out surfing.' He leaned towards her, whispering conspiratorially. She could smell the liquor and cigarettes on his breath. 'Or, more precisely, I was hanging out at the surf shack, but don't go telling the old lady that, OK?'

She nodded mutely, shrinking away, worried already about the implications of being his confidante.

'So we're going to be brother and sister then?' he continued. 'That's exciting.' He picked a lock of her hair from her forehead and brushed it slowly

45

away from her face. 'You have nice hair, don't you?' he said. He rested his hand on the curve of her hip, beneath the sheet. 'Good,' he said, leaving his hand there for a whole second longer. 'Isn't that good.'

CHAPTER FOUR

DECEMBER 1983

Trembling, Romy sneaked along the dark, empty corridor to Professor Lemcke's office, gripping the piece of wire and the letter opener in her fists.

She watched her shadow stretch along the floor. She'd grown tall in the last three years. Tall and hungry and thin. Her chest was flat, but her hips were now curved. She'd had her first period two weeks ago and her best friend Claudia had given her wads of cotton and shown her what to do.

Tonight was New Year's Eve and she could hear the guards laughing drunkenly in the canteen. Passing a window, she saw that it was still snowing outside and her breath froze in the stillness. She had to hurry. She had to focus on the plan. She and Claudia were going to escape in the early-morning laundry truck. The guards would be far too hungover to check. Then once they were down in the town, they'd slip away.

Klaus, the laundry manager, who for these past three years had taught Romy to read, had retired from work, sick with bronchitis. His parting gift to her had been a dictionary and in it he'd left the name and address of a clothing factory in Berlin.

There'd been no explanation, but Romy hadn't needed one. She'd heard his stories of his happy days as a machinist there, and now she planned for herself and Claudia to escape and find work there themselves.

She held the small torch in her mouth as she knelt by the Professor's door, waggling the wire into the lock and hearing it give. She quickly opened the door and stepped inside, before closing it behind her and pressing herself against it. She stood there hardly daring to breathe, listening to see if anyone had followed her.

It took less than a minute to get the desk drawer open. Romy's eyes grew wide when she saw what was inside.

Money.

Nearly a thousand marks, she quickly counted. She fanned out the notes in awe, then folded them and stuffed them deep in the pocket of her dungarees.

There was a cardboard folder inside the drawer too, but as she flipped it open, hoping for more cash, her breath caught. She put her torch on the desk and flicked through the photographs in the weak light. Each image made her heart stutter. They showed the terrified faces of girls being made to do disgusting things to grown men.

For an instant, Romy's fist tightened around the letter opener and she wished Lemcke would walk in right now. She'd slit the bastard's throat. But as she started to rip the photos in half, she hesitated. She'd just recognized one of the girls. Marieke. She'd left the orphanage more than a year ago. To work in the steel factory, they'd all been told.

Another lie then. Another terrible promise of

what awaited Romy if she stayed. Another reason why she and Claudia, the two oldest girls left in the orphanage now, had to get of here. Tonight.

She stuffed the photos back in the folder and slipped it inside her jacket. She'd post it to the police the first opportunity she got, and would include an anonymous note to say where she'd found it. She'd make sure Lemcke paid for this sickening crime. But right now she had to get into the records room. She wasn't leaving without her papers.

It took another two minutes to break into the room next door. It was full of large filing cabinets. Alphabetized by surname. The one thing she could thank Lemcke for was his thoroughness.

She went to the cabinet marked 'N' for Neumann, her given surname, and started rifling through its contents, her hands shaking with cold and adrenaline. The torch beam flickered maddeningly across the worn photographs and documentation.

Finally she got to her name. Gerte Neumann, written in faded black ink on a cardboard file with her date of birth.

Inside was a thick manila envelope. Eagerly, she lifted it out. It felt light and yet strangely bulky. But it would contain all the answers. She was certain.

Her heart was in her throat as she tore it open. But instead of the sheaves of papers and photos she was expecting, all that was inside was an old green blanket.

Was that it? No explanation? No birth certificate? Documents? Details? Nothing? *Just an old green blanket?*

48

Romy rushed back to the filing cabinet, scrambling through the other 'N' files, tipping their contents out one by one, determined to find something . . . anything. Because there must have been a mistake. Everyone had paperwork, didn't they? Everyone. Even orphans. Details of her parents' names. Details of where she'd been found.

But there was nothing.

She stared at the mess she'd made, winded with disappointment.

In the silence, the exercise-yard clock outside chimed midnight. She heard a faint cheer from the guards.

Romy hugged the blanket to herself and made herself a promise. A New Year vow. If she had no past, then she was going make sure she had a future. No matter what. And it was going to start right now.

*   *   *

But back at the dormitory, Claudia wasn't waiting for her as they'd agreed. She wasn't in bed. Or in the bathrooms.

'Where is she?' Romy demanded, not caring who she woke up. 'Where's Claudia?'

Tara was shaking as she sat up in bed. Tears were running down her face, and her cheek was blotchy and red from where it had clearly been slapped. 'The boys took her, Romy. Fox and Pieter. Up to the top floor.'

Romy wasn't the only one taking advantage of the fact that the guards were distracted tonight.

'Shit,' she muttered, already sensing trouble as she raced out of the dormitory. She'd never been

49

up to the top floor before. It was where the eldest orphanage boys lived, the ones who were practically men. The first thing that struck Romy as she sneaked in through the dormitory door was the warmth. A heater blasted out. A radio played and an electric kettle steamed on a unit by the sink. The four empty beds each had clean blankets and sheets, with reading lamps on little tables next to each one.

Romy felt the injustice of it all, like a wasp sting. All this luxury. Right above her head. All this time.

She heard a low rumble of voices behind a door at the far end of the room. Laughter. Then what she'd dreaded—a cry—a voice that she recognized straight away as Claudia's.

She hurried to the door and strained on tiptoe to look through its small square of glass.

Claudia was lying spread-eagled on a cast-iron bed, her nightdress pulled up around her waist. Her mouth was bound with a gag, her wrists tied to the bedposts. She was twisting and bucking her legs in a futile attempt to get away.

Romy saw Fox—six foot tall now and set to join the army in less than a year—unbuckle and kick off his trousers. Pieter, Monk and Heinrich clapped and cheered him on.

Romy's legs were shaking so hard she couldn't move. She squeezed her eyes shut and desperately tried to come up with a plan. But there were four of them in there. All bigger and stronger than her. What chance would she have?

She thought of the guards downstairs, but then she thought again of the photos inside her jacket. The guards would not help her. They'd probably just join in.

She could hear Claudia's muffled screams now. Suppressing a sob, she sneaked a peak through the window once more. Claudia's eyes were widening with terror. Fox was hunched over her open legs and was thrusting violently against her.

Enough!

Romy bust the door open and ran through it, yelling with all her might.

Fox had just pulled away. His back was to Claudia. He was flushed and sweating and was just swigging from a vodka bottle when Romy charged at him, ramming the letter opener with all her might into his abdomen.

He punched her hard in the face, knocking her to the floor. She curled up, waiting for the first blow to land. She knew she was never going to get out of this room alive.

But the attack never came. Instead, Fox moaned softly. She looked up to see that he was staring down at his bare stomach in disbelief. The handle of the letter opener was sticking out of it. Its blade was buried inside him.

The vodka bottle slid from his grasp and shattered. He staggered back, knocking an oil lamp off the bedside table. Its green glass smashed as it hit the floor. Flames began licking hungrily across the dry wooden boards.

Heinrich, Pieter and Monk fled past Romy, running for help. Fox lurched towards her, but then sank to his knees. His naked legs and shrunken genitals were now soaked and dripping with his own blood.

'You fucking evil bitch,' he said. 'I'm going to—'

He reached out for her, to seize her, but even that exertion proved too much. He slumped back

51

against the wall, groaning, twisting the silver handle of the letter opener, trying and failing to pull it free. A thin rivulet of blood trickled from his mouth.

'Burn in hell,' Romy told him, getting quickly to her feet.

Smoke was filling the room. The corner of the bedspread over the mattress caught fire.

Coughing, Romy grabbed Claudia, untying her bindings with shaking hands. Claudia was bleeding, a circle of red widening across her nightdress. Her glazed eyes stared right through Romy, as if she wasn't even there.

'Claudia! Clau!' Romy shouted.

No response. It was as if she was in a trance. Romy growled with exertion, pulling Claudia off the bed and hauling her towards the door.

Fox had started making a horrible gurgling sound and Romy was choking too now, as the smoke grew thicker. A sudden whoosh of flames behind her. A crackling of varnish burning on wood.

Romy pushed Claudia through the door, into the deserted dormitory beyond, just in the nick of time. She turned to see flames and smoke engulfing the room.

The fire alarm rang out as Romy hurried down the stairs, half-carrying Claudia now, determined that she would not leave her behind. She could hear men's voices shouting below. Any minute now and the guards would be here. If she and Claudia carried on this way, then they'd run straight into them.

Halfway down the stairs a small window was set into the landing wall. Romy stood back and kicked straight through it, before stamping out the remaining shards of glass. Icy wind blew in at her. The darkness beckoned outside. Cover. A chance to escape.

'We have to get out and up onto the roof,' she said. 'Now,' she told Claudia, pushing her towards the small opening. 'Please, Claudia. Or we're dead . . .'

Finally Claudia seemed to break free from her trance. She stared into Romy's eyes, then nodded and began squeezing herself through the tiny windowframe and sideways onto the thin window ledge.

Romy edged out after her. Before them was a sheer drop into a deep ventilation shaft, thirty foot deep. Fall down it and they'd most likely break their necks.

Claudia began shaking uncontrollably, as the thick snow swarmed furiously all around. Romy took off her jacket and gave it to her friend. But as she did so, the folder inside slipped and fell. The photographs got caught up in the flurry of snow, black on white, disappearing into the night.

But Romy had no time to worry about that now. Even over the wind, she heard the thunder of footsteps in the stairwell behind them.

'We have to get across,' she told Claudia, focusing on the flat roof ahead, four feet away, across the shaft. 'I'll go first.'

She didn't give herself time to think about it. She didn't look down. Kicking off the ledge, she launched herself across the gap and made it— just—hooking her shoulders over the far roof lip, before quickly hauling herself up.

Claudia hadn't moved. The ledge glistened in

the moonlight beneath her bare feet. Romy cursed herself. She should have given Claudia her boots too.

Shouts. Louder. Closer.

'Now!' she screamed to Claudia. Any second and she'd be seen.

Another shout, this time right behind her, finally spurred Claudia into flight.

One second she was just standing there, quaking, and the next she'd thrown herself forward and was flailing mid-air, desperately reaching out for the lip of the roof.

She missed. But Romy didn't. Coiled and ready, she seized Claudia's wrist as the older girl's body slammed into the wall where Romy now stood. The weight of most children of Claudia's age would have been sufficient to drag Romy down into a pile of broken bones at the bottom of the shaft. But Claudia was light—little more than a bag of bones herself. Romy would not let her go. She hauled Claudia up and got her onto the roof beside her.

They ran across the roof of the refectory, slipping and sliding all the way to the end. Then down the metal ladder onto the roof of the laundry office to its edge.

'Now! Jump!' Romy said, taking Claudia's hand this time and not giving her time to think. They plummeted down onto the laundry van in the yard. Its canvas roof shrieked and gave way with a giant rip. They landed with a thump on the bare metal bottom of the truck, a pile of snow cascading down around them.

'I can't go on,' Claudia cried, but Romy was already scrambling up.

Blood was running down the inside of Claudia's

legs. Her nightdress was soaked, translucent.

'Here, take my boots,' she told Claudia, unlacing them and hurriedly jamming them onto her friend's feet. Romy pulled her jacket tighter around Claudia's shoulder, tenderly brushing the sweat-soaked hair from her friend's face.

'Stay with me,' she said. 'We can do it.'

She forced her way through the hatch into the driver's cabin and leant in. Through the windscreen and the dancing snow beyond was the service gate. If only she knew how to drive, she could start up this truck, ram right through those gates and drive them both to safety. But she couldn't drive. In fact, it was only now, staring at the gates, that she realized she knew nothing of the outside world. Nothing but the views she'd glimpsed from the roof. Even if she did make it out of here, what chance did she really have of surviving?

But just as these doubts threatened to overwhelm her, she remembered something else. Another view from the roof. The woods. Just there outside the orphanage. Get as far as the woods in this storm, and she and Claudia might just give their pursuers the slip.

She grabbed Claudia's hand and shuffled to the back of the van, then jumped down into the yard. She held out her arms to help Claudia.

She could hear alarms ringing out all around now. Flames licked out into the darkness from the top of the building. The lights inside the orphanage were all coming on. Dark silhouettes were appearing in the windows, the faces of orphans pressed up against the grubby glass panes, peering out into the blizzard to try and see what

55

was going on.

Romy couldn't think about the children now. They knew the fire drill, she reassured herself. They'd all be out here soon. And so would Lemcke and the guards.

Lemcke. The very word rang out like a whip-crack in her mind. She'd rather die trying to escape than let him get hold of her.

Hauling Claudia, who stumbled after her across the concrete, leaving drops of blood in their footprints in the snow, they reached the gates and started to climb. Romy's sodden socks slipped on the ice-cold metal bars. But she kept going and soon reached the top.

The single-track road ahead was a tapestry of black ice and snow.

She and Claudia dropped down onto it. Romy pulled Claudia with her over into the trees. They fell into a ditch, landing thigh-deep in snow, and fought their way through it and out the other side.

'Our only chance is to disappear into the woods,' Romy said, cold gripping her feet like a vice.

They ran on, the orphanage alarms still ringing out behind them. Romy delved in her pocket and clicked on her torch, desperate not to get caught in another drift. She immediately saw that to the left the woods were thicker and the snow less deep, as the land dipped sharply towards what looked like a river valley below.

Behind them, she heard a shout. She looked back. Through the trees she glimpsed a flicker of torches at the orphanage gates. Boots clattered on the icy road. She thought she heard Ulrich's voice and his whistle blowing, and then the sound she'd most feared. The dogs.

A howl went up. Another. Snarling. A yelp. The creatures were desperate to be let off the leash.

Then silence.

'Run!' Romy said, but it was already too late.

A hiss of barrelling motion. Of muscle crashing past bushes and trees.

Then the dogs were upon them. Two Alsatians. Ulrich's pride and joy. Both of them drawn by the scent of Claudia's blood.

Claudia screamed as the dogs piled into her and knocked her to the ground.

Romy snatched up a heavy branch and swung it hard, two-fisted, down onto the nearest beast's spine. It yelped, twisting to one side, but then only tore back all the more fiercely into Claudia, who'd now curled up in a tight ball.

A lattice of torch beams criss-crossed through the trees. The guards had realized where they were.

Romy brought the branch crashing down on the dog again. This time she struck the creature hard across its brow. It slumped sideways in the snow and did not move again.

But the second dog now had its jaws locked around Claudia's neck.

Claudia stared wide-eyed up at Romy. Her cheek was torn open. Her back was arched, her whole body stretched, as if at any second she might actually snap.

'Go,' she mouthed at Romy.

And this time Romy knew she had no choice. She turned and fled into the dark, just as Ulrich burst triumphantly into the clearing and stared down at Claudia's bloodied body in the snow.

But Romy was already gone. Stumbling deeper into the dark wood, with tears pouring down her face, Romy was running for her life.

CHAPTER FIVE

JUNE 1984

On the hotly anticipated day that Griffin Maddox was destined to tie the knot with Storm Haileux-Maitlin the New England sky was a cloudless aquamarine blue and the rolling lawns of the Little Elms estate shone emerald in the sunshine.

Inside the house Thea picked up the net-fluffed skirts of her baby-pink bridesmaid's dress and tiptoed over the brand-new carpet, careful not to trip over the photographer's lighting cables, which snaked across her path.

The recently refurbished top floor had the frenzied backstage panic of a catwalk show, as Mimi, the wedding planner from New York, shouted into a walkie-talkie about a time-check, marching out of the adjacent bedroom where Storm was being dressed in a cloud of cream taffeta by a coterie of hangers-on.

Thea scooted out of the way and looked through the round picture window down to the gardens at the back of the house, where the yew-tree walk had been made into an outdoor chapel, complete with a white wrought-iron altar and canopy.

As well as many New York acquaintances and Griffin Maddox's business associates, the glamorous rich set that Thea had met at Crofters were all jetting in for the wedding. Storm had spared no expense in her effort to impress them. It was as if she were some kind of blushing virgin bride and not a twice-married divorcee. Thea fought down her sense of injustice. She'd always imagined that a wedding at Little Elms like this would be hers—in time—not Storm's.

Now Thea saw a familiar figure placing the fancy, embossed order-of-service booklets out on the velvet chairs and she knocked on the window, but Michael was so far below her he couldn't possibly hear.

Even though she was thirteen and he was nearly fifteen, Thea had noticed how much older he seemed these days. He'd grown tall and had started shaving the fluffy moustache she'd teased him about. His face was tanned and his honey-blond hair was slicked back, making it seem darker and his face more handsome. He was wearing a navy tuxedo and Thea saw how the tie constricted his neck, how the whole outfit made him look as if he wanted to burst free and ride with the wind in his hair.

She pictured them together as they had been yesterday, riding for miles in the early morning. How, when they'd stopped, he'd told her to be brave about today. She knew he'd meant it in the kindest possible way. After all, Thea had offloaded to him countless times in these last few months of wedding planning. About how she couldn't shake the feeling that Storm didn't like her. About how upsetting it was that Storm always promised shopping days and spa trips, but always cancelled right at the last moment. About how she didn't trust Brett and how he intimidated her. Her lists of

59

doubts had gone on and on. Michael had listened, soothing and agreeing with her.

But now the day was here and she was in this dress, and Thea felt nervous about the wedding for an altogether different reason. There would be dancing later and she'd be able to be in Michael's arms. Just as she'd daydreamed.

She stood back and gazed at her reflection in one of the three full-length white mirrors set up by the doorway. What would he think when he saw her? she wondered. She hardly recognized herself in all the eyeliner and mascara, her blonde hair sprayed up away from her forehead and plaited with ribbons at the back. Did she look like one of those ghastly pageant queens? Or beautiful, as the make-up girl had said? She couldn't be sure.

She went over to the table to pick up her pink posy of roses and eyed the door, waiting for the opportunity to present itself for her to sneak away and see her father. She'd be able to tell how she looked from his reaction. She could always see from his eyes whether he was pleased with what he saw.

But there was another reason too. She wanted to know whether getting married brought back painful memories of her mother. Somehow, hearing him say just a few words to acknowledge the past seemed so important today.

But just as she reached the door, Storm called out to her from the bedroom. Thea turned and walked towards her. From the coos of the dressers, who were standing back to admire the vision before them, it was clear that Storm was finally ready.

Storm's much fussed-over designer dress was

similar to the wedding Barbie that Thea had played with as a child: layers upon layers of frills nipped in to show off Storm's formidably small waist. Storm, with her never-ending desire for the theatrical, had made no secret of the fact that she'd drawn inspiration for the design from the wedding dress Princess Diana had worn three years earlier, although thankfully she'd ditched the twenty-five-foot train, Thea thought. But even without it, the dress was a big enough number to make Thea wonder whether she'd fit down the aisle outside.

'Wow,' Thea breathed. 'You look amazing.' Up close, she saw that the jewel-encrusted bodice of Storm's dress led to puffy sleeves, which complemented the shape of the neckline perfectly and framed a dazzling diamond necklace.

'Thank you,' Storm said, as if genuinely touched. Then she waved for the others to go. 'Give us a minute, will you?'

Storm watched them leave the room, her hands clasped in front of her, as regal as a queen. Sunlight poured in through the window, making the diamond necklace and the jewels in her hair light up the walls of the room with sparkling dots.

She walked towards the fireplace, making the dots jump.

'Griff and I were going to give this to you later, but I think now is the right moment,' Storm said, taking a duck-egg-blue box with a white ribbon from the mantelpiece. She turned with the box and smiled at Thea. 'Open it.'

Thea didn't move for a second. If this was a gift from Storm and her father, then why wasn't he here, giving it to her as well? But she took the box and slipped off the ribbon.

'It's lovely,' she said, pulling out the silver Tiffany locket. She meant it. It was exactly the kind of thing her mother would have worn, and she guessed that her father must have picked it out, not Storm.

'I want you to wear it today,' Storm said, coming forward and helping Thea with the clasp. Then she put her hands on Thea's shoulders and looked right into her eyes. 'I know this is hard for you, hon,' she said in her husky southern drawl, 'being a teenager was never easy for anyone. But you and I . . . we'll have something so special. You'll see,' Storm said, fastening the locket behind Thea's neck and kissing her cheek.

And right at that moment she remembered Storm's very first promise: that she intended to be more of a fairy godmother than an evil stepmother. Now, in that dress, dazzling with jewels, her beautiful face soft with affection, Storm really did look as if she was going to finally come good on her word.

Thea felt something inside her shift. She put her fingers around the cool silver heart and smiled back at Storm. Maybe she'd seen her father's marriage in the wrong light . . . because she'd been jealous, she thought.

Well, she would change, she vowed. She'd reach out back to Storm. She'd be her perfect stepdaughter. She would. She wouldn't let any doubts get in the way of her father's happiness. Not ever again.

'Let's go, people,' Mimi, the wedding organizer said, marching in and breaking the moment. 'The press photographers can't wait any more.'

62

Thea slipped out of the door onto the landing and tiptoed down what had once been the nursery stairs to the first floor. A lighting rig for the grand photos on the sweeping staircase had transformed her home into a film set. The whole interior of the hall was filled with the heady perfume of close on 2,000 roses.

She stopped for a moment to take in the scene, but Mimi pushed her out of the way, scooting past her down the stairs in a flurry of panic.

Griffin Maddox was coming out of the door of his room, wearing a grey-striped morning suit, and he was whistling, as if he didn't have a care in the world.

'How's it going up there?' he asked, a baffled smile on his face as he watched Mimi. Then he winked at Thea and nodded up the stairs, and she knew that she couldn't ask about her mother. Not today. He simply looked too happy to be reminded of any pain.

'It's crazy,' Thea said honestly, stepping forward to straighten the cream rose in his buttonhole.

'Look at you,' he said, with an impressed whistle.

Thea did a little curtsey in her pink dress, feeling a flush of satisfaction. He really did think she looked great.

'Oh? She gave it to you already?' he asked, reaching out to touch the locket. She noticed a hint of disappointment in his voice.

'It's lovely,' Thea said. 'Thank you.'

'Did you read the engraving? Here.'

He opened it so that she could read the tiny engraved writing inside. 'To Thea, with all our love from Mom and Dad,' he said.

Mom? He and Storm had chosen those words for Thea? But . . . but she already had a mom. No matter how nice Storm was being, she couldn't just step into her mom's shoes . . .

But before Thea could say anything, Mimi's shrill voice and accompanying finger-clicking made her look down to where a line of photographers was snaking up the stairs, pointing their cameras towards them.

'Nervous?' her father asked, patting her hand in the crook of his arm. She looked down and noticed his bare hand and wondered what he'd done with the wedding ring he'd worn when her mother was alive. She hoped he'd saved it for her. She hoped he hadn't thrown it away.

Behind them, she noticed her father's bedroom door opening. Justin Ennestein, the family lawyer, was coming out, straightening papers in a leather folder. He was small and rotund, with brown hair that Thea saw was already flecked with grey. He adjusted his heavy-framed glasses on his beaked nose and looked directly at Thea. He looked caught out, or maybe he was just embarrassed, Thea thought, that her father was still working today of all days. He turned quickly away.

Brett bounded up the stairs towards them. 'Wait for me,' he said.

He was wearing a matching suit to Griffin Maddox, but he'd bulked out in the last few years and looked uncomfortable and constrained, a fold of his neck spilling over his collar. Despite his cheery manner, his cold eyes looked Thea up and down for a second, making her skin crawl.

'This is the shot to use,' Brett called out, grinning down to the photographers, hoisting his arm around Thea's father's shoulder. 'Griffin Maddox and his children.'

'Children? But you're not—' Thea began, unable to stop herself.

'Did you tell her, Griff?' Brett interrupted, looking at the camera and grinning. 'Your dad's going to adopt me officially. Which means that, as of today, I'm changing my name to Brett Maddox and then I'll be your brother for real. Isn't that cool?'

*   *   *

The next part of the day passed in a blur, as Thea's head was reeling from the implications of Brett's announcement, even as she followed Storm down the aisle towards her father. Why did it matter so much that Brett had taken her name? Why was the fact that Brett was now officially family so much worse than her father getting married in the first place? She couldn't place her sense of betrayal, only that it felt very real. As if once again she'd been somehow demoted or overlooked.

But as the pastor talked about the importance of family and how much Griffin and Storm cared about uniting Brett and Thea with them, Thea found herself having to put on a brave face, despite Brett's smug grin.

And afterwards, seeing her father so happy, she couldn't help but be affected by the atmosphere, not to mention the sheer sense of occasion and glamour of the wedding. It was the first time she'd

65

seen so many of her father's colleagues since her mother's funeral, and the various family friends who came to congratulate her couldn't have been more flattering. She'd been shocked to realize the power of her dress and her make-up and how they caused everyone to tell her how grown-up she looked, how sophisticated, how she was no longer a child, but was becoming a woman.

As the wedding spilled from the reception into the evening, the night seemed to be filled with magic. The sides of the marquee were open, letting the balmy air waft through, like a caress after the fierce glare of the day. The trees were lit by fairy lights, as the big-band orchestra played 'My Everything' and Thea joined the crowd to watch, as Storm took to the dance-floor with Thea's father.

'Come on, you,' Justin Ennestein said, taking her hand and leading her out to join them. As she danced with him, Thea realized that she was almost the same height as him now. 'You were brilliant today,' he whispered, as he held her formally. 'Social glue.'

Thea smiled, flattered.

'So how do you like your new stepmom?' he asked. She noticed a hint of something in his voice—as if he thought it was baffling that Griffin had married Storm. Five hours ago Thea would have agreed with him, maybe even confided in him, but now she felt a new-found sense of family loyalty rising up in her, as she remembered her vow not to ruin Griffin's day.

'Oh, she's lovely,' Thea said quickly, smiling at her father and Storm as they twirled by.

Justin nodded. 'That's good,' he said, as if relieved. 'Just never forget who you are, Thea. I promised your mother before she died that I'd always look out for you.'

Had he? Thea tried to picture the conversation. Once again, she felt a pang of sadness . . . and respect, too. Her mama had known she was going to die. Somehow, that bald fact made her mother seem so incredibly brave. But now Thea longed to know what else she'd discussed with Justin. Why had her mother felt it necessary to tell someone like Justin to protect her daughter? Had Alyssa Maddox sensed that her husband might remarry one day? Or—the realization suddenly came to Thea—maybe Alyssa Maddox had insisted that he did? Maybe she'd made Griffin Maddox make promises too. Ones Thea had no way of knowing about.

'Mind if I cut in, old man?' Griffin Maddox asked, leaving Storm to Brett, who leant her back across his arm dramatically, causing a smattering of applause.

'My pleasure,' Justin said, kissing Thea's hand and looking into her eyes for just a fraction of a second.

Griffin Maddox held Thea in his arms and pulled her close. She breathed in his familiar aftershave.

'Oh, my Thea. My gift from God,' he whispered. It had always been the sentiment her mother had uttered, and Thea feel a pang of something so bittersweet that it took her breath away. 'See, it wasn't so bad. I told you. I know you hate change, darling. But the world goes on. It doesn't end.'

Thea laughed, blinking away tears, as he kissed her on her forehead. There were so many things she wanted to say, but somehow she couldn't say

67

any of them. She wished she could apologize for being so offhand and surly these past months. That she hadn't really understood before, but now she did. That she'd seen for herself that he and Storm were in love. And love was all that mattered.

'You'll always be my number-one girl,' he said.

And at that moment Thea felt as if he'd grounded her back to something she'd lost for the past few months. More than just a sense of well-being, but a certainty of her place in the world—in *his* world—that had been missing.

She was Thea Maddox. His only daughter. His true flesh and blood. Nothing . . . nobody could change that. Not even Brett.

*　　*　　*

Michael Pryor stood at the bar in the ballroom and filled up another glass of champagne. These people were unstoppable, he thought, smiling at the woman in the backless purple dress as she sashayed away, her laughter high and shrill. He'd never seen such excess, so much wealth on display.

He supposed it would always be the same. The rich were the rich, the poor were the poor. He'd always known he was in a different class to the likes of Griffin Maddox, but days like today made it all the more painful.

He hoped that he'd get a tip later on for working so hard all night. His mom had managed to get three tickets for the show-jumping event at the Olympics in Los Angeles in August in the ballot. Michael was saving up for Greyhound tickets to get there and planned to ask Thea and Johnny to come with him, if Thea's father would

68

let her. He knew all too well that if he told Thea of his plan, she'd immediately ask her father for the money for them all to fly there, but Michael desperately wanted to do this by himself, without her money or charity. That way it would mean so much more.

'What are you doing? There's staff for that,' Thea said, sidling up beside him and pinching him playfully, as Michael replaced the champagne in the bucket of ice behind the bar.

'I *am* staff, Thea.'

He watched as she bit her lip. He knew that his bold declaration had drawn a line in the sand between them, but sometimes she needed reminding.

'You look like you're having a good time?' he said, his tone making it obvious that he'd been watching her all day. He suspected her of faking her way through the whole thing, and maybe she'd been caught out, because he noticed a blush rising in her cheeks.

'There's fireworks, then they leave at midnight. Then everything can go back to normal,' she said.

Normal. What was normal about any of this? Michael wondered. But even though he knew what she meant, he wondered how long he could go on faking 'normal' for her.

'Well, you must be tired,' he said. 'I promised Johnny I'd check on the horses before I turn in. They've been inside all day.'

Storm hadn't wanted 'those ghastly beasts', as she'd put it, ruining her wedding shots, but Michael didn't tell Thea that.

'I'll come with you, if you like?' she said.

And there it was again. That look he'd seen

69

increasingly often in the last few months. The one that made his stomach feel funny. He'd thought about doing something about it countless times—confirming what he suspected she might feel for him. But Thea was just a kid, and he couldn't imagine the trouble he'd get into if he so much as laid one finger on Thea Maddox. But sometimes the temptation to kiss her was overwhelming, especially when she looked like she did right now. He wondered whether it was a good idea for them to be alone later.

A firework lit up the sky, breaking the moment.

'I'll be right back,' Thea said, her infectious smile making him laugh. 'Wait for me. Promise?'

'I promise,' Michael said, watching her go. Then he picked up the cloth, a sigh heavy in his chest. He'd promise her everything, if she asked him.

*   *   *

Thea ran upstairs to call Storm. She wanted to say goodbye to her before she set off with Griffin on their luxury honeymoon. She wanted to show them both that there really were no hard feelings, and that she wished them both a bright and happy future together.

But just as she was running up the final flight of nursery stairs, she heard raised voices. Thea opened the bedroom door just the tiniest crack. In the reflection of the white mirrors inside, Brett was pacing, staring at Storm, who had changed again from her evening dress into her going-away outfit. It was a gorgeous green velvet suit with gold buttons and big shoulder pads, and Thea felt momentarily disappointed that Storm hadn't

70

waited for her. But she was much more shocked by what was going on.

'Calm down, Brett, please,' Storm pleaded, as she pulled on her gloves. 'What more can you want?'

'You know what I want. I had it spelled out in black and white.' She saw Brett shaking a sheaf of papers in Storm's face. 'Do you know how hard the lawyers worked on that pre-nup? You told me he'd sign it.'

Thea flinched, amazed to see the fury in Brett's eyes and the terror they inspired in Storm. What was Brett talking about? A pre-nup? What was that?

Behind Storm, through the window, fireworks lit up the night sky. The fireworks were for the new Mrs Maddox. Storm glanced anxiously at the door and Thea flinched away.

'He wouldn't budge, Brett,' Storm said urgently. 'I tried, believe me. If I'd pushed him more, he'd have gotten suspicious. But I trust him, OK?'

Thea squeezed her eyes shut for a moment, longing for this conversation not to be happening, for the sickening suspicion to go away. She put her eye once more against the crack of the door.

'Trust? Trust Griffin Maddox. What? Are you crazy? You trusted the last two losers, and look what happened. We ended up with nothing,' Brett said.

'It's not going to happen again. I'm happy and we're rich.'

'Until you blow it,' Brett snapped. 'What happens then?'

'He'll give you a job. Make you successful. The past doesn't matter. You're family now.'

71

Thea held her breath, her heart pounding as she watched Storm lean in to soothe Brett's temper. She put her hand on his chest, her voice changing.

'Do you think I've put in all this work for it to go wrong? Christ, Brett. I've had to put up with living in this mausoleum. And *marrying* here. When I think of all those venues I could have had, it makes me weep. I've even tolerated that freakish brat of his.'

Thea recoiled as if Storm had slapped her face. Through the blur of tears that now clouded her vision she could see Brett softening.

'Ah, yeah. Thea. Now she's one of the good things about this place,' he said.

At first Thea thought she'd misheard. Was Brett really standing up for her? But then she saw his sneer.

'Don't you touch her,' Storm said. 'Not a finger, you hear?' She pointed in Brett's face, as if she'd resumed control. 'Don't you dare.'

'Then you'd better pack Thea Maddox off to boarding school, far, far away. Soon,' he warned. 'Or I might just not be able to hold myself back.'

CHAPTER SIX

APRIL 1985

Romy woke in the dark, with a gasp, her fist clutched around the closed penknife. She felt her dream evaporating into the cold air, but her breath still stuttered in her chest.

The same dream *again*.

The fear. The fear always woke her.

But now she exhaled, reminding herself of the facts, forcing herself to retrace the past, in order to let hard facts guide her step-by-step out of her nightmare.

In a second, she was back in the woods outside the orphanage. The sound of her raggedy breath, the crackle of ice, the menacing blue shadows as she'd lurched through the funnel of snow. But just as she'd run out of hope, she'd stumbled upon a hunter's cabin. She remembered how she'd burrowed underneath it, how the snow had caved in after her, burying her in the freezing crawl space.

Moments later she'd heard the muffled noise of Ulrich and the others arriving. Arriving, then stopping, shaking the cabin's padlocked door and rattling its locked shutters, her heartbeat crashing in her ears, before they'd given up and run on again. Whistles, shouting, the snarl of the dogs, gradually fading into the night.

Only when she'd been certain that they wouldn't be coming back, that they'd given her up for dead—already frozen, or devoured by wolves—had she started kicking upwards. Harder and harder. Bloodying her bare heels against the cabin floor's rotten wooden boards. Finally she'd burst up, smashing through the floorboards, like a corpse from a coffin, into the still air above.

She'd lain there huddled on the floor, too afraid to move. She'd fought the urge to sleep, to keep her limbs moving, to keep herself alive. She'd been shaking so hard, it had taken half an hour to light a match in order to see around the cabin in the dark. She'd thought about lighting a fire, but she knew the smoke from the chimney would give her away. Fumbling in the dark, she'd ransacked the cabin, finding spare clothes and boots and a pile of rags, which she wrapped herself up in on the hard bunk.

But she was too scared to sleep. As the dawn light had crept in through the dirty windows, she'd shaved off her hair with a blunt razor that she'd found, changing her appearance as much as she could. When she'd stared at herself in the small shard of mirror by the basin, she'd been sickened by her haunted eyes.

She'd limped through the woods in the oversized boots, her cut, bruised feet bound in the rags that had kept her from freezing the night before, until the land had fallen away to the railway line. For the whole of the day and into the next night she had stumbled along the snowy track, before she'd found a place where the trains stopped at a signal junction, where she'd climbed unseen aboard a freight train.

She'd been hauled into consciousness by a stationmaster who had gripped her in an armlock and frogmarched her along the platform, muttering about calling the *Polizei*. But Romy had remembered Lemcke's cash and had offered a bribe that had made the man's eyes widen. Keen to get shot of her without implicating himself, he'd put her on the right train to Berlin, with an ID that would allow her to survive a cursory inspection.

And that's where Romy had met Ursula.

Thank God for Ursula, Romy thought, starting her daily ritual before her shift downstairs. She listened to the sound of her fellow workers in the clothing factory's dorm waking up around her. Quietly and carefully she stored the penknife under her pillow, touching the picture of the ocean view that was taped to the board behind her bed, then working her fingers into the split in the mattress, checking for the plastic bag with Lemke's cash inside.

Yes, how different life might have been without clever Ursula, Romy thought, remembering now how Ursula had boarded that train at a stop halfway to Berlin and had swung her hips into the empty seat opposite Romy. She had frizzy auburn hair and was wearing a man's military coat, but despite that she'd exuded femininity, and a knowingness that Romy had found captivating.

Romy had gazed, entranced, as the girl had opened her knapsack and pulled out a bundle of brown paper, oil already soaking through in patches. Inside were fresh schnitzel and, as Ursula had started to eat, she'd caught Romy's eye.

She'd told Romy afterwards that Romy had practically been drooling, which is what had prompted the kind Ursula to share her picnic.

Romy would always remember the taste of that crumbly, oily fresh schnitzel, the meat inside still warm. Ursula had joked about how ironic it was that her mother had given her such a large picnic, when the truth was that, with so many other children to feed, Ursula had been sent packing to fend for herself in Berlin. Not that she had the first clue where she'd find work.

So Romy had produced the slip of paper from the dictionary that Karl had given her all those years ago, with the address of the clothing factory in which he'd once worked. But as Ursula had inspected it, it had occurred to Romy for the first time that the factory might no longer even exist.

75

That Karl's information must have been old. She had been about to declare as much when Ursula had announced that they'd go together. Then she'd given Romy a bottle of beer and clinked it with her own to seal the deal. Romy had taken a sip, then burped loudly and they'd both laughed.

'You're just like my brother,' Ursula had told Romy, who realized that Ursula had assumed she was a boy. 'It's safer to travel if you're with family. You can be my cousin,' Ursula had told Romy. 'What's your name?'

Romy had looked at the ID the stationmaster had given her, for more of Lemcke's cash. 'Jorgen,' she'd told Ursula.

'We're more likely to find work together, Jorgen. Stick with me. I'll keep you safe.'

Now, over a year since that day, Romy swung her feet out of bed and flattened down her chest with the grubby length of crepe and tied it tightly, before pulling on her trousers and overall, ready for the day's shift in the factory.

The others complained all the time about the harsh working conditions, the lack of light, the fact that the factory was a fire hazard, but compared to the orphanage, this place felt like heaven.

The only problem was that now Romy's disguise was starting to wear thin. She'd lied about her age, so that everyone here thought she was younger than she was. She'd thought it would be easier to pose as a boy that way. The problem was that now her voice should be starting to break, and stubble appearing on her chin. It wasn't long before questions would be asked. What then? Where would she go? She had money, but to spend any of it would arouse suspicion anywhere she went. And she didn't want to go anywhere. Not yet. Not until she'd worked out a plan.

She tiptoed out of her cubicle in the dormitory in the dark. Franz, the security guard, was pulling on his boots. He gestured for Romy to wait and she rolled her eyes at him, smiling as he hopped along after her.

Franz was in his twenties, with dark hair and a thin moustache. He slapped Romy on the back as they walked together into the corridor, past the steam of the shower room, where Lutz was whistling loudly.

'She's quite something,' Franz whispered to Romy, conspiratorially, nodding over his shoulder, back in the direction of Ursula's cubicle.

'I heard,' Romy said, keeping her voice jovial.

She'd learnt to put on an act of camaraderie with the boys. But the truth was that the sound of Ursula and Franz's frenzied panting had made Romy pull the pillow over her head.

She felt confused—and jealous—of the escapism that Ursula found through sex and of the comfort Franz found in her soft arms.

Franz chuckled. 'You should have a go on her yourself. I know you're distant cousins, but it doesn't matter. You know she likes you.'

Romy shook her head, taking one of the smokes Franz offered him. 'She's not my type.'

'Believe me, that girl is *everyone's* type.' He leant in closer, his arm around Romy's shoulder. 'She told me her mother was once a prostitute. Good fucking is in her blood. She knows how to squeeze,' he added, elongating the word, as if reliving a delicious sensation. 'I'll see you tomorrow for poker?'

77

Romy nodded, trying not to show how eager she was. Franz and the other guards could pick up the same radio station where she'd heard that Madonna track 'Crazy for You' a couple of times. She couldn't get it out of her head.

'Sure. You'd better watch out this time,' Romy called after him, hauling up the grey bag of material samples and taking it into the lift and closing the grille door, as Franz's laughter echoed down the corridor. Then the lift clanked as it shifted between the floors.

She knew that Franz had a Sony Walkman—his prized possession—and some tapes for learning English. Whatever it took, Romy was going to win them from him.

*   *   *

Two hours later the windowless warehouse was starting to fill with the day-shift workers, despite it being a Sunday. Romy studied each one of them. The women with hard, hungry faces who had children at home to feed, who worked in the deafening noise of the machine room, with muted, disciplined devotion. Nobody could afford to lose their job here.

Despite the spring weather outside, inside it was cold, as if the building couldn't shake off the winter damp. Occasionally an industrial alarm would sound off and the workers would tip their finished garments into the blue bin, which they took it in turns to push in the narrow strip between the rows of machines.

'You're late,' Anna-Maria said, marking a sheet on her clipboard and glaring at Ursula as she slid

78

in next to Romy.

Ursula poked her tongue out at the prim floor manager as she turned her back.

'Sour-faced cow,' Ursula said to Romy, tying her curly auburn hair up into one of the regulation grey scarves. She picked up the white material of the vests they were to sew. 'Relax,' she read, looking at the large orange letters on the white jersey cloth. 'If only.'

Romy smiled. Now that Ursula was here, she felt happy. 'I saw Franz this morning and I heard you two last night,' she said, wriggling the material under the foot of the machine and applying the power. The stitches whirred away from her in a straight line.

'Stupid oaf! He thinks he's God's gift to women,' Ursula said, threading her machine, eyeing up the needle with a professional knack. 'You OK to come out on the bikes this afternoon?'

'Sure.' Romy smiled. She turned back to her machine, but now the weight of the lies she'd told pressed on Romy's conscience. How she'd spun yarns about how her family had been taken away and falsely imprisoned, but she'd managed to escape to her aunt's, and how she'd grown up in a happy home. How she remembered their family Christmases together and sledging with her little cousins. This afternoon alone would require more tall tales.

But the closer she and Ursula became, the more terrified Romy was of her finding out the truth.

Stop it, Romy told herself, forcing her fear away. She wouldn't think about it. Not today. Today was going to be a good day.

79

The whirring of the machines soon made it impossible to chat, but when Ursula's foot reached out for Romy's, she looked up to see Herr Mulcher, the floor manager, come into the warehouse. He was a fat fifty-year-old with weary, weepy eyes and a bulbous red nose.

'Jorgen?' he called as he shrugged off his overcoat. 'I need to see you in my office. Now.'

Romy stared at Ursula, feeling her heart racing.

'What have you done?' Ursula mouthed, alarmed.

Romy shrugged and got up from the bench as if it were no big deal, but inwardly she was cursing herself. She should have taken the money out of the mattress this morning and hidden it in her clothes, just as she'd painstakingly done every day for the first six months here. If she had to run, she'd have no time to get it now.

Mulcher's cramped office was filled with material samples, the walls covered in invoices and notices, the window covered by a blind with dusty kinked slats. A broken umbrella was propped up next to a grey filing cabinet, its drawers overflowing with papers. A newspaper—today's—slid off the top and Romy picked it up to replace it, noticing the headlines about the new Russian leader, Mikhail Gorbachev, and the picture of him with a distinctive birthmark on his head.

'Sit,' Mulcher said, pointing to the orange plastic chair opposite his untidy desk as he searched for something. He chewed an unlit cigarette between his lips.

'If I've done something wrong, I can explain,'

Romy began, memories of Professor Lemcke looming large in her mind.

Mulcher looked at her for the first time. He took the cigarette from his mouth. 'I'm not here to tell you off, but to thank you.'

Romy gawped at him as he laughed.

'Thank me?'

'Yes, lad. It's not often in this low-life load of scum that I get someone with something up here.' He jabbed his temple with his finger. 'Anna-Maria told me what you did last month. And so now I'm going to promote you to pattern-cutting.'

'You are?' Romy felt a stab of panic. That would mean being away from Ursula.

'You have no idea, do you? You see, it's like this . . .'

Mulcher pulled his chair in beneath him, lowering his considerable bulk into it with a grunt. The air escaping from the leatherette seat made a hiss.

'You changing the design on the pattern for the trousers saved me a hundred yards of material.' He leaned in across the desk. His breath smelt of garlic. 'Can I tell you a secret?' he asked. 'Man-to-man?'

Romy nodded. Mulcher's bulbous eyes bored into Romy's, as if he were trying to see inside her head, weighing up the consequences of talking to her, of sharing the secret he wanted to.

'If you save me material, I use it to make the same garments, but I ship out those ones to my contact to the West. Pure profit, my boy. Pure profit.'

Romy felt relief balloon inside her. She already knew about the secret shipments from Franz's

81

coded chats with the other guards. But Mulcher telling her made her officially in the inner circle. One step closer to the West. To where she wanted to be.

'I can save you more,' Romy said. 'More materials. The design patterns—they're sloppy. Look . . .'

She grabbed a piece of paper and a pencil on the desk, clearing a space. She drew the shift-shirt they'd been making all week. 'Bring it in at the waist here,' she drew, her tongue sticking out of the corner of her mouth as she concentrated, 'and take it up by half an inch, which will be more flattering, and you can cut the pattern the other way. See?'

Mulcher rubbed his hands together greedily. 'You, my boy, are going to go far.'

*   *   *

Ursula had laughed when she'd found out that Romy hadn't been able to ride a bike, but Romy had soon picked it up, thanks to Ursula's gentle patience, and in the last few months they'd explored the whole of East Berlin. They'd gone along the river path, to the centre of town, to the boating lake to see the ornate fountains, to the business district with its restaurants and the space-age TV tower, and over the bridges to museum island, where the grand buildings of a bygone era were derelict and covered in weeping ivy.

That afternoon Romy was still riding high after her meeting with Mulcher as she joined Ursula outside the factory.

'Come on, slowcoach,' Ursula called, already

hitching up her skirt and riding down the potholed road away from the factory, the shadow of her wheels whirring across the piles of debris on the roadside.

They crossed the overpass of the busy road and soon dropped down into the residential area, where the streets on a Sunday were quiet. They raced now, laughing and weaving past each other, as they rattled towards the city centre, following the line of the huge grey wall that separated them from West Berlin. Here they had to be more cautious.

'Relax, will you,' Ursula tutted as they spotted two police men up ahead. She was always scolding Romy for being so jumpy. 'I'll handle this.'

They slowed to a stop.

'Where are you two going?' one of the policemen asked.

'Just around. We're exercising,' Ursula said. 'It's been a long week at the factory.'

And there it was again. That cock of the head, the soft knowing smile, the way she put her hand on her hip, as if promising a caress. Romy watched, amazed, as Ursula lured in the young police officer.

'It's a nice day for it,' she said, her voice suggesting so much and yet seeming so innocent at the same time.

The policeman's expression softened from suspicion to indulgence.

'Well, then. Have fun,' he told Ursula, barely looking at Romy, as Ursula flashed their papers from the factory and the officers waved them on their way.

They cycled on, stopping only once, so that

83

Romy could listen to someone playing a violin through an open window. The sound, mixed with the sunshine and the birdsong, filled Romy with joy.

Eventually they stopped in Romy's favourite spot. Across the plaza from the Brandenburg Gate. They leant their bikes up against a tree, its bark stripped off to reveal tan and yellow patches.

'How do you do that . . . thing?' Romy asked, as Ursula peeled off her sweater and tugged at the front of her vest top. Her ample cleavage shone with perspiration.

'What thing?' she asked, still out of breath.

'You know. The way you are with men?'

Ursula shrugged and put the sunglasses down over her eyes. 'It's easy. It's a girl trick. You boys can't tell if I'm putting it on or not. Why?' Ursula asked, suddenly lifting the glasses again and cocking her head in a coquettish way at Romy. 'You jealous?'

'No,' Romy scoffed, but something about the way Ursula looked at her made her blush.

'Franz gave me this,' Ursula said, revealing a bar of chocolate in her skirt pocket. 'You want some?'

'You don't have to share it with me,' Romy said, but the chocolate looked so delicious that her mouth was already salivating.

She wanted to tell her friend so badly about how happy such little treats made her. How hard life had been at the orphanage. How even seeing chocolate made her feel guilty—made her think of the kids she'd left behind. Had any of them survived? she wondered, remembering the faces at the window. Snow and flames. She forced the memories away.

84

'You're different from the others, Jorgen. Sweeter. You know that? Sweet like chocolate,' Ursula said. She broke a bit of chocolate off and slipped it to Romy. Then she licked her lips, her blue eyes widening mischievously as she took the chocolate in her mouth.

Romy leant back against the tree and gazed up at the columns of the gate and the proud statues on top against the backdrop of clear blue sky. The wall was at its lowest at this point and Romy stared through the gate, as she felt the sweet chocolate soften against her tongue.

'What are you looking at?' Ursula asked, coming to stand next to Romy and mimicking her stance. One foot against the tree.

'The gate and what's beyond it.'

'It'll never open and we'll never find out what's on the other side. So there's no point in worrying about it.'

But Romy continued to stare.

'Poor sweet Jorgen,' Ursula said, taking Romy by surprise. She rolled around closer now, pinning Romy back against the tree. 'Why so serious?'

She smelt of sunshine and chocolate.

'Come on. Let's stop all this flirting,' Ursula breathed in her ear. 'You know I don't care about that fool, Franz. Let me make a man of *you*.' Suddenly she started singing—the Madonna song Romy had thought about earlier, 'Crazy for You'.

'Don't. Someone will see us,' Romy said.

It was too late. Ursula was still singing as she slid her hand over Romy's crotch. She giggled, delighting in her power to shock, as she gave Romy a squeeze.

'Don't!' Romy said, trying to shove her away,

but Ursula's hand had already stopped. She recoiled as if she'd been burnt.

'Oh my . . . oh my . . .' she gasped, the song forgotten. Her eyes widened as they met Romy's. 'You're, you're not—you're a . . .'

Romy felt her cheeks burning. 'It's not like you think. It's . . .'

But Ursula just shook her head, backing away. Her face was drawn with shock. 'All these months together,' she gulped.

'I couldn't tell you,' Romy said, trying to stop her backing away. Trying to stop her from making a scene out here in the open air, where anyone could be looking.

'You're not . . . I mean, you're a *girl*? Why have you lied to me all this time?' Ursula demanded, her eyes raking over Romy's face and chest.

'Something happened—I had to run . . .'

Romy cursed herself. Cursed herself for lying. Cursed herself for the look of pain on Ursula's face. Romy pulled Ursula towards her, desperate now not to let her go. Not until she understood.

'You're *that* girl, aren't you?' Ursula gasped, blocking Romy's embrace. 'Franz told me they're looking for a girl. A girl from Bolkav, the orphanage—she burnt it down to cover up a murder.'

Romy felt her legs shaking. Lemcke . . . Ulrich . . . the other boys. Of course they'd try to blame her. The photos she'd stolen from Lemcke's desk—all that evidence of what was going on at the orphanage. Of course they wouldn't rest until they found her body. Or killed her, if she was still alive. And now that Ursula knew, they'd kill her too.

But it was too late. Ursula had seen the look of

86

admission in her eyes. And fear.

'Ursula, please,' Romy begged.

'Get away from me,' Ursula said, then grabbed her bike.

'Ursula, wait,' Romy called out, but it was too late. With a sob Ursula was cycling away, back towards the factory, as fast as she could.

CHAPTER SEVEN

DECEMBER 1985

Thea stood in the choir stalls, looking around the stained glass of the softly lit school chapel listening as the choirgirl—Annabelle Atkins, a bully from the sixth form—sung the first verse of 'Once in Royal David's City', her clear voice soaring above the hushed congregation of staff and parents. *How terribly English*, Thea thought, thinking of the snow outside and the reception with mulled wine and mince pies that she'd have to help at when the service was over.

Her father had chosen St Win's because Thea's mom, Alyssa Maddox, had boarded here as a child before she'd moved to America. At first Thea had comforted herself with the thought that it would give her a spiritual connection to her mother. But the only trace of Alyssa McAdams, as she had been then—apart from a glowing eulogy in the 'Notable Alumni' section of the school's prospectus—was a tiny blurred spec in a school photograph. Her mother wasn't in any of the school drama-society or sports photos. Most likely because she'd spent

87

most of her free time at home or out riding, learning how to jump. She probably hated the over-traditional hotbed of bitchiness then, just as much as Thea did now.

Everyone would be going home later tonight with their parents, except Thea, who would be boarding a flight to New York tomorrow alone. She couldn't help but picture all those girls back in their childhood bedrooms, back with their family pets, surrounded by siblings and friends and warmth. It made her ache for Little Elms and all she had lost.

Griffin and Storm had been busy finishing the top two storeys of the newly built Maddox Tower in New York since their wedding last year, and Thea guessed that it was where she was expected to join them. Her father had sent a curt letter about Christmas being a time for families and he expected her to come home. But nowhere could ever be home when it contained Storm and Brett. Not for Thea.

Her home had gone.

It still seemed unbelievable that her father had sold Little Elms so fast and had moved on without so much as a hint of regret. Or without mentioning once that it was Thea's inheritance that he'd sold. Much more than that too. Her past. Her memories. Her heritage. Her happy childhood. All of that had been woven into the brickwork and turf of Little Elms. They'd just thrown it away. A fact that had started to rankle more and more.

But the worst part was losing Michael. The awkward public goodbye with him still made Thea shudder when she remembered it. The way Michael had looked at her standing next to her father. She'd known what he'd been thinking. She'd read it in his face as clearly as if he'd spoken the words out loud. He thought Thea was the same as Griffin and Storm Maddox. That she'd cast him and his mother out of their home, without so much as a second thought. When nothing could have been further from the truth.

If you're there, God, she prayed silently, *please make sure Michael is safe*.

*   *   *

Forty-eight hours later, weary with delays and the boredom of the long journey, Thea was stepping out of her father's limousine onto the pavement outside Maddox Tower. She slid the headphones from her head. She'd been listening to Madonna's 'Crazy for You' track non-stop, but now the sounds of the city assaulted her and the smell of roasting chestnuts and icy pavements.

'It's impressive, huh?' Anthony, her father's driver, said, looking up at the mammoth steel and glass structure, his breath condensing in the cold. A gold M was on the top—a recent addition, Thea noticed.

'Yeah, I guess,' Thea said nervously. How could a skyscraper ever really be home?

But that's exactly what Storm considered it to be, Thea thought, as a few minutes later she arrived at the penthouse in the express elevator.

'You're here. You're home,' Storm said. She threw out her arms, not to embrace Thea, but as a gesture to encompass the sheer grandness of the atrium. 'I mean, isn't it totally, like, *wow*?' she prompted.

89

'It's . . . big,' Thea managed, her heavy book-laden bags landing with a thud on the marble tiles. She'd ransacked the school library to swat up on economics over the Christmas break.

From where she was standing she had a clear view up a staircase, to a vast atrium with a glass roof above. This wasn't a home. This was more like standing in a spaceship. A very gold spaceship, she noted.

Everywhere she looked there were flashes of gold—clocks, mirrors, even a golden Buddha, of all things. But it wasn't just gold that was on display. It was money. In all its forms. Paintings, tapestries, vases. A white grand piano. The whole place was a gaudy shrine to newly acquired—and spent—wealth.

There were people everywhere too. Corridors stretched off to both left and right—along one a penguin-suited waiter seemed to skate along the marble floor, with a giant tray full of champagne glasses held aloft.

'You're having a party?' Thea asked, noticing the extravagance of Storm's floor-length sequinned dress for the first time. Did they really think so little of her that they'd organized a party the night she came home from school?

'Oh, don't sound like that, sweetie,' Storm said. 'It's just a little soirée. In your honour,' she added, but even as she did so, it sounded like a lie. 'Brett's girlfriend Susie is coming too. You'll like her.'

'Brett has a girlfriend?'

'Oh, and they're so good together,' Storm said. 'Just you wait.'

Thea felt a small bloom of relief. If Brett had a girlfriend . . . then maybe, just maybe, this vacation

90

wouldn't be so bad after all. But once again she felt the sting of Storm's betrayal. This was the woman who had called Thea a 'freakish brat' behind her back and had sent her away to boarding school. No amount of twinkly-eyed smiles could ever erase that.

But maybe those harsh words had just been Storm's stress talking? For Brett's benefit. Because Brett had been so argumentative and aggressive on her wedding day. Maybe she hadn't really meant what she'd said—it had just slipped out.

'Oh, darling, it's so wonderful to see you,' Storm said, finally enveloping Thea in a hug. Her scent—the exotic perfume that Thea had once found so beguiling—now made her nose tickle with its overwhelming saccharine smell.

Did she mean it? Was this love and affection that she felt? Or some other kind of connection? An altogether darker grip. Thea couldn't tell.

'My, you've put on some pounds,' Storm said, pulling back and appraising Thea, who felt her cheeks burning. Was it really that obvious? 'We'll have to shift those, won't we. Being fat is just too sloppy,' Storm continued with a bright smile. 'Oh, there's so much to show you, honey, and I just can't wait to catch up. How's school. Is it a riot?' Storm continued, keeping her hands on Thea's shoulders and her smile fixed in place.

'Yeah,' Thea lied, noticing that something odd had happened to Storm's face. Her lips seemed to have changed shape since the summer. They were puffier. More pouty.

'See?' Storm said, beaming. She rubbed her knuckle on Thea's cheek. 'I knew you'd love it.'

Thea smiled weakly and followed Storm along

91

the hall, noticing how the heavy sequins of her dress crackled around her curves.

'Griff's still at the office downstairs,' Storm announced, 'but he should be here soon. Although these days all he does is work, work, work.'

Thea picked up a petulance in her tone. So much for being the perfect corporate wife, she thought, as Storm threw open a door to what was clearly a guest room.

It had bronze-patterned wallpaper and bronzy-gold flouncy silk curtains over the windows. Three sepia aerial photographs of *Alyssa*, her father's yacht, in full sail were framed on the wall. When had he commissioned those? Thea wondered. Her father was smiling, stretching out to wave at the camera. Was that *Brett* with him? Is that what they'd been doing whilst she'd been at boarding school?

'There's boxes and boxes of your things,' Storm said. 'We've put them in storage until you've decided which room you want.'

There was a choice? Thea wondered. How big was this place?

'Oh, look, there's my baby,' Storm gasped.

A small shih-tzu dog with a diamanté collar jumped up at Storm. She let the dog lick her face as she petted him.

'Oh, my baby, my baby,' Storm cooed. She turned to Thea. 'This is Cha-Chi. My Christmas present from Griff.'

Her father had given Storm a puppy? Thea thought. Why had he never given *her* a puppy, when she'd wanted one all her life?

'He's very . . . er . . . cute?' Thea said, trying to find the right word. Cha-Chi snarled, baring his needle-sharp teeth.

'He doesn't like strangers, do you, my handsome?' Storm said, hugging him tighter.

Strangers. So I'm now one of those, am I? Thea thought. *Even here in my father's home.*

'If only he was a real baby,' Storm added wistfully, smooching the dog on the lips, setting it back down on the floor. 'Now *that* would have been the perfect Christmas present.'

*   *   *

Thea took a long shower, then put mousse in her hair and switched on the TV. As she tipped her hair upside-down, scrunching it to dry it with the hair-dryer, she looked at the pictures of the President, Ronald Reagan, at some sort of Christmas party with Nancy, stick-thin in a red dress next to a huge twinkling tree. Then, once again, the video came on for 'We Are the World' and all the pictures of the dying children in Africa, and she switched off the TV. She'd seen it so many times and had helped the charity do the fund-raiser in school, but the images left her depressed. What with nuclear missiles and famine and AIDS, she wondered how everyone was so upbeat about the future.

She rifled through her suitcase for the black cocktail dress Storm had bought Thea to take with her to England for 'all the parties' at school. What a joke. There had been no parties. Well, certainly not ones Thea had been invited to. She thought of Bridget Lawson and Alicia Montgomery and all those girls who giggled about Thea behind her back, and who made it abundantly clear how left out Thea was from their inner clique. They did everything together—from quoting *Back to the Future* and religiously watching *Fame*, to shopping for the same black miniskirts and metallic pink lipstick. Thea was glad to be away from them for a while.

Now she smoothed out the wrinkles on the much-travelled—never worn—dress. She hoped she could still squeeze into it. Was it that obvious how much weight she'd put on? But that wasn't all. In the last year her breasts had grown three cup sizes and, judging from the length of her jeans, she'd grown several inches too.

She quickly drained a bottle of Coca-Cola from her backpack in the hope of staying awake and put on some blue eyeshadow in the bathroom and her black velvet headband, fluffing out her hair behind it.

'Come on,' she told herself, forcing a smile in the mirror, 'you can do this. It's only a party.'

And tomorrow . . . tomorrow she could spend time with her father and she could ask him what he'd done with everything from Little Elms. But right now she had to concentrate on fitting into this weird new family.

Steeling herself to be on show once again, she slipped out of the bedroom towards the sound of music and laughter. But just as she was about to go up the wide staircase to the mezzanine floor, she heard an insistent knocking. It must be some kind of private entrance from the Tower's service-lift elevator, she figured, trying to work out the vast geography of the apartment as she walked towards the door.

Opening the tricky bolts, she saw a woman in a

94

fawn cashmere coat on the threshold.

'Can I help you?' she asked.

The woman looked far too sensible to be one of Storm's guests. She had no make-up on, which only exaggerated her anxious expression.

'Is this the Maddox household?' the woman asked.

Thea nodded. 'I'm Thea Maddox.'

The woman was craning her neck to look into the apartment. 'Is your father here? May I see him? It's a personal matter.'

A personal matter? Thea looked at the woman, but her soft grey eyes didn't seem threatening. 'I think he is. Yeah, sure. Come in.'

As the woman talked politely about the snow outside, Thea took her upstairs into the living room. There were already lots of people—more than Thea had expected—about fifty guests, standing around with colourful cocktail and champagne glasses, and the hubbub of chatter and laughter filled the air. A man was playing the grand piano in a corner and singing 'Have Yourself a Merry Little Christmas', next to an enormous Christmas tree, which was lit up in gold lights.

'There you are,' Griffin Maddox said, breaking away from a conversation and coming over to greet Thea, kissing her on both cheeks. He was wearing a red smoking jacket—a garment Thea didn't even know he possessed.

'Oh. Hello?' he said, his look demanding an explanation as he greeted the woman.

'Is Brett . . . Brett Maddox here?' the woman asked.

'Sure. He's over there.'

The woman stiffened as she followed Griffin's

95

glance across the room to the sofa where Brett sat, his arm spread out along the back of the seat. He was wearing pink jeans and a white shirt with the collar turned up. A pretty blonde girl in a miniskirt was sitting in the crook of his arm. Brett was feeding her caviar canapés and laughing.

In an instant the woman had crossed the room and stood facing him.

'You—you . . . monster,' Thea heard her say.

'Hey . . . hey, what's going on?' Griffin Maddox asked, quickly catching up.

Thea followed, feeling her cheeks burning with apprehension. The whole atmosphere of the room had suddenly changed, as tension radiated out of the woman. Storm was striding across the room.

'He . . .' the woman said, her eyes glittering with fury as they bored into Griffin Maddox and then back at Brett, '. . . he did something unspeakable to my daughter.'

Storm arrived at Griffin's side. 'Who is she? Who let this woman in?' Then she glared at Thea. She must have seen her introducing the woman to Maddox. Her eyes blazed with fury.

But suddenly Thea didn't care. Whatever this stranger was saying Brett had done, Thea knew in an instant that it was true. That look in his eyes. She'd seen it that first night when he'd sat on her bed. The way he'd instructed Storm to send Thea away—it all made sense.

But now . . . now he'd been publicly caught out.

'Your daughter . . . ?' Griffin Maddox asked.

'Ally. Ally Munroe.' The woman's voice cracked.

Brett shrugged. 'Never heard of her,' he said. He didn't get out of his chair, or take his arm from around the blonde.

'You come in here and *dare* to accuse my son—' Storm's voice rose in outrage.

'He's a liar,' the woman snapped back. 'An animal.'

'And you,' Brett said, stiffening now, his face beginning to flush, 'should know that accusing people you don't know, of things you know nothing about, could get you into a whole world of trouble.'

Undeterred by the threat in his voice, the woman stepped towards him, her arm raised to strike. It was Griffin Maddox who held her back.

'Griff!' Storm's hands flew to her mouth. 'Oh my God!'

'Please,' he said. 'We'll talk about this downstairs,' he told the woman, as her composure crumpled.

'Get her out of here. Get her out,' Storm screeched.

'Storm, let me handle this. I'm terribly sorry,' Griffin Maddox said icily, smiling at the guests and ushering the woman away.

Brett's girlfriend Susie sat in the crook of his arm, her hands on her knees. She looked at the carpet as Griffin Maddox escorted the woman from the room. Thea saw that her chest had gone dappled and her cheeks were burning.

'Now look what you've done,' Storm hissed at Thea, watching them go. 'You can't stop yourself from poisoning everything, can you?' She could barely get the words out, she was so angry. 'How dare you let that woman in. How dare you ruin my party.'

Thea stared defiantly at her. So much for it being a party in Thea's honour then. Here was the real Storm. Any doubt—any hope—that there was

97

another Storm, a Storm who really did care about Thea and who would treat her as an equal to her son, all that was washed away in one look.

Not only did this Storm resent her, Thea realized. *This* Storm—the real Storm—was frightened of Brett. Just as she had been on her wedding night. And she would always put him first.

Or you'll try, Thea thought, as she continued to stare right back at her. *But now I know you . . . now I see you. I might find a way to stop you.*

But Brett . . . Brett gave nothing away. He stretched his leg out along the large couch and shrugged.

'She's probably after money,' he said, totally unfazed, popping another canapé into his mouth. He smiled widely at Storm, who smoothed down her dress as if mentally brushing herself off.

'Of course she was, darling. She's not the first, and I'm sure she won't be the last. It's the price you pay for being rich and handsome,' she said. Then she clapped her hands and smiled brightly, turning to her guests. 'Let's have some more cocktails, everyone.'

Thea stared as Storm disappeared into the crowd, reigniting her party with another anecdote about how she'd inspired Sylvester at Crofters to make *Rocky IV*, as if its recent success was all down to Storm herself.

'Bad call, Thea,' Brett said, his eyes glittering with menace. 'Tut-tut. Rule one: you really should leave it to the staff to open the door. Unless, of course, you fancy ending up one day as staff yourself.'

* * *

98

Much later Thea was exhausted, but she couldn't sleep, her mind whirring with injustice and jetlag. The party had gone from bad to worse. Storm had got drunk and had started singing along with the pianist.

Brett had left early with Susie, thankfully, but Thea hadn't felt able to excuse herself. Just as Brett had predicted, Griffin Maddox was furious that Thea had let the woman into the party. Whatever Brett may or may not have done seemed to be outweighed by Thea's own lack of judgement, in her father's eyes. He'd been frosty and disapproving of her all evening. Whenever she'd been in earshot he'd done nothing but trumpet Brett's academic and sporting successes to anyone who'd listen.

As for the woman's outburst and accusation, the whole thing had been brushed over, and Thea was left both outraged and baffled. How had her father let Brett get away with it? Where was *his* moral judgement? Why couldn't he see that the woman had been telling the truth and that Brett was a liar?

Now Thea felt the humiliation of it all overwhelm her. She felt soiled. As if her silence had made her complicit in family secrets of which she wanted no part.

Too upset to lie in the shadows of her room, she got up and walked silently to the kitchen. She was ravenous. She'd been too nervous to eat in front of Storm. Her catty comment about Thea's weight had stung. So what if she'd put on a few pounds? What else did she have to do at school but eat? What other comfort *was* there?

Upstairs on the mezzanine floor, where the

99

party had been, the blue glow of a security light made this supposed new 'home' feel more like a prison.

It could not feel more different from Little Elms. She'd never once felt scared in the big house that had been her playground for all of her childhood. She'd never once felt spooked out or threatened there. She remembered how, when she couldn't sleep, she'd go down to the kitchen to find Mrs Pryor, who'd make her warm milk and fill a hot-water bottle from the kettle.

Without turning on the lights, Thea started opening cupboards in the sterile designer kitchen, until she found the fridge and poured herself a glass of icy-cold milk.

'You waiting up for me? How sweet.' The voice behind her made her spill the milk over the side of the glass.

Brett staggered against the kitchen doorway. He was drunk. Thea backed away and clutched the neck of her robe.

'I thought you were staying with Susie?' she said.

He laughed, humourlessly. 'Ah, Susie. Not tonight. I had to let her go.' He shook his head, as if the letting-go to which he referred had been a battle he was glad to be out of. Thea shuddered to think what he'd done to the poor girl, if she'd challenged him at home about the accusations made at the party.

'I'm just going to bed,' Thea said, trying to dodge around him.

'Ah-ah-ah. Not so fast.' His arm barred her exit. 'Stay a while. Let's catch up.' He trailed his finger along her arm. She flinched away.

100

'I don't want to speak to you,' she said, suddenly feeling terrified. She backed up against the sink.

'What a perfect Christmas present,' he said, ignoring her. He pushed off the doorframe and came towards her. 'You've ripened up, just as I knew you would. You know, I pleaded for you to come home. Christmas is a time for family, I told them,' he went on. 'I made them promise to stay in Manhattan. Just to get you here.'

Thea felt a sinking sense of dread as she remembered her father's letter, clearly puppet-written by him for Storm. Thea should never have got on the plane.

'What's the matter?' Brett said. 'You still upset about that little scene earlier? You know, what that woman said. About her kid. It wasn't rape.' He waved his hand, as if it were all a big fuss. 'OK, so I did fuck her, and I guess she didn't like it much.' He laughed as if it were a big joke. 'But that's the power of being a Maddox, I guess. You can make everything nasty go away,' Brett said, clicking his fingers, taking the final steps so that he was right in front of Thea. 'Just like that. Gone.'

'You're not a Maddox.' The words were out before Thea could stop herself. But they were true.

'That's not a very nice thing to say,' Brett said. He picked at his tooth, and then suddenly he put his arm around her, pinning her arms to her sides.

She screwed her eyes tight shut as Brett pushed his face into her hair. He kissed her throat tenderly, making her shiver with revulsion and fear. Thea heard a whimper escape her lips.

'Don't,' she managed to say.

'But I want to.'

His breath smelt of whisky. He pushed his body

101

up against her, so that the worktop dug hard into her spine. He gripped her jaw to stop her crying out. Then he stuffed his hand inside her robe, lifting up her Snoopy nightshirt. 'Oh, won't you look at that,' he leered, forcing her legs apart and his hand between them. 'You're all wet for me. Fat girls are always so much more grateful.'

'Don't,' Thea gulped, her eyes bulging with tears. 'Please don't.'

'Or what? You'll tell on me? You think they'll believe you? The hysterical hormonal schoolgirl?' he whispered. Then put his wet tongue in her ear.

She closed her eyes, willing this not to be happening. She felt him slide his fingers inside her. She flinched, nausea rising in her throat as he pressed against her and she felt his erection rubbing through the thin material of his trousers up against her trembling thigh.

'Nobody will believe you, Thea. I'm your father's protégé. Didn't you know that? Which means that everything with a Maddox name on it will be mine for the taking. Even . . .' he said, '. . . you.'

CHAPTER EIGHT

OCTOBER 1986

The plane's wheels screeched as they hit the tarmac, the brakes making a furious roar, the engines, which had been so constant for so long, beginning their deafening fight to make the plane stop. Inside the wooden crate deep in the bowels

102

of the cargo hold Romy stiffened, her limbs mimicking the plane's wheels, bracing against the thin wood.

She licked her dry lips and rearranged her aching body, pressing her eye against the peephole, but it was still too dark to see anything. She'd got used to the noise of the engines, but now the sound of the plane taxiing along the runway just a few feet below her made all her nerves jangle.

She tried to imagine all the passengers on board the plane sitting above her. The holidaymakers and business people who'd boarded the short flight from West Berlin to Heathrow, never thinking that there was a stowaway just below their feet.

Romy felt her heart pounding. If she could just survive this next part, then she'd be free.

Free.

Her throat constricted at the thought of what it would all mean. To be in London. The city of her dreams. She couldn't wait to get out there and see the buses and the taxis, the theatres, shops and bars.

Now that she'd come this far, failure wasn't an option. Do that and she'd have failed Ursula, and she'd promised her friend that she'd make it.

Poor Ursula. It was probably worse for her, being left behind, Romy thought, remembering their tearful goodbye. But it had to be this way. Once Ursula was in on Romy's secret, the clock had been ticking. Lemcke's net had been closing in around her. She'd been able to feel it.

It had taken serious explaining to make Ursula understand that she'd had to lie to protect them both, but after Ursula had eventually forgiven her for her deception, they'd both agreed that Romy

103

had to get out of East Berlin. Fast. The only problem had been, how.

They'd both known it would have been too dangerous to cross the border at any of the normal crossings. Half the border police were Stasi, and they had new body-scanning equipment and trained sniffer dogs. There'd been constant reports about people getting caught. Or killed.

For months they'd deliberated, until, just after Christmas, Ursula had told Franz about Lemcke's money. Once Franz had been in on the secret, he'd organized for Romy to escape in a crate of black-market clothing from the factory.

The plan they'd formulated had been risky, but Franz's brother had a contact at the Bulgarian crossing, who'd known how to bribe one shift of the border guards. All it would take was money, Franz had told Romy. Most of Lemcke's money, and precision timing. As well as one hell of a lot of luck.

The first time, in the spring, the plan had failed and they'd had to abandon all hope of Romy getting out until after the summer. But now, this time, miraculously, the plan had worked. Once in Bulgaria, the lorry had travelled on a twelve-hour straight route into West Germany, terminating at a freight depot, where Romy's crate had been put with the air cargo bound for London. More palms had been greased with cash, and the crate bearing Romy had been waved through the customs check and onto the plane early this morning.

And now here she was, half-starved, parched and aching, feeling as crumpled and twisted as the rags she'd made her nest in, all that time ago in the cabin in the woods.

The plane slowed to a stop. The engines died. The moment of silence was so acute that it felt to Romy as if her ears had been boxed.

Then the cargo-hold door swung open. A thin shaft of grey light came through the peephole, illuminating the cramped living quarters in which Romy had been folded up for the last three days. She was surrounded by the detritus of biscuit rations and water bottles, the last of which she'd finished yesterday, and a large bottle full of urine, which she'd spent half of last night resisting the temptation to drink.

She'd trained herself to ignore the claustrophobia that had threatened to overwhelm her in the past few days by considering the alternative. But now that she was so close to escaping from the rancid, confined space, spending even a second more in it seemed unbearable.

Footsteps came towards her. Two knocks on the top of the crate. A pause. Another. Finally, she knocked back. Her arm felt like lead as she lifted it.

A grunt. Then the splintering of wood as the crate was crowbarred open.

'Hello?' she heard someone whisper.

Romy stood up, gasping in pain as her spine straightened for the first time in days. She blinked into the weak light. The silhouette of a man came into focus. There behind him—a block of thin daylight, the open cargo hatch of the plane. Beyond that a silver patch of tarmac.

Freedom.

The man's clothing came into focus next. An insignia on his overall sleeve. A uniform.

Romy felt her heart skip a beat. Where she

came from, uniforms meant imprisonment, or punishment, or death. Her hands balled automatically into fists.

Please, she silently begged. *Please don't send me back.*

*　　　*　　　*

Paulo Santini stared at the girl. They were all the same, these stowaways. Scared, hungry. Ready to fight.

He never ceased to be amazed by the force of the human instinct to survive. Now his nose crinkled at the sour smell of the girl, and he wondered how long she'd been holed up in there. Not that it mattered. All that mattered was that she'd risked everything to make it to Britain. As so many of them did, fleeing persecution and injustice. Who could blame them?

The girl seemed to slump. He put his arm out to steady her, helping her from the crate. Her arms were thin, but her skin was soft. So soft. And those legs. Boy, oh boy. They kept on coming from the crate.

Paulo glanced behind him. Time was tight, but he knew the drill. He had to get her into the baggage trolley fast. Then out to the loading dock, where he'd hide her under the tarpaulin in the maintenance truck. He'd drive her into town later this afternoon when his shift finished.

If she didn't have any contacts in London, as most of them didn't, he'd take her to his second cousin, Carlos. He'd get her cleaned up at his apartment, then put her to work. Oh yeah. This one looked like she'd do well for Carlos. And

106

Paulo would get another kickback for that.

He rubbed his thumb across his fingertips—the international sign for money. The girl quickly delved into the pocket of her denim skirt and handed over the notes he was expecting. He checked the money, then stuffed the notes into his overalls, before helping her get into a grey baggage trolley. He quickly loaded up bags around her. On top of her. Burying her from sight again.

Pushing the trolley down the ramp and onto the baggage truck, he began to whistle. 'How Will I Know?' That Whitney Houston song had been in his head all morning.

Oh yes, she was a pretty one, this one, Paulo thought. After he'd taken her to Carlos, he'd ask his cousin for a favour. Perhaps he could be the first man in the queue to help break her in.

*   *   *

Romy immersed herself in the hot water, feeling her hair seeping out into the bubbly water of the deep bath. Then she pushed herself up again, wiping the water from her face.

No, it wasn't a dream. She was still here. Boy, this had to be the craziest day ever. In a matter of hours her life had changed beyond even her wildest imaginings. Was everyone in London this rich? she wondered, looking at the pink tiles around the bath and the fancy gold taps and mirror. What would she have to do to be this rich herself?

Her mind was whirring with possibilities. From what she could understand from Paulo's heavily accented English, which was so much more difficult to understand than the language tapes she'd listened to hundreds of times back in the clothing factory, Carlos, his cousin, was something to do with fashion. Maybe he had some kind of factory, Romy thought. Paulo had said he had good opportunities for girls who were prepared to work.

Well, one thing was for sure: Romy was a good worker. She had relevant experience too. What if Carlos did give her a job? Wouldn't that be something? Perhaps she could stay here in this apartment.

Yes, she thought—picking up the bar of pink soap with the word LUX on it, and lathering it between her hands, before spreading the bubbles over her skin to wash away her horrible journey— she could get used to this.

Conscious that she mustn't spend too long in the bathroom, Romy got out of the bath and dried herself on the fluffy pink towel, pressing her face into the soft fragrance of it, amazed that something so simple as a towel could be so lovely. Then she looked inside the plastic bag that Carlos had given her, pulling out the clothes that she was going to change into.

But these clothes . . . . she'd never even seen anything like them. But perhaps this was the English fashion, she thought, wriggling her thin hips into the short leatherette miniskirt and pulling the mesh top over her bra. Did it matter that the bra didn't fit? she wondered, looking in the mirror and feeling painfully self-conscious. She towel-dried her hair and tried to style it in the mirror. Then she slipped on the high white heels, unlocked the bathroom door and tottered into the kitchen.

Carlos stood by a steamed-up window, leaning

on the cooker and smoking a cigarette. The radio was playing pop music. She smiled nervously.

'Feel better?' he asked and she nodded.

He was wearing black leather jeans and a leather jacket. A thick gold chain nestled in the hair poking over the V of his jumper. He had olive skin, like Paulo, and from the look of his stomach, he liked his food and drink. But he seemed friendly enough.

'Eat,' Carlos said, nodding down at the table. 'You must be hungry.'

Romy smiled and pulled the bowl towards her. She didn't know what it was. Some kind of pasta. Long and thin, in a rich red, meaty sauce. But it smelt good. So good.

She started to shovel it into her mouth, but it kept slipping and sliding from her fork and spoon. She twisted in her chair so that Carlos could not see. She was ashamed of her manners, embarrassed in front of him, a sophisticated man from the West.

The door buzzer went. Carlos looked at his chunky gold watch—worth enough by itself, she thought, to have paid for Ursula to have crossed the border too—and stubbed his half-smoked cigarette into the metal ashtray on the table in front of Romy. He glanced at her as he exhaled. Then he went into the hall to open the door.

Romy looked at the cigarette, then sat on her hands. Every instinct told her to steal the cigarette and put it in her pocket. That was far too much tobacco to waste. But what if Carlos wanted to relight it? Then she'd be caught out and, if she made him cross, he might ask her to leave.

A moment later Carlos came back, jangling a set

of car keys in his hands. Three other girls were in the corridor behind him. One of them had a black eye, which she'd tried to cover up with make-up. They all stared at Romy in silence. She froze, the pasta dangling from her mouth.

'Time to go,' Carlos said, swinging the car keys around his finger and catching them in his hand.

Realizing that he meant right now, Romy reluctantly left the pasta, wiping her mouth on a towel on the cooker rail, and followed the girls along the corridor and down the front steps to a big car with blacked-out windows. Carlos held open the door for her, looking nervously up and down the street.

Romy got in the back with the girls, who were all chattering in an Eastern European language she could only make out the odd word of. Where were they going? Who had given that girl a black eye? Why didn't she seem to care? And why did another one not mind her dimpled thighs showing?

But they all ignored her and instead Romy looked out of the window, her eyes feasting on all the London sights she'd been longing to see—the red buses, the phone boxes, the tall plane trees. There was even a royal horse . . . Oh, and that must be Buckingham Palace, she thought, twisting in her seat as Carlos drove down a wide avenue. If only Ursula could see *this*.

Everything was so shiny here, Romy thought, staring out at the colourful hoardings advertising gorgeous Max Factor lipsticks. If only she were rich enough to buy one of them. Or to shop in the stores, she thought, her hand going to the glass window as they passed a huge music store, the windows filled with pictures of Whitney Houston

110

and Prince.

Soon they crossed a river and, just as she was expecting more sights, the city seemed to change. The tall buildings gave way to streets of shabby-looking crammed-together houses and grim-looking tower blocks. Litter was piled up in the gutter and soon there was a row of boarded-up shops covered in graffiti. Two African-looking black children were fighting on the street.

By the time they'd stopped, ten minutes later, Romy's nails were digging into the car seat. They pulled up on the kerb outside a house with a bump. A grey mesh grille covered every window. The door was steel and heavily bolted.

'Your first time?' one of the girls asked her, in English as heavily accented as Paulo's and Carlos's. Romy stepped, shivering, onto the pavement and nodded, wrapping her arms around her mesh top.

'Don't talk to her,' Carlos said from the front.

Inside was a large open-plan sitting room with chunky black-leather seats filled with men. Romy coughed. She was used to smoke, but nothing like this. The air smelt acrid. She looked across at a black man in a hat sitting by a table. He had a yellow plastic frisbee in front of him piled high with what looked like green weed. He nodded, as if he knew her, and Romy quickly turned away, watching as the girls arrived, their high heels clicking against the steel-capped stairs.

Carlos smiled at Romy, but his eyes were no longer friendly, giving her no choice but to move ahead and follow them. At the top of the first flight of stairs he grabbed her arm. 'You. In here. Room two.'

There was a door reinforced with plywood. A

111

green light shone above it.

He pushed her inside. He closed the door and Romy felt as if prison bars had clanked shut.

Panicking, she backed up against the wall.

How could she have been such a fool? She should never have got in that car with Carlos. What other kind of work did she think was available to penniless illegal immigrants? So what if Carlos been kind to her? He'd just assumed her to be a prostitute all along. From the second Paulo had dropped her off at Carlos's flat.

She clawed at her hair, a growl of frustration escaping her.

After everything . . . *everything* she'd been through, she'd walked into *this*? She'd killed Fox to defend herself and Claudia, she'd lied to Ursula, escaped to Britain, putting her life at risk, enduring a horrendous journey, and now she'd walked in here?

Desperately she looked around. There was a bed with a stained purple cover, a cracked basin next to it and a red scarf over the lamp. A joss-stick burnt on the bedside table, filling the air with the sickly smell of patchouli. There were thick bars over the window and the frame was bolted. She flung open the door next to her and saw a small windowless bathroom with a toilet and little shower cubicle. No way out there, either.

Suddenly the door opened and a man came in. He was tall, with a tattoo of a bird on his neck.

'Carlos says you're new. The German chick, right?' he said, baring crooked brown teeth. 'I'm Jimmy.' He pulled a note out of his pocket, put it on the bedside table and tapped it with his finger. 'So come on. Let's see what you're made of.'

112

He grinned at Romy and cast his eyes down at the bed and then back at her.

She glanced at the door, then back at Jimmy. Then she looked at the bin. Could she swing it at his head? But Jimmy was too big. And he was moving towards her.

*   *   *

Later, sore and sickened, Romy stumbled through the dark streets. All the girls had left the house barely two hours after they'd arrived. No one had said anything to her, or acted as if anything important had happened at all.

She'd taken her chance, telling Carlos she was going to be sick so that he'd unlock the car doors. As soon as he had, she'd made a break for it, jumping out of the car by a big set of traffic lights near the river. The other girls had screamed as Romy had leapt from the car, dodging through lanes of traffic to the central reservation, where she'd tripped over the kerb, skinning her knees. She hadn't cared if she'd been run over—only that she got away.

Carlos had shouted after her, and for a second she thought he would run her down, but the other traffic had been blaring its horns at him. She'd watched the car roar away into the distance.

Now, as she stumbled along the kerb in her high heels, her bruised knees smarted, and her palms were bleeding and gritty. She ached to be back with Ursula. Ursula who had loved her.

Shivering in the cold night, she followed the meandering path of the river. Several times cars slowed down and pulled alongside her as she stumbled along the pavement. Each time Jimmy's face loomed in her mind. She thought about that creaky bed and his heavy weight on top of her. How she'd closed her mind, shut herself away in a tiny place, imagining that she was back in the crate, as he'd thrust inside her. How he'd laughed afterwards, and Carlos had come in and taken the money from the bedside and told her they were leaving for another house. How Romy had known then that she'd rather kill him than let him make her do that again.

Romy turned south away from the river, her eyes scouring the ground for coins, but before long she was in some sort of concrete underpass. In the middle of it, a fire in an oil drum illuminated people warming themselves around it. Romy stared at their hollow, hungry faces.

How could this be? People in London didn't starve, did they? People were rich. Why were all these people here? Living in cardboard boxes? It was like the kind of post-apocalyptic scene everyone had been dreading since the nuclear explosion at Chernobyl had released its radioactive cloud. She thought she'd escaped all that when she'd left Berlin. But here . . . this was horrible.

Her heels echoed through the tunnel. Jeers and whispers prickled her from the darkness as she stumbled past the people. She felt terror rising up in her as she hugged her arms around her thin mesh top. Terror that her bravado had deserted her. That her luck had finally run out. She had no means of survival. She was in a strange city, where she knew nobody and had nothing. She'd starve on the street. She'd have to live rough, like those people in the underpass. Or freeze to death.

Whichever came first.

Maybe she should go back to Carlos. Say sorry. Tell him she'd work for him. Maybe that was the only choice. Maybe she couldn't escape her fate. Maybe those photos in Lemcke's office were where she'd been heading all along.

Shivering uncontrollably now, she half-walked, half-ran out of the underpass towards a big building with a clock above its wide-open entrance. She headed up the steps and inside into the comfort of the brightly lit train station. The black boards above her head clattered as the destinations changed.

She walked on, looking at the commuters, and stopped by the entrance to some sort of underground train system. She saw that to reach it you had to first pass through a row of electronic gates with some kind of ticket that she didn't have. Not that she had an idea where she would go, if she did. But the thought of being on an underground train, like the one she'd seen on that TV show *Hill Street Blues* in the guards' office back at the factory, was tempting. She could ride round and round and fall asleep. At least it would be warm.

She looked at the crowds coming up the steps towards her. Normal people, affluent people, with homes and friends and places to go. She looked each one in the eye, challenging them to meet her gaze. But none of them did.

How much braver did she have to be? Romy wondered, feeling dizzy with tiredness. How much braver *could* she be, before someone somewhere gave her a break?

All she needed was just one piece of luck.

Just one piece of luck . . .

'Here,' she heard.

A girl with blonde hair in a red coat stopped, bent down and dropped something in her lap. Romy looked at the money, the crisp note, then up at the girl, but she'd already walked quickly on.

CHAPTER NINE

OCTOBER 1986

'Why did you do that?' the voice behind Thea said.

Thea turned to see Bridget Lawson coming up behind her out of the Tube station. She was one of the most popular girls in Thea's year, and she broke away from the other girls to catch up.

'Do what?' Thea asked.

'Why did you give that girl some money back there? Paying beggars isn't the solution, you know.'

Thea turned and looked back at the girl outside the station. 'She just looked . . . I don't know . . .' Thea didn't know how to put it into words. It was something about the girl's look, in the tiny moment they'd made eye contact, that had caused Thea to take out her purse. Perhaps it was because she looked so hopeless. So alone.

But now her stupidity had been enough to grab the attention of Bridget Lawson. Bridget with her dark curly hair coming from underneath the black beret. Bridget with her pretty freckles and inquisitive eyes.

Their class was on a school trip to see a play at the National Theatre on the South Bank here in

116

London, and Bridget had sat with all the other girls on the Tube here, fussing and primping over their appearance, leaving Thea to read her Sidney Sheldon further up the carriage, alone. Now Thea felt a pang of jealousy for Bridget's electric-blue mascara. She'd never have the confidence to wear something like that.

But confidence was something Bridget Lawson possessed in buckets. She'd played Annie, Tallulah and Lady Macbeth in the school productions. She was also short and nimble and played centre in the school netball team. She had a Benetton jumper in every colour of the rainbow and had never spoken to Thea alone even once before.

But Thea didn't blame her. Ever since Brett's assault last Christmas she felt as if any confidence she'd ever had had been drained out of her.

She tried to console herself with the thought that it could have been so much worse. Just as Brett had been kissing her and reaching for his fly, Cha-Chi, Storm's dog, had nosed around the door and started yapping. Thea, grabbing her opportunity, had chucked her glass of milk in Brett's face, before sprinting to her room and barricading herself in.

She'd stayed awake all night, waiting for the morning when she'd tell her father exactly what Brett had done. But Brett had been waiting for her.

'You breathe a word,' he'd whispered, 'and I'll do much worse.'

'Stay away from me,' she'd managed.

He'd laughed then. 'No problem. You're one of those girls, anyway. You'd let anyone do anything to you.'

At that moment Storm had appeared in the corridor with an ice-pack pressed to her forehead and had announced that she was so stressed after the party that she was going to Crofters for Christmas after all. Brett had whooped with delight and had said he'd go too.

Thea had feigned a stomach bug so that she could stay in New York with Griffin Maddox, hoping he'd protect her. Hoping for the right moment to tell her father. But the moment never came, and when she ended up on the private plane with him to the Caribbean on Christmas Eve to join Storm and Brett, he'd spent the whole time chatting to two businessmen who'd joined them in the plane at the last moment.

So she'd feigned her stomach bug at Crofters too, making sure she stayed locked in the turret room. And as the days and nights had blended into weeks, her resolve to tell her father and expose Brett had weakened.

What if Brett had been right? What if her father didn't believe her? Storm would certainly stick up for Brett, no matter what. And maybe Brett had been right on another account too. Maybe it was somehow her fault. Maybe she had provoked his attack. Maybe, being 'one of those girls', she'd unwittingly given off the wrong signals.

The way her mind had veered back and forth between indignation and guilt had been exhausting. And it had only increased her sense of isolation and the realization that she had nobody— nobody she could confide in. Not any more. Once upon a time she'd had Michael. But even if she knew where Michael was, how could someone good and wholesome like he was ever respect her after what Brett had done?

Thea had felt relieved to go back to school in England. But in the dead of night, alone in the dorm with no real friends, she'd felt desperate at times. And as the slow months had turned into school terms, Thea had become more and more withdrawn, opting to go to a tennis camp in France for the summer holidays, instead of going back to America where she might have bumped into Brett. And even though the immediate horror of his attack had faded, now in the autumn term Thea still felt desperate at times. As desperate as that girl at the Tube station just now had looked.

But Bridget didn't seem to be judging her at all, Thea thought. Well, at least not negatively. She'd expected Bridget to move away, back to the others, but she didn't seem in any hurry to go. In fact, she stayed right by Thea's side as they crossed the road and walked on until the river was in sight.

'Ah,' Bridget said, taking in a deep lungful of crisp London air. 'I love this time of year.'

'Me too,' Thea admitted.

The crisp evening reminded her of her childhood in Little Elms. The leaves swaying down from the plane trees, the skyline faded to a silhouette, the cast-iron lamps shining light on the pavement, the boats sliding under the bridges on the Thames. Suddenly the evening she'd been dreading was infused with possibility.

Now she glanced at Bridget, embarrassed by her scrutiny.

'We've never really talked before, have we?' Bridget said, smiling.

Thea shook her head. She didn't want to say the wrong thing, or mess it up. 'We sit next to each other in biology.'

'Ah. Well, I can't talk to you then, I'm always too busy copying your answers,' Bridget said. Then she laughed, looking at the shock on Thea's face. 'I'm kidding.'

Thea smiled back, feeling unsure of herself. 'I wouldn't mind. I know Poppy copies me, too.'

'Poppy copies everyone. She'll ace us all in the exams, though.'

'Really?'

Bridget laughed. 'Yes, really. That's what I like about you, Thea. You're so out there and American. Haven't you worked it out yet?' Bridget leant in and whispered, 'It's not cool to work hard. Or . . .' she held up her finger, 'to be seen to be working hard. They all swat like crazy in the holidays.'

'Hey, Bridget. Who's your new girlfriend?' one of the girls called from behind them.

Bridget turned and hoisted up her two fingers. 'Drop dead,' she said, linking her arm through Thea's as if they were long-lost friends.

*   *   *

As they walked towards the theatre Bridget Lawson slowed down, letting the others overtake them. But for once Arabella and Marcia could take a running jump, Bridget thought. After Marcia's party in the summer, she had been having second thoughts about hanging out with her set anyway. They were such spiteful bitches. All they did was criticize other people, as if they were the most perfect girls in the world.

And Thea Maddox wasn't half as bad as they

had made out. Giving that girl at the Tube station money was kind of cool. All the other girls wouldn't dare do anything spontaneous and ballsy like that. But Thea was different. Probably good breeding, Bridget thought, thinking of what her father might say about someone like Thea. He'd approve. In fact there'd almost certainly be a horse metaphor, Bridget thought, smiling to herself.

Of course Bridget had to admit that she'd played her own role in goading the American girl, especially when she'd first arrived at St Win's. Who hadn't? She was a sitting duck for being teased, and hardly ever retaliated. She had that funny way of calling jam 'jelly' and holidays 'vacations'. She was so *serious*. Such a bookish swat. But no matter what they said to her, Thea never seemed to get her parents involved, so the girls knew they were safe.

In fact Thea had been so cool in not reacting to all the taunts that Bridget had considered palling up with her that first term, but somehow the moment had passed. She'd been in with Marcia and Poppy then, who hated Thea and had told Bridget all about Thea's mother, Alyssa McAdams, and her grim death from cancer. Marcia, who wasn't the sharpest tool in the box, had told the others that cancer was catching and that Thea would probably die of it too.

She knew that was all hogwash, but Bridget couldn't imagine anything worse than her own mother dying, and had steered clear of Thea. But she noticed now that Thea carried a sadness about her and she wondered whether it was lingering grief. Or maybe something more recent had happened? Come to think of it, Thea had been a bit subdued since the start of term and she'd lost all that weight in the last few months.

Out of the context of school, the Maddox girl took on a different light, Bridget thought. In fact, seeing her now in her red coat, she noticed for the first time just how pretty Thea was. She was tall, with high cheekbones and piercing pale-blue eyes, which complemented her flawless skin and long blonde hair. She was elegant, like a swan. The best part was that she was totally unaware of it.

Yes, she needed a new project, and Thea would be just right, Bridget thought. So what if freaky Thea Maddox was the most unpopular girl in school? Bridget was going to single-handedly make her the most popular. All Thea needed was some trendy clothes and a new haircut and—bingo, Bridget would have a reinvention on her hands. Maybe she could persuade Thea to get her hair permed, then she'd be a dead ringer for Kelly McGillis in *Top Gun* (God, how Bridget adored that film). Or she could even go more punky and get a bob like Debbie Harry, who'd looked awesome on *Top of the Pops* last night. Whatever they decided, Bridget couldn't wait to get started.

Checking to see that there were no teachers nearby, she reached into her pocket and opened her packet of Marlboro cigarettes.

'No, thanks,' Thea muttered, backing away. 'I . . . I don't smoke.'

Bridget took two out of the packet and lit them both with her Zippo lighter. She inhaled on both, then handed one to Thea.

'Go on, give it a try,' she said, talking through the smoke and handing over the cigarette. She watched as Thea took it, unsure how to hold it. She

122

put it between her lips. Bridget smiled and watched Thea take a tentative puff and blow the smoke out. She coughed and spluttered, putting her fist over her mouth.

'Don't worry. That always happens,' Bridget assured her. 'You'll soon get the hang of it.'

So Thea Maddox was just as innocent as she looked, Bridget surmised, regarding the taller girl through the smoke-ring she herself now blew out. But hats off to her: she'd taken a cigarette. As Bridget had suspected, there was clearly some spirit under there after all.

'Why are they all racing to the theatre?' Thea asked, as they walked on, watching the other girls giggling and jostling through the glass doors ahead.

'Two reasons,' Bridget explained. 'Amanda's just got her allowance from her dad and will be bulk buying vodka tonics at the bar as soon as the teachers are distracted. Second, we happen to know that the King Edward boys are coming tonight to the production.'

'Oh,' said Thea.

'You ever had a boyfriend?' Bridget asked.

Thea shook her head.

'Seriously?'

Thea shook her head again. But Bridget saw that she was blushing.

'I don't think you're telling me the truth,' Bridget said.

'I told you *no*,' Thea snapped the words. Bridget saw fury in her eyes.

'Hey, it's cool,' she said. 'I don't want to hear about it anyway. I mean, it's only stupid boy-stuff, right?'

'Right,' Thea said, looking relieved, the colour

fading from her cheeks once more.

Bridget linked arms with her. 'Hey, I just thought of something,' Bridget said, stopping and looking at Thea. 'Do you ride? Horses, I mean? Like your mother?'

She noticed a tensing in Thea's muscles at the mention of her mother. She thought she'd crossed another line, but this time Thea smiled.

'Yes. Well, I used to. I haven't for a while, but I'd love to again.'

'OK, cool,' Bridget said. 'You're coming home with me this weekend. It's settled.'

'Really?'

'Really.'

'What about your other friends? Won't they—'

'Oh yes,' Bridget said, 'but you see, that's the first thing you need to learn, if we're going to start hanging out . . .'

'What?'

'Being important enough to be bitched about by other people is the most fun any girl can have. So long as you learn how to play it just right.'

* * *

By Friday night Thea could hardly remember life before Bridget. It only took one person to think she was cool for Thea actually to *be* cool. She felt hopelessly and pathetically grateful, as if this happiness was a dream and she would pinch herself and wake up.

At night in the dormitory Thea was no longer alone. She was 'in' on the inner circle, listening to Bridget and Tracy and Suze as they sat on Bridget's bed, surrounded by posters of Culture

Club and Duran Duran, whilst flicking through Suze's collection of *Jackie* magazines. They talked about boys they secretly fancied, and Thea found herself sharing her childhood stories about Michael and they all listened attentively, telling her how wonderful it sounded and how lovely Michael must have been.

But the best thing of all was that Bridget had somehow made it possible for what Brett had done to stop occupying Thea's waking thoughts. Bridget's positive energy now filled the place that had only been filled by Thea's doubts and anxiety. She vowed that she would stop thinking about Brett. She vowed that she'd never, ever tell Bridget or anyone else what he'd done.

For the first time since leaving Little Elms, Thea finally felt normal. As if she deserved to be normal. With Bridget's help, she soon learnt how to stick two fingers up to Alicia and all the other bitchy girls who called out nasty comments as she and Bridget linked arms along the corridor. But Bridget seemed to delight in ruffling their feathers and only held onto Thea tighter. It was all to do with attitude, Thea realized. And Bridget Lawson had plenty of that.

When Friday night came around, the two of them could hardly stop talking and giggling, as they set out on the train for Bridget's home. Thea couldn't wait to see the tumbledown Cotswolds flint house where Bridget had grown up.

They were picked up by a farm worker called Joe in a draughty Land Rover, which bumped so vigorously down the lane that Thea wondered whether she'd arrive with any teeth.

'Ah, Pipsqueak,' a man in tweed said, coming

out of a stable door and hugging Bridget, to a cacophony of barking dogs.

'Daddy, this is Thea from school,' Bridget said.

'Ah. Our gold-medal-winner's daughter. An honour.'

Thea smiled at him, feeling something she hadn't felt about her mother for a long time. Not just loss, but something warmer, fiercer: pride.

'And Bridget tells me you ride yourself?' her father continued, looking Thea up and down approvingly. He had a bushy moustache and a tweed hat and twinkly eyes, like Bridget's. 'Marvellous. The hunt meets at eleven. Bridge will find you the proper togs.'

'There'll be a hunt ball up at the manor tomorrow night.' Bridget said, linking arms with Thea and leading her through the hissing geese to the front door. 'You absolutely must wear my green dress.'

They walked through the door and into a homely kitchen. A pretty woman with dark-brown wavy hair—clearly Bridget's mother—wiped her hands on a tea towel.

'Bridgey,' she smiled, embracing Bridget and kissing her cheeks, before holding her face. 'Oh, look at you,' she said, her eyes glistening with love. 'My darling.'

'Mum,' Bridget said, embarrassed. 'This is Thea Maddox. My friend from school.'

'Call me Shelley,' Bridget's mum said, shaking Thea's hand. She was wearing a multicoloured baggy woollen cardigan and a long buttoned-up denim skirt. Bangles jangled on her wrist. 'Your mother was my absolute riding heroine. We were at St Win's together for a while,' she said.

126

'You mean you knew her?' Thea asked, amazed by this news. 'You were friends?'

Shelley nodded. 'I'll dig out all my old school photos later.'

'I'd like that,' Thea smiled, adoring Shelley Lawson already.

She looked around the kitchen. Photographs of Bridget at various horse shows and events graced the walls. The radio blared and a cat meowed around three little kittens in a basket in the corner. On the long wooden dining table were piles of newspapers, as well as eggs, flour and milk, a fruit bowl and a typewriter surrounded by papers.

'How's the novel going, Ma?' Bridget asked, lifting up a tea towel that was covering a tray of cakes, and Shelley gave her hand a loving slap.

'Fine. I'm nearly finished.'

The phone rang, adding to the homely hubbub, and Shelley went to answer it.

'Your mum's a novelist?' Thea asked, impressed, crouching down to pet the kittens.

'Bridge has just come home with a girlfriend from school,' she heard Shelley say, holding a mixing bowl against her, the phone jammed against her shoulder. 'No. Not at all stuck-up like the others.' She winked at Thea. 'Be here early then. You know what your father's like.'

She rang off. 'Tom,' she said in explanation to Thea and Bridget.

Bridget put her fingers in her mouth, simulating retching, when Shelley wasn't looking. 'My brother.'

'The Lanes and the Exmoors are coming for supper tonight,' Shelley said. 'Show Thea around, and then be ready to help me lay the table.'

127

Thea followed Bridget through the latched wooden door and the low stone lintel into the drawing room. There was a thick blue carpet and chintzy curtains and an old wood-burner roaring in the hearth. A battered upright piano stood in the corner. Sofas and chairs were dotted all around the room. Even empty, Thea could imagine it filled up with people. It was the kind of room she imagined playing charades in at Christmas.

'I love your house,' she told Bridget, walking over to a dresser and inspecting the photographs in silver frames.

'That's Tom,' Bridget said, as Thea picked up a picture of a boy. He looked about seventeen and had Bridget's dark hair and freckles.

Thea stared at the photo for a moment longer, until Bridget snatched it away.

'He's a horror,' Bridget said. 'Don't fall for his charms. Promise me? He's totally unscrupulous when it comes to women. He'll lure you in and then hurt you.'

'Wow,' Thea said, stunned by how adamant Bridget seemed to be.

'Seriously. I'm not joking. I absolutely insist you totally avoid him. If we're to be best friends, then that's the deal.'

Thea laughed and shook hands with Bridget, thrilled at the thought of finally having a best friend. 'Deal.'

* * *

But despite Bridget's warning, Thea couldn't help but look out for Tom Lawson early the next morning. She was curious to know if he really was

128

as handsome in the flesh as his photo implied.

She'd never been out on a proper English hunt and loved the atmosphere as the horses gathered in front of the ancient manor house up the road, with its diamond-patterned windows and Elizabethan chimneystacks. There were about forty riders or so, the men dressed in white jodhpurs and pink jackets. The earlier mist that had hung over the fields had evaporated, but the trees were still blurry against the pale sky.

'Down the hatch,' Bridget said, grinning from beneath her black riding hat, as she handed Thea a silver goblet of sherry, which was being offered around by men in long brown Barbours. Thea downed the sherry like Bridget, gasping and laughing.

Thea had been given a young mare, Frollick, from the Lawson stables. Shelley waved at Thea and Bridget and rode up. Dressed like the others in her hunting attire, Shelley looked younger than she had done last night, as they'd sat around the cosy kitchen table laughing and talking late into the night.

Thea had stayed up even later alone in her comfortable guest bed, studying the photographs of her mother that Shelley had given her. Thea had always imagined her mama to look just like she did now, at the same age. But they were so different. Both tall, yes, but Alyssa had always had dark hair, even as a child. Thea adored these images of her young mother and couldn't wait to show them to her father.

'She's jittery at first, but you'll soon get the hang of her,' Shelley said, circling round with her own shiny chestnut mare. 'Oh, it's so wonderful having you here, Thea,' she beamed. 'It's just like the old days and having Lis around.'

'You hunted with her?'

'Once or twice.' Shelley smiled, looking up as if trying to remember something. 'What was that boy who was always around her?' She bit her lip and squinted. 'They were quite a pair. Ah,' she said, her eyes bright. 'Johnny. Johnny Faraday. That was it. He was quite a dish.'

'Johnny?' Thea asked. She couldn't possibly mean the same Johnny. Her Johnny at Little Elms?

Thea's mind whirred. What did she mean by 'quite a pair'? Was she saying that her mother and Johnny had been boyfriend and girlfriend?

But before Thea could even start to contemplate any of these thoughts, a horn blasted out, signalling for the hunt to follow the hounds. Thea's heart was racing as she galloped after Bridget, jumping the first fence and racing into the countryside beyond.

The pace was frenetic, but Frollick seemed to have a mind of her own and soon she'd veered off, taking an alternate route across the fields. Thea held on, seeing the hedgerow coming up fast towards her. Kicking her heels in, she tried to steer Frollick towards the gap, realizing too late that she had to jump the ditch.

'Shit!' Thea yelled, almost going over Frollick's head and saving herself just in time, as they came to a halt in the muddy water. She tried to coax the stubborn beast out of the deep ditch, but Frollick wouldn't budge. Instead she whinnied, annoyed, trying to stamp her back foot, which was stuck.

Thea looked around her frantically, but she

could hear that the hunt had moved off ahead. If she didn't get going soon, she'd be completely lost.

She jumped down, the cold water making her gasp as it poured over the top of her boots. She scrambled out of the ditch the other side, mud splattering into her hair and all over her face. Grabbing the reins, she heaved with all her might, but only succeeded in slipping down the bank on her bottom, back into the water.

She scrambled up onto the bank again and pushed her hair out of her face. She looked down at her once-pristine jodhpurs and jacket. They were ruined.

'I didn't realize there was mud-wrestling too?'

Mortified, Thea looked up to see another rider trotting up on his horse. He dismounted and came over.

'Oh dear,' he laughed. 'Quite a pickle you two are in.'

He helped Thea to her feet, then took Frollick's reins and, clicking his tongue and yanking the leather straps, got Frollick to move up out of the ditch and into the ploughed field beyond. He leant in close and smoothed Frollick's mane, whispering, 'It's OK, girl.' The horse nudged him, clearly familiar with his voice.

Then he turned to Thea, who had scrambled to her feet. Her teeth had started to chatter.

'Hi. I'm Tom, Bridget's brother. You must be her friend from school?' His voice was deep and his eyes bored into her, until she felt herself flushing a deep red. She recognized him now, from his photo. But he was even more handsome in the flesh. He had floppy dark hair and big green eyes with long lashes.

131

Of all the ways to be introduced. She looked down at herself, ashamed. Then back at Tom, who was still staring at her. 'I'm Thea Maddox,' she mumbled.

Right at that moment, as Thea's eyes connected with his, she felt something strange happening, as if she were driving fast over a hump-backed bridge. *Oh my God*, she thought, her promise to Bridget forgotten. *This is Tom Lawson?*

CHAPTER TEN

JULY 1987

The horn of the cruise ship *Norway* blasted out, making Romy jump. She leant over the top railing, hearing its echo across the Hudson River.

'Wow,' she gasped out loud. It wasn't every day a girl arrived in New York.

She was so high up, it was like staring down from a cloud. She looked past the red and white lifeboats, past the fluttering bunting, past the vast blue mass of *Norway*'s hull, to the wide channel where five tugs were spraying huge plumes of water into the air, welcoming the biggest cruise ship in the world to America, as they helped steer her into port.

It was magical, Romy thought, looking out at the Statue of Liberty in the heat-haze. In the other direction the whole of Manhattan stretched out before her, the familiar skyline even more glamorous and enticing than she'd ever imagined. She could feel the sheer buzz of the place, even

132

just standing here.

She glanced behind her, knowing that she was stealing these precious moments alone. Donna and the others would be waiting for her below deck. Whenever they docked somewhere new, the ship was a hive of activity, and Romy and her fellow crew members were expected to help out, cleaning the five-star berths, ready for the new influx of guests.

But look at it, she thought. She couldn't miss a moment like this.

She ached to go ashore, but she knew the crew were forbidden shore leave without permission from the Chief Purser, Mic. Romy knew it was sensible to keep her head down and not draw attention to herself. In the last six months Mic had handed over all the crew passports to each new customs authority they'd encountered, and hers had been stamped along with the others, without question. So far her luck hadn't run out, but she wasn't about to tempt fate.

The fake British passport had cost her four months' wages, but it had been worth every penny. She'd taken the opportunity to change her name for good. Gerte Neumann no longer existed. Now she was Romy Jane Valentine. Romy because it was the name Claudia had given to her and was the only thing that she really felt was hers; Jane because it sounded English; and Valentine because Romy liked the romance of it. With a name like that, she was pretty sure nobody from Germany would ever be able to track her down.

She'd faked her birth certificate too, stating her place of birth as a little village near Reading in England—a nothing kind of place; Christian had told her he'd passed through it on a train once.

She sighed again, sending a little prayer of good fortune to her friend on the breeze. Christian would have loved it here, she thought. But since his diagnosis of AIDS, his own travels had been traded in for an exhausting regime of experimental treatments and counselling in London. Not that it had stopped him from encouraging Romy to travel the world. She was his chance to do something with his life, he'd told her. Even if it was only vicariously.

She'd send him a postcard in the morning, she vowed. She pictured his familiar room in the hotel near Tottenham Court Road, decorated with the postcards she'd sent over the last six months: Puerto Rico, Miami, St Barts, St Lucia. She knew how important each one was to him, and she remembered now the postcard she'd kept for years of the Hotel Amalfi in Italy.

She'd left the postcard with her clothes in that horrible place of Carlos's. That was the night she'd met Christian. That night he'd rescued her in London. The night her luck had changed. *That sure seems a million miles away now.*

She'd been wandering the streets through the dead of night, she remembered, when she'd found a guy in kitchen whites smoking a cigarette by some big steel bins. She'd stopped, levering her white shoe off to relieve the giant blister, when he'd kicked the bin next to her. Then, when he'd seen her, he'd apologized. In German.

Romy, still in shock from her ordeal in the brothel, had been relieved to find someone having a worse night than her and had struck up a conversation with Christian. Glad to be talking in

134

her native language, she'd asked him what he was doing and why he was annoyed.

'I'm playing cards,' he'd said. 'I'm losing.'

She'd peeked around him through the open doors into the warm kitchens beyond. She'd been willing to bet anything there'd be hot food in there.

'Why don't you let me play in your place?' she'd suggested, seizing her chance.

'You?' The German guy had looked her up and down.

Romy had held up the note the girl at the Tube station gave her. 'I'm good. An expert. I'll split my winnings fifty-fifty with you.'

He'd nodded. 'OK, you're in. Don't let me down.'

That night Romy had cleaned up, to the delight of Christian and the amazement of Dieter, Gazim, Harry, Bernard and Luca. After the game, when the guys had discovered that Romy was homeless and she'd told them about her journey from Germany, Christian had taken pity on her and smuggled her up the staff stairwell to a spare room, where she'd broken down and told Christian what had happened to her with Carlos and about her horrible ordeal with Jimmy.

Christian had given her a big hug. 'You make your own luck,' he'd told her. 'You just made yours, by finding me.'

The next morning he'd woken her gently, given her a staff uniform and taken her hooker's clothes to burn in the incinerator.

'It didn't happen,' he'd told her. 'I've made you an appointment with a doctor to check you're OK, then you're going to forget all about last night. Forever. But for now, you'd better get up. I've got you an interview lined up with the hotel manager at nine. Here's a list of places I want you to memorize to tell him that you've worked.' He handed her a piece of paper. 'The fact that I've vouched for you should seal it, I think.'

He'd been right. Romy had started work at the hotel that very afternoon. Christian had even fudged some typed references for her. Two days later her results from the doctor had come back clean. More of that luck that Christian had told her was hers.

Romy had loved her time at the hotel. Working out with Christian, she'd learnt how to use the weights in the gym and build up her stamina. She'd learnt to cook and clean properly and had improved her English beyond measure, obliterating her crude German accent, by mimicking the snatches of television soaps that she caught every day, until she could do a perfect Bet Lynch from *Coronation Street* and Sharon Gless from *Cagney & Lacey*.

But most of all she loved hearing all the stories from the guys when they played poker at night. Secret relationships, tales of being an outcast— Romy related to them all. As the hotel guests came and went, she'd strike up conversations with them, and later identified all the places they'd been in the atlas she'd bought in a second-hand charity shop, along with a growing assortment of funky second-hand clothes and boots.

When Christian had discovered her thirst for knowledge of the world, he'd put her in touch with one of his friends, a chef on the cruise ship *Norway*. Once Romy's passport had come through from Yanos, the Pole who could procure anything for the right price, she'd got a job as crew.

Yes, she was on her way, she thought, looking out again at New York and the cars in the distance glinting along the edge of Central Park. And those buildings. They were amazing, she thought, looking at one of the skyscrapers with a big gold M on the top. What would it be like to stand on the top of there? she wondered.

Closer to, on the *Norway*, she could hear the whoops of the kids jumping in the pool on the aft upper deck, and a band playing 'When the Saints Come Marching In' wafting towards her on the breeze. Then a noise right behind her made her jump.

'What are you doing out here?' Donna asked, in her rough Australian accent. She flopped against the railings breathlessly. 'I've been looking everywhere for you.'

Donna was Romy's friend and room-mate on board *Norway*. She was small with blonde hair, tapered up the back of her head, with a long fringe that she liked to backcomb. She had an infectious laugh and the drinking capacity of a man three times her size.

'There'll be a party later on, when we dock. Clark's got some mates he can hook you up with,' Donna said, wiggling her eyebrows.

Romy couldn't think of anything worse than being match-made with one of Clark's buddies. Affairs amongst the crew were rife and carried out in public, and Romy had managed to steer clear of becoming involved with anyone. Sure, there were nice enough guys, but Romy didn't ever seem to fancy any of them. Not like Donna, who permanently had a crush on someone.

137

'What about Dwight?' Donna asked, widening her eyes. 'He's single now.'

Romy laughed, thinking of the pimply bartender. 'You think I'd go for Dwight?'

'He's a great guy, and he thinks you're hot. He told me.' She fixed Romy with a look. 'Beggars can't be choosers, you know.'

'Who says I'm begging?' Romy said, playfully punching her arm. Donna had no idea about the kind of man she secretly dreamt of ending up with. It would sound silly to say it out loud, but Romy had read too many novels to be swayed from the idea that one day she'd be swept off her feet. Instead she gave a practical reason for turning Dwight down. 'Aren't you forgetting the bunny-boiler?'

Donna nodded, taking Romy's point on board. Susie, Dwight's ex-girlfriend, had got her nickname after *Fatal Attraction*—the favourite movie in the crew mess at the moment—when Susie had publicly shredded the teddy that Dwight had given her, in a fit of hysteria. Romy was happy to steer well clear.

'Thank you. But no,' she said firmly, closing the subject.

'Aww, come on, Romy. You're young and you're OK-looking, for a Pom. If you can't live a little now, when can you?' Donna asked, and Romy laughed at her familiar refrain. 'Pah, I'm wasting my breath. We'd better get back to work. Anyway, I forgot. You're working the tables tonight, right?'

'Yes, thanks to you,' Romy said.

Two of the American crew members had applied for immediate shore leave on compassionate grounds, meaning that Romy had temporarily been promoted to junior croupier, when Donna had grassed to Heston, the Casino Manager, about Romy's card skills and her quick head for numbers. Tonight was her first night in the Monte Carlo casino.

'Think of all the tips,' Donna said. 'You'll be able to save them for the day when you finally decide to have fun.'

* * *

That evening the casino was full and Romy couldn't get enough of the atmosphere, the sheer noise and exhilaration of the room, the whirring roulette wheel and the clatter of chips. As well as the high-flying guests on the *Norway*, people came from Manhattan to sample the delights of the famous cruise ship, and Heston, the Manager, had already given her way more responsibility than she was expecting.

'So far so good,' Heston said, after she'd finished croupiering a long game of seven-card stud. He waved over to a man in a croupier's jacket. 'Meet Xavier,' Heston shouted over the din, introducing the Spanish-looking man with a floppy fringe and brown eyes. 'Lives here in New York. He's helping us out for the night.' He clapped Xavier on the shoulder. 'Can't we tempt you back to *Norway*, Xav?'

'Maybe,' Xavier said.

Romy felt a wave of something so unexpectedly physical that she had to rip her eyes away from his to the floor. Who *was* this guy? Had the heat just turned up in the room? Why did she suddenly feel so hot?

She felt tongue-tied and shy, as she and Xavier prepared the table. She couldn't seem to stop looking at him and the way his strong, nimble fingers caressed and stacked the chips. Suddenly everything seemed heightened—Whitney Houston singing 'I Wanna Dance With Somebody' on the sound system, the smell of cigarette smoke and perfume, the bright-green baize, the heat of the room, the sweat on her glass of icy water.

And then Xavier was talking to her, as if they'd known each other for ages. She couldn't stop staring at his lips and his trendy goatee beard, as he told her about how he was once head croupier on the *Norway* and how he was starting his own bar in Brooklyn.

Take me there, she found herself thinking. Yet she hardly knew the guy, she told herself, unnerved by the feeling that was growing inside her. So what if Xavier was cooler and more sophisticated than anyone she'd met on the *Norway* so far? She was here to work.

But as the play began she couldn't seem to stop looking at him and the easy way he charmed the guests. He was always professional, but he had a way of complimenting the women and congratulating the men, when they won a hand, that made everyone warm to him. No wonder Heston had been delighted to get Xavier back for an evening.

'You'll have to go to that table, Romy,' Heston said, nodding over towards the table by the bar, where a group of guys was raucously drinking cocktails. 'They're up next.'

Reluctantly Romy tore herself away and went to stand by the far table, smiling nervously as she sorted the stacks of cards and chips. These guys looked like city hotshots—yuppies, she'd read people called them now—with their slicked-back hair and sharp, shiny suits. She looked over at Xavier, who winked at her reassuringly, and she smiled back.

'Is it a special occasion, gentlemen?' she asked, quelling her nerves and taking Xavier's confidence on board, as she dealt out the cards for the first round.

'Sean here is getting hitched next weekend,' one of the guys slurred, putting his arm drunkenly around his friend.

They played badly, roaring loudly when they lost their hands against the house. But still they kept on playing, thanks to the beefy blond one, who got more chips from the cashier. He had a swagger about him, an arrogance, that was only backed up by the fact that all the other men looked up to him.

Romy noticed him watching her as she handed out the chips. He was drunk too. A mean drunk. Not good-natured, like Sean, who could barely keep himself upright on his stool.

'Have we met before?' the blond one asked her, in a break between games, when the boys were getting their drinks from the hostess. 'You seem familiar.'

'No,' she said, trying to smile. But something about his eyes unnerved her. They were cold and assessing. She'd seen eyes like that before.

Fox's.

That never happened.

But the buried memory had punctured through her wall of lies and she felt her heart thumping hard, as the blond guy continued to stare at her.

She watched him taking out one of those brand-new mobile phones and pretending to make a call on it, before putting it back in his pocket, clearly assuming that she'd be impressed.

In the next break, again when his friends were distracted, he grabbed her hand.

'I'll pay you five hundred dollars to come back to my apartment,' he said in a low voice.

Romy ripped her hand away, colour rising to her cheeks.

At that moment Sean let out a whoop as he won the hand, his arm flailing out and catching the tray of drinks that the waitress was holding, sending shot glasses and a bottle of tequila flying.

'OK, my friend. Time to go,' Xavier said, twisting Sean round on the stool and letting him stumble off into his arms.

'Come on, man. It was an accident,' one of Sean's friends protested.

'Sorry. House rules. You gotta be able to sit upright to play. You better take your buddy somewhere else, boys.'

He helped Sean to the door, the others around him pro testing, but good-naturedly. The blond guy was last to leave.

'If you change your mind, it'll be a thousand,' the guy added, leaning in close. She could smell whisky on his breath. 'You are very beautiful.'

He slid a card, with its embossed gold name, across the green baize towards her.

*   *   *

When the shift was finished and the last gamblers had staggered to bed, Romy lingered so that she

142

could walk out with Xavier. Tiredness pinched her eyes, as she watched the sun lightening the skyline of New York, glinting on the top of the Twin Towers.

'You OK?' Xavier asked, as she sighed, looking out at the city.

'Sure,' Romy smiled.

'You did great tonight,' he said, taking off his jacket. 'It was tough—even for an old-timer like me.' He held his jacket over his shoulder. She hadn't noticed how broad and strong his shoulders were, despite his slim frame. He obviously worked out.

'Are you going back now?'

He nodded. 'I've got an apartment downtown.'

The words sounded so impossibly glamorous. She trailed her hand along the wooden railing, noticing the way the sunlight was turning it gold.

'So you wouldn't consider signing back on with the *Norway*?' she asked, hopefully.

Xavier laughed. 'There's lots about it I miss. But you can't stay too long. People go stir-crazy if they stay too long.'

'Is that what happened to you?'

'I got shacked up with a waitress. She was a nice girl, but it didn't work on dry land. The ship gives you a warped perspective of what people are really like.'

Is that what he thought she had? Romy wondered. A warped perspective? She hoped not. Because she couldn't bear to take her eyes from his face.

'You were great dealing with those guys earlier. Heston was impressed.'

Romy picked out the card from her pocket and

143

the cash that the blond guy had given her.

'One of them even had the nerve to give me his card. To ask me back with him.'

'People like that think they can get anything—and anyone.'

'Yeah, well he was wrong,' Romy said. 'Brett Maddox,' she read. 'MD Media Division, Maddox Inc.' She ripped it up into little pieces and let them go. They fluttered away like confetti on their long descent to the water.

'He was right about one thing, though,' Xavier said, as they stopped at the top of the staircase.

'What's that?'

'You are incredibly beautiful, Romy.'

Romy stared at him. The way he'd said it, the hushed intimate tone of his voice, cut through all their chitchat. She saw in his eyes an attraction she couldn't resist. She stepped forward and tiptoed up to kiss him.

'I'm sorry,' she whispered, 'I don't know why I did that.'

But he just smiled. Stroking her cheek, he leant forward and took her in his arms. Slowly and sensually he kissed her again.

'Come on,' she said. 'Let's go to my cabin.'

They hardly spoke as Romy led him through the warren of corridors to the cabin. She felt caught up in something over which she had no control. Her mind was spinning with thoughts—what all this meant, and what he must think of her. Why this had happened so suddenly?

She unlocked the door, relieved that Donna was out and that the tiny cabin was relatively tidy. She took two steps over to her bottom bunk, tidying up the stack of novels next to it, adding the Danielle

Steel that lay open on the pillow to the top of it, and hurriedly smoothing down the blanket and pillow. She could feel herself trembling all over.

'Come here,' he said, coming up behind her. She felt his hardness against her thigh through his trousers as he started to kiss her neck. She turned around in his arms, kissing him back. Then they moved onto the small bunk and he lay on top of her, but he didn't squash her, like Jimmy had. Instead he stroked the hair from her face, staring into her eyes, giving his mind to her.

'Are you sure?' he asked her.

'Yes,' she breathed. 'Yes.'

*   *   *

It was five in the morning and Donna laughed outside the door, drunkenly trying to fit her key in the lock. She'd nipped out of the party in Clark's room to come back for her secret bottle of vodka.

She finally opened the door, fell into the small cabin and turned on the light.

Romy was naked and asleep, a soft smile on her face, and she didn't stir. Neither did the gorgeous naked hunk spooning her tightly.

'Good on yer, girl,' Donna whispered, grabbing the bottle and tiptoeing out backwards.

CHAPTER ELEVEN

AUGUST 1989

'Thirty-love,' Thea called with a grin, running back to the baseline, high-fiving Bridget on the way.

Across from them, on the other side of the tennis court, Tom Lawson and his friend Finn made eyes at each other and then Tom threw his arms out wide, looking at the service line, from where Thea had just served her second ace of the match.

'It's not fair,' he called over the net. 'Tell her, Bridge.'

'Stop being a bad sport,' Bridget called back, before jogging over and picking up a bottle of water by the net and taking a swig.

Thea looked up as she wiped away the sweat from below her visor and peered at the early-morning sun, which was already marinating the court, a shimmer of heat rising up from the baseline. She rolled her tennis-racket handle in her hands.

'I thought we'd have beaten it, but it's getting too hot already,' Bridget panted, handing her the water bottle. 'You'll burn.'

Thea smiled. 'Just a few more games. We've got them licked,' she said. She was enjoying herself far too much to stop now.

'You know we can't put it off any longer. It's nearly time,' Bridget said.

'Put off what?' Thea asked as she got ready to serve again.

'*Thea?*' Bridget squealed, exasperated. 'The results. We've got to ring school.'

'In a while,' Thea said, bouncing the yellow ball on the hot court.

The last thing she wanted to think about was school and telephoning the secretary for their A-level results. She wanted to put off reality as long as possible. Or thinking about the future and what that held.

She wanted to enjoy this moment. Right now.

The last few weeks had been magical. Sailing on the Lawsons' family friend's yacht, hopping around the ports of southern Italy. But the best part of all was that, now they were in the Hotel Amalfi, Bridget's brother Tom and his friend, Finn, had joined them for the week and she was determined that this, their third game, should end in victory for her and Bridget.

Thea glanced up at Tom now on the other side of the net, his tanned legs wide apart, crouched down, waiting for her serve. He had an incredibly athletic body, but it wasn't just that. He radiated the kind of sexual charisma that made women notice him wherever he went. Bridget and Thea teased him about it, but whilst Bridget was genuinely annoyed by him, Thea couldn't help but be secretly fascinated. It was as if he had a thirst for girls—all types of girls—that was insatiable. He noticed every single one of them, except Thea.

Each night she went to bed, tossing and turning, going over every single tiny moment of private contact between them, and reading meaning into it. Did he like her? Didn't he? But then she'd turn over, furious with herself for having fallen for his charms in the first place.

But maybe she didn't deserve Tom. She'd been so careful not to send out the wrong signals—Brett's horrible words still preying on her mind. Just like she couldn't shake the memory of Brett pressing against her in the kitchen, violating her as he had. She felt soiled. Unworthy of someone as wonderful as Tom.

And yet at the same time, another thought persisted. It wouldn't be like that with Tom . . . would it? He'd be sensitive, caring, if anything ever happened.

If.

She was crazy, she knew. She got plenty of attention from other men, or boys at least, so why was she so hung up on the one person she couldn't have? But somehow that only made her secret obsession worse.

She stretched up as the ball sailed over her head and smashed it, running forward. Tom desperately tried a passing shot. She watched in delight as it sailed harmlessly over the tramlines and landed out.

'I give up,' Tom said. 'You're just too good for me.'

Thea beamed at him. If only that were really true.

*   *   *

On the wrought-iron white swing chair on the terrace Shelley Lawson pretended to read the page proofs of her latest novel. But she couldn't help staring through the door into the reception area, where Thea and Bridget were telephoning the school.

She knew how much the exam results meant to both girls. She wasn't worried so much about Bridget. Shelley knew that Bridget was as tough as she herself was. She had been since she was a baby. Apart from some of her bolshie behaviour in her early teens, she'd been a doddle.

No, Shelley was more worried about Thea. There was something so fragile about her, and now Shelley felt the enormity of her responsibility. What if Thea didn't get her results? What if she couldn't fulfil her dreams? What if only one of the girls got into Oxford, and not both of them?

Poor Thea. She didn't have much of a home life to speak of. Shelley couldn't help but feel it was somehow her own duty to fill the void. She owed it to Lis. Her dear old friend, Lis, who had loved this little girl. This little girl Thea, who was on the cusp of becoming a beautiful woman.

Alyssa McAdams. Memories of her crashed into Shelley's mind, making it impossible to concentrate. How strange that the past should come up after all these years. And how bloody infuriating that she'd been so unprepared to deal with it, Shelley thought. It seemed ironic that she spent her days writing novels about people's pasts and their secrets, and yet she'd been totally shocked by Thea's sudden arrival in her life. Because with her had come all those memories of Lis and everything that had happened.

Poor old Alyssa. Looking back now, Shelley guessed she'd been a little bit in love with Lis McAdams from the start, in the way girls can be. So she'd totally understood that Bridget had fallen for Thea.

But now Shelley remembered how Lis had

turned to her in her hour of need, making her swear to keep her secret. And Shelley had. All these years. Even when Lis had gone to the States and left it all behind her.

That had hurt, of course—especially when she hadn't been invited to Lis's wedding, but Shelley had understood her friend's need to move on and forget.

And Shelley had forgotten too. She'd never even told her husband, Duke, the thing she'd done for Lis all those years ago.

But now she felt the weight of the secret, like some kind of test. But she wouldn't break. She'd come so unthinkingly close to making a stupid blunder when she'd told Thea about her mother and Johnny. She hoped that Thea hadn't understood or taken it to heart. But it wasn't a mistake she would ever make again. She'd been lucky that Thea hadn't asked her more about it. Perhaps she hadn't heard what Shelley had said properly. Hopefully enough time had passed for Shelley to feign ignorance or forgetfulness about the slip entirely, if it ever came up again.

Now she clenched her fists, watching the girls. They were so young. Their whole lives ahead of them. All she prayed for was that nothing unpleasant would ever come between them, as it had between her and Lis. That they'd never have a test of their friendship. A test that would break them, as it had broken Thea's poor mother.

Suddenly she stood up, seeing Bridget's expression, which could only mean one thing.

*   *   *

In the reception area Bridget screamed, flung down the phone to the school office and jumped up and down.

'Oh my God!' she gasped.

Thea could feel her heart hammering. 'Oh my God,' Thea said back, her mouth wide open with shock. She couldn't believe it. She wanted to cry, she felt so relieved.

Thea hugged her and they jumped up and down together.

'You've got to call your father,' Bridget said, retrieving the handset from the loopy chord where she'd dropped it. She dialled an outside line. Then handed the phone to Thea, her eyes shining.

'Go on.'

Thea dialled her father's direct line in the apartment in Maddox Tower, biting her lip as she looked at Bridget.

He'd seemed so far away these past months. She could hardly believe he'd be there. But suddenly there was a click and, one ring later, her father's voice.

'It's me,' Thea said.

'Thea? What's the matter?' Griffin Maddox asked. She realized it must be very late at night in New York. She felt butterflies in her stomach as she pictured his face.

'Nothing's the matter.' She gripped the receiver and glanced at Bridget. 'I called because . . . because I'm into Oxford,' she said.

'Storm . . . Storm, can you take this dog away. I can't hear for the yapping.'

'It's Oxford, Daddy. You know. England— university. I passed my exams. Straight As.'

'But I thought you were going to apply to

American universities?' he said. 'I can get you a place anywhere you want to go.'

She could hear the disapproval in his tone, could picture the frown on his brow. When was the last time she'd seen him smile? When was the last time *she'd* made him smile?

She felt tears tighten her throat. 'No. I said I wanted to stay in England.'

'But it's so far away,' her father said. 'Where are you now anyway?'

'Italy. Remember? Didn't you get my postcard? I sent it to the office.'

Thea felt Bridget reach out and touch her hand.

'Ring off,' Bridget mouthed. 'It doesn't matter.'

She pointed through the open door to the terrace, where Duke and Shelley were waiting expectantly, a bottle of champagne sweating in a bucket on the table.

'OK. Well, I've got to go,' Thea said. 'I'll call you soon.' She hastily put down the phone. 'That went well,' she said, feeling more emotional than she wanted to. Griffin Maddox's decidedly flat reaction felt like a bad omen.

'Forget it,' Bridget said, gripping her elbow. 'Don't worry. Let's go and tell Mum and Dad.'

Thea took a breath, trying to steady herself as Bridget ran outside to her parents on the terrace, yelling with delight. She felt jealousy burning through her as Bridget's parents folded her in their arms.

Why hadn't her father reacted better? Why didn't he care? Thea wondered. He didn't have a clue how hard she had worked to get those results. All he cared about was business. Well, she would show him, Thea vowed. She'd take Oxford by storm with Bridget. She'd come out with her own contacts and her own qualifications. He could shove Maddox Inc.

But almost as soon as she thought it, she remembered Brett. She shuddered and forced the thought of him away. But she also knew that if she really did walk away from her father's business, everything that was rightly hers would be Brett's. *Don't think about it now*, she told herself. *Don't let them ruin your moment.*

Thea caught up with Bridget. Shelley had a tear on her cheek as she squeezed Bridget, and then broke away to kiss Thea.

'Hey. What's all the fuss?' Tom asked, coming up the steps onto the terrace to join them.

'The girls have done it,' Bridget's father Duke said, winking at Thea. 'A right clever bunch. They've made us very proud.'

Without warning, Tom grabbed Thea and twirled her round. Thea landed breathless in his arms and stared up at him. Her flushed face was reflected in the lenses of his Ray-Bans.

Tom leant in and kissed her cheek. She breathed in his fresh smell and the hint of aftershave and felt her knees weakening in his embrace.

'Hey, congratulations,' he said softly.

And right at that moment all the hard work, all the worry, was worth it. Tom Lawson had noticed her at last.

*　　　*　　　*

Sitting at the café on the harbourside later that night, Thea felt the scene was impossibly

153

glamorous. Tom and Finn had come here because they wanted to 'people-watch', but Bridget scoffed that it was they who wanted to be seen themselves. And perhaps she was right. Tom and his friend Finn were sporting a preppy look, both with sweaters knotted around their polo shirts and both wearing blue and white loafers, and they were sitting at the best table as if they owned the place.

They'd both insisted that Thea and Bridget look out to sea, but Thea suspected that Tom was embarrassed by his sister's latest 'look'. Despite the heat, Bridget had squeezed into a white lace dress, which she wore with Doc Martens and black nail-varnish. Thea had opted for her favourite Laura Ashley dress and Gap pumps, but the skirt was so short that she tugged at the floral material self-consciously.

'Look at the size of that thing,' Thea said, pointing to the cruise ship on the horizon, its lights twinkling against the black sky. It was probably heading for Naples, just up the coast.

'An abomination, if you ask me,' Finn said, turning to look at where she was pointing. 'I don't see why they have to let the plebs ruin this place.'

Thea felt herself bristle. She didn't like Finn's attitude. He had red curly hair and small beady blue eyes, which somehow always seemed to be making a judgement on other people. But Tom seemed committed to him, despite his caustic personality. According to Bridget, they'd been up Kilimanjaro on one of their expeditions together— a trip that had, according to Tom, bonded them for life.

'Surely they have just as much right to be here as us?' Thea said.

154

'That's a damned noble thing of you to say, Thea,' Finn said nastily. 'When your father is one of the richest men in America.'

'What do you know about my father?' she asked.

'Enough to know that you'll walk into any job you want. Not that a girl like you *will* ever work. A place at such a good English university seems a bit wasted on an American like you.'

'I should shut up, if I were you, Finn,' Tom warned, glancing between Finn and Thea. 'You don't want the company lawyers after you.'

He changed the subject, but the evening was soured. And it only took a further turn for the worse when Finn and Bridget ordered mussels for dinner and afterwards both felt queasy. By the time Tom and Thea had driven them back to the hotel, the pair of them were green.

Thea helped Bridget into her room, and after she was sick for what had to be the last time, Thea helped her take off her Doc Martens and get into bed.

'Oh, you poor thing,' Thea said, wiping her glistening forehead with a damp flannel. 'What a dreadful way to end the day. Go to sleep.'

'Will you be OK?' Bridget asked.

Thea smiled. 'Of course I will. It's late. I'll probably go to bed myself,' she assured her friend, although she knew that she needed to clear her head first.

'Well, do. I don't want you to be alone with Tom.' Bridget lay back on the pillow, her head glistening with sweat.

'Tom? Why ever not?' Thea asked, but her voice sounded shrill.

'Because . . .' Bridget said, 'you promised.'

155

'Tom? Me and Tom?' Thea said. 'Don't be crazy, Bridge. You're delirious.'

*   *   *

But out on the terrace, with its ropes of soft lights, the warm breeze coming in from the bay and the sound of the silver waves breaking on the beach far below, Thea forgot her resolve. Tom was sitting alone by the bar, reading the book she'd lent him—*The Magus* by John Fowles. Thea felt her heart racing as she quickly tried to slip past him down the steps through the garden to the beach, but he looked up and caught her eye.

'How is she?' he called over to Thea.

She walked over to the bar towards him. 'Weak. How's Finn?'

'Finn?' Tom asked, staring at Thea, as if he'd forgotten the conversation already. 'Oh, he'll be fine.'

Thea bit her lip, breaking his gaze. Something about his stare was so intimate that it was making her blush.

'After all that vomit, I just wanted some air,' she said, putting her arm out in the direction of the gardens. 'I suppose I should turn in really.'

Tom pulled another seat towards his. He patted it. 'Stay and have a drink with me.'

Thea looked at the seat and at Tom's expectant face. Why shouldn't she have a drink? What was so wrong in that? She tried to dismiss Bridget's face, which loomed large in her mind.

Because you promised . . .

And yet his family were paying for her holiday, Thea reminded herself. It wasn't as if he had any

156

idea how she felt. Besides, to leave now would be so rude. Tom ordered her a glass of white wine and Thea sat down. In the distance she could hear music from the bar inside, the INXS song 'Need You Tonight', which she knew Tom liked just as much as she did.

'Weird evening,' she said, trying not to sound as nervous as she felt.

'It's better now,' Tom said. He raised his glass to clink with hers. Thea took a sip of her wine and laughed nervously.

'So, I'm sorry about Finn earlier. Being rude. I guess he must be jealous. He has issues about being the only kid from his group of friends at school not to make it to Oxbridge.'

'It's OK,' Thea said.

'You don't talk about your family much.'

'There's not much to say. My father is Griffin Maddox. He barely notices me. My family isn't like yours, Tom. You have no idea how lucky you are. Your mom is . . . well, she's like I think my mom might have been, if she was still alive.'

'She was a good mother?' Tom asked.

Thea looked at him. She shouldn't be talking about this stuff with Tom. But somehow he seemed so easy to talk to.

Thea sighed. 'Of course she was. When she was alive. From what I remember, at least. But now . . .?' She paused, looking at the stem of her glass.

'Now?' Tom prompted.

'She feels like a mystery.'

'What do you mean? Tell me about her. What do you remember about her?'

'She always said I was her gift from God,' Thea said. 'I've never told anyone that before.' She smiled at Tom, her stomach fluttering when she saw that he was staring right at her. 'She always seemed so solid. Like . . . I always thought she was the love of my father's life.'

'And now you're not sure?'

Thea shrugged. 'It just seems so odd that my father was so quick to marry her complete opposite. Then there was a comment that your mum made about Johnny once.'

'Who's Johnny?'

Thea explained. And as she told him all about Johnny and Little Elms, she remembered how idyllic her childhood had been, and how painful it was that it had gone forever. Before she could stop herself, she found herself talking about Michael too.

'It sounds like you really cared about him,' Tom said, 'loved him even . . .'

'No,' she said quickly, embarrassed. 'Not loved. I was much too young. Nothing but a kid.'

But had what she felt for Michael been love? she wondered now. And not just the kind of love you might feel for a friend or an almost-brother, but something more consuming and much more adult than that?

'I took it all for granted, and then it all got ripped away,' she told Tom, feeling more emotional than she meant to.

'So you want to track down this Johnny fella then?' Tom asked.

'I want to know what happened. You know . . . before. When he and Mom were young. I think there's a story there I need to find out.'

'Old family skeletons really don't interest me. I bet Mum has loads of gossip stacked up, but I'd

158

rather not know,' Tom said.

Thea laughed at the ridiculousness of the idea. 'Your parents?' she said.

'Don't be so sure. Everyone has dark secrets.'

'Oh, really?' Thea said, 'Even you?'

He seemed to think about this for a moment, a twinkle of amusement or—Thea wondered—uncertainty in his eyes.

'Maybe. Just the one.'

'Oh?' she asked, smiling. 'And what's that?'

He sighed, looked down at his fingers holding the base of his glass. Thea thought how handsome he was, his face lit in profile, his dark hair falling carelessly into his eyes.

'I'm crazily in love with someone I shouldn't be in love with,' he said.

He sighed, leant forward and put his hands over hers. This time she didn't move away. She could feel herself being dragged. Dragged somewhere she knew she shouldn't go, but it was like being dragged over velvet.

'Don't you feel it too?' he whispered, his eyes locking with Thea's. 'This thing between us?'

'Tom. Don't . . . I can't,' she said, feeling like a fool.

'Can't what?'

'Do this . . . with you,' she said, but as she stared into his eyes, her words withered on her lips. She wished she had the courage to tell him about Brett. To tell him the truth about herself and how inexperienced she was, as a result of his abuse. How naive, when it came to anything sexual. How terrified the thought of being intimate with anyone made her.

She felt herself trembling. Was this real? Or had

159

she given Tom the wrong signals. Could it really be true that he wanted her? What if he rejected her?

'You mean, you don't want to?' he asked quietly, his eyes boring into hers. 'Because I haven't been able to stop thinking about you every second of this week.'

But she couldn't answer. She felt the truth radiating out of her, and she was powerless to stop it.

'But what about Bridget?'

'What about her?'

'I . . . I promised her, I wouldn't. I mean . . .' she fizzled out. Her promise to Bridget suddenly seemed so childish.

'How we feel is our business, not hers.'

Thea tried to find an answer, a way to protest, but then Tom stood up. Without even losing eye contact with her for a second, he left some notes on the bar from the inside of his jacket and took her hand.

'Don't say anything,' he said as they walked inside the hotel and across the marble lobby. 'And don't stop.'

She felt her heart pounding as he led her up the stairs, taking the keys out of his pocket. They stopped outside a door with a brass number on it. Again Brett flashed into her mind, the revulsion and fear mixing now with excitement about this new experience of being here with Tom. Well, she would do it, she decided, daring herself to be bold. She would not let Brett ruin this. And as Tom held out his hand to her, she took it, stepping over the threshold and into the moonlit room beyond.

160

CHAPTER TWELVE

AUGUST 1989

It was just after dawn when Romy stepped down the gangplank of *Spirit of the Seas*. She smiled, patting the leather bag she'd bought in Venice, with her passport inside. She had a whole twelve hours until her shift started again.

They were only here in Naples for a day and tonight they'd leave Italy for Sardinia. But she couldn't leave knowing that she'd been so close and hadn't tried to find the place she'd always dreamt about. Amalfi was only five miles down the coast and she planned to be there and back by this evening.

Xavier was right when he'd told her that spending too long on board a ship could warp your perspective of the world. It was only now, acting on her own whim, stepping alone onto dry land, that she realized just how bad her cabin fever had become in these last few months.

She still missed Xavier. He'd been the best thing about her time on the *Norway*, by far. She'd tried to keep up her relationship with him, after that first night together, but it had been too hard. He was busy in New York, and the *Norway* had whisked Romy away and, after a few letters, she'd stopped writing, resigning herself to the idea that their one-night stand was as much as there was ever going to be between them.

But she had taken his advice and had applied to work on the *Spirit of the Seas*, which had taken over

161

from *Norway* as the biggest cruise ship in the world. At the time, it had felt daring and brave to make such a huge career change, yet two years on, life on board was pretty much the same as it had been aboard *Norway* and had lost its allure. She felt claustrophobic and hemmed in.

Yet again she was the only female working as a croupier on the floor. She'd never before minded being one of the guys, but unlike Christian and the others that she used to play cards with in London, this lot were a load of sexist pigs. Especially Marco, the boss, who always blamed his mistakes on Romy.

Romy didn't want a boss. She wanted to work for herself. She was fed up with constantly being put in her place. She wanted to live the kind of life that the guests on board had. She wanted to wear gorgeous clothes and gorgeous shoes. She wanted to be *free*.

Truly free. She wanted freedom from being a wage-slave. Freedom not just to go where she chose, but to be as she chose when she got there. Thoughts of freedom and independence had cemented as one inside her mind.

Which is why she'd been saving every cent she made and putting aside every tip so that she'd have enough to go and study. The only problem was, she had no idea where she wanted to live. She was tempted to go back to London, but life aboard the *Spirit* was so relentless, it was hard to make any decisions. And at least she was safe on board. Lemcke, Ulrich and his dogs still haunted her dreams, and she still slept with a penknife under her pillow.

Yes, you could travel all around the world, she

162

thought, but you could never escape from what was inside your own mind. But today she was damn well going to try and find some peace.

She turned and looked up at the vast ship, thinking as she always did that it was as ridiculous as a fancy wedding cake. Then, with a resolute skip in her step and hugging her soft peppermint-green cardigan around her shoulders in the chill dawn air, she set off towards the town.

* * *

She followed the fruit-haulers to a low building along the port. Inside, the market was in full swing. Romy drank it all in, revelling in the vibrant colours, fingering the fat grapes that dripped from the stalls and the sweet yellow melons piled high. Above it all was the smell of rough cigarette smoke and the shouting of the men, as the traders bartered with the fishermen, and forklift trucks whined as they shunted crates of produce at break-neck speed. A black pig on a leash ran by, dragging a man in boots, while another man walked past shouldering two cured ham legs.

No wonder the pig was running, she thought.

She stopped to buy a peach, but when she smiled, the man gave it to her for free. 'Where are you going, lady?' he shouted above the din.

Romy, delighting at understanding the basic phrase and seeing the opportunity to try out a few of her own stock phrases that she'd learnt, explained that she needed to get to Amalfi. She asked him directions to the bus stop, feeling every inch the guidebook novice she was. The man pulled a face, impressed.

163

Suddenly he whistled through his teeth to the guy on the fish stall and talked in rapid-fire Italian.

'The best way is by boat,' he said eventually in flawlessly pronounced English, bringing a smile to Romy's lips. 'Around the coast. Pietro will take you.' He nodded over to the toothless man on the fish stall, who grinned at Romy.

Twenty minutes later Romy found herself clinging to the rigging, as the small fishing tug nipped through the water. Pietro grinned again over his shoulder at her, as he headed out away from the port, driving the boat at full tilt, as if it were a bumper-car in a fairground.

They went right out into the Bay of Naples, and Romy felt the wind blowing her hair back from her face as she took in the spectacular view and the cliffs of the rocky coastline. She turned her face into the hot sunshine, suddenly not caring how she would ever get back to Naples by this evening. Below her the boat cut through the clear greeny-blue water and she saw the shadows of fish chasing the boat, as if they were daring each other not to get caught.

Soon they rounded the headland and Amalfi came into view. The engine changed gear and, as they got closer, slowed to chug towards the port with its pretty pastel houses along the quayside.

The fishing boat slowed and stopped at the end of one of the long wooden jetties. Pietro nodded for her to get off and explained it was faster into town from there than if she went all the way with him to the port.

She waved to the fishing boat as it travelled on towards the high harbour wall and she set off down the jetty, past the sleek white yachts.

164

At the end, where the quayside was packed with cars, she saw a guard in the office by the barrier reading the paper, stuffing his face with a sugar-coated pastry, and she waved to him as she strode past, as if she owned the place, enjoying the way her yellow sun-dress flapped around her thighs.

As Romy stopped and ordered a cappuccino at a small café she wanted to pinch herself. She was really here. In Amalfi. There was no one telling her what to do. No shift to be on anytime soon. No one snoring, or talking in her cabin.

This was what real life was like for everyone else, she thought. This is what it really felt like to be free. As she stared out at the street and at the small cafés opening up, she understood that deep down she was always waiting. Always expecting someone from her past to spot her. But as she breathed in, feeling the rising heat of the sun, she remembered the cold orphanage a world away, and let herself say the words, 'They can't find me here. They will never find me.'

When she'd finished her coffee, she went to the shop to ask directions, pushing through the plastic strip-curtain. It was cool inside like a church. In the sudden dimness, Romy could make out shelves stacked sparsely with provisions.

A man carrying several awkward black bags was buying lots of packets of cigarettes. He looked hassled. He took off his baseball cap and she saw that he had closely cropped dark hair, which only made his eyelashes look longer. He glanced over at Romy as he dug in his jacket for his wallet.

Romy stood by the postcard rack and turned it slowly round. Dust-motes swirled down from the high window above the door.

165

And suddenly, there it was. Her picture. Identical to the one she'd had in the orphanage all those years ago. She felt her heart in her throat as she reached out and plucked it from the stand. As she held it, staring at the bright colours, Romy felt as if she were reclaiming something precious for herself. Her chance to dream.

Because if one of her dreams—if *this* dream—could come true and she could stand in that picture and look out at that view, then she'd know anything was possible.

The curtain rattled as the man left the shop, and Romy was alone. She looked out and saw that he was climbing into a waiting yellow taxi. Maybe she could get a taxi too.

She paid for the postcard, handing the coins over to the woman in the grey dress, a black shawl draped over her shoulder at the counter. A black cat wound around Romy's heels, tickling her ankles.

'Where is this?' Romy asked the woman, pointing to the picture.

The woman took the card, putting thick brown-framed glasses over her eyes.

'Hotel Amalfi, along the coast from here.'

Romy's stomach jumped at the words. 'How do I get there?'

'You don't have a car? The last taxi just left.'

Romy shook her head.

'Go by moped. You can hire one from Rene, my grandson.'

*   *   *

Romy had driven a moped once before, when she

166

and her friend Donna on the *Norway* had gone ashore in St Barts, but she was surprised at how speedy this one was, as she followed Rene's directions out of town, along the road dappled with shadows, the glittering sea flickering between the Cyprus trees as the dusty road curved up and away out of town.

The more the open road unravelled before her and she climbed the steep bends, the more she felt her ties with the cruise ship breaking. The staff, her responsibilities, fading into the distance, lost on the twinkling expanse of ocean.

Now a delicious thought occurred to her. What if she never went back?

But she couldn't just leave, she thought. She needed a reference to get another job. And besides, what other job could give her the opportunity to travel as much, and to earn and save so much, until she decided what to study?

So much for the University of Life, she thought, remembering what Christian had told her in the hotel in London all those years ago. She'd thought travelling on a cruise ship would give her proper life experience, but she'd been just as institutionalized and protected as she had been in the orphanage.

She hadn't really been *living* her life at all. Not until today.

Soon, at the top of the cliff, Romy saw the sign and, indicating, she turned down the lane leading to the lavish gates of the Hotel Amalfi.

Romy had seen some high living on *Norway* and *Spirit*, but this place was opulent to a whole other degree. Romy stopped the moped and stared at the palatial frontage, with its pretty paintwork and

167

fancy shutters. Neat box-hedges lined the gravel driveway.

She took a deep breath, feeling her nerves threatening to overtake her resolve. What if someone stopped her? How could she explain why she'd come?

But she was here now. She'd been carried here by fate. She couldn't stop now.

She walked up the smooth stone steps, and a porter opened the green wooden and glass doors from inside and bowed to her.

Nervously she walked across the marble hallway, glancing up at the enormous chandelier above her head. It's a confidence trick, she told herself. Act like you belong here and nobody will stop you.

She made her way over towards the desk. A man and woman were standing with a girl with dark curly hair. The girl was wearing silly Doc Marten boots and tie-dyed trousers and was crying.

'You're overreacting,' the woman said. She had a posh English accent and put her arm maternally around the girl.

'I found them together,' the girl said, stuffing a wad of tissue against her eye. 'I knew he'd do this to me. He's always done this to me. He's always stolen everything I cared about.'

'I'm sure it's just a misunderstanding,' the woman said. She mouthed something over the girl to the man with the bushy moustache. He shrugged, clearly not knowing what to do. 'Tell her, Duke.'

'You always take his side,' the girl shouted suddenly, her raw eyes turning to the woman's.

'Please, Bridgey, calm down,' the man said. 'I'm

168

terribly sorry about this,' he added to the concierge, who smiled at Romy.

'Could I help you?' the woman asked Romy in Italian in an embarrassed whisper. This obviously wasn't the kind of place that this sort of thing happened.

'I'm meeting a guest here,' Romy lied quietly, making it clear to the concierge that she was just as shy of getting involved with the other guests. 'Would you mind if I waited on the terrace?'

'Of course.' The concierge pointed to the door and Romy headed outside, feeling each step lighter than the other, as she saw the familiar balustrade and the ocean stretching twinkling into the distance.

*   *   *

Nico Rilla sat on the terrace, squinting in the early-morning sunshine as he threw his baseball cap onto the table. His head thumped as he reread the fax he'd just picked up at reception and cursed.

Fucking movie directors, he thought. *They were so unreliable.*

He'd slogged his guts out to get enough time in his schedule to meet the great Carlos Antonio, who summered here at his favourite hotel, but his assistant had sent a message to say that Antonio had been delayed in LA for the foreseeable future.

God damn it, Nico thought. Antonio might have won a score of Oscars for his last movie and was a busy guy, but even so. To let Nico down like this was bad form. He'd been relying on that commission for *Vanity Fair*.

And without the job he had no idea now how

169

he'd ever pay for his rent in Milan—one more missed payment and Signor Ziglioni would be bound to throw him out. Nico rather liked his rooftop apartment, even though it was barely large enough to swing a cat and the pigeons woke him in the morning. But it was all he had. The place he called home.

He lit his sixth cigarette of the morning and drained the black espresso in front of him. Then he ran his hand over his new buzz-cut, trying to get used to the feeling of not having any hair. It was the only way to go, he told himself again, unable to ignore how much he was thinning on top. It pained him that he'd lost his hair so young, and working around beautiful people all the time only added to his sense of inadequacy. It didn't help that after his last relationship with Misha six months ago, he was still single. He wondered what Misha would make of his hair now.

But suddenly his attention was caught by a blonde girl, her hair messed up, her face streaming with tears, running after another girl with short dark hair. Why the hell was she wearing boots in this weather?

'Wait,' the blonde girl called in English. 'You don't understand—'

'You don't get to come on holiday and do this to me,' the other girl shouted back. 'You broke your promise.'

Automatically Nico appraised them with a photographer's eye. He was always doing it. It was his job to find talent wherever he could.

Neither of those girls would cut it in his business, he thought, inhaling on his cigarette. The spoilt ones never could. Not enough need. Not

170

enough hunger. The short freckly one was too furious-looking, and the blonde one was tall and had a good figure, but it was hard to tell what her face was like, as it was blotched with tears.

Teenage girls, Nico thought, puffing out smoke sardonically. They were all the same. Hysterical. They had no life experience to ground them. He should know, he was an expert on the species. It amazed him that he was only just twenty-six and yet he felt old already.

That's why he'd been so glad to get off the catwalks and do some portraits for a change. To be one step closer to doing photography as art. Proper art. Like he'd dreamt about at college. The portrait of Carlos Antonio had felt like the first step on the ladder. But he might have known this commission was too good to be true.

He took out his mobile phone from his jacket pocket. There was nothing for it. He was going to have to grovel to Simona.

Simona Fiore ran one of the biggest European modelling agencies and she was ferocious. But she also happened to be the most-connected person in the fashion world, and Nico had done her more favours than he cared to remember. If there was any shoot that needed a photographer fast, then Simona would know about it. As long as there was a cut in it for her.

He sighed, looking up and then back at the phone, but as he did so, something caught his eye. A girl was leaning on the stone balustrade, her dark hair blowing softly in the breeze. Nico's cigarette paused midway to his lips.

Christ, was that the girl he'd seen earlier in the kiosk in Amalfi? The girl who'd caught his eye as

171

she'd stood in the shop looking at him.

And she was here?

Nico felt a tingle start inside him as he stared at the girl, watching the expression on her face. Backlit by the sun, he could see her fine bone structure. Hell, with those long legs, Nico was willing to bet she had one hell of a body underneath that sun-dress.

But there was something about her. Something that he'd known in his gut the moment he'd seen her. Something that made him unable to take his eyes off her now. It was just that expression on her face . . . as if nothing else in the world mattered except this moment.

He watched as she guiltily looked back behind her, towards reception. Then she quickly walked along to where the steps led down towards the beach.

Jeez, Nico thought, shaking his head and rubbing his eyes. Maybe he was being crazy and desperate, but if he was right . . . ? He felt his hairs tingling on the back of his neck again.

A gut feeling was a gut feeling. *What are you waiting for, stupid*? He'd not had the time to speak to her in the shop, as he'd been in such a rush to get here to meet his goddamn Houdini of a director, but now he had all the time in the world and a rare second chance. He stabbed his thumb down to disconnect the phone. Then he quickly ground out his cigarette and grabbed his camera bag.

*   *   *

Romy breathed in deeply, feeling the sun on her

172

face. Even though she'd been awake all night, she felt more alive than ever as she tripped down the stone steps, through the fragrant bushes towards the twinkling ocean.

All her life she'd longed to find out what was on the other side of the balustrade and now here she was, alone amongst the olive trees, on the hot stone path, her fingertips trailing over the flowering cacti nestled in the rocks.

It was so weird to be here. She'd imagined it for so long, but now it felt illicit, as if she didn't deserve it. As if she might get found out any minute. It felt like she was in a dream.

The path got steeper and steeper and soon the steps led down to the beach.

A tiny sliver of sand framed the perfect cove, set amongst the craggy rocks. The water was crystal-clear. She gasped, jumping down onto the rocks, then flinging her bag on the sand. She checked around her to make sure she was alone, then ripped off her sun-dress and threw it beside her bag. Then a crazy idea hit her. She checked again. If this was a baptism, then she needed to be naked.

She stripped off her bikini and stared out at the horizon.

This was it. She was going to walk into the water and cleanse herself. Cleanse herself of her past. The orphanage, Lemcke, Ulrich, that horrible night with Fox. Her terrifying ordeal in London. She would wash away all the bad memories and make only good ones in their place.

She took one step into the water. Sunlight danced on the surface, but it felt cool. Her feet sunk into the sand; she could feel some small pebbles grazing her toes. A shoal of grey fish wriggled past in the clear water. It was perfectly still and quiet except for the lapping waves and the trilling of some birds in the trees.

Romy stepped forward—up to her knees, her waist. Her hands flapped and she laughed out loud as the water made her back tingle.

With a yelp of triumph she held her nose and plunged under the water. Coming up for air, she gasped, grinning, her eyes closing as she spread her arms out to the sun.

She was eighteen years old, she was here and she was free.

PART TWO

CHAPTER THIRTEEN

NOVEMBER 1991

In the Oxford lecture hall third-year under-graduate Thea Maddox screwed the lid back on the engraved fountain pen that her father had given her, her hand aching from writing hurried notes. She gathered her books and notepads together, as the 500 students erupted into chatter.

Way down the banks of seating at the front of the hall Professor Doubleday, Thea's main tutor on her Modern European History course, took the board rubber and wiped away the writing behind him. He turned, shielding his eyes to look up at the students. Seeing Thea and catching her eye, he smiled and beckoned her to come down to him. She waved back and nodded, feeling a swell of satisfaction. He must have marked her essay, she thought, gratified that out of all of these students he'd picked her.

Just below her in the row in front Oliver Mountefort turned round and grinned up at her. Thea knew Ollie had a thing for her and she tried to avoid his puppy-dog stares in their seminars. If things had been different, she might have considered dating him. He had a big quiff of a hairdo and always got parts in the drama-society plays, and he was the kind of joker who always had people laughing around him.

'Hey, Thea. I'm expecting you in the debating chamber later,' he said. 'You'll be on our side, I take it?'

177

'I'll try and be there,' she said, but she knew she would probably duck out of going. The debating chamber at the Oxford Union was just the kind of place where she would bump into Bridget, and Thea did whatever she could to avoid that happening.

Trying to avoid Bridget Lawson had been her biggest pastime since she'd been here at Oxford. Just as she had been at school, Bridget was everywhere: in the drama society, the debating club, at every party. It seemed crazy that they didn't speak, when they had applied to Oxford together and had vowed to be best friends all through university and life beyond. But that summer in Italy had changed everything.

Thea's first year had been a nightmare, the second hardly better, and she'd promised herself that now at the start of her third year all this nonsense should stop. But Bridget's sense of betrayal had hardened into spitefulness and quite often people said to her, 'Oh you're *that* Thea Maddox.' And she knew that Bridget had got to them first.

She secretly longed to confront her old friend, to tell her how much it hurt that they no longer spoke. Apart from Michael, Bridget had been the only person who'd ever really known her properly. And just as losing Michael had hurt so deeply, now the situation with Bridget felt almost as bad.

There must be a way to be reconciled, Thea thought, if only Bridget wanted it. But the truth was that Bridget seemed just as happy hating Thea now as she had been liking her then. That hurt. Oh, how it hurt. Thea had to remind herself constantly that this wasn't school and that they were grown-ups now. She mustn't give Bridget the power to make her feel like that fat, unhappy teenager she'd once been, but it was so hard. Thea had seen Bridget arm-in-arm with a good-looking guy last week. She'd waved, trying to look friendly, but Bridget had crossed the road to avoid Thea, deliberately ignoring her.

Yet despite Bridget's childish behaviour, Thea was hopelessly in love with Oxford. She loved the academic challenge and the college traditions. She liked the feeling of belonging to a club that had nothing to do with her father, of being a million miles away from where Brett could get to her.

And she liked it too that, here, her money didn't matter. Everyone lived in the same style of room as her. Everyone wore similar types of clothes. You proved yourself through work and, from the first, Thea had set out to excel.

She hugged her books to her and shuffled to the end of the row of desks and then down the stairs to Professor Doubleday's desk.

'Hi,' Thea said, smiling.

Professor Doubleday hitched up his glasses and smoothed his white hair over his bald patch. He had probably been quite good-looking in his day, Thea thought. He reminded her a bit of Harrison Ford, and she suddenly remembered how she and Bridget had been obsessed with *Indiana Jones and the Last Crusade*. She brushed the memory away. There would be more Bridgets in time, she assured herself. Someone to giggle in the cinema with. One day.

The Professor slid Thea's essay on the reunification of Germany across the green leather top of the desk towards her.

'Very good, Thea,' he said. 'I gave it an easy first. I particularly liked your insights into the East Berliner's socio-economic disadvantages and their polarization in the labour market. Very good research.'

Thea felt her cheeks blushing with pride. She'd stayed up half the night working on that essay, trawling through the microfiche in the library, reading the eyewitness accounts. She'd even unearthed videotapes of the news reports in the new media suite in the library. The tears of joy of one girl almost her own age—was it Ursula?—had inspired the whole essay; she'd been interviewed on the night the Berlin Wall came down. She'd spoken so movingly about how she'd had a friend who'd escaped across the border. The terror and danger of such a journey had been so real for Ursula, and she had no way of knowing whether her friend had survived. That all this hardship had gone on so recently had moved her profoundly.

'You know, I wish you would join my Modern History seminar group,' the professor said, doing up the leather buckle on his briefcase. 'It's never too late to join in here, Thea. It's part of what makes Oxford unique. I hate to think that you're missing out.'

There was a question in his voice, but she batted it away with a shy smile. How could she tell him that she'd like nothing more than to join in. But that she couldn't. Because of Bridget.

But his words were on her mind as she left the lecture hall and shivered in the crisp evening air. She unlocked her bike and then, wrapping her stripy woollen scarf inside her duffel coat, headed off.

180

Thea loved cycling through the streets of Oxford. Both in the summer, when the punts slid through the willows on the river, or now, when the leaves were falling and she could see her breath in the cold air. A gang of students in black tie laughed, falling into the road. Thea laughed too and rang her bell, swerving to avoid them. One of them was carrying a sparkler and she remembered that tonight was Guy Fawkes night, as he shouted after her, and another of his friends let out a leery wolf-whistle.

She whizzed over the bridge, feeling her stomach jump, her brakes screeching as she slowed down to reach the sprawling racks of bikes outside her college, smelling the roast from the back of the college dining hall. If she was quick she'd catch the evening sitting.

She stepped over the high step and through the door with its ornate stone college crest into the Porter's Lodge. It smelt of tea and toast, and the music from *The Archers* crackled on the radio. Mr Brown, the porter, stood behind the high desk studying the visitors' ledger.

As usual he was wearing a bowler hat and a waistcoat and had the air about him of someone who considered himself to be a guardian of the college's many traditions. He polished the glossy mahogany pigeonholes, never missing the opportunity to tell anyone who would listen that they bore the history of 500 years' worth of alumni.

Still out of breath from her bike ride, her cheeks smarting in the warmth, Thea went along the line

181

to where Maddox was spelt out in neat gold letters. A fax on thin yellowish paper was rolled up neatly inside.

'Where's my key?' she asked, looking at the empty hook.

'Ah, Miss Maddox,' Mr Brown said, in his clipped English. 'A young gentleman took it.'

'Who?'

'Well, your brother of course. He says he's staying with you,' Mr Brown prompted, his look over the half-moon spectacles making it clear that he'd heard it all before.

'My *brother*. Here?'

'Yes, Miss. He was most insistent. Obviously, I'm sure you're aware of the college rules on gentlemen callers in the women's colleges—'

But Thea didn't wait to hear the rest. She was out through the other door in a flash, running across the cobbled courtyard, with its neat square of grass and the dark shadow of the ancient bronze sundial, to the corner door, taking the wooden stairs two at a time, her mind spinning with fury . . . with fear.

Not Brett. Not in Oxford. In her rooms. He couldn't do that to her. Could he? How could he possibly be here?

But she knew the answer.

What was he going to do to her *this* time?

No, no, no, no, she screamed inside her head. She would not let this happen. He would not spoil this precious place for her. Since leaving Little Elms, this was the closest place to feel like home. A real home. A place where she felt safe. She'd defend it—and herself—no matter what it took.

She ran along the short corridor on the second

182

floor and flung open her door, her hands already balling into fists. But the thick wool curtains were drawn across the latticed windows, blocking out all the light.

Suddenly a hand grabbed her from behind in the darkness, across her mouth, pulling her backwards. She jerked as she heard the door being kicked shut and then locked.

With a furious yell, Thea broke free and turned, swinging her bag with full force. Whoever it was, she hit them hard. She heard them scramble back and grunt as they let go.

'Don't you fucking dare,' she spat into the dark.

Already she wished she'd brought Mr Brown with her. The darkness closed in. She scrabbled to switch on the lamp, which smashed to the floor, but stayed on. A naked man was curled up in the corner behind the door, cradling his balls with one hand, his head with the other.

'Oh . . . oh shit,' she breathed, tears of exasperation and relief bursting from her.

'Jesus!' Tom Lawson said, sitting up. 'That hurt.'

Thea crouched down by him. 'Oh, Tom. Oh God. I'm so sorry.'

Tom staggered to his feet and Thea took a shuddering breath as she flung herself into his arms and clung on.

'Hey, hey, calm down,' Tom said.

'I was so scared.'

'Clearly,' he said, with a small laugh.

She took a deep breath, embarrassed now, and sniffed loudly, brushing away her tears.

'What were you doing anyway?' she asked, looking down at his naked body.

It was only now that she saw that her room was

tidied and unusually warm. The small fan heater must have been on for hours. The stereo was playing her favourite Beverley Craven album. Fresh pink roses were in a pint glass on the small table. The bed had a new red silk cover on it and a silk blindfold to match. Four silk men's neckties were hanging from the brass bedsteads. A bottle of champagne and two glasses sweated on the bedside table, beneath the black-and-white poster of Robert Doisneau's 'The Kiss'.

'It was supposed to be a fantasy,' Tom said gruffly, 'like we wrote in our letters. You know. I was going to lead you to the bed, tie you up. Ice-cubes and feathers. It's firework night.' He stared at her, his familiar features dark with disappointment. 'I was going to give you fireworks.'

'Oh, Tom. Oh God, I'm so sorry,' she mumbled.

This was her own fault, she thought, her cheeks burning. She was so aware of how experienced he was with other woman, so cripplingly insecure in her passion for him, that she'd gone out of her way to impress him, plundering scenes from books and plagiarizing fantasies from the movies.

But now she felt the weight of her own naivety come crashing down on her. And something else too. A nagging sense that this was the moment she should own up. That she should stop trying to present herself in a false light. She should tell Tom the truth about her sexual past. About Brett, and what he'd done . . . what he'd said.

She'd thought so often of telling Tom her secret. Now that she was in a proper relationship with him, Brett's power over her had dwindled. And yet somehow that made the secret so much worse. And

184

the longer she kept it to herself, the more it ate at her.

With the benefit of hindsight, the fact that Brett had violated her and threatened her like that, in her own home, was unforgivable. But worse than all of that was that he'd got away with it. And if he'd done that to other girls, then surely that made Thea complicit in his crimes too?

But it was too late to say anything . . . do anything. She was too much of a coward to come clean to anyone, let alone Tom, who might make her confront her father. What if he made her blow apart the whole facade of the happy family behind the huge Maddox corporation? An image (false as it may be) that kept the company together and the shares trading high.

No, Thea couldn't expose Brett. Not now. She couldn't risk it. She couldn't risk hurting her father like that.

Instead she did what she always did, burying the secret, determined to put Brett where he belonged: out of her mind.

She stepped forward and cupped Tom's face.

'I'm so sorry. Forgive me.' She kissed his lips softly. 'You know, we can still . . .'

Tom shook his head. 'The moment's passed. Forget it.' He snatched her blue and white striped dressing gown from the hook by the cupboard and put it on.

Inwardly wincing at her cowardliness, Thea decided to let the matter drop. She watched as he went over to the champagne bottle.

'What are we celebrating?'

'Certainly not my erectile function at this particular moment,' Tom said.

Thea let out an embarrassed laugh. 'You're never going to forgive me, are you?'

'At least I know that you'd handle a burglar,' he said, and she knew he was softening. The cork popped and hit one of the diamond patterns on the painted ceiling, landing in the worn leather armchair.

Tom poured her a glass of champagne and she accepted it, smoothing her hair behind her ear.

God, she loved him, she thought. She loved every single tiny hair on his head. She loved his long, dark eyelashes and the pattern of freckles on the bridge of his nose. And she loved being in love with him.

'So . . . how long can you stay this time?' she asked.

'Longer than before. I quit.'

She stared at him, stunned. His father, Duke, had fixed him up with a graduate position at Lloyd's in London, a job most people his age would kill for.

'It's so fucking soulless. I can't stand it. My parents are furious, but the good news is that I'm free to hang out with you. If you'll let me, that is. I'm going to take a year out and then reapply to do law. Just like you said I should.'

My God, she thought, he really means it. She noticed his bags then in the corner of her room. He really was planning on moving here to Oxford. Nerves writhed inside her. What about her studies? What about all the societies she'd joined? And what about Bridget? What the hell would she say?

But in spite of her apprehension, another kind of excitement filled her too. Tom had come to *her*.

186

This beautiful boy, whom she sometimes felt she'd loved her entire life, had left London and changed his entire future to be with her. Because he believed in her. Because he believed in *them*.

She threw her arms around him—at the same time throwing all her doubts aside. She kissed him hard on the lips. She believed in him too. Together they'd make this work. Still kissing him, she pushed him back towards her bed. He laughed as she tumbled on top of him, then he moaned, grabbing her and kissing her.

Afterwards, as they lay there together, their naked bodies still entwined, his soft fingers gently trailed across her breasts. *I could stay here forever*, she thought. Just here and now in this beautiful room.

He finally pulled away and went to his jacket and lit up a cigarette. She smiled, watching him walk back towards her, luxuriating in the way the candlelight flickered across his perfect smooth skin. She picked up the glass of champagne, took a sip and held the bubbles in her mouth.

He crouched down by the bed, then stood, the fax she'd picked up from her pigeonhole in his hand.

He opened it out. 'It looks like it's from your father,' Tom said.

Thea took it from him and read it. It was typed in her father's usual gruff tone, telling her that he wanted her to start making plans for her twenty-first birthday. But she knew what he wanted and, as she pictured what a party in Maddox Towers would entail, she shuddered. There was no doubt he was calling her to step in line, but Thea had perfected the art of wriggling out of all the family events that might have involved the photo opportunity her father craved. By meeting Griffin Maddox in Europe and being flightily and exasperatingly too busy to get back to New York when he had requested her presence, Thea had managed to avoid being in the same building as Brett for nearly six years.

'Oh God,' she groaned. 'Why can't he just leave me alone?'

'It's just a party. I think it's sweet.'

'Yeah, with all of his and Storm's friends. It will have nothing to do with me.'

'It might be fun,' Tom said. 'I wouldn't turn it down, if I were you.'

Thea looked at the fax again, then up at Tom.

'I'll agree to it, if you come with me,' she said.

The words were out before she could stop herself. Her birthday wasn't until next March. It was months away. They had the whole ordeal of Christmas to get through first. The last thing she wanted to do was put him off by pressuring him.

'What? Meet the parents,' he said, speech-marking the phrase with his fingers.

'You don't have to,' she said quickly, putting down her champagne. 'In fact, it's probably a very bad idea—'

'I'd love to,' he said, stopping her excuses with a kiss. She put her arms around his neck, pulling him back down towards the bed, loving the way his hips automatically snaked against hers.

'Are you sure? You'll come back to America with me?'

'You think I'd let you celebrate your birthday on your own? I want to spend every second I can with you,' he said, kissing her.

'Right answer,' she said, smiling and kissing him back.

Outside a firework exploded, making them both jump, and Thea laughed. But as she rolled him onto his back and positioned herself astride him, she remembered the night of fireworks a long time ago when she'd overheard Storm telling Brett that she was a freakish little brat.

What had she done, inviting Tom to meet her family? What if he ended up thinking that she was a freakish little brat too? Or, worse, what if Tom saw through them? Through Brett and Storm, and Thea too? What if he glimpsed the dark secrets behind the perfect Maddox facade?

CHAPTER FOURTEEN

MARCH 1992

Romy yanked at the handcuffs that were chaining her to the prison bars behind her. She rattled them again, crying out. Pressing her bare feet up against the bars, she flexed, flipping her head back and pulling with all her might, as if she could break the thick metal.

Exhausted, she flattened herself against the bars, looking at the tiny cell, with its shiny white floor and black bunk, the scene blurring for a moment in her vision.

'Sensational,' Nico said, coming in low with the camera, the shutter flickering in her face. 'That's it, darling. Keep going.'

But as Romy looked into the lens, seeing her

own reflection, a memory flickered in her mind. Black-and-white photographs floating into the darkness, a figure in a blood-stained gown jumping in slow motion like a ghost.

Romy's eyes snapped open. 'Stop,' she said.

'What's the matter?' Nico asked, alarmed, as he peered up from behind the camera. 'It's going great. You look terrific. Are the handcuffs too tight?'

Romy shook her head, wriggling her wrists out of them, so that they clattered to the floor around the mocked-up bars. She bent her wrists round. 'No.'

'Then what?'

Romy moved away and stood in the centre of the set, her hand on her hip. Her hair had been backcombed beyond recognition and her false eyelashes weighed down her eyes. She fingered the diamond top of the ripped designer vest that barely covered her bronze-dusted chest.

Beyond the fake prison cell, in the darkness of Nico's studio, she knew there were a whole host of observers watching today's shoot. Nico's assistant, Florence, the make-up and hair crew, as well as the agency people and the client from the cosmetics giant. None of them were going to miss this—the big shoot for the launch of the new fragrance. Nico had been planning it for weeks.

'I'm uncomfortable with this whole . . . prison thing. I think this is the wrong message,' she said, shielding her eyes from the bright lights.

'Darling, you don't get to have a view,' Nico said, through clenched teeth. 'And we agreed . . . this is what the Art Director wants. *This is what they're paying us for.*'

Nico might be nervous, but he was the talent here, not these people. *He* was the one they were paying. But that's what he forgot sometimes, even though Nico had more persuasive powers than anyone she'd ever met, when he wanted to. After all, it had been Nico who'd talked her into modelling in the first place. It was thanks to him that her life had changed beyond all recognition in the last two-and-a-half years.

Which is why she eyeballed him back now, telling him to hold his nerve, as the Art Director Lorenzo and the ad-agency people strode onset, as well as the pinstriped grey suit who—Romy assumed from the way the others' panicked looks focused on him—was the client.

Lorenzo was wearing tight leather jeans and had sculpted facial hair and little black-framed glasses. He spoke in rapid Italian to Nico. Romy looked furious.

'He wants to know why you have stopped,' Nico said, his tone making it perfectly clear that once again Romy had overstepped her position. He widened his eyes at her, but she brazened it out. She hoped her strength would give him confidence.

'I like this fragrance, but I wouldn't wear it with this imagery. My point is that there are so many women in prison,' she said as the crowd of men assembled around her, 'women who suffer real incarceration—physically and mentally. There is nothing sexy about the smell of fear.'

For a second she pictured herself standing up in the crate in the aeroplane hold, after her terrifying journey from East Berlin. Stinking and scrawny. None of these people would ever know what they were trying to glorify here. Let alone understand.

191

A stunned silence followed. Romy didn't flinch. They needed her, whatever it was they thought she had. This was the same as poker. It was all a confidence trick. Make them think you held the winning card, and they'd bend to your will.

Lorenzo started talking rapidly to the man in the pinstriped suit. But Romy interrupted.

'Let *me* explain,' she said. 'Please.'

The fat man in the suit stepped forward and Romy shook his hand, then led him away from the others by the arm. She was much taller than him, something that clearly intimidated him, as he straightened his back now and attempted to stare her down.

'Listen,' she said, neutralizing him with a smile and a look—that look, the doe-eyed come-and-get-me look that she was already famous for across Italy. As she continued to talk, in Italian— something that clearly delighted and surprised him in equal measure—she watched his shoulders relax.

Her tutor in her evening classes had told her that she had a gift for languages, the like of which he'd never come across before. Romy didn't tell him that she'd made it through this far by becoming a chameleon, and it was always languages that had helped her fit in, allowing her to win and now to keep her precious freedom.

She used this ability now to get on first-name terms with Tomaz, the suit. Then, once she'd brought a blush to his flabby cheeks, she grilled him about his demographic for the perfume, and explained in his native language why she thought the message was wrong. Then she told him her idea.

192

'But that's a whole change of the campaign dynamic,' Lorenzo spluttered, when Romy explained it to him a few minutes later. But it didn't matter what he thought now. The fat client, Tomaz, was already convinced. He was gazing across the studio at Romy even now, his eyes glittering. Was he having fantasies, she wondered, of inviting her onto his yacht? Romy knew plenty of models who went out with filthy-rich, ugly men, but she wasn't ever going to become one of them. She was too busy earning her own money to bother with anyone else's.

'If that's what the client—thanks to you—now wants, then that's what we'll give him,' Lorenzo said. His eyes flashed a warning. 'I just hope, for both of our arses,' he said, deliberately slipping into English so that no one would understand, 'you're right.'

She knew she was taking a risk, putting her own views on the line like this. Adrenaline burst through her as Lorenzo clapped his hands to get everyone's attention.

Romy turned to Florence, Nico's assistant. She was wearing leggings and an oversized baggy jumper, which accentuated her mop of peroxide-white hair and elfin-like features. 'Get the doorman up here. Jovo's his name. Tell him Romy needs a favour.'

'What are you planning now?' Nico asked.

'You'll see.'

Jovo was exactly what she needed. They'd always chatted whenever she came to Nico's studio, and Romy often brought him cherries from the fruit stall on the corner by her apartment. This morning they'd talked about the crisis in Bosnia, where his family was originally from, and how he was expecting trouble between the Serbs and Croats. He'd once been a boxer back there, he'd told Romy. Now, in his sixties, he was decidedly more fat than muscle. Perfect for what she had in mind. 'Trust me. It'll be OK.'

Ten minutes later Romy had Jovo lying on the floor of the cell on his considerable belly, his hands handcuffed behind his back. Then Romy sat on him, the keys of the handcuffs dangling on her finger.

'Now shoot,' she told Nico. 'And Florence, honey, could you get me those Gucci heels we had before, please, darling? I don't want to do any more shots with bare feet. Not when those shoes are so gorgeous.'

She let Nico direct her, flicking her head triumphantly. Out of the corner of her eye she noticed Lorenzo nodding approvingly, his arms folded across his shirt. She even thought she saw him smile.

*   *   *

At the back of the studio, dressed in her regulation black polo-neck jumper and designer slacks, Simona Fiore sucked on her cigarette, concealing with her normal scowl the frisson of excitement that she felt. She didn't usually come along to her models' shoots, but she had some special news that she was looking forward to breaking to Romy after the job had finished. Very special news indeed.

Perez Vadim had requested Romy for his Paris catwalk show on Friday. *Perez Vadim.* What's more, the hot designer of the moment had personally called Simona, and she'd wasted no time in demanding a ludicrously high price for Romy's services. Such a commission would really propel Romy into supermodel status.

She just hoped that Romy could toe the line before then. It was unheard of for a model to call the shots. But Simona had been in the business long enough for nothing to surprise her. Especially as far as *this* girl was concerned. But what the hell? She obviously had good instincts, because in a single suggestion Romy suddenly had a room full of self-important men running round her, doing her bidding.

Romy—the girl was special all right. She had an aura of attitude around her, of toughness that offset her beauty in the most unusual way. Simona had noticed it the very first moment she'd seen those shots Nico had sent her, of Romy drying her hair on the beach after taking a swim. She'd called him straight away and told him to sign up the girl on the spot. Offer her triple her salary from whatever stinkpot cruise ship she was working on, and do everything in his power to make sure she didn't go back.

By the time Nico had dragged the poor starstruck girl to Madrid, the guy had been as hopelessly and completely besotted with Romy as she had been with him. It had been a tough conversation to break the news to Romy that Nico was gay.

But that was Romy all over—worldly in some respects way beyond her years, but as naive as a child in others. Perhaps that was why Simona had fallen for Romy too. She'd never had a daughter, or ever bonded with any of the models on her

195

books, but this kid—there was something about her that made Simona favour her above all the others.

So what if her story about her normal childhood in England didn't wash? Simona didn't care where she came from. Romy had a freshness about her that had enabled Simona to orchestrate a total reinvention. She'd styled the girl and shaved a couple of years off her actual age and, looking at Romy flicking her hair, Simona knew in her gut that Romy was *the one*. The one she'd been waiting for. The one Simona intended to propel right to the very, very top.

* * *

But despite Simona's reassurances, none of Romy's new-found modelling experience had prepared her for Paris fashion week. Romy had thought that live modelling would be a similar kind of deal to the studio sessions she'd done, but the second she walked backstage and saw the frenzy of activity, she knew that she was totally out of her depth. Within minutes she was hustled through to the hair stylists, who slicked her hair back with Brylcreem, then hacked some of it off, before she could protest.

Then after the make-up team had done their extraordinary job on her face, she was dressed in a corset dress, yanked in and trussed up. Everyone spoke in rapid French all around her.

'Fur and lace?' she said to the designer's assistant, tugging at the thin mesh top. 'That's got to be a first on me.' But the guy just scowled at Romy as he pinned an elaborate headpiece on her head, his face creased in concentration as he gripped the pins between his lips.

Almost ready now, Romy peeped through a tiny slit in the blackout curtain, into the cavernous venue where the expectant crowd of fashion aficionados gathered in the darkened auditorium along the sides of an elevated runway. Prince's 'Diamonds and Pearls' boomed out and dramatic lights strobed the stage, illuminating the V-hologram of Perez Vadim's famous logo.

'Don't,' a girl whispered, tugging at Romy's arm. 'If Pierre sees you peeping, he'll go nuts.'

'Who?' Romy asked, turning to talk to the demure English girl with white skin, who flicked her tawny eyes in the direction of the skinny Frenchman who was concentrating on the skirt of one of the models' dresses. Even from a distance she could feel the tension radiating from him. Romy hadn't realized they'd take it all this seriously, but it was more like an art show than a fashion parade.

'He's in charge,' the girl hissed. 'I'm Emma, by the way,' she added, more kindly. She took out a packet of gum from the pocket of her voluminous denim outfit and offered some to Romy. 'I'm so pleased to meet another English girl.'

Romy took the gum and the girl smiled shyly. There was something so vulnerable about her. And she saw something else in the girl's eyes—something more than just nerves, something closer to fear.

'Hey, you OK? What's up?' Romy asked, instinctively reaching out to touch the girl's shoulder.

'It's Tia,' the girl said in a frightened, hushed

197

whisper.

'Who's Tia?' Romy asked.

Emma's eyes brimming with tears were wide, looking at someone behind Romy. She turned to see a girl in high boots, with a sharp fringe of jet-black hair and the piercing green eyes of a snake.

'She scares me,' Emma said.

'She's just a model—the same as you. You have as much right to be here.'

Emma shook her head. 'You don't understand. It's not like that with her. Look at this,' she whispered, turning over her arm. There were purple bruises on either side of what looked like nail-marks.

'She did that?' Romy asked.

Emma nodded. 'She does it to everyone.'

Romy stared over in the direction of Tia again, but she was strutting into the makeshift bathroom. Romy went to follow.

'Don't,' Emma begged. 'Don't say I said anything.'

But Romy was already pushing her way through the crowd of bodies and models to the bathroom door.

For a second Romy stopped dead in her tracks when she saw her own reflection in the long mirror. Her eyes were surrounded in thick black and fluorescent shadows, but the elaborate headdress somehow finished the whole look. It was elegant and yet playful, punky and somehow extremely feminine. The messy fur and lace top tapered into a tweed ra-ra skirt with pink-net petticoats underneath. Then there were slashed fishnets leading down to skyscraping open-toed boots. But considering how outlandish the whole ensemble was, Romy felt oddly comfortable.

Then she noticed Tia was snorting a long line of white powder from a mirror that she'd rested on the side of the sink.

'Who the fuck are you?' Tia said, rubbing her nostril and noticing Romy staring.

So *this* was Tia, Romy thought. A bully. She'd seen enough at the orphanage to spot this one a mile off.

'What's it to you?' Romy said, suddenly aware that the girl was assessing her too.

'Oh, I know . . . you're that new English chick from Italy.' She had a low French accent. 'The way I heard it, you only got the Perez gig at all because my friend Lula broke her ankle, and I was too busy. But she'll be back and then you'll be gone,' she said, flicking her fingers at Romy, as if she were an annoying insect. Then she brazenly snorted another line of cocaine. 'So don't get used to any of this, because, after today, I'll make sure you're history. I mean, Christ . . . who told you— *you*—could be a model anyway? Freak.'

Romy stood perfectly still, forcing herself to stay calm. She shouldn't pick a fight. Not here. Not on such an important job, but it was a while since she'd encountered someone so arrogant and rude. No wonder Emma was frightened of her.

A few moments later, when Tia came back out of the bathroom, Romy heard Tia's voice above all the others.

'Hey, Pierre,' she called, without turning round. She shouted in rapid French and Romy became aware that everyone had turned and was staring at her headdress.

'That headdress is better. Give me her

199

headdress,' Tia said in English, strutting over and trying to rip it from Romy's head.

And all of a sudden Romy felt as if she were nine years old again, fighting Fox in the refectory in the orphanage. She shoved Tia backwards.

Pierre was by Tia's side in a second, trying to calm her down. Tia snarled at Romy, before turning on her heel and stamping away.

Pierre glared at Romy.

'What?' Romy shrugged, adjusting her headdress. 'You saw what she did.'

'She's Tia Blanche. She can do what the hell she likes,' Pierre said. 'Now get in line. We're on in less than a minute. Please, *new girl*, do not upset our top model again. Monsieur Vadim will not be happy.'

But Tia clearly hadn't finished with Romy. When Romy saw that they were models one and two out on the catwalk, she knew there'd be trouble.

'Wow,' Emma said to Romy as they hustled into line, being checked and primped. 'You really stood up to her.'

'Yeah, well, she doesn't frighten me,' Romy said.

Romy saw Tia preparing herself in the darkness, waiting for the music cue to step into the spotlight.

'You don't get to walk in front of me, bitch,' Tia hissed to Romy, as she took her position behind her. 'You don't get to be near me. You don't get to touch me. You do not even step foot out here until I am on my way back and give you my signal. *Capiche?*'

Romy didn't say anything, but she felt every nerve-end bristling. Then the lights came on and the music boomed out. It was Tia's cue to move.

Just before she went onstage she deliberately took a step backwards, plunging her stiletto heel into Romy's big toe.

The pain was so intense that Romy couldn't stop herself. She gave Tia a massive shove, making her lose her balance and sending her flying. Tia landed in a heap in the spotlight at the back end of the runway.

Romy heard the audience gasp.

Everyone backstage froze. Then Tia was up, coming for Romy, screeching with fury. There was an almighty tear, as Romy's fur-and-lace bodice ripped and Tia pulled her into the spotlight too.

Romy punched her full in the face, the music thumping out as the audience got to their feet.

Romy was up first. Shaking her head free, she pulled up the mesh top and secured it in place with the gum from her mouth. Then she marched down the runway, her head held high, working the catwalk, giving it her all in the bright lights, to whoops and applause.

*   *   *

The rest of the show passed in a blur. Nico came backstage and, having found a first-aid kit, dabbed at the wound on Romy's toe. It had gone an angry purplish-red and was swollen. But adrenaline still coursed through her body.

'Hey, it was fun to have a catwalk moment,' she said. 'In Paris.'

'I think it will be your last,' Nico said grimly, not rising to her gallows humour. 'Do you have any idea how furious Simona is?'

'Tia started it, Nico,' Romy protested, but she

201

knew her outburst had caused a tearful row between Tia and Pierre, and the star model had left the venue before the end of the show. 'Maybe I'm just not cut out for this.'

'Don't say that,' Nico said.

They both looked up as Pierre shouted, running towards them. 'You. You're on. Final bows,' he said to Romy, his cold look making it clear just how angry he was with her.

Her knees were shaking as she was hustled to the front of the line of silent models. Judging by their wide eyes, she was in no doubt that she'd just committed the ultimate modelling faux pas. But there, waiting to walk with his models for the final bow, was Perez Vadim.

She'd never seen him in person before. It was his protégé, Milo, who'd interviewed her in Vadim's Milan headquarters. There'd been plenty of photos of Perez Vadim around the place, some going way back, spanning his thirty-year career.

Looking at him now, he was much older than she'd expected, with watery blue eyes. Dark shades were pushed into his thinning hair. He wore trousers covered in zips and a cape attached to his cowboy shirt.

'I am very sorry, Monsieur Vadim,' she said, expecting the worst. 'I guess I made a bad impression.'

'Au contraire,' the great designer said, taking her hand and kissing it, leading her out to the standing ovation. His eyes sparkled with amusement. 'You've made my show the most talked-about one of the whole season. You, Romy, are a triumph.'

CHAPTER FIFTEEN

MARCH 1992

Thea stood outside the back door of the Swiss ski chalet and grinned. The conditions for her twenty-first birthday weekend couldn't be more perfect. Bright-blue sky and a clear powder run stretching from their very front door straight down the mountain.

'Come on, what you waiting for?' Tom called as he whooped away through the snow.

Thea skied after him, laughing as she overtook him, and he raced again to be in front. When he came to a stop, showering her in powder, he took off his goggles and his face was flushed. Sometimes his sheer beauty took her breath away and she wanted to pinch herself that a man so wonderful could love her the way he did. She kissed him, glad that she'd brought him here. Then she laughed as he expertly tripped her over so that he was lying on top of her in the powder snow.

'I love you, Thea Maddox,' he said, kissing her.

'I love you too,' she said.

'So will you stop being so nervous?' he said, smiling at her.

'Nervous? I'm not being nervous, am I?'

He laughed. 'You always plait your hair when you're nervous,' he said, toying with her thick rope of blonde hair.

She blushed, amazed that he'd noticed. 'I'll take it out,' she said.

'Don't. I like your *Fräulein* look,' he said. 'But . . .

Thea, just relax, will you? We're here to have fun. You've got your own way. You've managed to wriggle out of a big party. They've all come over to Europe. So stop acting like it's such a big deal. What can really be so bad about me meeting your folks?'

'I know. I'm sorry,' she said. Then she kissed him again and he hauled her to her feet before skiing away laughing.

He's right, she told herself. She should relax. It was just a weekend and then she'd be back in Oxford with plenty of time to revise before her finals. One weekend of fun wasn't going to ruin her chances of a first.

Besides, it was great to be on holiday with Tom, and she knew how much he'd been looking forward to this weekend. She mustn't ruin it with her doubts. So far it had been brilliant. They'd arrived to find that everyone at the chalet was already out on the slopes, so they had this time to themselves.

So why did she feel so goddamn tense?

But further on, down the slopes, a familiar trill of laughter brought Thea to a stop outside the Krug champagne bar.

'Thea?' Storm called, waving her over. 'Thea, honey. Over here.'

Storm was wearing a fluorescent-pink one-piece ski suit with designer glasses and fur ear-muffs, and several empty bottles littered her crowded table. As was usual for Storm and her ever-changing entourage, there were only one or two faces whom Thea recognized. Griffin Maddox was nowhere to be seen.

'Tom, this is my stepmom, Storm Maddox,'

Thea said, watching as Storm outstretched her manicured hand. Her fingers glinted with diamonds in the sunshine.

'So you must be Thea's college hunk,' Storm drawled, her heavily made-up eyes raking over Tom's features. She looked as if she wanted to eat him. From the ripple of laughter around the table, Thea knew that she and Tom had been a recent topic of conversation.

But all Thea could do was stare at Storm. What had she done to her face? Since last summer Storm's lips had changed shape again, and the skin over her cheekbones was taut. Had she had *another* facelift already?

Thea watched Storm's white teeth gleaming in the sun, amazed once again that her father could ever have chosen her. Or that anyone could find someone who was so brazen attractive. As she and Tom joined them for a drink, the conversation progressed. Storm declared herself to be too hot and, fully aware of what she was doing, undid her front zipper to reveal some new assets. Thea blushed, disappointed to see that Tom had noticed them too. But the conversation quickly moved on, as one of Storm's friends noticed a girl on the next table.

She was unusually tall, with striking black hair, but from where they were sitting it was clear that she had a black eye beneath her designer shades. Tom winked at Thea, as if Thea should know who the girl was. But Thea just shrugged.

'Tia Blanche,' Tom whispered, 'The model.' The name meant nothing to Thea. 'She was all over the tabloids last week,' he explained. 'She had a massive fight with another model in Paris.'

Thea smiled despite herself. Tom's time at the bar in Oxford where he worked had given him a keen ear for gossip, and time to read the papers. Whereas the only papers Thea had been reading recently were economic migration trends in twentieth-century Europe.

Storm had clearly overheard Tom's explanation, because she leant in now, slipped her arm around Tom's waist and pulled him close. 'Well, at least *one* of you knows about the real world.'

But instead of defending her, Tom just laughed. 'The way I heard it,' he said, 'it was the bitch-fight of the century. The other girl—Romy-something— she totally kicked her arse.'

'Oh, I do like a man with his finger on the pulse,' Storm said, pulling Tom in even tighter, flashing her green eyes at him. Her hint that she wouldn't mind Tom putting his finger on her pulse was implicit, and Thea noticed him blushing.

At the first chance she had, Thea made an excuse and dragged him away. The last thing she wanted was to be stuck with Storm and her friends all afternoon, despite their protestations that they wanted Tom to stay and chat. Besides, there would be a big dinner later, when there would be plenty of time.

'Storm seems nice,' Tom said, as they skied to the lift, but Thea was mortified.

'Stop it. She's awful. Just say it.'

'You're jealous of her,' Tom said. 'It's a dominant-female thing.'

'Jealous? Of all that hair and those new boobs of hers . . .'

'Yeah, those things are something else,' he said, blowing his hair upwards, as if he was too hot.

Thea hit him on the arm, but Tom grabbed her and kissed her.

'Don't worry,' he grinned. 'She's not really my type. I prefer someone smart as well as beautiful. Someone real. Someone exactly like you.'

*　　　*　　　*

They left it to the last possible moment to get back for supper, Thea having persuaded Tom to go all the way up the mountain in the gondola. By the time they arrived at the chalet, lights were blazing from every room and the guests had gathered for dinner.

As Thea had suspected, her intimate family weekend had expanded to include at least twenty strangers who made up Storm's current inner circle. Thea had no doubt that, by the end of the season, Storm would have jettisoned at least half of them and they would join the ranks of the countless others who had briefly found favour with the powerful first lady of the media-set in New York.

Thea felt her face tight with sunburn, as she quickly changed into her baggy jeans and a polo neck and joined the others in the main sitting room, realizing too late that all the other women were dressed up. She'd thought the smart dinner would be tomorrow night. But it was too late to change now.

'About time,' her father said.

Thea kissed him and apologized, but she noticed that he looked more stressed than he had done for a while, and his dark hair was much greyer than she remembered.

207

Feeling nervous, she introduced Tom to her father, biting her lip and smiling as they shook hands. She'd expected him to be pleased that Tom's mother and Alyssa Maddox had once been friends. It was a trump-card that she'd been looking forward to playing face-to-face. After all, he was the one who always talked so much about the importance of networking. Wasn't the fact that she and Tom were linked by a past family friendship important to him?

But Griffin Maddox hardly paid any attention at all. Instead he was abrupt with Tom, almost to the point of rudeness, and Thea was left baffled. She'd painted a picture to Tom of her charming father, but now she felt ashamed of him for being so dismissive. Worse, when the staff led them through to the dining room and showed each guest their allotted seat, far from putting Tom in any position of honour—beside him, Thea or even Storm—Thea saw that he'd been seated amongst some of Storm's cronies whom Thea had never laid eyes on before.

She was trying to think of a way to politely complain when Storm did some quick reshuffling of her own, slipping in beside Tom and turning the full beam of her attention on him. 'Now tell me all about your Princess Diana,' she said loudly, laying her hands on Tom's arm. 'I just can't believe she's gonna split with Charles . . .'

Thea couldn't help noticing how low-cut her black dress was, but after his comment earlier, Thea was determined to show Tom that she absolutely wasn't jealous of Storm in any way. Besides, she thought, glancing up for what she was determined would be the last time, it was no bad thing if Tom got to know the real Storm. New boobs or no new boobs, he'd soon grow weary of her after that.

Thea sat next to her father, who was deep in conversation with Justin Ennestein, his lawyer, about his contribution to the Clinton campaign—determined as he was that his friend from Arkansas should oust Bush from the White House.

She wished they would stop talking, or at least include her; and, as the meal progressed, Thea couldn't help looking down the table to where Tom was surrounded by women, each of them seemingly leaning further across the table to be in earshot of whatever he said. She loved the fact that he was handsome and could make people laugh. But she loved it more when she alone was the subject of that attention. Watching him now, she felt strangely that he was no longer just hers.

'Thea?' Griffin Maddox asked, eventually putting his knife and fork together. 'What's got into you? You're miles away. You've hardly joined in at all.'

She wanted to protest that he'd hardly given her the chance, but she knew he'd only see that as weakness. He spent so much of his energy and time talking business these days that sometimes she felt he treated her like a business associate too. Sometimes—like now, on the eve of her twenty-first birthday—she just wanted him to treat her like his only daughter again.

'Yes, Thea. I've been meaning to ask. How's it all going at Oxford?' Justin asked.

'Fine . . . thanks.'

'There are plenty of good universities in the States,' Griffin Maddox said.

'It's history you're studying, right?' Justin checked, ignoring him.

'Modern European History.'

'Why study Europe's past? The future is America,' her father muttered.

Thea felt his words like a slap. She caught Justin's eye.

'Oh, come on, Griff. Don't be so inflammatory,' he said.

Griffin Maddox sighed. 'I just wish you were closer to home, Thea. That's all. I hardly see you these days.'

The only home I ever had was the one you sold, Thea thought. But she forced a smile instead. That was an old argument now. One she'd never even been consulted on.

But his attention was now drawn to Storm. 'It's true isn't it, Griff?' she trilled. 'Tom doesn't believe me that Thea was a fat teenager.'

There was a ripple of laughter. Griffin pulled a face to show that he was simultaneously irked by Storm and nevertheless duty-bound to indulge her.

'Puppy-fat,' he said patting Thea's hand. 'She was always a beauty underneath.'

But despite his kind words Thea felt ice in her stomach as she saw the glint in Storm's eye. She saw Tom pick up his napkin and wipe his mouth. Over the top of it he caught Thea's eye, and she knew that he might be down there at the mercy of Storm and her friends, but he clearly saw through Storm's barbed comments. His eyes gently smiled at Thea and she knew that he loved her. Nothing Storm could say could alter that. Soon she'd graduate from Oxford with a first, and she'd leave Storm and her warped childhood far behind her.

'She's only teasing,' Thea heard her father say.

'I think she's had one glass of wine too many,' Thea said, just loud enough, she hoped, for Storm to hear.

'So . . . what are you planning to do with all these qualifications of yours?' Justin Ennestein said, getting their conversation back on track.

Thea took a breath. This was her moment. The conversation she'd been waiting for. How perfect that Justin should bring it up, when he and her father were the very people she needed to speak to about her plans.

But just as she was about to start her pitch there was a commotion in the hall and Brett walked in, fresh from the airport, snow in his hair, a bag over his shoulder. There was an immediate round of applause. Thea watched, horrified, as her father stood up, smiling broadly for the first time since Thea had got there.

'Ah . . . there he is,' Griffin Maddox said, beaming at Brett and clapping him on the back as they hugged. 'You made it.'

'Hey, Thea,' Brett said, 'birthday surprise.'

His look of triumph sent shivers down her spine. He playfully punched her shoulder, as if they were the best of buddies.

She watched as Brett put his bag down, and Storm engulfed him in a hug and he twirled her round, as if he were some prodigal son returning from the war.

'This is my Brett,' Storm told Tom, kissing Brett lavishly, her bright-red talons against his cheek.

'Her brother,' Brett said, nodding towards Thea.

Tom smiled at him, before glancing at Thea as if to say: *Who*? Thea winced as they shook hands.

Her father had told her that Brett wouldn't be here, so she hadn't told Tom she had a stepbrother, assuming that he must have heard of Brett through the press. Whenever the subject of her family had come up, Thea had concentrated the facts on her father, and had taken Tom's lack of questions about Brett as lack of interest. But now she could see that Tom had questions. Lots of questions. Like why Thea had never mentioned this obviously important family member.

She felt soiled, as if he could already sense her guilt.

'Nice to meet you, man,' Brett said, all charm. 'Tom, right? Come and have a drink with me, buddy.'

And as Brett led Tom away, Thea felt tears of impotence pricking her eyes. Was this how Bridget had felt when Thea had fallen for Tom? she now wondered, suddenly understanding. She stared down at her glass, then drained the contents. When she looked up again she saw her father standing by the glass doors onto the balcony.

'Fancy some air?' he called to her, and she followed him out into the darkness.

*   *   *

The view from the chalet was breathtaking. The full moon was bathing everything in silver and the snow twinkled like a vast diamanté cloak. Her father had lit a cigar and, as he blew smoke out into the liquid black air, it felt to Thea like a filmset and that she should have rehearsed this.

'So I suppose you're going to tell me you're in love with this Lawson guy?' Griffin Maddox asked,

212

as they leant against the wooden balustrade. The question startled Thea. She was still smarting about Brett turning up, uninvited and unannounced.

'Yes.' Thea stared at him, already feeling defensive.

'First love never lasts,' he said. 'It's just one of those mistakes young people keep on making.'

How dare he be so patronizing? Thea smarted. Love was love.

'You were young when you met Mom. You loved each other.'

'That was different,' he said firmly.

'How? What's wrong with Tom?' she demanded.

'I don't trust him.'

Thea took a breath and forced herself to stay calm. 'Well, I don't see why you should say that,' she said, trying to keep her voice even. *Why are you talking like this*? she wanted to scream. 'You're wrong. I'll prove it.'

Griffin sighed, his great wide shoulders sagging. 'Maybe you're right.'

He put his strong arm around her. She was still trying hard not to cry. Was he drunk? she wondered. Is that why he was being like this?

'I just want to protect you, that's all,' he said. 'I won't say any more.'

Thea softened. Such an admission of fatherly emotion, coming from him, stunned her. They were silent for a moment, looking up at the stars.

'So . . . you never answered Justin. What *are* you intending to do with all these fancy qualifications of yours?' he asked.

Thea steeled herself. She'd been ready a few

minutes ago, but Brett had unnerved her and now she felt lacking in confidence.

'Do you remember how you always used to tell me that one day you'd teach me everything you knew?' she said.

And that everything that is mine will be yours, she wanted to add, remembering his familiar mantra. But she stopped herself.

Her father stayed deep in thought. 'Those days were a long time ago, and things—well, everything has changed,' he said quietly. 'Your mother always thought that you'd never have to work. That's what she wanted. And I've made that possible.'

'And I'm grateful for everything I have,' Thea said quickly, 'but I'm not going to sit around for the rest of my life.'

'But you could find a *suitable* husband. Have children?'

'How very modern of you,' she said, gently digging him in the ribs, finally coaxing a chuckle out of him. Then she paused, stepping away from his hug and standing firmly facing him. 'I'd like to stay in London. I was hoping you'd give me a job?'

She tried to sound meek and grateful as she told him about her research into the Maddox Inc. newspaper group in London, and how she'd like to take an active role in the company. It was something she'd thought long and hard about. For a long time she'd considered walking away and doing something else, but Tom had told her she was crazy to.

Besides, it was her inheritance. Something she'd been planning on doing all her life. It was what she'd been born to do. And if she didn't? Well—*everything with a Maddox name will be mine for the*

214

taking. Brett's mocking voice rang in her memory as if he were speaking in her ear.

'Thea, I'm not sure working for me would suit you.'

'Why not? Brett does.'

She suddenly felt childish, her jealousy was so overpowering.

'Brett is a very talented young man,' her father said. 'Even if he wasn't family, I'd want him in the organization. He's proved himself to be a very valuable asset.'

Thea fell into silence, into a darkness blacker than the night. A voice deep down inside her wanted to scream at him, to tell him what Brett had done. But another part of her strangled those practised words in her throat, telling her that she was disgusting, that her father would find her disgusting, that he'd think what had happened had somehow been her fault.

It was her father's voice that pulled her back from the void. It felt as if a hypnotist had just snapped his finger and broken her free from a trance.

'If you like studying, I could organize for you to do some kind of postgrad?'

She stared at him, marvelling at his ability to trivialize her life whilst simultaneously expecting her to be grateful. Well, Brett might have stepped into a position on the board without question, but she was damned if she was going to be so nepotistic.

No, she'd find a way to prove herself to him. She'd succeed *despite* him. Show him what a valuable asset *she* was. No matter what it took, she would claim her place as his rightful heir. And it wouldn't involve a postgrad course that he'd bought for her.

'I'll think about it,' she mumbled.

He patted her shoulder. 'I'm giving you more shares for your birthday,' he said. 'I thought you'd like that more than money.'

'Thank you,' she said. She didn't add 'Daddy' and she didn't give him a hug.

*　　　*　　　*

Later the party at the chalet was in full swing, but Griffin Maddox slipped off early to bed, Thea noticed. She wanted to go to bed too, but Tom wouldn't hear of it, DJ-ing on the decks in the den to the delight of Storm, who danced with her friends until they were so hot and sweaty that they went outside to plunge into the snow, whooping and giggling.

Brett stayed in the den, deep in conversation with Justin Ennestein, and Thea couldn't help but wonder what they were discussing. She didn't want to be on the outside any longer. She wanted to know what was going on.

Working at Maddox Inc. had been something she'd been expecting to do since she could remember. Her father blocking her, for what she could only surmise were sexist reasons, only made her ambition stronger.

And OK, yes, it would be easy to walk away. Admit defeat. Accept that Brett had filled the role that her father had always told her would be hers. But she already knew she wasn't going to. She wasn't going to accept her father's 'No'.

She flicked her head at Tom, hoping he'd sneak

216

off to their room, where they could discuss her conversation with her father. But Tom was already too drunk to be as serious as she needed him to be. Besides, Storm was clearly on a mission to prove to him that she was the most fun anyone could be. Thea noticed how she kept filling up his drink and laughing at everything he said, her hand with its long talons resting on his arm as she shrieked with fresh peels of mirth. It wasn't long before Storm and her equally exuberant friends had persuaded Tom to go outside, where they were diving into the snow. He shrugged helplessly at Thea as they dragged him along.

Thea laughed weakly, refusing to join in and calling him 'crazy' as she watched from the doorway. In a minute, at the first chance he had to extricate himself, he was back, shivering. Storm was calling him from the outdoor hot-tub, but Tom appealed to Thea. 'Let's go to the sauna,' he said, his teeth chattering.

She was about to refuse, but decided against it. It was much better for her to be in the sauna with him than leave Tom with Storm and her friends. Some heat might sober him up. She took him downstairs.

* * *

Tom only lasted five minutes in the sauna before Thea was seriously worried about him. 'I'll be straight back,' he said, getting up. 'I'm going to get some water. Don't go away.'

'OK, I won't, but be quick,' she said.

Thea sat back in the heat. It had been a while since she'd skied, and she ached all over. She had to admit that her stiff muscles did feel better for being warmed up. She could hear the distant sounds of Storm and her friends putting on more music.

She stood up and wiped the steam off the window of the door, wondering whether to go and find Tom.

But just then a face at the door made her jump and she yelped, falling backwards onto the hot wooden slats as the door swung open and Brett came in. He was wearing a short white towel. She recoiled at the sight of the gingery blond hair on his chest and his pale-pink nipples.

'Where's Tom?' Thea asked, wiping the sweat-soaked hair back away from her face.

'He's gone to lie down,' Brett said. 'He told me to tell you. You shouldn't have let him get into the clutches of the old lady. He's wasted.'

He grinned at her. She pulled her knees up, upset that she was in a bikini in such a confined space with him.

But Brett was in no hurry to leave. He leant back against the door, crossing his feet.

'He's quite keen, that Tom guy.'

That Tom guy. Why wasn't anyone taking him seriously?

'Yeah,' Brett continued, clearly enjoying the way he was unnerving her. 'He showed me the ring he's going to give you tomorrow.'

Tom was going to give her a ring? Did that mean ...?

Thea felt her heart plummet through the floor. She stared at Brett, loathing him for the way he was enjoying ruining this for her.

Suddenly he plucked the scoop from the hook

218

on the wall and, dipping it in the small wooden barrel of water on the floor, carelessly splashed the water on the hot coals in the corner. There was a loud hiss and the temperature spiked. Thea squirmed on the seat, determined not to show him how scared he was making her feel.

'So. Dad told me you'd asked him for a job,' Brett said. He sounded amused, as if her request had already been the subject of a private joke between them.

Dad. Her father wasn't Brett's dad. God only knew who Brett's real father was. Storm had always been so evasive about her ex-husbands. So how dare Brett steal hers? She felt furious that her private conversation with her father had already been reported.

'You don't want to work for us, Thea,' Brett said. It sounded like a threat.

Us?

'Why? You're worried I'll expose you? Or outshine you?' she snapped back. 'You don't frighten me,' she went on, trying to sound much braver than she felt. She had to get out of here. Fast. She had to get back to Tom, where she'd be safe.

She got up and tried to push past him, but suddenly Brett whipped her around and pinned her up against the rough wooden boards of the sauna wall. Her cheek burnt as it pressed into the hot wood.

She felt dizzy in the heat, weak in his grasp, as he pushed her arm up her back, making her shoulder scream with pain.

This couldn't be happening. Not again.

Where was Tom?

219

'Don't,' she gasped, terrified. 'Let me go.'

She struggled harder this time, but he held her like a vice. Thea felt nausea rise in her mouth as he jerked off his towel.

'How d'you think your little boyfriend Tom would like it if I told him what you let me do to you?' Brett said. 'What a little slut you really are?'

She tried to scream, but he put his hand over her mouth, choking her violently.

Panic set in as he ripped down her bikini bottoms. She struggled much harder, her muffled screams lost in the heat. Brett hit her then, momentarily stunning her, before pressing her all the harder against the burning wood, his hand grasping her hair tightly. Then he pushed her legs apart and positioned himself against her. Then into her.

'Happy fucking birthday, little sister,' he said, thrusting with each word.

CHAPTER SIXTEEN

MAY 1993

It was a perfect spring day in Paris. The sidewalk cafés were jammed with people sipping chilled wine in the sunshine, and tourists dawdled through the Tuileries gardens snapping pictures of the majestic horse-chestnut blossom as the trill of birdsong filled the air.

On the Avenue George V, above the plush designer window and behind the billowing net curtain on the second floor, Romy stood on the polished parquet flooring of Perez Vadim's atelier, as the great designer walked around her, his bony, nicotine-stained fingers on his puckered lips.

A line of immaculately dressed assistants waited for his approval, as if this were an audience with a king. Behind them the enormous doors opened from Vadim's famous salon onto the pattern-cutting room, with high desks covered in drawings. Dressmaking mannequins draped in the finest silks were crammed in between the high tables, and the walls were covered in sketches of dresses and hats.

'What do you think?' Vadim asked Romy in his gnarled North African drawl, peering over his thick-framed black glasses. Since she'd last seen him he'd dyed his short hair blond. He was wearing electric-blue drainpipe trousers with low pointed cowboy boots and a black jacket with the tailor's stitches on the outside. A signature piece from his autumn collection, Romy remembered. She'd done hours of homework on the great designer before she'd come today.

She stared down at the mock-up of the exquisite evening dress she was wearing. This was the last in a long line of dresses in various stages of design that she'd modelled today from Vadim's forthcoming couture range.

'I like it,' she said, moving slightly and lifting off the fabric samples that had been draped across her shoulders. One of them—the favourite—was green. But Romy felt repelled by it. She didn't mind green generally, but this material was the same colour as that green blanket she'd found in Lemcke's office all those years ago. It reminded her of that moment of furious, impotent anger she'd felt. As if she'd opened a treasure chest and

221

found it full of sand.

Once again, she forced herself to lock the memory in the vault. She was a different person now, she reminded herself. All of that was in the past. And the past was a foreign country—a phrase she'd read in a book and one that had stuck with her.

'I don't like the green,' she said. 'Personally, I think the blue is better.'

Vadim nodded slowly. 'Yes, midnight-blue. Not the green. You're right,' he said.

Romy pulled a humble face at Jocelyn and Marie, who made hurried notes on their clipboards. She was amazed that Vadim had listened to her and, by the looks on their faces, they were too. Another assistant hurried over and collected the sample from Romy. The green silk fell to the floor in a pool by her feet.

Vadim stood staring at her. 'I'm still not sure about this neckline,' he said.

He put out his hand, gesturing for his assistant, Marcel, to come forward. He was wearing skin-tight drainpipes to match Vadim's, and his thick black eyebrows shot up at Romy as he handed his master the dressmaking shears.

'Still,' Perez told Romy. Then he put the scissors in the fine material near the armpit and slashed the arm of the dress away. Jocelyn and Marie came intrepidly around the front to look at Vadim's work.

'Better, huh?' he said. 'Diana will like this,' he said conclusively. 'She is here next week. Make sure it works by then. With the sequin-line down here,' he said, tracing a line down the skirt, his fingertip caressing Romy's thigh beneath. But he

222

didn't seem to notice. Instead he ruffled the skirt, and Romy imagined the dress moving when it was made up in the fabric for the newly single English princess.

He handed the scissors back to Marcel.

Romy cleared her throat. Vadim turned slowly and looked at her, his neck wrinkled like a turtle, his hooded eyes curious over his beaked nose.

'Yes?' he said.

'If you don't mind me saying, it feels too . . .' she began, then stopped. What had Nico told her this morning? She was to turn up at these studios and do as she was told. She wasn't to venture an opinion *at any point*.

'. . . too?' Vadim asked.

Romy sighed, shifting her weight onto her other leg. Those high heels were killing her. 'It's just . . . I once wore a bandage over my chest. It's a long story,' she continued hurriedly, with a nervous laugh. 'This feels like that. Just the line of it here,' she went on, looking at the straight line across her chest and remembering the bandage she'd worn in the clothing factory in Berlin so that she could pretend she was a boy.

Vadim walked back towards her and held his hand out for the scissors once again.

'Where?' he asked her, nodding at the dress.

Romy looked down. 'It needs to feel just slightly more at an angle,' she said, tracing the line with her finger.

'*Comme ça*?' Vadim chopped more of the fabric away. Then he stood back with a surprised smile.

*   *   *

223

The sun was low in the sky by the time Romy was finally allowed to leave, the streets bathed in a warm late-afternoon gold. Nico was waiting for her, standing smoking a cigarette against his old black Mercedes, which was parked underneath a cherry-blossom tree on the street. Romy's dog was on a lead by his feet, and Romy laughed at what a reluctant dog-sitter Nico had turned out to be.

'You should be a model yourself, posing like that,' Romy said, picking up Banjo and giving the delighted mutt a cuddle.

'You mean the dog should be a model, or me?' Nico asked.

'The dog, silly,' Romy laughed. 'What on earth are you wearing, anyway?'

Nico pulled at the green German-army jacket. Romy knew they were the height of fashion, but she couldn't get used to seeing people wearing them. They reminded her of the guards at the orphanage.

'Don't you like it?'

She could tell he was disappointed, so she changed the subject.

'Has he been any trouble?' she asked, tickling Banjo behind the ears and thinking that he actually looked as if he was grinning. It was no surprise, considering how he'd looked a few weeks ago when she'd found him, half-starved, a broken chain around his neck strangling him.

'He peed on my new Converse, but apart from that he was OK. Anyway, how did it go?' Nico asked, treading on his cigarette and opening the car door. 'Did you behave yourself?'

'I modelled a dress for Princess Diana. It was *so* sexy,' Romy said, ushering Banjo into the tiny back

224

seat, before running back and picking up her bags. 'What have you got there?' Nico asked, looking down at the designer names over the top of his sunglasses.

'Oh,' Romy grinned. 'I went shopping earlier.'

'But I dropped you off—'

'But I was early, so I had a snoop around. Oh my God, Nico, you won't believe the stuff in some of these shops.' She got into the car and put the bags on her knees, before delving inside. Nico sat in the driver's seat.

'There was this shirt,' Romy said, pulling the Oxford stripe out of the bag. 'I couldn't *not* buy it. You'll look amazing in it.' She held it up against Nico's face. 'Much better than this silly army look. You look great in classic stuff. I thought you'd like it in white too.'

Nico shook his head, pulling an exasperated grin. 'You shouldn't have. You have to stop. You have to save. The whole point about fashion is that people will give you everything for free.'

Romy took one of the skyscraping yellow heels out of the shoebox and showed it to Nico. 'But how could I leave them in the shop?'

Nico rolled his eyes at her, then took her bags and wedged them in next to Banjo, who clamped his sharp teeth around the fancy rope handles of the shoebox. 'You're going to have to keep them well away from this little fella,' he warned.

She petted Banjo, then grinned at Nico, pulling the Aviator sunglasses out of his hair and putting them on herself, as he started the car and drove down the wide avenue.

'I love Paris,' she told Nico. 'Isn't this amazing? Are you really sure you don't mind being here with

225

me?'

He shrugged. 'I'll make do,' he told her, turning up the neat car stereo, then grinning at her. It was the new acid-jazz CD Romy had brought from the buskers the other night, when they'd been having dinner.

Romy sat back in her seat, putting her sore feet up on the dashboard. She still had the scar from her run-in with Tia Blanche all that time ago, but it was fading now. Just as Tia herself was. Romy was gratified that she'd been chosen over Tia for several high-profile jobs in the last few months. The perfume campaign, with the shot of her dangling the keys on her finger as she sat on Jovo, was everywhere. She'd even seen it on a hoarding in Charles de Gaulle airport, right above Duty Free.

Romy had insisted on splitting her fee with Jovo, her co-model, who had made enough to send his granddaughter to university and to buy a new car, he'd told Romy in his last letter.

She was delighted, as was Tomaz, the client, who'd also been in contact to assure Romy that sales of the perfume were soaring and to tell her that if she was in the South of France in the summer to be sure to look him up in his chateau. Simona had already booked Romy in to be the face of their new make-up range, charging quadruple her normal fee. When Simona had told Romy how much she was going to get, she'd nearly fainted.

And now that she and Nico were going to be settled in Paris, she felt as if life couldn't get any better.

'So. I have a surprise,' Nico told her.

'Oh?'

'The apartment is ours.'

Nico reached into his jacket pocket and threw the keys to her. Romy squealed with delight as they entered the ninth arrondissement and moved into the warren of streets, past the Moulin Rouge and the row of clubs, cabarets and bars. Pigalle certainly wasn't the smartest place to live, but it was the most hip, and all the artists Nico knew were gathered here, where the apartments were much cheaper than in more salubrious neighbourhoods.

Romy looked up at the high building as they stopped near the kerb, and at the imposing black front door and the row of posters and flyers plastered on the wall next to it. A van had stopped further up the street and Nico nodded to a man who had clearly been waiting for him. The back grille of the van rattled as he pulled it up.

'I took the liberty of getting removal men to get all the furniture in. I rented that job-lot we saw. They weren't very pleased when I told them we were right at the top. Why did it have to be a penthouse apartment?' Nico said.

'The law of relativity. People at the top live longer than people at the bottom. It's a fact.'

'How much longer?'

'A trillionth of a second—over a lifetime,' Romy clarified, 'but it's the point that counts. We'll be living life faster up there, so time will go slower.'

She grinned at him and Nico rolled his eyes. 'The stuff you pick up from all those books you read,' he said, taking the keys back off her to open the front door. He pulled her out of the way as two men passed them, heaving the leather sofa up to the stairwell. 'We'll take the lift,' he said gesturing

227

her inside. She followed him and watched as he pulled back the grate of the old-fashioned lift. 'After you.'

Romy giggled. 'I feel like I'm in an Audrey Hepburn movie,' she said, as she watched the lights on the numbers above the grille light up. As they moved through the floors, she saw the shoes of a woman walking along the corridor with a small white dog on a lead. Banjo barked.

'Looks like there'll be a lady-friend or two for you,' she told him.

They arrived at the grand doors of the penthouse apartment a moment later.

'Well,' Romy said, pointing to herself and doing a cutesy hip-bend as she put Banjo down. 'You gotta carry me over the threshold. It's good luck.'

'Seriously?' Nico said, laughing, then she whooped with delight as he picked her up, threw her over his shoulder and took two nimble steps across the parquet flooring to the door.

He deposited her inside and she grinned at him in the giant gilt-framed mirror on the wall opposite. They'd seen this partially furnished show-apartment briefly last week and she knew how much Nico liked its old, bohemian charm. Looking round now, Romy thought it was even cooler than she remembered.

They both laughed as Banjo ran into the vast sitting room and onto the armchair that the workmen were putting by the fireplace.

'Which bedroom do you want?' Romy asked Nico, her eyes wide as they explored the flat. But now, for the first time, she realized the massive commitment that they'd made—to actually live together. But who better to live with than her best friend? It wasn't as if she had anyone else. Florence, Nico's assistant, had moved in with her boyfriend, and her other friends were all settled in their own places. It had been fine crashing with Emma and Terese, but Romy couldn't wait to have her own place and pay them back for their hospitality.

'You take the big one,' Nico said. 'You'll need the space for all those shoes you keep buying. Besides, I won't be here the whole time. I'll keep my studio things in the small room.'

Romy reached up and kissed his cheek. 'You are the perfect gentleman,' she said. 'If you romance a hot stud and bring him back here, I promise I'll let you use my room.'

Romy ran into the bedroom and jumped on the four-poster bed, touching the canopy above. 'Romy, be careful,' Nico laughed, calling after her. 'The deposit was huge.'

'Come on,' she laughed, holding her hands out for him.

He jumped once on the bed with her, then they fell over, giggling.

She was in his arms for a moment, nose-to-nose, and she breathed in the comforting smell of his aftershave. She grinned at him. She adored him so much, she wondered whether it would ever be possible to find a man she got on with as well. 'Show me the roof terrace again,' she said, scrambling away from him.

She ran barefoot over the floorboards into the vast living room with the circular staircase on the back wall. Then, unlocking the glass door, she was on the roof. Banjo's claws clattered on the metal stairs as he ran up behind her.

'This is amazing,' Romy said, leaning out over the railing and looking at the view. Montmartre was so close, it felt as if she could touch the white stone of Sacré Coeur Basilica at the top.

'Come and see this,' Nico said, and she followed him up some steps to the top of the roof terrace, where there was a barbecue area complete with a wooden hot-tub. There was even a small patch of turf, which Banjo was already scratching at.

'We're having a party. Call up everyone you know. This place is fantastic. After Boho,' she said, remembering her earlier conversation, 'I said we'd meet Anna there at ten.'

'No. I don't think we should trash it right away—' Nico began, but Romy held up her hand to stop him.

'Nico, Boho is practically downstairs. You can't move in here and then put a halt to partying. Think about it. We're right in the centre of everything. This will be like our own private-members' club.'

'OK, but do me a favour and give me a buzz before we go,' he said, smiling at her and running his hand bashfully over his hair. She laughed, knowing how much he liked her to play hairdresser to him.

'Why? Are you feeling lucky?' she asked him.

*   *   *

Anna was Romy's new friend in Paris. They'd met a few weeks ago on a shoot, and the Parisian model was happy to show Romy around and introduce her to her formidable social circle. It seemed Anna knew anyone who was anyone, and Romy was intrigued by this new set of funky, talented

230

people—all of them artists or models or actors. It made her feel like she was part of a hip gang. That, for the first time, she was on the inside looking out, and not the other way around.

Romy pulled Nico down the basement steps towards the bouncers outside the famous club, smiling and talking rapidly and loudly to them over the thump of the music, about her and Nico being on Anna's guest list.

'Are you really, seriously planning on dancing all night in those shoes?' Nico said. 'You can barely walk in them.'

Romy laughed, pulling him past the crowds to the dark, smoky club.

Inside the music was deafening, a DJ in a booth lit up above the heaving dance-floor.

'Come on,' she yelled to Nico. 'Let's head to the VIP area.' She took his hand and dragged him through the sea of dancing bodies to the industrial metal staircase.

Anna spotted her and waited at the top, her arms open wide in welcome. She was tall with long blonde hair, which she'd tied up in a big clip, so that it fell in wisps around her pretty face. She was wearing a miniskirt and high black boots, which showed off her long, tanned legs.

'Hey, girlfriend,' Anna said huskily. 'Take one of these. They're amazing.' She draped her arm around Romy's shoulders and popped a pill in her mouth.

Romy waved to Nico, wanting him to get one too, but she saw him talking to a guy in a blue silk shirt and smiled. She'd probably lost him for the evening.

Anna squeezed Romy in on the purple

231

banquette, next to a dark-haired guy with a stubbly beard called Bernard, and handed her a glass of champagne.

Soon there was more champagne, and then Romy felt Bernard rubbing his hand up her thigh and felt herself shuddering all over. The flashing lights, the beat of the music in sync with her heartbeat—she suddenly felt as if her nerve endings were tentacles soaking it all up. When Bernard suggested that they move away from the banquette to dance, Romy let him hold her hand and lead her.

She felt the rhythm of the music pounding through her as she surrendered herself to the darkness and the mass of bobbing bodies around her. Bernard pressed against her, his hand moving up her thigh. Then the next thing she knew she was kissing him.

Later she couldn't remember how they'd all got back to her apartment, or who half the people were whom Anna had invited. But Nico wasn't there when they got home. Romy felt a momentary worry, but there were too many people stumbling, laughing into the apartment. Gil and his friend Max, who set up music in the living room whilst Anna's friends Paulie and Jules sorted out more tequila shots. Then a guy on a motorbike turned up with more pills.

And then there was Bernard. Sexy Bernard, who snaked his arms around Romy and kissed her again, until she was lost in his kiss, moving towards the bedroom, already not caring that he was undressing her, knowing only that she wanted more of his touch, more of his skin.

It was nine o'clock in the morning when Romy heard the insistent buzzing, followed by Banjo yelping and scratching at the door.

Sitting up in bed, rubbing her eyes, she saw that Bernard was naked beside her, the curve of his torso making her instinctively want to touch him. *God, he has a great body*, she thought. Pulling on her robe, she picked through the debris of the sitting room and hallway, then giggled when she saw Nico passed out on the new sofa, red lipstick on his mouth. She ruffled his hair affectionately.

Romy picked up Banjo and opened the door.

'Am I late?' Simona asked, in her rasping drawl.

'A bit. Or early. Depending on your view,' Romy said, hugging her.

'What happened in here?' Simona said, stepping over the threshold. 'I thought this was supposed to be your chic new apartment.'

'Shhh,' Romy said. 'You'll wake everyone up. Come on. Why don't we go out for coffee? I have to take Banjo out anyway.'

They wandered together through the local streets and Romy breathed in the fresh morning air, still amazed that she had stayed up all night, her mind reeling from just how crazy the party had been. She was quite glad to be out of the apartment and leave the carnage to Nico. She had no idea how much he'd joined in, or how much he'd seen, but she suspected she might be in a lot of trouble with him—and the neighbours.

Soon they passed a small park, where a guy who'd been sleeping rough held out a crumpled polystyrene cup. Romy delved in her pocket,

233

pulled out a ten-franc note and popped it in the cup. The guy's eyes widened, then he muttered *'Merci, merci.'*

'That was a bit generous,' Simona said.

Romy shrugged. She didn't tell Simona, but she'd never forgotten the girl who had given her money at the Tube station, that night she'd arrived in London all those years ago. Ever since, whenever Romy had seen someone begging, she'd always given them money. You never knew what difference it might make.

'Let's go to the flea-market,' Simona said, heading off towards the Left Bank. 'My favourite handbag of all time is from there,' she said. 'But that is a fashion secret. *D'accord?*'

'OK,' Romy agreed, holding on to Simona, glad to have her cashmere-clad arm for support. Romy was wearing her Birkenstocks, but her feet were aching from all the dancing last night. Maybe she should have listened to Nico after all, about her shoes. Banjo yanked at the lead, sniffing all the trees.

Suddenly a flashback of her and Anna dancing on the podium in the club made Romy bite her smile. She'd never behaved so outrageously. God only knew what were in those pills Anna had given her. Even with her shades on, the colours seemed so bright, as if all her senses were still altered, like they had been last night. The old-fashioned Metro sign and the rubbery smell coming up from the ventilation shafts; the plane trees with their dappled trunks and leafy canopy; the rippled surface of the river and the pigeons pecking the pavement—all of it seemed so vivid.

A café owner was sweeping up the pavement,

the tan wicker chairs piled up on round tables. He was whistling tunefully, but stopped and smiled at Simona and Romy to let them pass.

'Like mother, like daughter,' he said. 'A fine sight.'

Romy laughed. She liked the idea of people thinking Simona was her mother, and hugged her arm tighter. Was this what it would be like to have a real mother? she wondered. She'd never really thought about it before. She'd got so used to being on her own, so used to the fact that she was an orphan. But now she was starting to have an inkling of what she might have been missing.

A church bell rang out in the clear morning, and Romy breathed in a deep lungful of fresh air. This really couldn't be more different from the smoky club she'd been in just a few hours ago.

But Romy didn't have time to dwell on it any longer, because they were going down the steps towards the flea-market. There were African vendors with bootleg tapes, and Moroccans with leather handbags. But mostly it was Parisians, with stalls of bric-a-brac stretching in every direction. Old gramophone players, sewing machines, oil paintings and saucepans, kettles, dolls, machinery of all sorts. As they wandered through the aisles, Romy couldn't get over how much stuff was here and how many people were bartering for it all.

Soon they came to the clothes stalls. Simona was rifling through the items, like a professional, feeling the fabric and looking at bags, and soon Romy joined her, searching through the piles of clothes. She put Banjo in her shoulder bag to stop him running off and he panted, looking at all the people from his elevated position.

235

Romy stopped at one stall, looking at the T-shirts piled high. Then a voice speaking in an unmistakable Germanic accent made her look up.

'Is it you?'

The voice cut through Romy's hungover haze.

Romy looked up slowly, directly at the woman behind the stall, her fingerless gloves wrapped around a mug of steaming tea, which was paused halfway to her mouth. But there was no doubt who it was.

Ursula.

Romy froze, her heart pounding, her mouth suddenly dry.

Ursula was staring right at her, trying to see beyond the dark lenses of Romy's sunglasses. Time had etched lines across her forehead, her bright-red hair had lost some of its bouncy frizz and her curves had filled out, but it was Ursula all right.

And yet in that split second that followed, when Romy ought to have taken off her sunglasses and embraced her old friend—the very person responsible for her freedom—she hesitated.

To acknowledge Ursula would make Romy beholden to her. Responsible for her. Embrace Ursula, and she had to embrace the past and make it all come back. She would have to come clean and explain it all to Simona. She'd have to relive those dark days. Reclaim the person she'd left behind.

Worse, if Ursula knew where she lived, then Franz might too. Ursula was a link in the chain to her past that she thought she'd broken. And at the end of that chain was Ulrich, Lemcke . . . people who wanted her dead.

And of course they could find her more easily now that they could travel. Now that the Wall had

236

come down. Of course Ursula would have come to the West to Paris. Like she'd always dreamt of. And now here she was.

How long would it be before Ulrich or the others showed up here too?

In a second Romy had replaced the T-shirt and had moved away from the stall. She didn't stop.

Simona eventually caught up with her as she was running out of the flea-market, up the old stone steps.

'What is it, Romy? Where are you going?' Simona asked.

'I've got to go,' she told Simona, hurrying on, her head down, tears seeping from below her sunglasses.

She dared not look back. She dared not see the look of hurt in Ursula's eyes. She felt utterly torn. Torn with guilt; torn that her better life had not made her a better person.

Simona grabbed her arm and stopped her. Then she gently lifted up Romy's glasses.

'Oh God. What's the matter, Romy? You look like someone walked over your grave.'

Simona Fiore felt a glimmer of understanding for the first time. Something back there—someone had scared the hell out of Romy. Whatever, or whoever, it was had obliterated Romy's buoyant after-party mood. She'd been shocked to see the girl so high when she'd arrived. Thank God she had. After her conversation with Perez Vadim, Simona had hot-footed it straight to Paris. Opportunities like the one he wanted to give Romy came once in a career. Simona was here to make sure Romy took it.

But she hadn't expected this, and now she

wondered whether Romy would finally open up. Because whatever it was she was hiding, Simona knew it would always be there, until she confessed to someone.

'You don't get to be like you are, Romy, without a past,' she said carefully. She took Romy's arm and walked on with her. 'Everyone successful has a past they've left behind. But it's OK, because there comes a point when nobody can touch you,' Simona explained. 'All you have to do is work hard and get there. Then you'll be safe. Untouchable.'

'You really think so?'

'I know so. Dry your eyes. I have a plan, but it's going to need all your commitment, all your passion.'

Romy nodded eagerly, soaking up her words, clearly keen to hear more.

'Do you know what a muse is?' she asked.

'Sort of.'

'Perez Vadim needs a muse.'

'What does that mean?'

'It means that Vadim will possess you.'

'You mean . . .' Romy didn't like the sound of that at all.

Simona laughed. 'No, nothing sexual. He'll possess you in the fashion world. You need to share all your ideas with him. Generate a creative flow. If you do that, my darling, you really will be untouchable.'

'You think so?' Romy asked, sniffing.

'I know so,' Simona said, patting her arm, feeling a sense of great satisfaction. So Romy had an Achilles heel after all. Her past. Simona knew that she had to make Romy successful enough, and rich enough, for her past never to cloud her future again.

CHAPTER SEVENTEEN

AUGUST 1995

Usually it was the bin men at the end of the smart Belgravia mews that woke Thea. But this morning she'd already been awake for an hour, the light seeping around the corners of the handmade blinds. Yet the uplifting shade of blue she'd chosen was doing nothing to stop the fat tear plopping out of her eye across the bridge of her nose to join the others on the soft cotton pillow.

She stared at the brown bottle of pills on the bedside table, feeling the fuzzy, dull ache in her head that the pills were supposed to take away. But Thea knew this was a pain that couldn't be reached by pills, no matter what the doctor said.

Of course he'd referred her to a shrink when he'd prescribed them, but Thea had refused to go. What was the point? She didn't need a doctor to tell her why she was depressed.

She knew it was useless torturing herself, but she couldn't help it. Just as surely as she couldn't help herself working out the dates that were etched in her mind. Which is why she knew that it would have been two years old by now.

It.

Her baby.

The baby that might have been Tom's, but might also have been Brett's.

A son. The baby would have been a little boy.

239

She was sure of it. She felt the familiar wrench of remorse and guilt, like a twist in the guts.

What would have happened if she hadn't booked herself into that Harley Street clinic, she wondered now? What if she'd taken a different path—kept the child, abandoned her career? Would she be happier now, with someone to love? Someone of her own?

But what child could love a mother who couldn't even say for sure who their father was? What child could cope with a mother who had been raped by her own brother? What kind of child could respect a mother who had allowed that to happen?

Which is why Thea had taken the decision to terminate the pregnancy. She'd insisted on a local anaesthetic so that she could leave the clinic as quickly as possible. Which meant that she'd met the abortioner with the butcher's hands. She'd watched him scraping out the contents of her womb, lifting out the bloody instrument as her insides contracted in labour pains.

Unable to bear the memory, she sat up in bed, reaching out to stunt the alarm clock before it went off. Then she tipped the pills from the bottle into her hand and stared at them.

How easy it would be to take them all, she thought. To swallow them all down and to forget. But then *he* would have won, she remembered, tipping the pills back into the bottle, except for one. Then she swept the bottle into the drawer in the small bedside table, but the lid wasn't on properly and they spilled.

Cursing, she sat up and opened the drawer fully, collecting the pills. At the back of the drawer she saw a photograph in a small frame and pulled it out now. It was one she'd always kept, of her and Michael outside the stables at Little Elms when they were kids.

Where had that happy, grinning little girl gone? Thea wondered, rubbing the dust away with her fingertip. That was probably the last time she'd been conscience-free. When everything was shining and pure in her world. Just her and Michael, and her horse, when that had been all she'd really needed.

With a sigh she got out of bed and went into the shower, letting the water pummel her into numbness, remembering the similar shower she'd taken after Brett had raped her in Switzerland on her twenty-first birthday. When all she'd been able to think about was how lucky she'd been to get away, how satisfied she'd been that she'd locked him in the sauna, wedging the door shut and turning off the alarm.

She'd had every intention of leaving him there to die of heat exhaustion. Such was her loathing, her fury, her shame. Which is why she'd stayed in the shower, ignoring the banging on the sauna door and Brett's muffled shouts.

But then he'd gone quiet. When she'd turned off the shower, the terrible silence had attacked Thea's conscience. And at the crucial moment, when she should have gone to get Tom, she'd gone back and opened the door of the sauna and saved Brett.

She remembered now the blur of paramedics, Storm freaking out. Griffin Maddox staring at Brett's body on the stretcher. Through his parched lips, Brett had managed to speak to Thea.

'You breathe a word of what happened and I'll

241

get you for attempted murder.'

'The next time you touch me, I *will* kill you,' she'd replied. And she'd meant it.

Tom had woken up as the helicopter was leaving to take Brett to hospital. Unaware of the drama that had happened, he'd tried to apologize for his behaviour, keen—despite his hangover—to make Thea's birthday special. He'd even gone as far as producing the diamond ring he'd brought for her, but Thea had just looked at the slushy snow on the ground and told him that it was over between them.

She'd loved him then, more than ever. But she couldn't be with him, because she'd known that she could never tell him the truth. Even though she knew it hadn't been Tom's fault, she knew that if he'd been there in the sauna—with her—then she and Brett would never have ended up alone. Tom would never be able to truly protect her. She'd been a fool to think he could.

So she'd told him she'd made a mistake. That he wasn't the right person for her. As the words had come out of her mouth, she'd been unemotional, hard, as if her heart was locked away somewhere that she couldn't access. As if she was watching herself from above. Watching his aghast face, as fat snowflakes settled in his hair, like ash.

Poor Tom. He hadn't understood. How could he? He hadn't been able to believe that she could stand there and callously break his heart. He'd blustered, argued, then left angrily, telling Thea that Bridget had been right about her all along.

Back at Oxford, Thea had stayed in her rooms, venturing out only for lectures. The rest of the time she'd worked, trying to forget the terrible thing Brett had done.

Then she'd found out she was pregnant.

Now Thea stepped out of the shower, towelling the body she no longer felt belonged to her. She stared at herself in the mirror, seeing her older, more serious face. When was the last time she'd smiled? she wondered. When was the last time she'd laughed—truly laughed—like she used to with Tom?

Tom. There it was. Just the thought of him, his name forming in her mind, was a touchpaper to fill the numbness with a burning ache.

Don't think about it, she told herself, forcing herself to forget before more tears came. Don't think about it. Just think about work.

She plucked out a neat work suit from her cupboard and quickly got dressed. It was time to put on her mask, she thought. Time to get through another day.

*   *   *

Downstairs Ollie Mountefort was in the open-plan lounge in a shabby dressing gown, a plate of toast in his hand. He was watching the breakfast headlines, the news blaring out more twists and turns in the O.J. Simpson trial. No doubt there would be a load more O.J. gags circling the office by lunchtime, Thea thought. Even though she didn't join in, she liked all the banter and the British sense of humour she'd grown accustomed to.

And there was no funnier guy than Ollie. He was her only friend still left from Oxford and, when he'd called her a few weeks ago and asked her if he

243

could 'crash' whilst he applied for acting jobs, she'd been so shocked to hear from him that she'd agreed, and he'd moved into her pristine, hardly-ever-used guest suite.

She hadn't ever considered what it might be like to have a housemate, but she couldn't complain. It was better having him here than an empty house to come home to.

'You're up early,' he said.

'They're signing off my cover today, remember?' she said, fetching her scooter helmet from the cupboard.

'I don't know why you work so hard, Thea,' Ollie said, sitting down on the big couch and putting his feet up. 'You should tell them you're the big boss's daughter.'

'No. I told you. I want to work my way up. Prove to them that I have talent, before they find out who I am.'

'I still think you're mad. You've got a Porsche in the garage. You should be cruising up and down the King's Road in it.'

'What? Like *you* want to?' Thea said. 'Nice try, roomy.'

Ollie laughed. 'You see through me every time.' He grinned at her and took a big bite of toast. 'Want some? You should start eating something, you know.'

'I'm fine,' Thea said quickly. She'd have a coffee at the office. That would do for breakfast. She knew Ollie was concerned that she was so thin these days, and he'd hinted at it more than once. She thought back to the days in Oxford when he used to fancy her. She worried that he just pitied her now instead.

244

'You out at any auditions today?' Thea asked, fastening her helmet under her chin. Ollie was still as handsome as he had been at college, although his dark hair was in less of a quiff these days. Certainly leading-man material, she thought—just not for her. She couldn't even remember the last time she'd looked at a man and felt aroused.

'There might be something. In the meantime I'll be here waiting for my agent to call.'

'Don't you ever get . . .' Thea asked. 'Don't you ever want to give up? Acting seems so hard. So cruel.'

Ollie stared at her. 'And that's the appeal of it. It's worth fighting for. You never give up, Thea. No matter what. No matter who stands in your way. You keep going until you get where you want to be.'

'I guess.'

'Well, you'd know,' he said, laughing. 'You're the most driven person I know.'

Suddenly embarrassed, he swung the remote at the TV to change channels. The room filled with the noise of Formula One racing cars.

'Wow! There he is,' Ollie said, his face lighting up. 'Alfonso Scolari. Amazing driver. I've got a tenner on him to win.'

'Any chance of any rent then?' Thea asked, hopefully. She didn't need it, but it was the principle that mattered.

'If he wins, yes, and dinner on me.'

*   *   *

Thea was on her moped and driving along the river within five minutes, her mind focusing on the day

245

ahead. Within ten minutes she was walking into the grand Thames-side office block that housed the Maddox Inc. operation in London.

She'd had the job for nearly two years, having applied after graduating, faking her CV and changing her name to Tina Jones. It had been harder and considerably more expensive than she'd thought to change her identity. She'd had to consult a lawyer to get a National Insurance number in her fake name, as well as references and a bank account for Miss T. Jones.

But Thea was pretty sure that she'd covered her tracks, so much so that Griffin Maddox remained totally unaware that she was working for one of his companies. He was under the assumption that she was doing a PhD at Oxford and that her workload was keeping her too busy to go home to New York until the summer vacation.

Instead she'd immersed herself in life as Tina Jones. She'd dyed her hair red and wore it in a short bob and, so far, her disguise was wearing well.

She knew her ruse annoyed Ollie, whom she'd sworn to secrecy, but it was true what she'd told him earlier. She was banking on the fact that by the time her true identity was revealed, her colleagues would be so impressed with her work that they would applaud her for wanting her talent to be seen without prejudice. She fantasized about going to the board meeting in New York next spring, with several triumphs under her belt. Her father couldn't ignore her talent then.

And Thea knew she was well on her way. After her help during the coverage of the collapse of Barings Bank earlier in the year, and her opinion piece on how securities broker Nick Leeson could have lost $1.4 billion by speculating on the Tokyo Stock Exchange, Andy Bellson, the Editor-in-Chief, had finally acknowledged her presence.

In the last few weeks she'd been promoted to the journalistic team of the *Sunday Bulletin*, the biggest UK Sunday newspaper. It was a prestigious job, and one that she was never allowed to forget could be someone else's in the blink of an eye. Even better, this week, with staff on holiday, Judith, her boss, had asked Thea to help out with the editorial team of the Culture section, the cover of which would be flagged up on the front page of the paper.

All Thea had to do was have it signed off at today's meeting and she would have her first issue under her belt. With the exclusive article on Perez Vadim that she'd commissioned featuring strongly in the Fashion section, Thea had fought for the cover image: a striking picture of a dark-haired girl, by fashion-photography hotshot Nico Rilla. His subject, Romy Valentine, was the model Vadim had described as his muse and responsible for inspiring his latest groundbreaking collection, which—Thea's copy argued—had altered the course of fashion. She found it ridiculous that she'd had to go from the financial pages to immersing herself in the fripperies of the fashion industry in order to get her first shot at a lead article, but she was pleased with the way it had turned out.

Andy Bellson strode through the open-plan office, tugging at his tie, as he made his way to the boardroom, like a general going into war. Judith, a small mousy-haired woman with a permanent frown on her forehead, pulled a face of concern at Thea and gestured for her to hurry up and fall into line behind the editorial team who were following him to large glass-walled boardroom.

'We've got the head honcho in. Move it, people,' Bellson growled as they all scurried to take their seats at the oval blond-wood table.

'Head honcho?' Thea asked Jack, her contemporary, in a hushed whisper, gathering up her things.

'Some guy from the holding company. Management. Bellson hates it when they descend. Rumour is that they're looking at streamlining the papers. Cutting down the London operation.' Jack pulled a grim face at her as Thea followed him into the boardroom.

'Actually, sir, he's already here,' Thea heard Susan say in a meek voice.

Thea felt her heart racing as they all sat down in the boardroom. With any luck the meeting would be quick and brutal, as they always were, and then she could hide until whichever 'head honcho' was out of the way. She just prayed it wasn't one of her father's team, who might recognize her.

But almost as soon as she thought it, a movement through the glass window snagged her attention.

He was coming out of the lift, surrounded by five men in suits who were all talking. Even just seeing a glimpse of the side of Brett Maddox's face made nausea rise in her throat. She'd spent so long trying to forget him. Trying to forget what he'd done to her in that sauna. But there he was—just the same cocky, arrogant guy everyone loved, never suspecting that underneath he was a sadistic pervert.

Thea tried to steady her nerves, but her mouth had already filled with saliva, the hairs on her neck bristling.

Brett was wearing jeans and a stripy shirt and was deeply tanned. He grinned at everyone, knocking on the glass of the boardroom and walking in, as if he was some kind of entertainer rather than the person who could fire them all.

Andy Bellson introduced him and sat back down—a rarity in itself. Everyone in the room knew how tense he was. They all knew that this meeting had to go well.

Thea shrunk behind Judith, using Judith's body to hide her from Brett's line of sight. She drew her leather folder up high in front of her, but she could feel her pulse in her cheeks.

Bellson went through the other staff and they briefly outlined the news pages, until it was the turn of the Culture Bulletin.

'Cover,' Bellson said, nodding to Judith, who nudged Thea.

'Go for it, kiddo,' Judith whispered.

Thea stared at her. She knew she'd wanted to get noticed, but she was rather alarmed that Judith had dumped this on her at the last minute.

'Yes. Come on, let's hear it . . .'

Thea cleared her throat.

'Jones,' Bellson said. 'Get on with it. Don't keep our visitor waiting.'

'Yes, Miss Jones, I'd love to hear what you've got for us,' Brett said. And as Thea met his eyes and saw the cold glint in them, she knew that he *knew*. Somehow he'd found out. Now he'd come here to make her suffer, to watch her squirm. Well, she wasn't going to give him the pleasure, she decided. If he knew, then her father probably knew too.

So be it, she thought, standing up. The cover was as good as signed off. If she was going to be 'outed', now was as good a time as any.

Thea explained the article on Vadim and showed the mock-ups of the cover with the model on it.

'Fine. Looks good. Next,' Bellson said, and Thea felt a glow of pride.

But at that moment Brett spoke up. 'Hmm. I don't like it,' he said, standing and walking around the table.

'But we've got an interview with Vadim,' Thea protested to Bellson, ignoring Brett. 'Surely his muse should go on the front cover? That's the basis of the whole article. This is a major fashion scoop.'

'But I don't like her look,' Brett said, standing too close. Thea felt the hairs on the back of her neck standing up. She almost gagged at the all-too-familiar smell of his aftershave. 'She looks mean. She's not feminine enough. Women should look like women. There must be other models. What about her?' Brett pointed to the small picture in the article.

'Tia Blanche? But we can't,' Thea protested, panic rising. 'The article is all about Perez Vadim and how his collection has been inspired by this English model. We can't use Tia Blanche.'

'So? It's about aesthetics. We're in the business of selling newspapers. Or so I thought,' Brett said, looking up. 'The whole point is to get a pretty girl on the front cover. Especially in August,' Brett

250

said, grinning at the others around the boardroom. 'And gentlemen definitely prefer blondes.'

'But Tia Blanche isn't really blonde—this is just her latest look—'

'Mr Maddox is right,' Bellson interrupted, clearly alarmed that Thea was arguing with Brett. 'Put Tia Blanche on the cover. Rewrite it, Tina. Make it a general fashion piece.'

'Sir?' Thea said. 'There's something I want to say.'

'What is it?' Bellson asked, annoyed now.

'I'm not Tina Jones. I'm . . .' she glanced at Brett. He might have snatched the cover from her, but she'd do her own unmasking. She wouldn't let him humiliate her. She was proud of what she'd achieved, and sick of him walking all over her whenever he chose.

'What do you mean, you're not Tina Jones?'

Thea stared at Brett. 'He's here because he wants to expose me. Because I've been working here undercover.'

'Undercover?' Bellson spluttered, confused.

'Yes. You see, I'm really Thea Maddox. Griffin Maddox is my father.'

She stood, listening to the audible gasp and then the general burble of excited conversation around the table. Bellson was standing now.

'And for the record, Brett, you're wrong,' Thea continued. 'Romy Valentine *is* the story, not Tia Blanche. Everyone here knows I'm right. Which means you don't know what you're doing. Which is something my father's going to realize one day as well,' her voice started to shake, '. . . along with realizing what a fucking jerk you are.'

'Tina—whatever your name is . . .' Bellson

251

shouted. 'My office. *Now!*'

MAY 1998

Romy was ushered into the last seat in first class, relieved to have made the plane. This week's schedule had been hectic and she'd only got back from Tel Aviv to London just in time to catch the flight straight out to Monaco.

But she'd made it. She'd be there for Nico's birthday. She pictured the look on his face when they met in a few hours and smiled to herself, taking out the headphones of her Discman. She'd been listening to the new Alanis Morissette album that Max, the shoot Director, had given her as a leaving present last night. The music was immediately replaced by Celine Dion's 'My Heart Will Go On', from that *Titanic* movie, which was being piped softly into the cabin. *Jeez, that song sure does seem to be following me around*, Romy thought.

The stewardess stowed Romy's Louis Vuitton bag and she sat down in her seat with a relieved sigh, before edging off the silver platform shoes, her favourite from this year's Versace catwalk collection. She smiled to herself, wriggling her toes, remembering the wrap party in Tel Aviv, which was probably still going on, she thought—all the Israelis being determined that everyone should celebrate the fiftieth anniversary of the State of Israel. And, boy, they sure knew how to party.

She'd been lucky to get out of there.

She was so looking forward to this holiday. God knows she deserved one. Sometimes the fashion world seemed as if it had swallowed her whole. And whilst she couldn't complain about the luxury and the constant compliments, it sometimes didn't feel as if Romy had any time to live her real life at all.

It had been five years since she'd first modelled for Vadim in Paris. Five years. She could hardly believe it had gone so fast. She still missed Paris and her dog, poor little Banjo, whom she'd had to give away. Paris had been the last place that had felt really like home. Since then, Nico had moved back to Milan, and Romy kept her things in a room on the top floor of his house, but she was hardly ever there. She'd lost track of all the places she'd been already this year.

She stared out of the window at the tarmac, the noise of the plane igniting a sudden memory of being a stowaway in the cargo hold all that time ago. She shut down the thought, as she always did. For the most part it was easy, obliterating the memories by filling every second of her life with photo-shoots and travelling and parties. But sometimes—like now, when she stopped for a minute and was off-guard—a memory slipped back to take her unawares.

One day she'd do something with all this money she'd earnt, she vowed. She'd rescue people like the person she'd once been herself. She'd do something useful with her life. When all the madness stopped. When she had time to catch her breath.

But at least she still had Nico, she thought,

253

concentrating on what lay ahead.

Whilst she requested him to be there as often as she could on photo-shoots, she hadn't seen him for a couple of months. The last time was that night in Mexico, when they'd sat, exhausted, on the terrace of their luxury hotel, vowing that they'd spend this week together in Monaco. It helped that Nico had been given sole use of a power-yacht for the week. A small thank-you from the rich parents of a famously unphotogenic minor royal, whom Nico had made look like a supermodel on her wedding day. The offer of a holiday together had been too good to turn down.

'All I want for my birthday,' he'd told Romy, 'is to have you there, and for us to do nothing.'

'Nothing,' Romy had repeated, with a sceptical frown. Nico was even worse than she was when it came to making arrangements.

'Well, when I say nothing, I want us to stay on the yacht and be perfect slobs, and float around the Med away from the crowds.'

Now, as the plane took off and climbed steeply through the thick bank of clouds to the sunshine beyond, Romy turned her head and looked at the young woman sitting across from her. She was wearing a well-cut light-blue suit, and Romy smiled when she saw the book she was reading.

The stewardess came down the aisle, handing out elegant flutes of champagne, and Romy took one. The girl opposite did too, and they smiled at each other.

'Is that a new one?' Romy asked, nodding down at the book. 'I'm a big fan. I've read all Shelley Lawson's books.'

'Really?' the girl asked. She had an English

accent, but with her dark curly hair and freckles she could easily have been Israeli. She was pretty enough to be, Romy thought, thinking of the girl on her last shoot in Tel Aviv.

'Yeah,' Romy said. 'She's great. But *Sons and Daughters* is best.'

The girl spluttered her champagne and stared wide-eyed at Romy. 'What? You liked that one?'

'Yeah, sure. I thought the girl in it was really cool. I'd have done the same as her.'

'I'm Shelley Lawson's daughter. That was based on me.' The girl laughed, moping up the champagne. 'Sorry,' she went on. 'I'm used to meeting fans of Mum's, but not usually in first class. I'm Bridget,' she said, proffering her hand, apologizing for it being soaked in champagne. 'Bridget Lawson.'

An attentive air hostess arrived with a napkin.

'Hey, aren't you that model? The "catfight on the catwalk"?' Bridget asked, clearly quoting those famous headlines from when Romy had first started out.

'Yeah, yeah,' Romy interrupted. 'With Tia Blanche. My nemesis. I guess I'll always be infamous for slapping her. I wish I still could,' she added.

'Don't you work with Perez Vadim?'

'I did for a time,' Romy said, with a sigh. 'Until there was some big mix-up a while back with the press. It all started with the *Culture Bulletin* in London. Perez was furious about it and said I wasn't high-profile enough for him and, after that, we kind of fell out.' It had been a low point of her career, and Romy was surprised she could talk about it now without feeling that familiar burning

255

sense of injustice.

'Ah. The meddlesome Maddox Inc. I know all about them,' Bridget said.

'Excuse me?'

'The *Culture Bulletin* is part of the Maddox group of newspapers,' Bridget said, taking a sip of champagne.

Romy frowned, a sudden memory coming to her. 'I met a guy called Brett Maddox, once. He was some kind of Managing Director of Maddox Inc. He was a creep.'

'Yeah, well, I knew the daughter, Thea Maddox. She's a thief.'

'A creep and a thief. That's one very good reason why I haven't let any of my stuff go in the *Culture Bulletin* since.'

Romy took another sip of her champagne and the stewardess came back with a delicious-looking plate of canapés. Romy couldn't remember the last time she'd eaten and happily accepted. With no shoots booked for over two weeks, she fully intended to let herself off the hook this week.

'Is all that stuff your mum writes based on reality? I mean, the bit in *Sons and Daughters*—that last one—about the baby really made me cry. That's not true, is it?' Romy asked Bridget as they both started eating.

'No. Mum has always had a vivid imagination. But it's often uncomfortable reading for me,' Bridget said in a confidential way, closing the book and tucking it into the pocket of her rather nice Ferragamo handbag. Romy had almost bought the same one last season.

'So why Monaco?' Romy asked, intrigued by this confident young woman.

'I work in PR for a big oil company,' Bridget said, with a sigh. 'Which would be fine, except that they're the main sponsor of Alfonso Scolari in the Grand Prix.'

'He's that racing guy, right?'

Bridget rolled her eyes. 'He's a lunatic. He's been on the top of his game for two years, but now he's out of control. Gambling. Women. Drinking. The lot. The sponsors want to pull out, if he doesn't start towing the line soon.'

'And that's your job?' Romy asked, laughing. 'To make him tow the line?'

'You got it,' Bridget said, pulling a dubious face.

But as she appraised the English girl, Romy couldn't help thinking that if anyone could do it, she could. She had a forthrightness about her that Romy liked immediately. It was nice to have a real conversation and not be treated as a supermodel for once. She couldn't remember the last decent chat she'd had about anything other than fashion, hair and make-up for a while. Yes, she thought, she liked Bridget Lawson a lot.

*   *   *

Despite the sunny outlook for her holiday ahead, it was raining in Monaco when Romy arrived. She turned on her phone and picked up her messages as they walked off the plane, shielding her hair with her coat. There were three messages from Nico.

'Shit' she said. 'My friend has been delayed on a shoot. He was supposed to be picking me up.'

'Where are you going?' Bridget asked.

'The Marina in Monte Carlo, I guess.'

'I've got a car picking me up. I can give you a ride into town?' she offered, and Romy was grateful for their brief friendship not to be over yet.

And it wasn't just any car that had been sent to collect Bridget. As they stepped out of the arrivals lounge, Romy saw a shiny stretch-limo by the kerb and a liveried driver standing next to the back door, who was waving to Bridget.

But as they went over and the driver opened the door, Romy saw that there was already someone sitting on the fawn leather seat in the back.

'Hi, trouble,' Alfonso Scolari, the famous driver, said, kissing Bridget as she climbed in next to him.

'Oh, the irony,' Bridget said, making eyes at Romy.

'This is Romy, my friend,' Bridget said. 'We met on the plane. I said I'd give her a lift. You don't mind, do you?'

Romy shook Scolari's hand, smiling. He had scruffy dark hair and the cheekiest grin she'd ever seen. He was wearing jeans and a trendy Smashing Pumpkins tour T-shirt beneath his cream linen jacket. His dark-brown eyes bored into hers, and she felt something so unexpectedly physical that it made her cheeks burn.

But the guy was a terrible flake, Romy remembered, with a string of publicly broken-hearted girlfriends—including several well-known models—behind him. She looked out of the win dow as the limo pulled away. She had no intention of adding her name to his list. She couldn't wait to tell Nico about her ride from the airport. He was a Schumacher fan, but even so—meeting Alfonso Scolari was pretty impressive.

She listened to Bridget attempting to explain her own visit, and how she was here to tell Alfonso what the sponsors had told her that he needed to hear.

'Oh, Bridget,' Scolari cooed in his rolling Italian accent. 'You are so gorgeous when you are angry. What can I do, if beautiful women throw themselves at me?' he said with a shrug, his eyes now seeking Romy's reflection in the mirrored glass separating the driver's compartment from them. He stared at her so hard that she had to suppress a giggle, before—with obvious satisfaction—he turned back to Bridget and complained, 'How can I cope, when you are not there to protect me?'

His phone rang and Scolari went into a loud, expressive tirade.

Bridget turned to Romy. 'See what I mean?' she whispered. 'He's a nightmare.'

But as Romy got surreptitious glimpses of Alfonso Scolari, she could see why he'd been so successful. Both in romance and on the track. Whatever he was doing, he gave it 100 per cent of his attention and passion. She watched him bellowing into the phone, loving the cadence of the expletives he was using and the way his elegant hands gesticulated them. She tried to follow the rapid-fire Italian, but all she could really pick up was that something from Alfonso's point, at least, was deeply unfair.

Before long they were nearing the Marina.

'I can jump out here,' she said, and Bridget knocked on the window for the driver to stop.

'Hey, Romy, why don't you and your friend come to the Grand Prix tomorrow?' Bridget suddenly asked.

'Are you sure?'

'I have seats in the sponsor's box. It would be good to have you there.'

'OK, well, sure. Nico will be thrilled.'

Alfonso rang off the telephone. 'Excuse me,' he told Bridget and Romy, remembering his manners. 'My father's lawyer.' He shook his head, exasperated. 'He is like Mike Tyson,' he explained, 'chewing my ear off.'

Romy laughed.

'Thanks for the lift,' she said, smiling and getting out of the car. 'Oh, and good luck,' Romy told Alfonso, reaching back into the car and shaking his hand. When he looked at her again, she grinned back stupidly.

She got out onto the pavement and went around to where the driver was lifting her case from the boot. She was still smiling as she walked along the pavement towards the marina. Motor racing had never been her thing, but free tickets to the Grand Prix would surely be something that she and Nico could fit into their schedule. In fact it would be the perfect birthday surprise for him. Wasn't it typical that, just when they were supposed to be relaxing, there were more parties to go to.

* * *

As the limo drove off, Bridget Lawson sat back in her seat.

'Is the lecture over?' Alfonso asked, looking at her with puppy-dog eyes. 'I can't cope with any more abuse. My father has legally cut me off.'

Bridget knew Alfonso came from the Scolari

260

publishing and media dynasty. For a proud, politically connected man like Roberto Scolari to cut off his only son must mean that Alfonso had besmirched the good family name once too often. After all, Scolari was one of Alfonso's team's sponsors too. Perhaps Roberto Alfonso had been banking on the fact that, sooner or later, Alfonso's good old-fashioned Catholic guilt about his mamma back in Tuscany and his six sisters might kick in. But clearly it hadn't yet.

She decided to take a different tack.

'Look, *I* understand, but BK Oil are very cross. Why can't you just leave the delinquents and the call girls alone? Just for a while. Why not go on a proper date, with a real woman?'

'I would do, if I had a real woman who inspired me.' He grinned at Bridget and then sat up in his seat and twisted to look out of the back window at the departing figure of Romy.

'You want to take her out on a date?' she asked.

'If you could made it happen, Bridget, I would be the perfect gentleman,' Alfonso said, holding his hand against his chest. 'She is seriously gorgeous.'

Bridget smiled, pleased with herself.

Yes . . . Romy Valentine and Alfonso Scolari. Now *there* was an interesting proposition. And Romy was perfect. As far as Bridget could recall, there were no sex or drug scandals littering her past.

She'd have to do a bit of research, but at her age—what must Romy be: twenty-five or so?—she must be coming to the end of the peak of her catwalk career. She might be in the game for some serious international PR whilst she planned her next move. OK, so she said she was on holiday, but Bridget had a feeling that she might be able to persuade her.

Yes . . . she would set up the date in a restaurant. Somewhere classy. Somewhere that projected the right sort of image for a truly reformed and tamed man. Then she'd tip off all the journos and photographers she knew. She was already writing the press release in her head. This might just be the opportunity to project a more civilized image for Alfonso—and all the brands associated with him.

* * *

Romy sat in the plush downstairs salon of the power-yacht, drawing her knees up to her chest. Then she covered her face with her hands and groaned.

It was the fourth day of their holiday and so far it wasn't going well. Nico had been late on their first night, and on the second day, his birthday, they'd gone to the Grand Prix, which had been fun, but it had rained all day. Caught up in a sponsor's party, they'd both drunk too much champagne and Romy had come home with a terrible headache.

Then yesterday Romy had been on the date that Bridget had persuaded her to go on with Alfonso Scolari.

'"I know what my reputation is,"' Nico continued to read from the front page of the newspaper, '"but it's all been a tissue of lies to protect my real feelings for this wonderful woman. The last three months together have been the most magical of my life." Wow, this guy is some smooth

262

talker.'

Romy wailed. 'Three months? Three months? How could he even say that? I've known him for, like, twenty-five seconds.'

'But look at these photos. Quite the romantic dinner,' Nico said, holding up the tabloid paper that he lifted from the couch. 'Holding hands.' His face was mocking, but Romy noticed something hurt in his tone. 'You said it was just a quick pizza.'

'That was *for a second*,' Romy protested, standing up and pacing. 'I can't believe he's done this to me. It's all that girl Bridget's fault.'

'What do you expect, if you get friendly with PR people, Romy,' Nico said. 'You can't trust any of them.'

'I think we should just get out of here,' Romy said. 'Besides, the weather is terrible. So much for sunbathing. My fake tan is all coming off.' She rubbed her smooth shin to avoid his gaze.

Nico lifted a telephone and had a word with the captain, who agreed to pull up the anchor and set off straight away, but Romy still felt a pang of sadness that they would be leaving Monte Carlo so soon. She'd had fun here, despite Nico's disapproval at her name being in the papers. But this wasn't about her, she reminded herself—this was Nico's birthday holiday. After everything he'd done for her, she owed it to him to give him her time and attention.

'You're not cross, are you?' Romy asked, standing up and touching Nico's cheek.

He'd lost weight recently and looked tanned and healthy. He stared into her eyes.

'I just don't want you to get hurt. That's all,' he said.

263

'What would I do without you?' she said.

Nico put his arm around her shoulder and walked towards the sliding doors. 'Look, the sun is coming out,' he said. 'I can't tell you how much I've been looking forward to this week. I've missed you, you know.'

Below them the engines started rumbling and the water churned, as the power-yacht started pulling away. They were going to zip round the coast to Nice, where Martin, Chris and Anna, some of Nico's other friends, would be joining them for the last few days.

Nico smiled, but then his expression clouded over.

'What?' she asked.

But just then she heard shouting. She turned to look towards the port and saw a speedboat racing towards them.

They both watched as the stylish red boat, with its shiny hull and wooden deck, drew up alongside them. Alfonso Scolari was standing up at the steering wheel, his hair wet with spray.

'Hi!' he called, waving to Romy and grinning wildly.

'Oh my God,' Romy said, laughing and blushing at the same time. 'That's him. He's here.'

'I guess he'll have to come on board,' Nico said.

He walked back inside to talk to the captain and Romy laughed, urging Alfonso to stay back. He zoomed off in a wide arc, then returned and the crew helped him come-to alongside the yacht. Throwing a rope to one of the deckhands, Alfonso hopped up on the back platform as if he were stepping onto a kerb, not out of a 200,000-dollar speedboat. He was wearing a loose cotton shirt and khaki shorts with soft leather loafers.

'Have you seen the papers?' Romy asked, as he bounded up the stairs two at a time and joined her on the deck.

'Yes. Isn't it wonderful?' Alfonso beamed. 'My father has read about us. They are willing to accept me back.'

Romy blew out a frustrated breath. This guy was unstoppable. 'Great, well, I'm pleased for you, but—'

'So we have to go there today.'

'Go where?'

'To my parents' place. In Tuscany.' Alfonso said it as if they'd already discussed it.

Romy stared at him, aghast. 'I can't just come with you to Tuscany. I'm kind of busy.'

She noticed Nico standing protectively by her side.

'I don't know what you're involved in here, but if you come with me, Romy, I'll pay for ten holidays for you and your friend,' Alfonso said, beaming a wide smile at them both.

'It's not about the money,' Romy protested. She could afford her own holidays. Besides, hadn't he noticed the boat they were on? Anyway, this *was* her holiday.

'One day in Tuscany. One day—that's all. Then I will bring you back. Once I have made peace with my father.'

He put his hands in a prayer position and looked at Romy and then, sensing a chink, Alfonso appealed directly to Nico.

'Romy tells me that you are simply friends. Is that the truth? I would not dishonour you, my friend?'

265

Romy saw Nico blush at Alfonso's Shakespearean declaration. She stepped in.

'I don't think this can work. I mean . . . I don't know anything about you,' Romy spluttered, staring wildly at Alfonso and then at Nico.

'You can learn it all on the way. I will drive you from the airport. I have the plane waiting. It will give us a couple of hours. You'll have plenty of time to find out everything there is to know about me.'

Romy laughed at his outrageous suggestion. 'And then what? I pose as your girlfriend, and you bring me back?'

'Exactly,' Alfonso said. Then he clapped his hands together. 'It's settled then.'

Then he clutched Nico's arms and kissed both of his cheeks. 'You are a true gentleman. I shall bring her back unharmed,' he said. Then he turned to Romy. His eyes made something stir inside her, as they had done the first time she'd met him. 'And you, darling, are my life-saver.'

CHAPTER NINETEEN

MARCH 1999

Thea was already late for the reception. In the chintzy suite of Vienna's grandest hotel she quickly checked her make-up, before growling in frustration. Grabbing a pin, she wound her hair up into a chignon and fastened it tight. Then she turned around, making sure her pale-yellow dress was done up at the back.

She looked more closely at the mirror, adding a touch more powder to her skin. She looked tired, she knew, but tonight's gala dinner for the European heads of the major publishing and media companies was her final chance to meet some valuable contacts, as well as the opportunity to get the last piece in the jigsaw that she needed to complete her report.

This time she knew she really was going to impress her father and make the Maddox Inc. board sit up and take notice. She was so close, she could almost taste the victory that she knew she'd feel when Brett realized how hard she'd worked. And how much she'd achieved. Enough, Thea hoped, to be considered for her own place on the board. One she knew she fully deserved.

For nearly four years she'd slogged her guts out. Ever since Brett had exposed her at the *Culture Bulletin* meeting, Thea had been determined to beat him. If his plan had been to scare Thea off, then he'd severely underestimated her.

At first Griffin Maddox had been furious when he'd heard about Thea posing as Tina Jones in London. Brett's version of events was that he'd caught her out quite by chance, when he'd requested photographs of all of Maddox Inc.'s staff for some private project of his. He hadn't elaborated on what the project involved, but Thea suspected that it had been exclusively to do with female employees. And there, in the *Culture Bulletin*'s staff line-up, Brett had spotted Thea. A different haircut. A suit. But Brett had seen straight through that . . . or so he'd said.

Had Brett had some kind of tip-off? Thea still wondered. Had the lawyer she'd used to help change her identity blown her cover? But she'd never know, and now it hardly mattered.

After that awful incident in London, Thea had flown straight to Crofters to confront her father. He'd heard her out, at her insistence, about why she'd done it. To prove that she could stand on her own two feet. To prove that she was every inch Brett's match. Without his interference she'd have done it too, without Brett spiking her feature the way he had.

Face-to-face, Griffin Maddox's fury quickly dissipated into something Thea hadn't witnessed for a long time: pride.

Then he had given her his verdict. She was fired. From the *Culture Bulletin* at least. After the way she'd spoken to Brett in front of the staff, he had no choice. But he wasn't kicking her out of Maddox Inc. altogether, which is what Brett had wanted. Instead he'd surprised her. He'd given Thea an altogether different role.

She'd moved to New York, where she'd been a junior on her father's troubleshooting marketing team, before being seconded to the European team, where Thea had relished her chance to shine. She knew that to secure the future of Maddox Inc. they needed to focus their energies on the predicted boom in digital and cable companies in mainland Europe.

And now, after all her time here in Europe, thoroughly researching and squaring up the Maddox alliances, Thea was sure her expansion plans would be a breath of fresh air to her father. He'd had a tough year, what with the Dow Jones crash last August, from which he was only just recovering, and then all this ongoing business with his friend, Bill Clinton, and that dreadful Lewinsky girl.

Not to mention Storm, who grew more demanding by the day and was exhausting her father with yet another revamp of Maddox Tower and the renovation of a fifty-acre estate in The Hamptons. Thea had followed the press on the recent divorce settlement payout to Jocelyn Wildenstein, a friend of Storm's, who'd been awarded 100 million dollars and thirteen million dollars a year for the next thirteen years—a verdict that Storm had celebrated with alarming glee. Thea had fantasized for so long about her father leaving Storm, but after the Wildenstein case she could see how potentially dangerous that could be. Besides, her father still seemed to adore Storm, despite the fact that she looked dangerously similar to the 'Bride of Wildenstein' herself these days. There'd been a photo of Storm and her father in the *New York Times* last week that had made Thea's jaw drop.

She turned now as the telephone rang next to the hotel bed, quickly fastening her dangling jade earrings, which she'd bought in Switzerland. The Germans she'd met so far were fastidious about punctuality and it was probably Reicke in the lobby, expecting her.

Reicke Schlinker was the head of the media company Maddox Inc. were about to buy, on Thea's recommendation. The deal would be announced in the next few months, and Thea was delighted when he'd accepted the Maddox offer in principle this morning. She smiled to herself, amused and flattered by his obvious attentiveness. She couldn't deny that they'd been flirting and it

269

had done her ego the world of good. She felt sad that this would be their last night together.

But it wasn't anyone from the lobby; it was Sarah, Thea's assistant, calling from the office in New York.

'I'm glad I didn't miss you,' Sarah said, her Brooklyn accent a blast of familiarity. 'How's it going?'

Thea smiled. 'It's exhausting, but this is the final day, then I'll be home.'

She pulled aside the thick brocade curtain and looked through the window. In the evening light the lights along the river twinkled romantically. Once again she wondered where home was these days. Her rented apartment in New York? The cold, unloved space that she'd hardly spent two consecutive nights in? She must start putting down some roots, Thea decided. Another item for her long list of resolutions for the new millennium.

'What are you doing for your birthday at the weekend?' Sarah asked.

Thea came away from the window and caught sight of herself in the mirror. After what Brett had done to her in Switzerland, she hadn't celebrated her birthday once in seven long years. And now she was going to be twenty-eight. It seemed so old, all of a sudden. She wondered what all those girls from school would be doing now. Would they have big careers like her? Or be settling down to get married and have children?

'I guess I'll be on a plane,' Thea replied. 'I can't really think about too much else before I've finished my report.'

'That's why I'm glad I caught you. You know you asked me ages ago to see if I could find some of

270

your old friends from Little Elms?'

Thea's heart leapt. *Michael* . . .

She'd been so busy, she'd almost forgotten that she'd asked Sarah to investigate.

Now she gripped the phone with both hands, as Sarah continued. 'Well, I've found one of them.'

*   *   *

Reicke was waiting for Thea in the crowded lobby.

'You look very beautiful this evening, Thea,' he said, kissing her hand and looking up at her with his blue eyes. He wasn't wearing his glasses, she noticed.

'Thank you,' she said, smiling back, thinking that he looked great in his impeccable tuxedo. He had sandy-blond hair and freckles, which made him look healthily tanned, and she noticed a few people looking at them together, as they arrived at the top of the grand carpeted stairway and Reicke held her arm as they walked down into the crowded reception, the hubbub of voices and the clink of champagne glasses loud in her ears.

'It feels weird that you're my new boss,' Reicke whispered to her and she laughed, enjoying the secret they were sharing.

Usually she excelled at handling events like tonight. She'd taught herself tricks for learning and remembering people's names and knew how to start conversations with even the most difficult of businessmen. But as she became embroiled in yet another conversation about whether the turn of the millennium would precipitate a global technology meltdown, rather than simply give the company line about everything Maddox Inc. had

271

done to protect their databases, Thea found herself tuning out and thinking instead about what Sarah had told her just now on the phone.

Because she'd found Johnny Faraday, the groom from Little Elms and the person Thea associated most with her childhood—apart from Michael, of course. According to Sarah, he was working as a manager in a famous South African horse stud. Thea's mind was reeling at how much his life had changed. Somehow, to her, he would forever be in the stables in Little Elms in her mind.

Did he even remember her? she wondered. Would he want to hear from her? How kind had life been to him since Little Elms? Did he still remember all the times they'd had together, just as Thea did?

Thea didn't know. But one thing she did know was that she'd spent so long wondering about her past that finally, after all this time, maybe this was a sign that she should do something about it. How often during this business trip had she been frustrated that people weren't quick enough to take action? Well, it was time to start being decisive herself, she thought. About her past and all the unanswered questions she couldn't lay to rest. And maybe, just maybe, Johnny might know where Michael was.

Her Michael. The boy with the hazel eyes and blond hair. She glanced across at Reicke. Was that why she found him so attractive? she suddenly realized. Because he reminded her of Michael?

A crackle of feedback rang out from the podium, where an elderly man in a dinner jacket was shuffling notes, ready to speak.

She sipped her champagne and turned the other

way, towards the stage, moving to stand next to an older, grey-haired man.

'A young girl like you, Fräulein, should be out having fun,' the man said after a moment to her, his English heavy with an Italian accent. 'These events tend to be very dry,' he added, turning and pulling a face, making her smile. 'You're with the German party, I believe?'

Thea shook her head, her attention caught by Reicke, who was looking over in her direction and waving. It wasn't the first time on this trip that someone had assumed she was German.

'I am amazed by how many people have turned up,' the man continued, 'but it's all for show. This unity,' the man added confidentially, 'this new-found belief in the euro, it's all because the Americans are on the prowl.'

'Oh?' Thea whispered, looking at the stage, where the Austrian Trade Minister had been introduced and was about to make his speech.

'Their desire is to make everything homogeneous. Americanized. Centralized. But that way there will be no character left. No national identity. I, for one, would fight with everything I had to stop Scolari being bought out by the Yanks.'

'I am very enlightened by your views, Signor,' Thea said, graciously bowing her head. *That's* why she vaguely recognized him. He was Roberto Scolari.

And now she felt it all slotting into place. Scolari's son was Alfonso Scolari, the F1 racing driver, who was now dating Romy Valentine seriously. Thea hadn't believed it when she'd heard from Andy Bellson at the *Culture Bulletin* in

273

London that Romy Valentine had refused three interviews with his paper. The word in-house was that the girl was a total princess, but Thea suspected the vendetta was to do with the *Culture Bulletin* piece that Brett had sabotaged, which had clearly put the supermodel's nose out of joint.

'I'm afraid I did not catch your name?' Scolari said.

'My name is Theadora Maddox. From Maddox Inc.' She smiled sweetly, watching the old man try to recover his composure.

'Miss Maddox . . . I . . . I . . .' he stumbled.

Scolari. Of course, she thought.

They would be perfect for her expansion plans.

*   *   *

Thea drank far too much champagne at the reception and, after the dinner, she got dragged onto the dance-floor. She danced to a few numbers, but was all too aware of the attention she was garnering, being one of the only women in the room. She knew she ought to retire gracefully, before she made a fool out of herself, and as the music changed to a slow Phil Collins number, she snuck off before she got asked to dance.

Reicke caught her just as she was getting into the lift. His bow tie was undone and his hair was more dishevelled than before and she found herself laughing at him, as he grinned at her and leant comically against the elevator door, to stop it closing.

'How about a nightcap?' he asked.

'No, I can't,' she said. 'I need to sleep.'

'Please. Just one,' Reicke said. 'I won't see you

again for ages.'

'OK,' she relented. 'Just one.'

He inserted his room card into a reader on the panel on the wall and took her to the penthouse floor. She caught sight of herself in the tinted mirrors of the lift as she stood next to him, holding her clutchbag. What am I doing? she thought, as she caught Reicke's eye. He grinned at her.

The penthouse was enormous. A thick cream carpet led into a sitting room with ornate silk armchairs and a dining room off it, with a fancy eighteenth-century wooden table with gold chairs. A very expensive-looking antique grandfather clock struck midnight now, the figurines inside shifting around in a scene from Mozart's *Marriage of Figaro*. 'Wow,' Thea said, admiring it.

'Isn't it great,' he said, coming to stand next to her and unbuttoning the top of his shirt. She caught a blast of his musky aftershave and felt a shimmer of desire. 'There was some kind of mix-up and they gave me the presidential suite.'

'You kept that quiet,' Thea teased him.

'I did. Until now.'

Thea followed him into the dark kitchen and, for a moment, felt her palms sweating, as she remembered the kitchen in Maddox Tower years ago, where Brett had first grabbed her. In the past few years, whenever she'd got anywhere near a physical situation with a man, something inside her had always shut down. She couldn't stop images of Brett rising up to ruin everything—like now—images of that sauna in Switzerland. Almost seven years ago to this day.

Thea took a breath, forcing the thoughts away, as Reicke turned on the light and peered inside the fridge.

'Gin, whisky, vodka or champagne? What can I get you?'

'More champagne, I guess.'

He lifted out a vintage bottle and unwrapped the cork. 'Find some glasses, could you?'

She opened some cupboards until she found some Tiffany flutes, and Reicke expertly popped the bottle and poured two glasses. She liked the feeling of playing 'house' with him, even if it was just in a hotel. Yes, she thought, she could do this. She must make herself relax. Why shouldn't she enjoy herself? Why shouldn't she have fun?

'I haven't shown you the best bit,' Reicke said, his eyes glittering as he nodded for her to follow him into the bedroom past the huge bed with its red brocade cover. He pulled back the matching curtains and slid back the tinted glass door. Outside was a private terrace with a hot-tub. Reicke flicked a switch and the lights in the water came on.

'Hang on,' Reicke said, going to a panel in the wall. 'That isn't it yet.'

He flicked another two switches and the water started bubbling. Music came on through the speakers—the New Radicals album that Thea loved.

'That's amazing,' Thea said, walking out onto the terrace to look closer and to see what was on the other side of the high wall. But when she turned round, she saw that Reicke was undressing.

'What are you doing?' Thea gasped.

'We've got to try it out,' he laughed, stamping out of his trousers. He stood on the wooden slats surrounding the hot-tub in his Calvin Klein underpants and stretched his arms out. She saw that, once out of his stiff dinner jacket and starched shirt, he was wearing a leather necklace with a small pendant, which nestled against his surprisingly toned chest. In fact his body was incredible, and Thea felt a dart of desire run through her. 'Don't leave me out here in the cold, Thea.'

She laughed, amazed at how comfortable he was in his own skin. But he had every right to be. She bit her lip as she watched him climbing into the water.

'There. See, it's easy,' he said. 'Pass me my champagne.'

Thea rolled her eyes and went to fetch him the glass he'd left on the bedside table. He grinned at her, the water in the hot-tub bubbling against his chin and steam rising into the night. He sighed as he stretched back.

'I'll close my eyes. Hop in,' he said. 'I promise I won't look.'

Thea looked up at the stars. She should leave right now. Reicke was her colleague. What was she even thinking of—getting into a hot-tub with him? And yet . . . and yet . . . she sighed, exasperated with herself. What, or more precisely *who*, was she saving herself for? Tom? Still? After all this time?

'Come on, it'll be fun,' Reicke coaxed. 'I'm still not looking . . .'

Putting her champagne down, Thea quickly undid the zip of her dress, watching it slip down around her hips. She stared at her stay-up stockings, wondering whether to keep them on. In the end she rolled them off, having difficulty balancing on one foot.

Then, giggling, she stepped into the water, in her thin lace bra and panties, staring at Reicke's face. She watched him peeping open one eye and squealed, clamping her arm against her breasts. 'Don't look,' she wailed, plunging down into the water.

'Can I open my eyes now?' Reicke asked, and Thea laughed.

She stared at him across the water, but Reicke just grinned back.

'You're so American,' he said. 'Us Germans strip off in front of each other all the time.'

'Yes, but this is different. We're all alone. And, as you said earlier, I'm your boss.'

Thea suddenly regretted pointing out that glaring fact, but Reicke didn't seem to be offended. He tipped his head back and looked at the stars.

'It is rather lovely, isn't it?' he said.

Then he looked at her, and this time his face was serious.

Under the water she felt Reicke's foot touch hers and then his leg. She held her breath. She could feel herself trembling, despite the warm water. But his closeness felt wonderful.

Then, before she knew it, he'd crossed the water and was next to her and his lips were on hers, kissing her. He took her in his arms and kissed her more passionately.

'Let's forget everything,' Reicke whispered. 'Let's just enjoy each other. You and me.'

CHAPTER TWENTY

MARCH 1999

Romy concentrated hard, as she wound the ancient pasta-maker on the worn wooden table. She felt Maria Scolari's strong, floury hands cup her own as the soft doughy mixture fell in folds.

'That's it,' Maria said, nodding her head.

Romy glanced up at Alfonso's mother and smiled. She had neatly curled salt-and-pepper hair and was wearing a striped apron made in the local pink and white patterned cloth. Despite being married to one of the richest men in Italy, when she was here at the family's Tuscan farmhouse the matriarch of the family liked to get her hands dirty in the way of all her ancestors before her.

Romy found it fascinating. Where she herself had done everything to sever all contact with her own roots, Maria positively embraced hers. In fact Romy had never been somewhere where family tradition was so obvious—from the hand-painted plates on the oak dresser to the tiniest rituals. Like the way in which Maria sang to the hens as she collected eggs in the morning, or the secret recipes for the giant dishes that Maria prepared for the family to eat in the evenings under the vine-covered terrace. Even the family dog was seventh-generation, from the same litter born in the farmhouse during the war.

Romy loved being amongst it all and learning the family ways from Maria, who treated all her children with total joy and devotion. And none more so than Alfonso, whom Maria—as well as Roberto, and all Alfonso's sisters—worshipped. Romy had thought when she'd first seen how they spoiled him that they'd never accept her, but somehow they had. Which was why she felt particularly blessed that Maria had singled her out to help in her kitchen this morning.

Alfonso swung round the kitchen door, the sunlight streaming in behind him. He was carrying a towel over his shoulder and announced that he was going for a swim in the lake with his father.

'It'll be freezing,' Maria said. 'You'll catch a chill,' she went on, tutting at him.

Alfonso smiled and came over and hugged Maria from behind, putting his arms around her shapely waist, making her bustle and slap his hand, and then tut as he stole a cherry tomato from the vine cuttings on the table. But there was no mistaking the love in her eyes as Maria watched her son, who now winked at Romy and kissed her dramatically, bending her over backwards in his arms. As usual she felt a dart of pleasure run through her, not dented for a minute by the fact that he was showing off in front of his mother.

She laughed as Alfonso started singing a loud opera aria as he made for the door.

'Did he tell you that he used to want to be a singer?' Maria said when he'd gone.

Romy felt herself blushing. 'Yes, of course . . .'

'Romy,' Maria said, putting her floury hand on Romy's wrist. 'Don't play games with me. Not any more. He can't sing for toffee.'

Romy felt the colour rise even more in her cheeks.

Maria chuckled at her. 'I knew the first time you

came here that you hardly knew a thing about my son. But it doesn't matter. All that matters is that you're still here now. Do you love him?' Maria asked, shocking Romy with her directness.

'Yes,' Romy told her, amazed that she was admitting it. But somehow this beautiful farmhouse kitchen demanded the truth. And Maria herself seemed to demand the truth too. 'I've never felt like this about anyone.'

Maria nodded, taking over the machine and letting another sheet of pasta spill expertly into her hand.

Romy couldn't help feel that this short exchange had propelled her relationship with Alfonso to a whole knew level. She wondered what he would say when she told him that his mother had seen through them all along. Would he be angry that she'd been so easily caught out?

But looking at Maria now, Romy realized that this formidable woman, who appeared so motherly and keen to please her husband, was in fact the backbone of the Scolari family. Nothing her children did had probably ever got past her.

Which is why her acceptance meant so much. But even so, Romy was surprised at how readily she'd admitted her own feelings. Not that there was any point in trying to hide them. She had been hopelessly besotted with Alfonso Scolari ever since he'd proposed the crazy trip to meet his parents for the first time, ten magical months ago.

It had felt so naughty, so illicit. As if they'd been on an adventure together, sharing a huge secret. She smiled, remembering how they'd talked the whole way—on the small private plane from Nice to Pisa. And then in the black Ferrari that was waiting for them on the private runway at the Galileo Galilei airport, which Alfonso drove at a terrifying speed onto the motorway and then along the winding roads north into the mountains. They'd spent the whole time trying to remember facts about each other.

'What do I like about you?' she'd asked him, as they drove through the countryside, the rolling poppy fields and the dark Cyprus trees across the landscape so perfect that she could barely take in its beauty.

'I have nice hair,' he'd replied. 'And I cook a fantastic *vongole*. Be sure to tell Mamma that.'

She'd laughed, nodding. Because it wouldn't be hard to remember, she thought. He did have great hair. Hair that she longed to run her fingers through.

'Oh, and I am a terrific lover,' he'd added. 'That's why you've fallen in love with me. But you can't tell Mamma that. Tell Flavia, my eldest sister.'

Romy had laughed again, but she'd found herself wondering whether that were true.

'What do you do, Romy? I mean . . . what are your hobbies?' he'd asked, turning his attention to her.

'I read books—romances especially,' she'd admitted. 'I take photographs of the places I've been, but I'm terrible at putting them in albums. I like shoes. Expensive shoes. My favourite ones are yellow, and this high.' She'd put her fingers out to show him and Alfonso had whistled, impressed.

'But you don't wear them that often,' he'd clarified. 'Because you're taller than me in them.'

Romy had shaken her head, alarmed and

amused by their deception and whether they'd ever pull it off. 'I have a thing for nice underwear. And stray dogs.'

'That's good. That all fits,' Alfonso had said. 'You chose me. A stray. You have tamed me.'

'Is that possible?' she'd asked.

He'd grinned over at her, putting his foot down on the accelerator, making her tummy jump. 'Anything is possible.'

And Romy had felt it right then, she remembered. That feeling. That feeling she'd had ever since. That this man was wonderful . . . amazing. That he had the power to make her happy in a way she'd never thought possible.

Now, as she watched Maria call to Alfonso's big sister, Flavia, who sauntered into the kitchen and stirred the meat sauce bubbling on the state-of-the art range in the ancient chimney-breast, Romy blanched, remembering the first time she'd ever eaten pasta in that seedy flat, on the first night she'd arrived in London. And once again she was assaulted by terror that these lovely people—that anyone in this, her new life—would ever know the truth about her past.

Now Flavia smiled at Romy. 'Mamma is teaching you how to sprinkle her magic into food then?' she asked.

Flavia had long wavy dark hair and rich olive skin and their father's proud nose. But she had her mother's softness of character and Romy had found herself feeling excited when Flavia had called her and suggested meeting for a coffee in Milan. She liked the fact that Alfonso's eldest sister wanted to be her friend, and they'd been on several shopping trips together. It had been the first time in Romy's life she'd ever thought how lovely it would be to have a sister of her own.

Romy was interrupted by a commotion in the hall, and Alfonso's other sister, Anna, came in with her two daughters. Maria threw out her arms to gather her granddaughters up. Romy smiled, watching as the family all kissed each other, talking and fussing over one another the whole time.

Did they realize how lucky they were? she wondered. To have all the money in the world *and* still to have this? This gorgeous family. This sense of belonging. Just being around it made Romy feel warm in a way she never had before. The more time she spent with the Scolaris, the more time she wanted.

When she'd told Alfonso how much she liked them all, he'd sulked and told her that they were annoying and nosy. She'd told him off and had been amazed at how he'd reacted. He'd been furious, she remembered—the first taste she'd had of his fiery temper. She didn't understand, he'd railed at her. Nobody understood how he felt. Romy had been so surprised by this childish outburst that she'd fallen about giggling, before doing an impression of him strutting about like an angry duck.

'Don't take their side,' he'd pleaded with her, softening only a little, his anger turning to embarrassment.

'Now, why would I do that?' she'd soothed, pinning his arms by his sides in a tight embrace and kissing him, marvelling that, even with his monstrous ego, he could still reveal his insecurities.

Anna too, by all accounts, had Alfonso's fiery

streak, but they'd never met until now, and Romy couldn't help but stare at the small, athletic-looking woman in tennis whites. She went to shake Anna's hand, but instead the smaller woman embraced Romy tightly, leaning up to kiss her. She smelt of a familiar perfume.

'You got Alfonso to come back. Thank you,' she said, looking relieved, and Romy saw immediately that they too would be friends.

'Are you the famous model?' Anna's daughter, Cesca asked, adding, 'You're just as pretty as Mamma said you would be,' as she stood with one hand on her hip.

'Thank you,' Romy laughed, bending down to kiss the little girl with dark curls in the white smock-dress. 'So are you. But being a model isn't about being pretty, it's just about being tall and having lots of luck.'

'I like your sparkly hairclip,' Cesca said, reaching out to touch it.

'Do you?' Romy said. 'Here. Why don't you have it?' she continued, taking it out of her hair.

'Cesca,' Anna scolded, apologizing to Romy for her daughter's forthrightness, but Romy wouldn't hear of it. She liked Cesca and, as she fastened the clip in her hair, she had a vision of being a mother herself. A mother to a Scolari. She stood up, shocked at how happy the thought made her. Just then her phone rang. She pulled it out of the back pocket of her jeans shorts.

It was Nico.

'Where are you?' he demanded. 'I've left you loads of messages.'

'I can't talk,' Romy said, turning away. 'I told you. I'm with Alfonso's family.' In the rustic farmhouse kitchen, with the hot sun streaming through the doors, her world of airports and model shoots seemed a million miles away.

'I don't care. Pack your bags now,' Nico said. 'I've got us an amazing job. We're doing an airline commercial. Filming in Peru. I've bent over backwards to see you in it, but they've agreed.'

'When would we have to leave?' Romy asked, thinking of Simona as much as Nico. Romy didn't want to get on the wrong side of her, especially after all Simona had done for her, and especially when she knew that Simona would do anything for Romy to keep her safe and happy.

'Tomorrow evening. I'm booking the flights now.'

'Nico, I can't . . . I've got to think about it. I can't just leave.'

'Romy,' Nico wailed. 'I've broken my back for this one. You can't let me down. Please, darling.'

Romy hung up, but as she put her phone back in her pocket, she caught the expression on Maria Scolari's face and realized, without a shadow of a doubt, that taking the job and leaving in the middle of this family weekend was the wrong decision.

She was either in the Scolari clan or out.

*   *   *

As the family gathered for supper under the vine on the terrace, later that evening, Romy was still in turmoil. She hadn't had a second to talk to Alfonso alone, but had been swept along by the arrival of all his sisters. Lola and Serena as well as blonde Bianca, the baby sister, who brooded in the corner and couldn't be won over until Romy started

286

discussing novels with her. Now she helped Cesca light all the candles on the table and laughed as Anna chattered, while she folded the napkins, filling Romy in on the family history and gossip. The only sister missing was Gloria, who Alfonso said had taken his gauntlet as the black sheep of the family. Maria arrived tight-lipped after talking to Gloria on the phone.

'She's not coming, Mamma?' Serena asked.

Maria shook her head. 'She won't come until your father accepts Marc.'

'Who's Marc?' Romy asked Anna.

'He's Gloria's latest squeeze,' Anna confided. 'Papa found out that he went to jail for drug-dealing when he was a kid, so he won't think about acknowledging him, or accepting him. It's breaking Mamma's heart. Gloria was always the brightest of us, but she's determined to stick by this Marc guy and has pulled out of her PhD.'

Now Romy watched as Roberto Scolari arrived at the table, smart as always in a pink shirt, which complemented his olive skin and silver hair. She squeezed Alfonso's hand under the table, secretly wondering whether he'd be as attractive as his father when he was old and grey.

'We're so lucky with the weather. So warm for March,' he declared. 'So. We are all here?' He smiled at everyone around the table. 'But where's Gloria?'

'She's not coming,' Maria said. 'You know that.'

Roberto sighed. 'Her loss.'

'Doesn't she deserve a second chance, Papa?' Alfonso said.

Roberto turned to him, his features stern. 'I will not have that boyfriend of hers associated with this

287

family. You know that.'

His tone was decisive, his eyes steely, and Romy saw then that Roberto Scolari was black and white. You were either in or out. There were no second chances. Romy watched Maria leave the table to collect something from the kitchen, but her silence spoke volumes about her disappointment.

The moment was diffused by the arrival through the kitchen door of another man.

'Who's that?' she whispered to Alfonso.

'It's Franco Moretti,' he replied, stiffening as the older man approached. 'He's known my father forever. The Morettis and Scolaris go way back,' he explained. 'Apart from Mamma, he's the only other shareholder of Scolari. He doesn't approve of me.'

Moretti was greeted like one of the family, the sisters kissing his cheeks, but Alfonso stood back.

'Romy,' Flavia called. 'Come and meet Franco.'

Romy went towards the older man and they shook hands. He was tall, with dark brown hair and a neat little moustache. His panama hat completed the look of an ageing matinee idol, Romy thought. They all followed as he walked over to the table, clapped Roberto on the shoulder and took his place next to him.

'Look who's here,' Roberto said, gesturing to Alfonso, and Franco shook his hand across the table. Romy immediately sensed the friction between them, as she retook her place next to Alfonso.

'You must come to the vineyard on Sunday,' Franco said. 'We have an exceptional vintage of the Chianti that you like. You must bring Miss Valentine,' he added.

'Oh . . . thank you, but I can't,' Romy said,

288

looking between Alfonso and Franco.

'What?' Alfonso turned to her as they all sat down. 'Why not?'

'I have to go.'

'Go? Go where?'

'I meant to tell you,' she said in a hushed voice. 'Something's come up. I have to fly to Peru.'

'Peru?' Serena interrupted, placing a platter of grilled aubergines and pine nuts down on the long table. 'I went travelling there.'

'I've never been,' Romy said, feeling the force of Alfonso's stare boring into her. His leg was pressing against hers, demanding an explanation. Roberto and Maria exchanged a look down the table.

'So, I hear you're a model,' Franco said matter-of-factly, looking at Romy, his eyes assessing her. 'Is that satisfying?' It sounded as if he just wanted to make polite conversation, but there was a hint in his voice that left Romy in no doubt that he considered her to be just another of Alfonso's meaningless conquests.

'It is when I get to influence the campaigns,' she said. 'And I've been very lucky to have travelled the world,' she added, looking at Serena.

'Don't you think the whole fashion industry is . . . well . . .' Franco continued, clearly not satisfied with her answer. He waved his hand in the air, '. . . silly little girls running about.'

Anna tutted loudly. 'Franco!' She made eyes at Romy as if to tell her that she was used to Franco being so provocative.

'Silly little girls,' Flavia added, taking her side. 'For goodness' sake.'

Romy was touched that they were springing to

her defence. She liked being part of their sisterhood.

'I am not just involved in fashion, although that is an important part of what I do,' Romy countered. 'And I would have to argue that it was far from "silly". Like the Ferragamo campaign I did recently.'

'Handbags,' Anna said, winking at Romy and taking her place next to Franco. 'Expensive ones.'

'Italians should be proud of their heritage of luxury goods,' Romy said to Franco. 'The brands count for so much on the world stage. If you look at the contribution of these designer goods as a percentage of your GDP, then the investment in expensive advertising campaigns really starts to make sense, especially with the burgeoning demand in Asia. The luxury sector represents a huge opportunity for Italy. That's why your new minister's tax policy seems to be sensible,' she added, smiling sweetly.

Roberto nodded, impressed. 'Is your business in Peru for an Italian campaign?' he asked.

Romy felt her cheeks burning. 'No, it's for British Airways.'

'Ah, *we* never use *them*, if we can help it,' Roberto said, his eyes meeting Romy's for just a second. But in that split second of silence, when she should have defended herself and her career, she smiled meekly and Roberto nodded, clearly taking her reaction as some sort of decision.

Romy looked at Alfonso. 'We'll talk about it later,' she whispered, giving his hand a reassuring squeeze.

Then Maria brought out the dish of spiced pumpkin pasta that she and Romy had made that morning, and the conversation moved on. She listened to Roberto tell Franco about his meeting last weekend in Vienna and how he'd bumped into Thea Maddox. Her name rang a bell. Hadn't that PR girl, Bridget, mentioned her once? Wasn't she from the Maddox corporation?

'She's certainly a good-looking girl,' he said, with a chuckle, 'but she'll never amount to much. The Americans are too hard-nosed for the likes of her.'

'He had a son, though? Maddox?' Franco checked.

Roberto nodded and said something Romy didn't catch, but she felt Alfonso stiffen. It was clear that his father assumed that Maddox's empire must be safe in the hands of his son, but not in the hands of his daughter, and Romy caught the inference. Roberto was very clear in his desire for Alfonso to join the family business—sooner rather than later.

Of course, Alfonso had mentioned it before— his father's insistence on the Scolari business being passed from father to son—but Romy hadn't really thought it was very serious until now. As far as she knew, Alfonso was focused on his driving career for the foreseeable future, but Roberto and Franco didn't seem to share that view. And as they tried to draw Alfonso into talking about business, Romy could feel him getting more and more wound up.

She took the first chance she could to leave the table and join Alfonso in the kitchen after the main course. So much for not eating too much before the campaign.

'So what's the story with you and Franco?' she asked.

'Nothing.'

'Really? You seem very annoyed by him. I thought he was supposed to be an old family friend?'

Alfonso looked bashful, then he puffed out his cheeks. 'If you must know, there's history between me and him.'

'What kind of history?'

'Just . . . there was a thing between me and his daughter once.'

'He broke her heart,' Flavia chipped in, piling the plates up on the counter. 'She's never got over it. Neither has her father.'

Romy stared at Alfonso, who looked embarrassed at being exposed by his sister.

'It wasn't my fault.'

'What? Someone forced you to be unfaithful, did they?' Flavia asked, enjoying her brother's discomfort.

'Will you leave me alone,' Alfonso said, flicking her with a tea towel. 'I had to get out of it. I couldn't have lived with that . . .' He gave Flavia a knowing look, then added to Romy, 'It doesn't matter.'

'You couldn't have lived with what?' Romy asked.

Alfonso shrugged. 'She had big nose, OK?' he said, looking at Flavia and Romy. 'Now leave me alone,' he told Flavia, before grabbing Romy's hand and pulling her out through the door.

He didn't stop, running with her through the gap in the box hedges towards the far vegetable garden.

'Hey, wait up,' she said. 'Where are we going? There's still dessert.'

'I'm fed up with them,' Alfonso said, 'and all their boring talk of business. I just want to be alone with you.'

Romy stepped forward and put her hand on his face. 'What's wrong. Why are you so upset?'

'Angelica Moretti was the reason I left in the first place. I just felt they were forcing me into something I didn't want to do. So I broke off the engagement.'

'You were engaged?' Romy asked. She was surprised by how jealous the news made her feel.

'So shoot me,' Alfonso said, throwing out his arms. Then he marched off.

'Where are you going?' she asked, following him.

'To get away,' he answered.

'Hey,' she said. 'Don't take it out on me. I didn't know about it, that's all. I don't care. It's nothing to do with me.'

'I told you when we met that I don't like discussing the past,' he said.

'But maybe we should, if stuff is going to come up,' she said. 'Especially if it's going to upset you.'

He stopped and turned to her.

'OK then, let's do this. Tell me, what's the worst thing you've ever done?' he demanded.

Romy felt the colour rise in her cheeks. Earlier in Maria's kitchen she'd felt compelled to tell the truth, but now, out here, she felt on slippery ground. There was no way she could tell Alfonso any of the truth about her past. Besides, her gut instinct told her that he wasn't really upset about the past at all, but about the future. He was reacting like this because he didn't want her to leave.

'I smacked another model once,' she told him. 'I got into big trouble for that.'

'But she deserved it, right?'

'Absolutely.' She paused, biting her lip. 'And what about you?' she asked.

'OK, so I'll admit it to you—there have been many women. But I don't regret it. If I were to tell you about them all . . .'

'What?'

'You'd be jealous.'

'How do you know I'd be jealous?'

'You're a woman.'

'I see.'

He checked for her reaction. 'All I'm saying,' he clarified, 'is that it's best if we don't discuss our sordid pasts. They are not relevant to us. Agreed?'

'Fine by me,' Romy replied.

'Come on then. I have to show you this,' Alfonso said.

He grabbed her hand and set off at speed again. He pulled her down the path through the garden, Romy's senses filling with the scent of night jasmine, as she tried to process this latest exchange.

She wished she could stop, go back, clarify what had just passed between them, but as usual Alfonso was speeding ahead, moving on, always racing, racing. He would always be like that. So what if he'd shut the door on his past and didn't want to discuss it with her? After all, wasn't that just what she'd always done?

He was right, Romy decided. They shouldn't discuss it. Any of it. Any of the dark secrets that haunted her at night. They were the past. What relevance did they have to her now? In the warm night air Romy felt exhilaration rushing through her as she ran to keep up. Alfonso had set her free. Free of her past. And it felt wonderful.

They came to a wall at the end with a gate in it and Alfonso opened it for Romy to let her pass.

They walked on in silence, until the trees gave way to a field and farm buildings in the distance.

'Where are we going?' Romy asked, but Alfonso just tugged at her hand.

'Nearly there,' he said, their shadows long in the tall grass.

They stopped by the trees and he pushed aside a branch for her to step through. On the other side, the land fell away and the view over the valley was breathtaking, the ancient town on the hilltop opposite shrouded in shadows from the huge orange-yellow moon low in the sky behind them.

An owl hooted. She watched the headlights of a car snaking up the hairpin bends to the town in the distance, blasting tunnels of silver onto the mauve hills. She stared up at the stars twinkling close above them. She'd never been somewhere so magical.

'I had my first fight there,' Alfonso said, pointing down towards the bottom of the field.

'Did you win?'

'No. They were much bigger than me. But then I beat them in a go-kart race.'

Romy had a sudden image of him as a small boy and how he must have been, and her heart contracted with love.

'Romy, don't go tomorrow,' he said.

'But I have to. I promised.'

'Then unpromise. Stay here. With me. I will talk to Nico. I will explain why he can't have you.'

He put his arms around her, then leant forward and kissed her.

'And why's that?' she asked.

'I have something I want to ask you, and I can't ask you if you go.'

'You can ask me anything,' she said. 'Why not now?'

'Because I want to ask you to marry me,' he said. 'In fact, what am I waiting for? I am asking you to marry me. I love you like crazy, Romy. So will you? Will you be my wife?'

CHAPTER TWENTY-ONE

FEBRUARY 2000

Thea was enjoying the drive north from the airport in Cape Town. After the snow in Manhattan, this Mediterranean climate in South Africa was wonderful. She checked the map on the passenger's seat once again, but she was still heading in the right direction towards the Franschhoek valley to the west of Stellenbosch.

As she pressed the button on the tortoiseshell dashboard, the roof of the Porsche glided up and away. Then, making sure her iPod was docked properly, she turned up the playlist, her favourite Oasis song 'Wonderwall' coming on, reminding her of her old friend Ollie from college, who'd been into that whole Britpop scene. She remembered the mews house they'd shared in Chelsea and how he'd played Blur all the time.

She wondered what he was doing now. The last

she'd seen of him was when she'd seen him in *Blood Brothers* in the West End a few years ago, when she'd been on a short stopover in London. She'd meant to go backstage and congratulate him, but she'd been crying so hard by the end that she'd had to hail a cab back to her hotel.

But there was nothing wrong with feeling nostalgic, she thought. Not today. Not when she was finally here and on her way to see Johnny.

She felt a buzz of excitement, wondering how her surprise visit would turn out. She'd thought about writing to Johnny many times, but she'd been so busy and, as the months had gone on and his address on a Post-it note in her leather organizer had started to annoy her, she'd booked a flight on a whim and decided to surprise him. That way Johnny wouldn't be able to make a fuss of her or, worse, make an excuse not to see her. And with a long-overdue week of holiday in her diary, Thea couldn't think of a better place to come than South Africa.

She'd read that the Leveaux estate was amongst the spooky-sounding Drakenstein Mountains, but as the afternoon sun started bathing everything in a golden glow, Thea couldn't help but think what a lovely place this was. As she arrived in the foothills, she knew she ought to carry on and check into the nearby Stellenbosch Country Club, but when she saw a sign for the Leveaux place, she was so excited that she decided to go there straight away.

As she turned off the main road, the private road to the estate was shaded with trees, just like the driveway to Little Elms had been, Thea thought. Glossy brown stallions cantered next to her in the green fields. Further up the slopes, rows of vines stood out in neat rows. According to what she'd found on the Internet, Marcel Leveaux had cultivated the upper slopes of the ranch into a vineyard as a hobby, seven years ago, but the wines were receiving so much attention that they'd become almost as famous as the stud-farm his wife ran.

Way ahead in the distance were brick buildings that were painted a bright white, but with the clock tower above, they looked as reverential as a church against the green fields and slopes. They must be the stables, she thought.

Thea parked in the car park near the white ranch building and stepped out of the car, feeling immediately hot and uncomfortable in her jeans. She shielded her eyes against the glare of the low sun and, looking round at the ranch, felt her heart fluttering with nerves.

She'd called ahead and said she was from a feed company and would be dropping in, so she knew that Johnny would be here, but now she wondered whether this really would be the surprise reunion she hoped for. *Well, I'll see soon enough how he's going to react*, she thought, plaiting her hair as she walked towards a man on the stoop to ask him for help.

*   *   *

Johnny Faraday was inside the stables, leading a glossy black stallion that was at least seventeen and a half hands high over the hay-strewn floor. Thea stood in the doorway, watching as he finished brushing the beast's impressive flank, before

298

producing an apple from the pocket of his green jacket and talking quietly, as the horse gently nuzzled it from his hand.

Well, well, well, Johnny Faraday hadn't changed at all, Thea thought, recognizing his manner with horses, as if she'd been with him in the stables only yesterday. It had been fifteen years since she'd seen him last, she realized, but the years had been kind. Johnny's tanned face was more lined, but just as she remembered it.

He stopped when he saw her standing in the doorway. He raised his hat, then wiped his forehead on the back of his hand. It was another so-familiar gesture that it made a small laugh bubble up inside Thea. She saw him looking at her, trying to make the connection, trying to work out why he recognized her. She bit her lip as he walked over to her.

'Thea?' Johnny said, as if he could hardly believe his eyes.

'Surprise,' she said, with a shrug.

'Oh, my . . .' Johnny said.

And as he burst into laughter and hugged her, Thea realized that it had all been worth it. The insecurity of coming here—all her doubts. She should have known everything would be all right.

*   *   *

It wasn't long before Thea felt as if she'd been at Leveaux for days rather than hours. She happily agreed as Johnny offered to take her up to the vineyards for a wine-tasting, keen to show off the place now that she was here.

There was a small restaurant at the wine cellar,

299

and soon Thea and Johnny were sitting on the wooden veranda with several tasting glasses, sampling a board of the house snacks that were selected to go with the wines.

Way below, the paddocks were fading into the cool evening. Thea sipped the delicious Sauvignon Blanc and sighed. She licked her fingers, having just enjoyed a delicious mouthful of cheese on crusty French bread.

'Do you remember the jumps in the paddock in Little Elms?' she asked Johnny. 'I can remember every detail as if it were yesterday.'

'You were so competitive,' Johnny laughed. 'You did it all to impress Michael.'

'Do you know what happened to him?' she asked. She was almost too afraid to ask. Too ashamed that she'd let Michael go, like Johnny.

'He joined the army. The last I heard he was out in Iraq.'

'Iraq?' Thea couldn't keep the shock from her voice.

'Quite a hero apparently. It's just a shame old Mrs Pryor can't see him.'

Thea felt her chest tighten. 'You don't mean she's—'

'No. But she might as well be, poor old girl. She's in a home. Alzheimer's. I think it broke Michael's heart to put her in there.'

She took a breath to steady herself.

'Sorry . . .' she said to Johnny. 'It's just . . . I feel so guilty.'

'Why?'

'Because I should have been there for Michael.'

Johnny shook his head. 'We were all your father's staff. His responsibility, not yours. When the house got sold—well, our jobs there ended too. We all moved on. That's just the way of the world.'

'I always thought of us as family,' Thea said, failing to hide the note of hope in her voice.

Johnny's eyes crinkled at that.

'I've missed you too, if that's what you're saying,' he told her.

No, I'm not just saying that, Thea wanted to explain. *It's more than just missed. Everything good ended back then, when Storm moved in and everyone started moving away.*

Johnny smiled, looking over Thea's shoulder, clearly not realizing how upset she was. Again she remembered what Shelley Lawson had told her all those years ago. That Johnny Faraday and Thea's mother had been inseparable. *No,* she told herself now, it was an absurd idea. Too crazy to ask Johnny about, particularly since he'd just told her that working for her parents had been nothing but a job.

'And who might this be?' a woman asked.

'Thea, meet Gaynor Leveaux,' Johnny said.

Thea forced herself to smile and let him introduce her to the tall woman with curly blonde hair, who was obviously not only Johnny's boss, but his friend. She was tanned, with deeply scored laughter lines around her eyes, and she exuded an earthy sort of healthiness, which immediately made Thea's jetlag and exhaustion from the long drive kick in.

Thea blushed as Johnny described her to Gaynor as his one-time protégée and the daughter of Alyssa McAdams, who had ridden in the Olympics. Impressed, Gaynor insisted that Thea take Lightning Strike out, to put him through his

301

paces, in the morning.

Thea happily accepted the offer and soon took her leave, telling Gaynor that she had some work to do. She was amazed by how quickly she made up the lie, giving the impression that she was passing by Leveaux because she was here on business.

But as she checked into the exclusive country club, where she'd been looking forward to a week of pampering, Thea felt foolish. She shouldn't have come here on a whim. Much as it was lovely to see Johnny, his life had so clearly moved on that Thea was left wondering what she'd really wanted from her spontaneous visit.

*　　　*　　　*

Later, after a long bath, Thea stood in her room, looking out at the craggy mountains in the moonlight, the silence only broken by the clinking of the ice-cubes in her water glass as she went over the past few hours.

Johnny had just been staff. That's what he'd told her. She was still surprised by how much that had stung. Did that apply to Michael too? Everything she'd felt for him—everything she thought she'd felt—had that been nothing but an illusion of family? Had her real family vanished, along with her mother? Were her father and her memories of them all together really all she had left?

Michael. She could picture his face so clearly, as if with one small step forward she could push her fingers back through his honey-coloured hair. Why, if he'd really meant so little to her, could she not push the thought of him away. Was *he* the real reason she'd come all along, she wondered?

She tried to picture her hazel-eyed blond boy in an army uniform, but she couldn't. But just the fact of it made her realize how much everyone's lives—*Michael's* life—had moved on. So why was she here? Why couldn't she move on too? Why was she still desperate to find that happy little girl she'd once been?

Was dredging up her memories really the answer? Would that really solve the problem of that empty feeling that she carried inside her all the time. The one that always resulted in her being lonely, as she had been at the turn of the millennium a few weeks ago, when she'd watched television alone in her apartment.

Maybe she was a freakish little brat after all, she thought, remembering how Storm had once described her. Maybe there was a fundamental part of her missing that stopped her forming proper relationships with people.

Like with Reicke. Thea was still puzzled over what had happened there. He'd never acknowledged that night they'd spent together in Vienna. She would have thought that the new head of Maddox Global Media in Germany might have found a moment to say something personal to her at the launch party a few months ago, but he'd stringently avoided becoming entangled in any situation where they might have to spend time together, just the two of them.

The way in which he continued to pretend they'd never had sex left Thea feeling insecure and paranoid. Hadn't it been as great for him as it had been for her? Hadn't she been worth pursuing emotionally too?

Maybe he was ashamed, she thought, because

she was so senior to him. Maybe he worried that she'd think he'd only seduced her to curry favour with her. And maybe that *had* been his motive after all. Or maybe, unlike her, he'd moved on, and was now in a proper relationship and didn't want to be reminded of what added up to nothing more significant than a one-night stand.

Whatever the reason, the end result was that Thea had been left feeling embarrassed, as if she'd let herself down. As if Reicke no longer respected her as much as she'd have liked. The fact that she'd been too busy even to think about getting into a relationship with anyone else since then had only heightened her sense of failure. Other people had someone special. Why couldn't she? Why did the thought of letting someone into her life always strike her as so complicated, so hard?

She thought about the magazine her father had shown her a few weeks ago. Thea had been named as the Most Resolutely Single Person in New York. Her picture had been put beside several high-powered businessmen as potential husbands, but Thea had been horrified. She told herself that it was just a journalist making up copy, but nevertheless her father's meaning had been more than clear. He, like everyone else, expected her to settle down. Not as someone's wife—her father knew her better than to think she'd quit her own career—but as someone's partner. Someone's matching half, or 'someone who'll love you and bring you happiness', as her father had actually said.

But it seemed so unfair to Thea. She was at the top of her game in business. Richer by far and, in some cases, more successful than the men she'd been linked to, but *they* didn't have the public pointing at them, expecting *them* to settle down. No, the onus was clearly on Thea—the implication being that she would only be truly happy if she was a brilliant wife and mother, as well as a brilliant businesswoman.

Well, screw them, she thought. I *am* happy. And I don't need anyone else to complete me. Especially a bunch of suits in a society mag. And least of all Michael Pryor, some kid she'd known half a lifetime ago.

She booted up her laptop. She knew the only way to stop thinking like this was to immerse herself in work. Sure enough, within minutes she was totally absorbed, her fingers flying over the keyboard as she fired off emails, making more demands on her staff.

It was time for action on Scolari, she decided. Time to make another bid for the company. She'd failed last time, but she wouldn't allow that to happen again. Italy was the only area where they were weak in Europe, and Thea was determined to focus everyone on getting the elusive media company.

That would bring her happiness. That would make her smile.

*   *   *

Thea was up just after dawn. It was chilly, the mist still settling over the hills as she joined Johnny at the stables and he introduced her to the black stallion she'd seen him with the day before. The pride of the stables, and destined to be sold to one of the greatest racing trainers in the States,

305

Lightning Strike was a formidable beast. Johnny assured Thea that she'd be OK, but as she mounted the powerful black stallion and he snorted and stamped at her unfamiliar touch, she felt her pulse racing. With a horse this valuable, she couldn't afford anything to go wrong.

'You know what you're doing,' Johnny assured her.

'But he's enormous.'

'Showbiz was bigger,' Johnny said, reminding Thea of the horse her mother had ridden.

Thea was immediately determined not to show him how scared she was, as Johnny mounted Gossip, another stallion from the stables, and they set out through the paddock and into the valley beyond. The sun was breaking through the mist, shafts of light illuminating the rich green grass. Her senses filled with the chirrup of birds and the breath of her horse, and Thea felt herself reconnecting with a part of herself that she'd forgotten.

'You should ride more at home,' Johnny told her when she told him how much she was enjoying herself.

'What, in Manhattan? No time,' she shrugged.

'Weekends?'

'What weekends? As I said, I have no personal time.'

'Then make time,' Johnny scolded her. 'Aren't you supposed to be the miracle-maker?'

He was quoting from a *Time* article a few years ago, when she'd talked about women's roles in corporations. She felt touched that he'd kept track of her, even from a distance.

'Come on. Get the engines running. Put your

foot down,' he said, making her gallop after him.

*　　　*　　　*

Thea was still exhilarated as she joined Johnny for lunch with Gaynor and Marcel in the ranch house, with their children Alice and Jack, along with a couple more of Johnny's colleagues. She wondered whether they too felt like she once had, as if Johnny were one of the family. Despite their warm welcome and the hearty banter around the table, Thea couldn't help feeling jealous of their closeness and of all the events stretching into the future that marked the calendar of the ranch and vineyard. With such a full life, when did Johnny ever have time to think about the past?

It was at the end of the lunch that Thea next got to chat to Johnny alone. Being last at the large kitchen table in the farmhouse, having helped clear away the dishes, they carried on where they'd left off their conversation yesterday. Before long Thea told him about school in England and how lonely she'd been. Then she told him about meeting Bridget and how she'd fallen in love with Tom.

'What happened?' Johnny asked.

Thea shrugged. 'It didn't work out,' she said, forcing her voice to stay calm, not to betray the emotion she felt, just talking about it. She was determined to keep her secret shame about Brett to herself, even though the urge to tell Johnny all about it felt so strong.

'But the good thing to come out of it was that Tom led me to you.'

'How do you mean?'

She explained the connection, about how Tom's

307

mother was Shelley Lawson, and how Shelley had mentioned Johnny to Thea. But rather than seem pleased, Johnny appeared subdued. When she'd finished talking, he got up and paced, rubbing his hand over his jaw. It was the second time Shelley Lawson's name had had an unexpected reaction. She remembered now how her father had looked strange when she'd introduced Tom to him and had explained the connection to Shelley.

'What else did she say?' Johnny asked. She was surprised by the harshness of his tone.

'That's all. Why?' Thea asked, staring at him.

'You really don't know?'

'Know what?'

Johnny shook his head and looked up to the beams. 'Isn't that why you're here, Thea? You know, I've wondered all these years whether this would ever come out.'

*   *   *

Johnny Faraday stared at Thea, weighing up what to do. Is this why she'd turned up out of the blue? Just when he thought his connection with the Maddoxes was over forever and his life had moved on?

After all the hours he'd spent thinking about her, wondering about her. And look at her! She'd grown up to be so beautiful. Lis would have been so proud. He'd missed his little Thea more than he could possibly tell her.

When she'd said she'd thought of Johnny as family—well, she'd hit the nail on the head. Thea *had* felt like family. It had ripped him apart to lose her.

308

So would it really be so awful to tell her the truth? After all, what could Maddox do to him now? After all these years? From what Thea had told him, he'd well and truly moved on with his life.

And hadn't he promised Lis that he'd always take care of Thea? In those dreadful secret moments they'd shared before she'd died.

But he hadn't. He'd been too intimidated by Maddox, just as Lis had been when she'd been alive. So he'd lived with the guilt all these years.

That seemed to be the story of his life, Johnny thought—letting the important things slip away. How could he possibly tell Thea the lifetime of regrets he'd had? How could he explain to this gorgeous young woman the pain of heartbreak? Of loss. What would a rich girl like Thea Maddox know about that?

'Please, Johnny,' Thea said, reaching out for his hand. 'I need to find out. I want to know the truth about my past. I want to understand why my father left it all behind.'

Johnny sighed. 'Let's walk. I talk better when I'm on the move.'

* * *

They left the house and walked down towards the paddock. Thea stopped by him as they rested on the white bars of the gate. Ahead of them, on the far side of the dusty expanse, Gossip, the stallion, whinnied and shook the flies away from his head. But Thea hardly took any of it in, concentrating instead on Johnny, who seemed to be lost in memories.

Memories of her mother.

309

And as he started to speak about those long-gone days, he talked of how he'd trained with Alyssa, how talented she was, how they spent as much time as they possibly could together. How horses were their lives.

'So it was true,' she said, remembering again what Shelley Lawson had told her. 'You and Mom were inseparable. Were you . . .?' Thea steeled herself, 'Were you lovers?'

'I loved her. She loved me. They were the happiest days of my life.'

He said it so simply that Thea realized how obvious it had been all along. Now she remembered that last day her mother had come to Little Elms to watch Thea jump. She hadn't come back to say goodbye just to Thea, but to see Johnny one last time too.

'What happened?'

'You really don't know? Shelley didn't tell you?'

Thea shook her head, trying not to betray how fast her heart was beating with anticipation. 'She hinted at something, but . . .'

He took another deep breath. 'I—we . . . well, we were kids and we . . . well, she got . . . Lis got pregnant.'

'Pregnant?' Thea felt her heart jolting.

'Lis was terrified. She was training hard. She wanted to get rid of the baby, but it went to full term. We were young. That's what happened back then.'

Thea stared at him, her mind whirring. 'She had the baby? Where? What happened to it?'

'Lis went to her schoolfriend Shelley's house. She had the baby there. Then she left the baby with Shelley. Lis felt it had to be that way.'

310

Thea felt her skin tingling all over. Shelley had known this about her mother? This enormous fact. Her mother had had a baby . . . in Shelley's house. Did that mean Bridget had known? Had *Tom*?

What if Thea hadn't ended things with Tom— how would things have played out? Would Shelley really have kept such a big secret, with Thea right under her nose?

Her head was flooded with questions, hundreds of questions, and her mind started scrambling for dates and timings. What if that baby . . . *Tom* . . . No, that couldn't possibly—

Thea felt adrenaline pumping through her. 'What kind of baby? What was it?'

'A little girl. We had a baby girl.'

She stood very still, letting the information sink in. Some where out there was a little girl—Thea's half-sister. Her own flesh and blood.

A sister.

And there and then Thea knew, without a doubt, that this was the reason her heart had brought her here. Had her sub conscious known all along that there had been something—someone— missing from her life?

A sister.

Her heart soared at the thought. Staring up at the fist-like mountain, Thea vowed that she would find her sister, no matter what. No matter how long it took.

CHAPTER TWENTY-TWO

SEPTEMBER 2001

'And then,' Alfonso was saying, 'you chop the oregano up very fine. See? Rub it between your fingers. Now smell.'

Romy smiled as Nico reluctantly dipped his head towards the proffered herbs. Alfonso's impromptu cookery lesson had already been going on for more than an hour.

They were in the kitchen of Villa Gasperi, Alfonso's family's home in the centre of Milan. Maria and Roberto had given Alfie and Romy a couple of months here alone whilst they were travelling. After their wedding in the summer, the press speculation on the couple had been so intense that the old convent, with its thick stone walls and large garden full of towering palm trees, was the only place they could truly be protected from the prying eyes of the press.

'And then you're going to stir it into the sauce right at the very last second, before you serve it up,' Alfonso said.

'It seems a lot of effort,' Nico complained, taking solace from another fortifying slug of wine. Romy smiled. He was the one who wanted to impress his new boyfriend, Pierre, who was arriving in Milan tomorrow.

It had made Romy's honeymoon even more special when Nico had fallen for the handsome Pierre. Nico had been there for the first week of their trip to the Maldives, to do the official honeymoon shots as the final part of the wedding deal that Romy and Alfonso had done with *Vogue* and *Grazia*. Out on the dive-shoot his romance with Pierre had sparked.

'Do you want to learn how to cook or not?' Alfonso demanded.

Nico winked at Romy, who was washing salad at the sink. 'Maybe it would just be easier to order a takeaway? A pizza?'

Romy smiled. It was good to see the two men in her life getting on so well. Together they formed a link between her past and her present. They made it feel as if her life had direction and consistency, and that the future too would be a clear path along which she could tread.

As she gazed out through the kitchen window at the sun setting across the orchard and the garden's cobbled wall, she thought back to her wedding day, less than two months ago, but already it felt like a lifetime away.

She remembered now how she'd walked from the house to the tiny church arm-in-arm with Nico, the clanking of the church bell breaking through the hazy afternoon as old ladies from the crowded balconies above threw flowers in her path.

Behind her, Alfonso's nieces in white dresses and lace gloves fussed around her dress, pulling the train out behind her. The same train that Maria had worn on her wedding day to Roberto, and his mother before her.

'This will take ages at this rate,' Nico had said.

'But it's nice,' Romy had squeezed his arm and then straightened the pink rose in his buttonhole. 'It's all part of it.'

'You're right. It *is* pretty amazing,' he'd said.

313

'I've never been big on weddings myself, but this . . . well, this is incredible. I can't believe how much work you've done to pull it all together.'

'I am doing the right thing, aren't I?'

'You're not sure?' Nico had asked, stopping her. 'Because if you're not—'

'No—it's not like that,' she'd said. 'It's just I'm scared that I love Alfonso too much. That I could never live without him. I don't know if it's possible to love someone this much. I feel so out of control. So strong, and yet so frightened.'

'The only thing you've got to be frightened of is not making it to the altar on time. And after that you can get worried about becoming fat on Mamma Scolari's pasta.'

Romy had smiled then, and had waved when she'd seen that Roberto Scolari was waiting for her at the doorway of the church.

'Were you worried I wouldn't come?' she'd teased him, noticing a tear in his eye. She'd touched his face affectionately. It had been Roberto she'd had to thank for the lavish wedding. He'd spared no expense, and she'd been able to tell how proud he was.

'Of course not.' Then he'd held her gaze and had said softly, 'You gave back my son.'

And as he'd hugged her, Romy knew that he really did love her like his own daughter, and that today had made him happier than he could possibly put into words. She'd turned and given her flowers to Cesca. Then she'd looked at Roberto.

'I'd like you to come with me,' she'd told him, taking his arm.

She'd winked at Nico, who'd instantly understood, and together all three of them had

314

walked up the aisle of the tiny church, each pew packed full of smiling guests. And Romy hadn't imagined that she could ever feel happier than she had right then.

She'd heard the majestic organ filling the church, the light flooding in through the high stained-glass rose window, sending shafts of colours onto the black and white tiles leading to the altar, where the priest stood with Alfonso, waiting for her. Behind him a flower arrangement of tumbling roses from Maria's very own garden had added sweet perfume to the heady incense.

It had felt as if every step of her life had been bringing her to this moment. She hadn't been able to stop grinning, as her favourite of Alfonso's nieces, Cesca, pulled back Romy's veil, and Alfonso had been able to see how happy Romy was.

'You look incredible,' he'd whispered and she saw tears in his eyes. 'Stunning.'

And Romy knew that, for all the compliments she'd ever been paid in her life, this had been the best one yet.

She had listened to the same priest who had baptized Alfonso here as a baby start the service, but her eyes had never left Alfonso's, the rest of the church forgotten. She'd wanted to pinch herself, she was so happy.

She'd dreamily smiled at Alfonso as he'd slipped the gold band onto her finger.

'I will love you forever, Mrs Scolari,' he'd whispered.

And as his lips had touched hers, Romy had known that she really was safe now.

Forever.

The CCTV intercom monitor lit up on the wall by the kitchen door, just as the CD on the huge sound system was changing. Alfonso picked up the silver remote and paused the familiar introduction to Robbie Williams's 'Rock DJ'.

The unsmiling face of Max, the burly security guard manning the gate, filled the small screen.

'There's a . . . woman . . . here who's insisting on seeing Mrs Scolari,' Max's gruff voice crackled through the speaker.

Mrs Scolari. Romy still adored the sound of those words. But it was clear from the way he'd hesitated before using the word 'woman' that forty-something, ex-paratrooper Max did not believe that whoever it was with him had any right to be here.

'We're not expecting anyone—are we?' Alfonso checked, glancing across at Romy.

'No.'

Alfonso crossed over to the monitor. 'Please tell her to go away. If she wishes to make contact with either of us, she can go through Father's office,' he said to Max before flicking the monitor off.

The screen faded into a grainy black. Probably just another journalist or photographer, Romy thought, as Alfonso flicked the remote. There'd not been a week since their honeymoon when they'd not been hounded by one tabloid hack or another.

But Villa Gasperi felt safe. It ought to, with the amount of security here—there were alarms and locks everywhere. That was because it was home to the renowned Scolari art collection. In the dining room alone there was a Titian and a priceless Da Vinci sketch. Its wine cellar wasn't bad either, she reflected, watching as Nico poured himself another full glass of Roberto's best Pinot.

Romy smiled as Alfonso started singing along with the song, sidling up behind her and dancing. She laughed, but then the intercom monitor flickered back into life.

'What now?' Alfonso said, irritated. He paused the music again and went to the monitor. Romy dried her hands on a tea towel and joined him.

'She's refusing to leave,' Max apologized. 'She wants me to tell you—to tell Mrs Scolari—that her name is Claudia Baumann. And that she knew Mrs Scolari many years ago, in Schwedt, when they were both still girls.'

Claudia. Schwedt . . . Even through the guard's mangled pronunciation, the word reached out and scraped like a talon across Romy's skin. The room seemed to sway before her eyes for a moment, as if she might faint. She steadied herself against the long wooden kitchen table—a table she'd spent Christmas at with Alfonso's noisy, chattering family.

Claudia. It could not be possible. Claudia was dead.

The dogs. The dogs had been there . . .

'What is it? Nico asked.

The shock must have shown in her face. She balled her hands into fists. She tried to speak, but no words came to her. She tried to think, but all she kept seeing were Ulrich's dogs in the woods; all she kept hearing were their snarls.

'Romy?' a voice broke through. 'Romy?' More

317

urgently now.

It was Alfonso. He was walking towards her now.

'Romy? Is this woman telling the truth? Do you know her? Do you want her to come in?'

* * *

It was past midnight. Romy took one last look at Claudia lying there asleep in the guest bedroom. She wore her hair severely short these days, shaved at the back. She looked so much older than she should.

It didn't seem possible that she was really here, really alive. Romy shivered, again thinking back to those dark, snowbound woods on that night, so many years ago, when they'd made their desperate bid for escape. She remembered red on white, blood on snow. Ulrich's dog had sunk its teeth into Claudia flesh. It had shaken her by the throat.

Ulrich's dogs. The ones that he'd fed on live rats.

I would have helped. I would have stayed and helped, if I'd thought you'd stood even a chance. If I'd not thought you were already as good as dead...

She stared at the familiar curve of Claudia's cheekbone, guilt welling up inside her as she turned and sighed in her sleep, the scar on her neck a livid red. One by one the other girls' names started coming back to Romy, their scared and tiny faces passing through her mind in a phantom parade. She pictured the photos she'd found in Lemcke's desk. What had become of them all, those lost girls? As Claudia was now, Romy prayed they'd one day been found.

318

'Let her sleep.'

It was Alfonso. He gently put an arm around Romy's waist and drew her back, before quietly closing the bedroom door.

'I'm sorry,' she whispered in the twilight of the corridor.

Sorry—the word wasn't enough. No matter how many times she said it to him, it could never undo all the lies she'd told.

'You've done nothing wrong,' was all that Alfonso said now. Her husband. This man she loved with all her being. Could he really just forgive her? Could it really be as simple as that?

He was leading her now by the hand down the long, winding corridor to their bedroom, passing Nico's room, from which the rumble of drunken snores could already be heard.

More guilt, more regrets, swelled up in Romy's chest. If anything, it was Nico rather than Alfonso who'd been the more hurt and confused by Claudia's arrival and the secrets from her past that had begun to spill out.

She'd read it in his eyes. What kind of friend lies to you from the first day they meet you? What kind of sick person does that? Why hadn't Romy respected him enough to tell him the truth?

She saw Nico thinking all of these things as she'd stood and admitted everything to him and Alfonso. There'd been no tears. Just bald statements: words falling like bricks from her mouth. Walling herself in. Cutting herself off. She'd told them about the orphanage. About how she'd caught Fox and the other boys raping Claudia. About how she'd attacked them—how she'd stabbed Fox—and had got Claudia out.

319

She'd told Alfonso and Nico all this in the time it had taken for Claudia to be escorted up the long gravel driveway to the house.

'I don't expect you to forgive me,' she'd told Alfonso when she'd finished, unable to look him in the eyes. 'But, please, let Claudia stay. If she needs to.'

He'd lifted her chin so that he could see her face. 'I don't care what you've done' was all he'd said. 'We agreed. Whatever happened before we met—it doesn't matter. I love you. That's all there is to it. And if this girl needs your help now, then I will help her too.'

Romy had hated herself then. Perhaps more than she'd ever hated herself in her life. Why hadn't she trusted him right from the start? Why hadn't she told Alfonso who she really was? Because she'd been afraid he'd judge her? That he'd find her wanting? That he'd throw her out? She was a fool. He'd always believed in her. So much more than she'd believed in him.

She'd vowed it then: she'd never keep a secret from him again. Everything she was, she'd give to him. There would be no more lies.

And then there'd been the door buzzer and Max had been there, a stick-thin blonde woman standing dwarfed by him.

Claudia.

The sight of her took Romy's breath away.

'It's OK,' Alfonso had told Max, taking charge of the situation. Then he'd welcomed Claudia in as if he'd been expecting her.

Romy stared at the girl who'd once been like a sister. But that innocent beauty had long gone. Mascara had smeared down Claudia's gaunt face,

320

her cheekbones pushing against the pockmarked skin there like two razor blades about to tear through a crumpled paper bag. Romy hadn't needed to see the track-marks on her forearms to know that they'd be there. She'd recognized the haunted look in her eye, had seen it plenty of times before, and not just on those poor London hookers she'd met when she'd escaped to the West, but on models too—girls with more money than sense, whose lives had slipped out of control.

Claudia had been clutching a magazine. In German. It had been folded open on two worn, once-glossy pages, showing Romy and Alfonso's wedding day. And there at the bottom—Claudia had pointed to it—had been this address, the Scolari family home where Romy and Alfonso were correctly rumoured to be holed up now.

'I knew it was you,' Claudia had said. 'I saw you in the magazine and I couldn't stop staring at you. You're so beautiful. My Romy . . .'

She'd stepped towards Romy then, her trembling hand extending as if Romy might not be real.

'You have no idea,' Claudia had said, her eyes pooling with tears, her voice cracking. 'I've searched for you for so long. It feels like I've been searching for you my whole life.'

Romy had swallowed down her own tears then, and as Claudia's hand had reached her arm, her touch had been like a feather.

'I can't believe I've made it here. I hitched the whole way, but I just wanted to see you one last time. Just to make sure you were OK.' Claudia's familiar eyes had filled Romy's vision. 'And to tell you that—to tell you that I escaped too.'

'You're alive. I thought . . . I thought . . .' A sob had burst from Romy. Then she'd reached out and pulled Claudia into her arms, not caring about the sour smell coming from her. Not caring about her thin, scrawny, tattoo-covered body. Only caring that she was living and breathing.

'I don't want to cause you any trouble,' Claudia had apologized eventually, pulling away. She'd glanced at Alfonso, as if suddenly becoming aware of her opulent surroundings and her own condition.

'It's OK,' Alfonso had reassured her, touching her bony arm.

'I'm sorry for coming to your home, Romy. I don't want anything from you. Really I don't. But maybe you could help me . . . just for tonight.'

She'd weakened then, and Nico and Alfonso had caught her and taken her to the couch. And as Romy had seen how desperately frail Claudia was, she'd realized that this was truly her second chance.

'Of course I'll help you,' she'd whispered to Claudia, smoothing her hair away from her face. 'And I will never let you down again. I'll give you a new life, a better life than you could ever imagine, to make up for the one those bastards at the orphanage took away.'

Now, hours later, after Romy had let Claudia bathe and had dressed her in clean pyjamas and Nico had tried out his pasta sauce on her, she was sleeping like a baby, but Romy still took one last glance along the corridor as she reached her bedroom door with Alfonso.

'Do you think she'll be OK?' Romy asked Alfonso.

'She'll be fine. She says she's clean. I think the worst of the withdrawal is over. She's one brave girl.'

Romy shuddered, thinking of Claudia's harrowing tales of life on the street in Hamburg. She knew all too well that the same situation could well have happened to her.

'She can stay for as long as you like,' Alfonso said gently. 'And when we go, you can bring her with us too. I will not mind.'

She nodded, feeling a sudden spurt of hope, as Alfonso closed their bedroom door behind them. The new racing season began in less than two weeks. For the next three months Alfonso would be moving from country to country with his team. Romy would travel with him, of course, but having a companion to spend time with whilst he was working would be no bad thing.

But what about Claudia? Is that something she might want too? Romy hoped so. She wanted to make it all up to her. Every second that had passed since she'd left her there in the woods. All the good fortune Romy had come into since, she wanted to share it with Claudia now. Poor, weak Claudia. Romy was determined to make her strong and healthy, probably for the first time in her whole life. That sweet little girl Claudia had once been—well, she was still there, Romy just knew it.

She undressed in silence, then slipped under the cool cotton duvet next to Alfonso. Her skin felt cold, as if she were made of stone. But then he reached out to her, taking her hand, entwining his fingers round hers.

'It's OK,' he told her in the dark. 'I know you've had a shock.'

Romy swallowed down more tears. 'I've been holding in this secret all of my life,' she said, feeling tears slide down her cheeks. 'But now Claudia is here and . . . well, I'm free of it, but I feel . . . I feel . . .' she tried, unable to put into words how she felt. 'I'm sorry.'

Alfonso took her in his arms, soothing her. 'Shhh. Stop saying that. You're a good person, Romy,' he whispered. 'I've always known that about you. In my heart.'

'But you don't understand. Fox, that boy—I killed him.'

'In self-defence. You had no choice. Romy you were a *child*,' Alfonso said. 'We can work all this out, OK? We can make sense of it in the morning.'

Alfonso kissed her neck and she wrapped herself around him. She felt his life, his strength, pouring into her. So long as he was here, so long as he was holding her, she knew that she could never, ever truly fall.

* * *

She woke to the sound of shouting. And something else: a noise. A sound that had invaded her dream and jerked her, heart pounding, wide awake into the cool night air.

Alfonso was sitting up beside her. Whatever it was that had woken her, he'd clearly heard it too. He snapped on the bedside lamp. Light stretched across the bedroom. Shadows reached out from the wardrobes and walls.

Romy could hear her breath coming in short, fast gasps. 'What is it? Did you hear something?' she said.

324

A shout. Distant. Muffled. Then another. It was coming from downstairs.

'Call the police,' Alfonso said.

'But—' Romy was terrified.

Alfonso was already on his feet, grabbing his jeans from the back of the chair. He stumbled for the door, pulling them on as he went, nearly falling as he did so.

Then he was gone. Out into the corridor, bouncing off the wall. Running in his bare feet.

Romy picked up the phone receiver from the bedside table and started to dial. But nothing happened. All she heard was a tinny crackling sound on the line. She grabbed her jacket and trousers, frantically searching through her pockets as she heard someone—a man . . . Alfonso?—shouting downstairs. But her mobile phone wasn't here. It was downstairs, she remembered then . . . it was downstairs in the kitchen with . . .

Claudia? Max? Nico? There was no one else here.

More shouting. Then nothing. Only the tick of the clock.

Romy dressed in a frenzy, tearing buttons and ripping a sleeve as she pulled her shirt over her head. She ran for the door and then stopped, holding it ajar, listening for a second, but hearing only silence in reply.

She walked out into the corridor. Where had Alfonso gone? Why was the house so quiet?

Then a figure stepped out of the shadows, making her jump.

It was Claudia. For a moment Romy felt a surge of relief that she was safe. Then she saw that Claudia was fully dressed in Romy's clothes, in her

325

jeans and jumper and loafers. Gone was the ravaged, weak look of earlier. With her hair pinned back in a clip, she looked business-like and aloof.

Then something glinted in the moonlight and, in the time it took Romy to realize that Claudia was holding one of the sharp knives from the block in the kitchen, Claudia had stepped to wards her and was pressing the tip of it against Romy's throat.

'Get downstairs, bitch,' she said. Her voice was cold and heartless. 'There's another old friend dying to see you,' she added, jabbing the knife tip in harder to make Romy start walking.

CHAPTER TWENTY-THREE

SEPTEMBER 2001

She was nearly there, Thea thought, straining to see through the crowds to the block of shops ahead, but at this hour the sidewalk was busy. She looked at all the people filling up the tables at the sidewalk cafés—couples and friends meeting after work in this trendy Manhattan neighbourhood.

When was the last time she'd come somewhere like this and just hung out at a bar? Thea wondered. Or gone to a restaurant with a friend? Or even, as her assistant Sarah had suggested, gone out on a date? There'd been that one guy last year—Alan someone (she couldn't even remember his full name). And he'd been nice enough, she supposed. Only the whole time she'd been with him, all she'd actually been thinking about was work. She'd become like her father in that respect,

326

she guessed.

But so what if Maddox Inc. meant everything to her now? Should that really come as a surprise? Wasn't it in her blood? And so what if she got lonely from time to time? she thought dismissively, telling herself at the same time to buck up. Wasn't that just the price one paid for being successful? So what if these people had more fun than her? To get where she was she'd had to use every second she'd been given. She'd had no time to waste.

She dropped a dime into a street performer's hat as she passed the subway entrance. His face was painted silver, along with his tailcoat, shirt and trousers. He suddenly, robotically, switched his position and winked.

'Good luck, lady,' he called after her.

It's got nothing to do with luck, Thea told herself. Her life, her career—everything she was—it was to do with strategizing. It was to do with competing just as hard as you could. All the time. Especially when faced with someone like Brett. It was to do with not being cheated out of your birthright. No matter what the personal cost.

Thea sucked in the smell of the hot New York air, the tang of the subway ventilation shaft mixing with the sweet odour coming from the cupcake café on the corner. She puffed out her chest and filled up her lungs. This city, she might not live so much in it as above it, but she still loved it nonetheless and was determined one day to make it hers.

Two rollerbladers slalomed past, almost crashing into a couple of thirty-something women who'd just stepped out onto the sidewalk from a bookstore, both clutching brand-new matching

327

hardbacks in their hands, and Thea smiled, glad she hadn't missed the signing.

After meeting Johnny last year, Thea had tried to find Shelley Lawson's home number in her old school diaries, but she and Duke had moved from their Cotswold house. So she'd got in touch with Shelley's publisher, who'd been kind enough to give her details of Shelley's book tour, starting with two days here in New York. Thea had cancelled three meetings today to make sure she got to this signing at the small, prestigious bookstore, rather than the new Borders store uptown. She joined the back of the line of people waiting.

Shelley Lawson was sitting behind a desk stacked high with copies of her latest novel. She was wearing a white linen suit, with her hair perfectly coiffed and her make-up smooth and professionally done. She looked totally different from the bustling English-countryside mom that Thea remembered. Thea wasn't the only one who'd become successful in the intervening years.

Shelley didn't see Thea until she was right in front of her and presenting her with a book to sign.

'My God,' she said. 'Thea . . .' But then the smile of recognition fell from her face. 'How nice to see you,' she continued, her voice much more formal and stilted now.

Tom—she was thinking about Tom, Thea guessed. She was remembering how Thea had dumped him and walked out of his life, without so much as a word of explanation as to why. And maybe she was thinking about Bridget too, and how Thea had let her best friend down. How she'd caused a rift between Shelley's children. Thea had no idea whether that rift had healed in her absence

328

from their lives or not. She hoped it had, but looking at Shelley now, it was clear it was still fresh in her mind.

'Can we talk?' Thea asked. 'I'd like to have a few minutes of your time, if I could.'

As she scribbled her name without any accompanying personal message on the title page of the book Thea had handed her, Shelley peeked behind her at the last few remaining people in the queue, and then over at her publicist.

'OK,' she said, pushing the signed copy back at Thea. 'Give me a few more minutes until I'm finished off here. But I haven't got long,' she glanced at her watch. 'Half an hour, then I'm due at a dinner.'

*   *   *

It was only two blocks to Thea's home, but even so she had a cab waiting when Shelley was ready. As they set off into the traffic, Shelley sat with her back straight as they made polite small-talk about the weather.

They drew up outside the stoop of Thea's brownstone a few moments later. Two perfectly manicured box trees stood on either side of the shiny black door. Splashes of red geraniums contrasted against the window ledges' cast-iron bars.

Sandy, Thea's trusted housekeeper, was just leaving, locking up the door. 'I picked up the dry-cleaning, like you asked, Thea,' she said. 'Supper is in the fridge.'

Thea thanked her and opened the front door.

'I would have thought you'd be living in Maddox

329

Tower. I hear the penthouse apartments are the most exclusive in the city,' Shelley said.

Meaning you have been keeping an eye on what's going on in my life, Thea thought, realizing that she really was going to have her work cut out to get Shelley to open up to her in any way.

'If I lived there too I don't think I'd ever leave my desk at all,' Thea said, leading her inside.

'You're not married then,' Shelley said, stepping into the neat hallway and looking round. It was a statement, not a question.

'No,' Thea said.

Thea had bought this house last year and had used the very top New York design firm to refurbish it completely. She watched Shelley look around the gunmetal-grey and white-striped walls of the hallway and at the swooping slate staircase.

'Minimalist,' Shelley said, but the way Thea heard it, it sounded like an insult, as if she were talking about Thea's life.

Thea let it pass, hoping Shelley might feel more inclined to talk after letting off some steam and needing to keep her on-side. She led her towards the back of the property and into the brightly lit kitchen, where she opened the huge steel fridge and took out one of the bottles of Sauvignon that she imported monthly from the Leveaux estate in South Africa.

She was glad that Sandy had gone home and they were alone, but even so, as Thea met Shelley's cool glance, she felt her nerves rising—not because she was in any way intimidated by Shelley, but because of what she was planning to discuss. She poured two glasses and handed one over.

'To old acquaintances,' Shelley said, raising her

330

glass. Thea could feel the tension radiating from her.

Thea raised her glass, determined to stay in control, but she didn't repeat Shelley's toast. She thought back to those magical holidays in Italy and how close she'd felt to Shelley and to all her family. How much she'd wanted her to be her surrogate mother. But, yes: *old acquaintances*—that was a fair description of what they were now.

'You've done very well for yourself. And you have a beautiful home,' Shelley said, following Thea through the far kitchen doorway and into the smart drawing room beyond.

Thea thought of Shelley's old home, that cosy, chaotic kitchen and how much she had fallen in love with it the first time she'd gone there with Bridget. The memory seemed so homely compared to Thea's own immaculate living space, where even the magazines on the table had been placed just so. Her own picture was on the cover of last month's *Time* magazine, just visible beneath this month's *Vogue*.

'So . . . I guess you want to know about Bridget and Tom?' Shelley traced her finger along the back of the candy-striped silk sofa.

'No. Actually I don't,' Thea said. 'I mean, I do hope they're both very happy. And I'm sure they are?'

'Yes.'

'But please,' Thea said, pointing to the sofa. 'There's something else entirely that I've brought you here to discuss.'

For the first time since they'd got here Shelley's self-assurance seemed to waver. But she did what she was asked and sat down.

'So what do you think of the wine?' Thea asked.

Shelley looked confused, but she took a sip. 'Very nice,' she said.

'I import it from an estate in South Africa,' Thea said. 'There's a famous stud-farm there too.' She locked her eyes on Shelley. 'It's where Johnny Faraday works.'

Something in Shelley's face altered. She looked away.

'So imagine my shock when I went to visit and Johnny told me about my mother's baby. Or how I felt when I realized that the scene you wrote in your book, *Sons and Daughters*, was true.'

Shelley pressed her lips together, then she closed her eyes. She slowly put her wine down on the glass-topped table in front of her. Thea held onto the edge of the high white marble mantel above the fireplace.

'But what I don't understand,' Thea went on, 'is, after my mother died, how could you have known that I had a sister and not have told me? When you knew how lonely I was. When you knew how much I missed Mom.'

She was trying to keep the anger from her voice, but her words had become sharp with it all the same. *Deceit.* This woman—this woman she'd thought of as a friend, whose son she might even, under different circumstances, have married—had kept the truth from her over something as important as this.

'It wasn't my place,' Shelley said quietly. 'It happened years ago, and I kept my promise to your mother to keep it a secret—'

'But you were there when she had my sister?'

Sister.

332

Shelley seemed to recoil from the word. She seemed to deflate right there in front of Thea. Then, slowly, she started to talk.

Her shoulders sagged further and further as she unburdened herself of her past. She described how the schoolfriend she'd most idolized, Alyssa McAdams, had come to her and begged her for help.

She'd been eight months pregnant—a fact Shelley had been astonished to discover as Lis had gone to huge lengths to conceal her condition.

She could have got rid of the baby before, she had known. But Lis had put it off and off until it had been too late. She'd been terrified that her parents would throw her out if they found out. She knew that they believed that having a child outside wedlock was a sin and a social disgrace. She'd been terrified too of what they might do to Johnny.

Shelley had comforted her friend. And then she'd got practical. Shelley's father, a doctor, had been running a local country medical practice at the time, so she'd told Alyssa that perhaps the best thing to do would be to go and talk to them, now that she was almost due, and ask them if she could have the baby at their house. Her father would know what to do. He'd either be able to talk to Alyssa's parents himself or arrange an adoption.

Alyssa had agreed and they'd left boarding school one afternoon and caught the train together to Shelley's parents. Their hope had been that Shelley's father would then call the school, making up an excuse for their sudden absence. But by the time the taxi had got them to Shelley's house, Alyssa had already gone into labour. Worse, Shelley's parents—Shelley had totally, *stupidly*, she

333

now said, forgotten—had gone away on holiday.

So together Shelley and Lis had battled through the whole terrifying ordeal of childbirth alone.

The baby and Alyssa had slept for ages afterwards, but then when Lis had woken up, she'd lain in bed and stared in silence at the bedroom wall, leaving Shelley to cope with the infant and feed her with powdered milk.

But the next day—the day Shelley's parents were coming home—Alyssa was up at dawn, her bags packed. She still wouldn't look at the baby. She'd said she couldn't help it, that keeping it would only make everything even worse. She'd told Shelley to lie to her parents and tell them that the baby had been left anonymously here at their home.

'She was such a sweet little thing,' Shelley said. 'When my parents came back that evening, they were horrified that a baby had been left on the doorstep. I lied to explain the fact I was there, by saying that Alyssa and I had run away from school because we'd been worried about our exams, but Alyssa had gone back now. And that much was true. She'd gone back and got on with her life. I'd find that out later. She'd shut it all out, as if it had never happened, as if that baby had never really been hers at all.'

'I got sent back to school while my mother looked after the baby. My father trawled the countryside looking for the baby's mother. A week later a lady from the adoption agency came round. She took the baby away.'

The baby, Thea thought. *My half-sister. Taken away.*

Those few words seemed so big to Thea. So

334

solid. Such a huge wrong, which she knew instinctively that she must right.

'After she went to America, your mother wrote to me. Only twice,' Shelley said. 'She'd got engaged to Griffin Maddox. Her family were over the moon about the match, but Lis had regrets.'

'She must have missed England. And Johnny.'

Shelley nodded. 'Yes.' She looked uncertain. 'But what had happened between her and Johnny—everything that had happened with the baby—it finished whatever chance she and Johnny had ever had.' Shelley smiled tentatively. 'And she did love your father, Thea. You need to know that. He came into her life at the right time. Together they moved on.'

But how far? Thea wondered, thinking of Johnny, always there, always near. Had her mother ever really truly belonged to her father at all?

'Did my father know?'

'When she had you, the doctors would have known that she'd had a baby previously. She might have told him she'd had a baby. But I doubt she'd ever have told him the father's name. Griffin Maddox—*your* father—I can't imagine a man like him would ever have let Johnny be near her, if he'd known that.' Shelley sighed. 'And that's it. That's all there is. You know it all now.'

'Did she ever mention the baby—my half-sister—to you?'

'No. She cut me out of her life after that.'

There was a small silence. Shelley took a sip of wine and sighed. Then she looked at her watch. Thea sensed that she wanted to leave now that she'd unburdened herself.

She stood up.

'I want to find her,' Thea said.

Shelley looked up at her, surprised.

'Don't you want to know what happened to her? To the baby?' Thea asked.

'Of course I do. But, Thea, it was a long time ago. She's probably living an ordinary life somewhere.'

'But what if she's not? What if she needs help?'

Shelley exhaled, clearly torn.

'Will you help me? The adoption agency in England. They must have records. Your mother must have known where the baby went.'

Shelley looked uncomfortable. 'I can try,' she said, unconvincingly.

'Would you?' Thea asked, her eyes searching out Shelley's. 'Please?'

Suddenly she felt overwhelmingly emotional. It had been so long since she'd asked anyone for anything. She swallowed back tears. 'It's just that finding her . . . my sister . . . would mean a great deal to me. A great deal.'

She saw Shelley soften. 'OK, I'll try and do what I can. But I want to know something too, since we seem to be getting everything off our chests.'

'What?'

She paused for a moment, then obviously decided to come right out with it. 'Thea, why did you break Tom's heart? Why did you just end it like you did? He suffered.'

Tom. Thea felt goosebumps rush up her spine, remembering how much she'd loved him.

He suffered.

Thea imagined Tom sitting at that long kitchen table being comforted by his parents, and the pain felt as raw as it had done when she was twenty-one.

But she'd never tell Shelley Lawson the truth. Never tell anyone about what Brett had done. Or the baby she'd aborted afterwards. Thea cleared her throat and stared down at her hands.

'I had a change of heart,' she said instead. 'And I know, I dealt with it badly. But I decided I had to move on.'

'Move on?' Shelley looked aghast, clearly shocked by the casualness of the phrase and its dishonesty. 'He really loved you.'

'I know. And I'm sorry I hurt him, Shelley,' Thea said, forcing herself to keep her voice level, 'but that's just the way that it was.' Thea wanted this interrogation over with. Tom—what a mess, what a terrible bloody mess, she'd made of it all. 'I'm sorry, but it was never meant to be.'

Shelley slowly shook her head. 'I remember you two together, right from the start. I remember the look in your eyes whenever you saw him. And you're telling me you never really cared?'

'It's the truth,' Thea said, starting to lose her cool now, feeling sweat break out across her brow. 'And anyway,' she said, defensively, 'Bridget wasn't exactly thrilled about it. It was probably best it ended.'

Shelley sighed heavily. 'Bridget was jealous because she loved you too.'

Bridget's behaviour had been so hurtful at the time that Thea couldn't help pulling a face, but Shelley's gaze was earnest and honest.

'She's come out, you know. She's living with her partner in London.'

Thea felt her cheeks reddening. She had never guessed Bridget had felt *that* way about her, but now it all started to make sense . . .

337

But she had no time to ponder on the magnitude of her own insensitivity, for Shelley was still talking.

'Obviously Duke and I are happy that she's happy, but I feel sad that grandchildren are not on the agenda.'

'You mean Tom . . .' Thea blurted, before she could help herself. Then she stopped. It was none of her business.

'No,' Shelley said resolutely. 'Tom is still single. He's here in Manhattan. A partner in his law firm already. He's very focused. Driven.' She reached into her handbag and pulled out a business card, then handed it to Thea. 'You should look him up,' she said. 'Tell him what you told me . . . if you really mean it. I don't know about you, but I think some closure would be very good for Tom. Young people like you two deserve to move on and to love again.' Shelley stared deep into Thea's eyes. 'Secrets are never the answer, you know. Your mother taught me that.'

Thea couldn't meet her eye as they walked together to her front door. She kissed Shelley on the cheek.

'I'll be in touch,' Thea said, reminding Shelley of her promise to help find her lost sister.

Shelley nodded, then looked pointedly at the card in Thea's hand. And Thea realized then that, without saying it, Shelley had made it clear that contacting Tom was a condition of her offer.

After an awkward goodbye Thea stood with her back to the closed front door and stared at the business card, thinking of everything Shelley had told her. About Bridget and Tom.

Tom. Wonderful, kind, gorgeous Tom.

338

So he'd qualified as a lawyer on her advice, she thought, memories of those blissful days in Oxford washing over her, when they'd both been so young and full of ambition.

Had he really never got over her, either? Was he—as Shelley had implied—just as much of a lonely workaholic as she was?

And he was here in Manhattan. Just a few blocks away.

Closure. Shelley had made it sound so simple. But maybe now she was an adult, she could make that bit of her life right. Especially if Tom was still suffering. Because of her.

Of course she wouldn't tell him the truth. She could never do that. But Shelley was right. He deserved to love again.

Her heart was pounding as Thea picked up the phone in her hall and dialled the number on the card, before she gave herself time to think.

'Could I make an appointment to see Tom Lawson?' she asked the secretary who answered.

'May I ask what it's regarding?'

'It's a professional matter. About one of his cases,' Thea lied. She wasn't sure what she could possibly achieve by such a meeting. She only knew that it felt miraculous to take a step like this into the unknown.

'Well—er, let's see.' Thea could hear the secretary turning over a page of a diary. 'He does have a cancellation. He could see you tomorrow morning at ten. Would that be convenient?'

'Yes, sure,' Thea said, trying to imagine what it would be like to walk into his office. To see his face . . .

'May I have your name?'

'Thea Maddox.'

The secretary obviously knew who she was. 'Oh . . . oh, Miss Maddox,' she simpered, keen to do her job well. 'Well, I'm not sure if you've been here before, but Mr Lawson's office is on the thirty-first floor of the South Tower. So we'll see you tomorrow, that's the eleventh of September at ten a.m.'

'I'll be there,' Thea said.

CHAPTER TWENTY-FOUR

SEPTEMBER 2001

Romy squeezed her eyes shut, jolting as the smashing continued below them. She tried her wrists again, but they were bound tight behind the chair, as they had been for the last hour. She felt the cut along her cheekbone congealing with blood. But she couldn't be a coward. She wouldn't shut her eyes, block this out. Not when it was her fault. Her heart hammered in her chest as her eyes snapped open and locked with Alfonso's.

He was sitting red-faced and trembling in a chair facing Romy, with a gun being pressed to the back of his head by a tall, thin boy with a shaven head and eyes wide with amphetamines, who couldn't have been more than fifteen. The same kid—Claudia's accomplice—who'd beaten Romy and tied her up too. Was he the old friend Claudia had referred to? Surely not. He was too young to be from her orphanage days.

Alfonso's eyes blazed with fury as the smashing

340

continued below them in the cellar. Row after row of the wines his father had collected over the years being systematically smashed with a baseball bat. His gaze didn't waver from hers, but she could tell he was feeling each blow, as if the bat were hitting him personally.

I'm sorry. I'm so sorry, she thought, beaming her heartbreak at him. And her terror.

In her peripheral vision she saw Max's body on the floor, fists tight like a felled boxer, as if even in death he was attempting to fight on. An obscene comma of blood had pooled beside his head on the white kitchen tiles.

On the other side of the kitchen Claudia stood, picking her nails with a kitchen knife. Beside her, crumpled in a heap by the white cooker doors, was Nico. There was blood on his face, but his chest was heaving, so he was still breathing, but his eyes were closed. Next to him was a bloodied poker, taken from the fireplace, with which he must have been beaten.

How many more of Claudia's accomplices were there in the house? More than three, Romy worked out. They'd been ransacking all the paintings, ripping them down from the walls, for the last hour or more. With nobody to raise the alarm, they were leaving no corner of Alfonso's family home unharmed.

Now she flinched as footsteps came towards the kitchen. Claudia stood to attention. She didn't look at Romy.

A dark, bulky figure stepped through the doorway into the light. He had a pistol in his hand. But it wasn't the weapon Romy's eyes now locked onto in terror. It was the man's face. Those eyes she knew so well—eyes she'd never been able to forget; eyes she'd somehow always known she'd see again one day. The eyes she'd been dreading that Claudia had meant when she'd said there was an old friend to see her.

The years slithered from her as she stared up at Ulrich Hubner. Suddenly Romy was a child again, back in the orphanage—a nothing, a nobody, and his to command.

'Hello again,' he snarled at her.

He nodded to the boy, who walked over and clipped the plastic ties binding Romy's wrists with some pliers. The blood rushed into her hands as Ulrich came over to her and pushed her off the chair. 'Now get on your knees, bitch,' Ulrich said, gripping Romy by the neck and forcing her down.

She strained to look up. She saw the boy with the pistol run his tongue across his lips, staring down at Romy. Excitement danced in his eyes. 'Tell her to strip,' he said, in German. 'Make her take off her clothes. Whore,' he added with a grin, in Italian, walking back and pressing the pistol even harder against Alfonso's head.

'I'll kill you,' Alfonso said.

The boy cracked him hard across the top of the head with the butt of the pistol. Alfonso's head slumped sideways and Romy screamed. For a sickening moment she thought he was dead. But then he slowly lifted his head once more, squeezing his eyes shut and gritting his teeth in pain. A trickle of blood ran down his forehead and splashed from his chin onto his bare chest.

An explosion of pain. Ulrich gripped Romy's hair and twisted her head round so that she was looking at him. 'First I want to know which of the paintings they keep here are real. All of them? Or only some?'

'Leave her alone,' Alfonso pleaded.

A dull thud. Alfonso groaned in pain.

'I said fucking shut up,' the boy screamed. 'You think I won't kill you? I will. I can't wait to kill you all.'

'Calm down,' another voice snapped. 'You'll get your turn.'

Claudia sounded totally in control as she moved to stand beside Ulrich, draping one arm across his broad shoulders. Gone was the helpless waif who'd stumbled gratefully into Romy's arms earlier that evening. This Claudia had the cockiness of a street-corner whore with her pimp by her side. She had nothing but triumph and contempt in her eyes.

'How could you?' Romy said, her voice paper-thin, a whisper. Even now she could see the scars at Claudia's throat. 'After what he did . . .'

'After what he did?' Claudia's voice rose in indignation. 'You were the one who left me there to die.'

'No, I . . .' But Romy's words dried up. Because it was true, wasn't it? She had given up on Claudia. She might have killed one dog, but she hadn't stayed to fight off the other, or Ulrich. She'd left Claudia there. She'd left her all alone.

But she'd thought Claudia had wanted her to go. That her last words had been a selfless act. That she'd wanted Romy to go . . . to run.

How wrong she'd been.

'After the orphanage burnt down,' Claudia said, 'he took some of us with him. He gave us work. He took care of me, Romy. All that I am, I owe to him.'

343

Romy could imagine right away what kind of work that must have been. Ulrich was at least five stone heavier than when she'd last seen him. Most of his hair was gone, with what little remained now being back from his smooth, wide brow. There was a dead man on the floor. Another dying man in the corner. And yet Ulrich's eyes betrayed no emotion at all. He was a monster. But Claudia—she could no longer see that.

'The paintings,' Ulrich reminded her.

They'd come here to steal her new family's paintings. And then to watch that boy rape and kill her. To have their revenge. Of that Romy had no doubt.

Then, through her fury, another memory of Ulrich rose up in her mind. Of the bumbling guard she'd once run circles around. And a memory of herself as well: of the little girl who'd refused ever to give in to her fear, no matter how cruel he'd been.

She made her decision then. She was not going to give them the pleasure of watching her beg for her life. If she was to die here tonight, she would die well. She would make her husband proud. And she would not betray the Scolaris—the people who had taken her in. Who had loved her like one of their own.

Ulrich tightened his grip on her scalp once more, taking a pistol from his jacket pocket. He leant down towards her and opened his mouth to speak.

'Go fuck yourself,' she told him, spitting in his face as hard as she could.

He roared in shock and anger, then smashed her violently across the face with the back of his hand.

344

She toppled sideways, cracking her head on the tiles. He grabbed her hair again and hauled her upwards. Her vision swam. The room tilted sideways. Bile rose up fast inside her throat.

Then two things happened at once.

Alfonso reared up without warning, catching completely by surprise the boy standing behind him and smashing the top of his head into the boy's jaw, sending him sprawling backwards. How he'd undone the tie around his wrist Romy had no idea, but suddenly he was free.

At the same time Nico staggered to his feet with a roar. He hurled the poker, spinning it end over end across the room. Romy knew in an instant that in the past hour they'd somehow communicated in secret and had planned this coordinated attack.

Ulrich saw too late the poker coming in his direction. Its handle smacked into the side of his skull as he attempted to duck out of its way. His grip on Romy slackened. She tore herself free, ramming her elbow hard into his gut. Claudia made a grab for her, but Romy shoved her violently aside as Ulrich's pistol fell from his fist and skittered across the floor.

A blur of motion: Nico threw his bloodied body at Ulrich. Both men fell into a twisted heap of struggling limbs. Romy spun, disoriented, searching for Claudia. Instead her eyes fixed on Alfonso. He had hold of the boy now. She watched Alfonso hit him once, then again. The boy sank to the floor, no longer struggling. No longer moving at all.

Claudia . . . .

Romy turned to see Nico and Ulrich back on their feet, still fighting, Ulrich with his fists now

345

tight around Nico's bulging neck. Claudia was on her hands and knees, reaching for the pistol, which had slid under the kitchen table. Romy saw a pair of nail clippers beneath Alfonso's chair. He must have got them out of his jeans pocket and used them to cut the plastic ties.

Romy lurched towards the gun. Reaching, stretching, but there was no way she could reach Claudia before she got it. As Claudia snatched up the weapon, twisted and stood, Alfonso reached Romy as she stood up from beneath the table. He threw himself between her and Claudia, as Claudia shakily aimed the pistol at Romy and screamed out the word 'Die!'

A gunshot. A grunt of pain.

But Alfonso didn't move. It was Ulrich who'd been shot. In the shoulder. He roared in pain and swore at Claudia, as another gunshot rang out from her shaking gun.

This time Nico's body bucked. He lurched sideways, grasping at his chest. A flower of blood bloomed across the back of his white shirt. He crashed into Ulrich, taking him down towards the cooker. Then Claudia turned to Romy.

She was going to kill them all. One by one. Claudia was crazy.

'No!' Romy roared, tipping up the heavy table with all her might, sending it crashing into Claudia and jamming her against the wall. Then she was running, being dragged by Alfonso, past Max's body and the wheezing, rising form of the boy, who was trying to get to his feet.

Romy and Alfonso's footsteps rang out in the service corridor as they raced for its end. Romy heard the jangle of snatched keys as they hurtled past a coat-rack. Alfonso tore the back door open. They burst out into the cold night air, nearly running straight into a black BMW, which had not been parked there before.

Beyond the gnarled silhouette of the ancient olive tree at the centre of the turning circle—a tree that Alfonso had told Romy had been there since Roman times—a classic white Mercedes convertible was parked. They reached it in less than ten strides.

He jerked open the door and pushed Romy inside. She scrabbled across the driver's seat and onto the passenger side. Across the courtyard, the back door of the villa swung violently open, casting a searchlight of bright light across the dark night.

Alfonso was already starting the engine.

'Keep down,' he barked at Romy, as she heard the first shot ring out.

It missed. With a screech of tyres, Alfonso pulled away. The engine screamed as he shifted up through the gears. Romy looked behind them. A set of headlights burst into life. Those of the black BMW.

A hundred yards up ahead were the villa's arched iron gates, the only way in or out. Past them, Romy knew, was safety. A city. Millions of other people—of witnesses. Get there, and surely Ulrich and the others would not dare to pursue them.

Fifty yards. Behind her Romy saw the BMW closing, Ulrich driving one-handed, Claudia next to him, leaning out of the window with the gun.

Alfonso stabbed a small black plastic box at the air before him. It was the remote for opening the gates. He repeatedly punched at its button, but the gates did not move.

'Put your belt on,' Alfonso yelled, struggling to do the same with his own.

He was planning on ramming through the gates. She braced herself for the impact.

Twenty yards.

Ten.

Just before the Mercedes smashed into the gates at sixty miles an hour Romy thought she heard a siren.

Then she heard and felt nothing. Her world turned black.

Her world turned dead.

PART THREE

PART THREE

CHAPTER TWENTY-FIVE

SEPTEMBER 2004

Thea had heard that the Landstuhl Regional Medical Center was the largest military hospital outside America, but it wasn't until she made her way from the car park to the pristine white reception block that she realized the sheer size of the place.

After her visit to South Africa in 2000 Thea had kept in touch with Johnny, and six months ago he'd written to her to say that he'd heard that Michael had been wounded in Afghanistan and had been sent back here to Landstuhl in Germany.

When she'd made enquiries, she'd found out that Michael had been caught up in a car bomb, which had killed scores of soldiers and civilians, and, even though he was relatively unscathed physically, he was suffering from Post-Traumatic Stress Disorder. She'd been advised not to visit for several months, and had chosen instead to write and send flowers on several occasions, although she hadn't ever received an acknowledgement that he'd got them.

But she hadn't minded. After 9/11 and that horrible day that had changed the world forever, Thea knew all about Post-Traumatic Stress Disorder. She knew Michael might still be experiencing any number of horrendous symptoms—from flashbacks to insomnia to uncontrolled rage.

She'd experienced it mildly herself for a year

after the Twin Towers came down. She'd needed tranquillizers to help her sleep. She couldn't help but focus on how close she'd come to tragedy, having almost made it to her appointment with Tom Lawson when the first aeroplane struck the tower. She'd seen the television pictures afterwards, but up close it hadn't been so clear. She only remembered the panic and the smoke and the dust.

She still had flashbacks, even now—those images seared on her brain. The sight of the tower with Tom Lawson in it, collapsing as he'd waited for her to arrive.

She'd sent her condolences to Shelley and Duke, but her card had seemed pathetic. After all what had she ever done but bring their son heartbreak? It was because of her that he was a lawyer, and because of her that he'd never found happiness. And she couldn't help feeling that it was because of her that he'd died. If she hadn't made that appointment to see him, who knew where else Tom Lawson might have been that day.

She felt that she had no right to grieve for him, when she hadn't seen him for nearly ten years, and yet in the aftermath of the Twin Towers privately Thea had broken apart.

So she understood perfectly that being involved in a car-bomb explosion might have affected Michael in ways she couldn't begin to imagine. But since Johnny's letter she'd thought of Michael so often, and now, on her latest trip to Germany, she had the perfect opportunity to see him.

She felt a shimmer of nerves as she stared up at the fluttering flags outside the hospital's main entrance. She steeled herself for the worst.

352

Young men in baggy hospital whites and Wayfarer sunglasses sat in small groups on the benches scattered amongst the flowerbeds, chatting in the sunshine, smoking cigarettes, some of them in wheelchairs, while others sat alone in silence.

Over to the right, between the rows of regimentally neat buildings, Thea glimpsed an exercise yard, where twenty or so soldiers were doing push-ups, egged on by an instructor with a loudhailer.

As she passed the chatting men on her way into the reception block, she heard one of them softly wolf-whistle. She'd assumed her grey Chanel suit with its short pencil-skirt was a sober enough outfit to wear, but she must look more sexy than she felt. She turned and saw the soldier smiling, a question in his eyes, and found herself thinking of Reicke and their formal goodbye this morning.

Once again he'd failed to say anything personal to her and, since their liaison, their relationship had become ever frostier. It annoyed her that the only thing he'd mentioned was how impressed he was by Brett, who'd just announced his controversial deal to buy out an Internet search engine. Brett had chosen the timing of his announcement, Thea was sure, to overshadow her achievements with Maddox in Germany.

Even more annoyingly, he'd chosen to use the publicity to crow about his new relationship with the actress Bethany Saunders. Their nauseating photo-shoot, which had been syndicated to magazines around the world, had made Thea's blood boil, especially because of the accompanying copy in which Bethany had simpered about Brett

353

being the most caring man in the universe. And
Reicke Schlinker had expected Thea to be
impressed! If only he knew.

She forced herself to put it out of her mind and
walked through the automatic doors to where
harassed-looking medical staff in green pyjamas
marched purposefully past her, pushing trolleys
and clutching clipboards to their chests. A
lingering smell of disinfectant permeated the air.
Air ducts hummed in the ceiling. Servicemen
limped on crutches along the corridors, and she
felt self-conscious as her high heels clattered on
the shiny white floor.

She asked for directions and soon she was
following an efficient-looking nurse through the
warren of corridors to Michael's wing. As they
passed a window overlooking the parade ground,
Thea's attention was snagged once more by the
men doing push-ups out there. Up close, she saw
that most of them were missing limbs. She thought
about the logo she'd seen on the way in: Selfless
Service. She felt ashamed right to her core.
Because when she'd seen those words it had
crossed her mind that she too gave selfless service
to Maddox Inc. But it was only watching the men
outside that she saw what a joke that was. Her
personal sacrifices for business were incomparable
to what these men had gone through.

The nurse stopped and smiled and pointed to a
glass-panelled door.

She said, 'You'll find Captain Pryor in there.'

*　　　*　　　*

As the nurse retreated back up the corridor, Thea

354

stepped up close to the door and peered through the soundproof glass. There Michael was, alone in a large, bright lounge, which had been furnished with sofas and armchairs and potted plastic plants.

A television mounted on the wall showed pictures of a press conference at the White House, no doubt more revelations about the weapons of mass destruction in Iraq and the dodgy evidence that had been uncovered. Whatever the so-called justification for the US invading Iraq last year, Thea—along with many others—had opposed the war, even though she had been so personally affected by 9/11.

But seeing Michael sitting on a stiff-backed chair by the window, gazing unblinkingly outside, she knew she wouldn't be able to share her anti-war politics with him. The rhetoric she dealt with on the international news desks controlled by Maddox Inc. suddenly seemed meaningless compared to the reality here.

As Thea put her hand on the door, she felt her palm sweating. She'd hoped today would be as joyful and happy a reunion as the one with Johnny had been, but she now understood with absolute certainty that this wouldn't be like that at all.

Michael turned slowly to face her, at the sound of the door swishing open. He gazed at her blankly. He had a deep scar running diagonally from just above his right eye across to his left cheek. Thea forced her smile not to waver, not wanting to betray her distress. 'Relatively unscathed physically' was what Johnny had told her. And by the standards around here, Thea thought, that was certainly true. Even so, Michael would clearly be scarred for life.

He'd grown a scruffy-looking beard that didn't suit him, she saw, perhaps in an attempt to conceal his injury, or perhaps, she worried, because he no longer cared about his appearance.

Even as she approached him from the other side of the room, she could see the grey steaks in his hair. It was this—how old he suddenly looked—that shocked her more than his scar, or the fact that he failed to acknowledge her arrival.

What had she expected? she wondered, still somehow managing to keep her smile tightly locked in place, putting her hand up in a pathetic wave as she reached him, before immediately regretting it and letting her arm flap uselessly back down by her side. Had she really thought Michael would be the same handsome sixteen-year-old of her dreams? Or that he'd smile at her now just as he'd smiled at her then? She saw now how foolish she'd been.

She murmured, 'Hello,' her confidence failing her now.

He said nothing. When she leant down to kiss him on the cheek—his right one; she was careful to avoid the scar on his left—he remained motionless. The skin her lips brushed against felt rough, almost brittle, like a newspaper that had been left out in the sun for too long.

Stepping back, she waited for him to speak. He stared past her, towards the door. A chill spread through her as she wondered whether he recognized her at all. She took a plastic chair, drew it up next to him and sat down.

'So how do I look, Thea?' he said.

Her breath caught in her throat. So he *did* remember her. He did know she was here.

She stared into his eyes as they locked on hers. His blank stare had vanished. But what, she wondered, had now taken its place? Certainly nothing friendly.

'Hideous?' he said. 'Disfigured?'

Thea felt her skin prickling as she recoiled at the bitterness of his tone. 'No . . .'

'Then what?'

Up close, she could see his bitten nails and the tired lines and heavy bags around his eyes. What did he want to hear? she thought. A lie? That he looked great? That he looked just as handsome as he always had? Michael was sick, not stupid. She decided to tell him the truth.

'You look exhausted,' she said. 'And angry.'

He stared down hard at the floor.

'They did tell you I was coming to visit you, didn't they?' Thea said. 'They did say I was coming today?' She felt terrible. If he hadn't wanted her here, then why hadn't he asked them to keep her away? The last thing she wanted was to upset him.

'Yes,' he said. 'They told me. They told me, but I didn't believe them.'

There was a roughness to his voice, but this time when he looked up into her eyes, she saw that the anger—the violence—was gone. Something else had replaced it, something warmer, gentler, something so familiar from so many years ago.

She felt her stomach contract as they held one another's gaze. A flare of hope rose up inside her. He was still here, the boy she'd once known. His hazel eyes were darker now, their yellow flecks having lost their sunshine. But he was still Michael. *Her* Michael.

'I didn't think I'd ever see you again,' he said.

'Apart from on the cover of *Forbes* . . . or *Vogue* . . .'

There was an awkward silence. But he was right, wasn't he? Their worlds really had grown that far apart.

Thea looked away, out through the window, at the leaves of a poplar tree shimmering in the breeze. She wondered how much Michael really knew about her, whether he'd read in the financial papers about her promotion to the board of Maddox Inc. Whether he'd seen any of those magazine articles speculating on her love-life—or lack of it. But most of all she wondered if he cared.

A thudding sound. The door burst open. Another patient staggered into the lounge shouting, clamping his hands over his ears, looking desperately behind him, back through the door, before curling up into a quivering, sobbing ball on the floor.

Thea stared in horror as two burly male orderlies rushed in and crouched down on either side of the man. One of them started trying to calm him, but the patient's only response was to start screaming the words 'Kill me' over and over. He twisted away, roaring, then froze. His eyes had locked on Thea. 'Sorry,' he whispered then, spittle stretching from his lip, before burying his face in his hands and starting to shake.

The orderlies gently lifted the man up under his armpits and led him back out of the room.

'Francis,' Michael explained, after they'd gone. 'Got hit by an IED, the same as me. They had to cut fragments of his best friend's skull out of his back. He was lucky to survive, but some days he thinks he never left there at all.'

Had Michael been like that six months ago?

358

Was that why she'd been told to keep away? *That poor man . . .* Thea didn't know what to say. All she could think about was how petty her life's traumas were compared with what the patients in here had gone through. It made her feel pathetic that she talked to her yoga trainer about how she longed for a proper relationship and how she had failed to get her work/life balance right, when the reality was that she was rich, successful and privileged. So much so that she wondered now whether she was brave enough to hear about the things that haunted Michael or the horrors he'd seen.

Not that she knew if he'd ever confide in her about any of that. Not that she knew what he might want from her, or how she might help. All she knew was that she'd do all she could.

'I'm sorry,' she mumbled.

'I don't know when they're going to let me out of here. Keeping me under observation, that's what they call it.' His expression darkened. 'They won't send me back out there, though,' he said. 'Not now. All that training, and I'm no longer wanted.' He smiled thinly. 'Story of my life, huh? People turning their backs on me and chucking me out, once they think I'm no longer any use . . .'

His words hit her like blows. It was as if they were right back where she'd last seen him—outside Little Elms with her father, saying a stiff, excruciating goodbye. It was just as Johnny had said: Michael thought of her, not as herself, but as Griffin Maddox's daughter after all. And he'd just been staff. Nothing more.

She should go, she supposed. But she couldn't bring herself to. She still needed . . . but *what* did she need? What had she come here for? she wondered. Forgiveness? For what her father had done? For the way he'd just let Michael and his mother and the rest of them go? Or for Michael to tell her that Johnny had been wrong? That their friendship *had* been real? And that somehow they could pick up where they'd left off—that some how they could still be friends.

Was that why she'd come here? Because she needed a friend? Because she still needed and wanted Michael, after all these years?

'I went to see Johnny,' she said, wanting Michael to know that she hadn't ever stopped caring about them, and that she still wanted them all in her life.

She opened her mouth to tell him all about the stud-farm and the vineyard and how well Johnny had looked, but stopped herself. Johnny's life in that beautiful place and Michael's here in this sterile limbo seemed too unbearable a contrast. She worried it would only upset him more.

Michael sighed wearily. 'Don't tell me you came all this way just to talk about Johnny?'

In part, Thea thought, *yes, I really did*. Because after seeing both Johnny and Shelley Lawson, she *did* want to tell Michael what she'd discovered— that Johnny and her mother had had a baby together, meaning that she now had a half-sister somewhere out there lost in the world. And she wanted to ask Michael if he'd ever known about Johnny and her mother. She wanted to *share* all this with him, because he was the only one who'd known them both. He was the only one she *could* now share it with.

But equally she now understood—with a great heaviness in her heart—that this wasn't the kind of

360

information you could ever discuss with a stranger. And that's what Michael had become.

She felt the memory of what he'd once been to her drifting away like smoke.

'I came here,' she said, 'because I wanted to tell you how sorry I was to hear about your mother . . .'

Michael looked down at his hands and Thea noticed them trembling. She had to force away the urge to lean forward and put her hands over his to still them.

'I'd like to help,' she told him. 'I mean, I'd like to offer to get her the best care possible—'

'We don't need your charity.' He practically spat out the words.

Indignation tore through her. 'It's not charity. Your mom practically brought me up,' she snapped. It had happened so long ago and yet, talking about it now, it felt as raw as it did back then. 'Do you think I didn't miss her when I was shipped off to boarding school? Do you really think I didn't care?'

She felt tears rising up and fought them down furiously. Why did she have to get emotional now? Michael was the one who needed support, yet here she was being weak.

'She wrote to you every week,' Michael said. 'You never replied.'

Thea stared at him, letting out a small gasp. 'I never got her letters,' she said, her mind racing over the fact that Storm must have thrown them away, or had simply not bothered to send them on. 'I had no idea where you were. Where either of you were. I was cut off, Michael. From everyone and everything I loved.'

She felt the colour blossoming in her cheeks,

361

but he looked away. He rubbed at his brow, confused.

'I'm sorry,' he said then, swallowing hard. 'I never knew. I never knew that at all.'

She did take his hand then. She clasped it between hers. She felt it trembling like a baby bird. She watched him close his eyes. His shoulders slumped.

'I can give you the name of the care-home she's in,' he said. 'It's not far from Little Elms. I'll be going there to see her as soon as they send me home.'

'And you'll let me help?'

He didn't answer. But why would he? she thought. He'd never ask for anything. That much about him, at least, hadn't changed one jot. He still had too much pride. And so what if he hadn't actually given her permission? Thea thought. He hadn't said no, either. And one thing she'd learnt as a businesswoman was this: not saying no was the same as saying yes.

She squeezed his hand tighter. In her mind the deal was now sealed.

A blonde-haired female soldier in dark-green fatigues pushed through the door and smiled at Michael.

'Hey, Mikey,' she said.

'Hey, yourself,' Michael replied, a sudden warmth in his voice. He sat up straighter in his chair. 'I hear you're shipping out,' he said.

Thea let go of Michael's hand. The woman— *strike that*, Thea thought, *she can't be much more than twenty-two*—had a Canadian accent. And was pretty with it.

Thea smiled, stepping aside and walking over to

362

the window as the girl came over to where Michael was sitting and started chatting about some mutual friend who'd just got hitched.

Thea watched them reflected in the glass. The girl liked Michael—that much was clear. She didn't stop smiling, not once. And Thea, much to her surprise, found herself smiling as well. Not at anything the two of them were saying. More because the girl kept glancing her way, clearly curious as to who she was, maybe even seeing her as some kind of competition. And for some reason Thea couldn't quite rationalize, that thought made her feel pretty good.

When the girl finally left a few minutes later, Thea went back to sit at Michael's side.

'She seemed nice,' she said.

'Yeah.'

'Attractive, too.'

'I suppose . . .'

Thea glimpsed it then, just a flicker, just a trace of the old smile he'd always given her whenever they'd been sharing a joke.

'So what *will* you do when you get home?' she asked.

'This and that. I have various leads. You don't have to start worrying about me, after all this time.'

'Well, that's the thing . . . I never stopped worrying about you, Michael.' She said it almost before thinking it.

Michael broke the awkward silence that followed.

'Thea,' he said. 'Thank you for coming. Would you let me have your number?'

She took one of her business cards out of her Gucci bag and handed it to him. He looked at it for a moment as if memorizing it, or not quite believing it was there. Then he sighed heavily, only not out of anger or frustration this time, she thought, but out of fatigue.

She had so many questions. About all the years they'd spent apart. About his life in the military. His personal life. And what he planned to do next. But she knew they could wait. This wasn't going to be their last conversation. It was going to be their first.

'I should get going,' she said, standing up. 'I've got a plane to catch.'

It was a white lie and he probably knew it. Her company jet would leave any time she chose. She leant down to kiss him goodbye. But this time he stood. He took her in his arms and hugged her close. She held him too and, given a choice right then, she would have stayed like that until the moment she died.

When they stepped back from one another she was smiling.

CHAPTER TWENTY-SIX

MAY 2005

Romy took a slug of wine as she slumped on the worn leather couch, surfing the channels on TV for anything mindless to watch, the remains of a tasteless microwave meal on the chipped metal tray in front of her. But *The Simpsons* had finished and the news was depressing, with earthquakes around the world and riots in Paris. The only story that had interested her was the introduction of a new act in the UK to make civil partnerships legal for same-sex couples, but it had only made her think of Nico and the boyfriend he'd had before he'd died. With a sad sigh, she switched off the TV.

She'd only been in this new apartment for two weeks. Removal boxes were still stacked up against the wall and she supposed she should start unpacking them. But she was too tired. Like every day these days, it just felt like she never stopped.

Through the open window of her top-floor apartment she could hear two people calling out to one another on the road below, their bikes hissing along the tarmac. Listening to the sound of their laughter drift off, she got up to draw the long wooden shutters over the windows, realizing as she looked outside that it was nearly ten o'clock already and the light had only just gone. The trees lining the Amsterdam canal below were all in blossom, but it seemed only yesterday that the city had been covered in snow.

It was a horrible fact of life, Romy thought, as she shut the night out, that time moved so fast, nothing lasted. Not even grief lasted forever. After it had eaten the essence of you, devoured a piece of your soul, it moved on somewhere else. Then life—at least a pale imitation of life—carried on, whether you wanted it to or not.

She knew she ought to be grateful. Across the world people had been scarred by the events of 11 September 2001, but the date would be forever etched on Romy's mind as the date that her life had been robbed too.

She remembered nothing of the crash itself, even now, nearly four years later. She only

365

remembered the terrifying, fragmented moments leading up to it. The insane look on Claudia's face as she'd levelled that pistol at Nico and fired. The echo of Romy's own footsteps in the corridor as she and Alfonso had fled for their lives. The roar of the Mercedes's engine. The BMW's headlights rushing up behind. The shriek of sirens.

She'd been told afterwards, when she'd surfaced from her week-long concussion, that Alfonso's Mercedes had crashed through the villa gates into the path of two fire engines, which had been hurtling towards an entirely separate incident.

The first had ploughed at sixty miles an hour into the driver's side of the car, crumpling it like a Coke can, killing Alfonso instantly and sending the car into an airborne spin. Romy, whose seatbelt had sprung open as the car had slammed into Villa Gasperi's garden wall, had been catapulted into a thicket of roadside shrubs, which had mercifully broken her fall, saving her life, but had left her with two broken legs and five broken ribs all the same.

The second fire engine had caught the BMW chasing after them, killing Ulrich, Claudia and their accomplice outright. After the fireball that had resulted, there had been so little left of the bodies that no identifications had ever been made.

Romy's recovery had been painfully slow. All she'd been able to think about, as she'd stared at the ceiling of the darkened hospital room hour after hour, had been that her husband—the only man she'd ever loved—was dead. And he'd died because of her. Because of her past. Which meant that it had been her fault.

And dear Nico . . . her talented, wonderful best

friend, who had tried so hard to protect her, the same way he always had. Brutally, cold-bloodedly murdered.

Her fault too.

At least in hospital Romy had been protected from the intense media scrutiny of the Scolari family. Even so, like a pack of baying dogs, the world's press had been camped outside, clamouring for information, waiting to get a picture of Romy's grieving face. The tragic end of her fairytale story was too much to resist.

But even just out of reach of the press, there had still been the questions from the police. Endless questions. Ones they'd felt only she could answer. Who were these killers? Why had they come here? How had they got past the guard? How had they stolen so much of the precious art that had been lost in the car crash?

Romy had told them nothing. None of what she'd admitted to Alfonso and Nico. If she'd admitted that she'd known Claudia and Ulrich, the police would soon have worked out the rest. About what she'd done to Fox. And the orphanage fire.

None of that would have brought Alfonso or Nico back. That's what Romy had told herself in the numbness of those first interrogations. And with Claudia and Ulrich already being nothing but charred bones and ash lost on the wind, what difference could knowing their names possibly have made to the police?

Instead, Romy had done what she'd always done. She'd buried her past down just as deep as she could.

She'd told herself that it was fairer, also, on Roberto and Maria to let them think that Ulrich and his gang had simply been nameless criminals, there to steal Roberto's paintings, nothing more. And as her lies had come thick and fast, she'd imagined that they were papering over the gaping hole of the truth of who she really was. Which was surely so much better than admitting to Alfonso's family that, right from the start, everything she'd ever told them about herself had been a lie.

But what she hadn't been able to deal with was Maria and Roberto's grief. Watching it, being close to it, feeling it mix in with her own misery and multiply. Rather than their proximity being a comfort, it had left her wishing herself dead.

They'd waited patiently—Maria and Roberto, the sisters—one of them coming each day to the hospital to visit her, encouraging her through her therapy sessions, ready to take her back with them the moment she was discharged. Flavia even bought her designer shoes, but Romy couldn't muster any enthusiasm for them. How could she think about shoes—how could she even bear to walk again—when Alfonso was dead?

For all their good intentions, Romy had felt suffocated by the Scolaris—the family she'd wanted as her own. For all their loyalty to her, she was a traitor to them. It had soon reached the point where she'd barely been able to look them in the eyes.

And there'd been another reason she'd kept silent too. Another reason that she didn't dare admit even to herself, until nearly three months after Alfonso's death.

But it had been reason enough to make up her mind. Reason enough to leave a note for Alfonso's family, check herself out of the hospital and sneak away. Reason enough to start again, somewhere new, on her own.

'Mamma?'

Romy quickly turned away from the window and went through the door behind the sofa.

Alfie was sitting up in bed, bathed in the soft glow of the night-light. He had long black eyelashes, just like his father, and Romy felt her heart contracting with love as she went to her son.

'Hey? What's the matter?' she asked, sitting beside him on his duvet and stroking his forehead.

'I can't sleep.'

Now she kicked off her slippers and tucked herself under the duvet with Alfie, cuddling him tight in his little bed.

'Is Papa with angels?' he asked her. She was amazed at his ability not only to express himself, but to ask such searching questions. Since he'd started talking at just eighteen months, he hadn't stopped. Now, at three, Romy was constantly surprised by his grasp on the world.

'Yes, he is.'

'Do the angels have cars?'

'Of course. Papa's got the fastest car in heaven. Didn't you see his tyre tracks across the sky earlier?'

It was an old joke between them that the vapour trails left by the planes taking off from Schiphol Airport, which often drifted this way over the town, were really left by Alfonso, who was constantly driving over the city to check that they were OK.

Romy had bought a new computer and spent her evenings trawling through old press cuttings and buying posters online. The one at the end of

Alfie's bed that they'd put up earlier was Romy's best find yet: a black-and-white poster of Alfonso spraying a magnum of champagne when he'd won the Japanese Grand Prix. They both stared at it now.

'What is he like?' Alfie asked, as if they might meet one day soon.

'He has nice hair. Just like yours,' she said, kissing his head. 'And he's funny, like you. When he was here and not in heaven, he could make great pasta.'

'Can I make pasta too?' Alfie said, yawning.

'Of course,' Romy said as she pressed her face into his hair, breathing him in.

She turned off the night-light and lay in the dark holding him, stroking the soft, downy skin on the back of his neck to get him off to sleep, the same way she'd done every night of his life. But in her head she felt words forming, as if Alfonso were speaking to her from the dead.

Mamma ... Maria ... she should be teaching him to make pasta. Papa ... Roberto ... should be reading him to sleep.

Memories of that wonderful Tuscan kitchen and the smell of that delicious spiced-pumpkin ravioli seemed to fill Romy's nostrils.

She knew it was wrong to deny Alfie his grandparents and his aunts. She'd thought about it so often. She'd even written to them dozens of times, but the first letter—a grovelling apology, telling them that she was fine and needed to be alone in order to heal—had been the only one she'd sent. She'd assured them that she'd be back soon. That she'd be in touch.

But once again it had all been lies. She hadn't

370

mentioned how the morning sickness and grief had assaulted her in wave after wave through the day and night, until she'd felt shipwrecked. So many times she'd wanted to call Flavia or Maria and beg them to rescue her. But she'd stopped herself. The Scolaris were wonderful people, and Romy had only brought them heartbreak and bad luck. They were better off without her.

But then Alfie had been born, and everything had changed. Her self-imposed rejection from the Scolaris had changed to self-imposed protection from them.

Because Alfie was *hers*—the only thing that had *ever* been just hers. And she couldn't, *wouldn't*, share him with anyone.

He'd felt like a miracle. A gift sent from Alfonso to heal her. She'd been so absorbed in him, so fascinated by him, that hours had flown by just watching his fist curl around her little finger. Then, all too soon, he'd sat up and she'd helped him to crawl. The months had flitted past like a sped-up calendar in a movie.

But now that time had gone and life was still moving on, faster and faster. And she knew it wouldn't be long before Alfie no longer accepted her standard explanation that his grandparents all lived a long, long way away. And then what? What would she tell him? How would she answer when Alfie told her that he wanted to meet Maria and Roberto? How could she risk letting him see them when, anonymous as she and Alfie were here in Amsterdam, they were both so safe?

And what about my own parents? she thought, rolling onto her back now, still holding Alfie as his breathing grew deeper and he drifted into sleep.

371

Parents. Whoever they were, they'd never been that. She felt a sickness in her stomach, the same sickness she'd used to feel in the orphanage, where each night she'd made herself push down the useless, poisonous hope that one day they'd arrive to take her back.

Had her own mother felt about her, as a baby, the way she did about Alfie? Surely she must have felt some kind of emotion when she'd held Romy for the first time? Maybe not as intense as Romy herself had felt, when she'd seen Alfie's face and had experienced falling in love in a way she'd never thought possible. But her mother must have felt something. How could she just have given up her baby? What horrible circumstances had driven her to dump Romy in an orphanage? Had she ever regretted not cuddling her as a little child, the way Romy cuddled Alfie now?

How could she not have? How could she have left me like that?

Wasn't there anyone in the world who ever thought about her? Any long-lost relatives out there who missed her?

*　　　*　　　*

Romy still felt unsettled when she woke up the next morning in her clothes, cramped up in Alfie's tiny bed. They both got up and ate cereal in the kitchen, and when Romy said they had a whole weekend stretching ahead of them, Alfie started to make plans to go to the zoo and on a boat trip. Romy laughed, marvelling at the way in which he so effortlessly filled their social agenda.

They struggled together down the crazily steep

stairs with Alfie's new scooter, which Romy had bought him for his birthday in March.

Lars, their new neighbour, was standing outside his apartment's open doorway downstairs. He waved and said hello, before staring back into his apartment and calling out, 'Hey, come on. Hurry up!'

Lars was probably around the same age as she was, Romy thought, and was tall and thin, with a friendly, lopsided smile, as well as terrible taste in jumpers, she'd noted. He might even be called handsome, she considered, under his thick reading glasses and unruly mop of dark hair.

Since she'd arrived in Amsterdam, Romy had kept a low profile and deliberately not made any friends. She'd cut her hair and dyed it and changed her name to Susan, terrified at first of the media finding her again, but then afterwards anxious to protect her own and Alfie's blissfully anonymous life together. She never went out without wearing large shades.

But Lars seemed harmless enough. Unobtrusive. The few conversations she'd had with him had been about the pros and cons of the local amenities and the lack of true musical talent displayed by their Austrian neighbour, who played his bongos late into the night and sang 'like a wounded pig' (Lars's words) whenever he got drunk. That was the other thing about Lars—he made Romy smile.

She didn't know him very well, but it was still a surprise now when she saw a little girl, probably just a few years older than Alfie, come charging out of his apartment into his arms, before giggling hysterically as he flipped her upside-down and

373

whipped her up into the air.

'This is Gretchen,' Lars explained to Romy and Alfie in English, putting the giggling little girl back down. He proudly placed his hand on the top of her head. 'It's my weekend with her.'

Was he divorced? Romy wondered, her curiosity aroused. She wondered what his wife was like and why they no longer lived together. She couldn't imagine living away from Alfie, surviving just on weekend visits.

'We're going to the park,' Alfie said and Romy ruffled his hair, amazed at his confidence with new people.

'Can *we* go, Daddy?' Gretchen asked. She was a sweet little thing, Romy thought, in a corduroy green jacket and jeans, her blonde hair in bunches. She was pretty, with big grey eyes—the same as Lars's, Romy now saw.

'I've got to go to the office, I told you. You've got to come with me. Not for long, but—'

'She can come with us,' Alfie said.

Romy looked at him and then at Lars, embarrassed. 'Oh, no, Alfie, um . . .'

'Please, can I?' Gretchen begged.

Alfie turned to Romy. 'Mamma?'

Romy was about to protest, but Alfie was so much like Alfonso, so trusting and sure that life would turn out all right. She recognized the forcefulness in his voice, and his eyes didn't waver from hers until she started speaking. Just like his father, he would get his way.

'Well . . . I don't . . . I don't mind,' Romy told Lars. 'We'll only be a couple of hours. I can bring Gretchen back here.'

Lars looked endearingly flummoxed, but when

Gretchen put her hands under her chin in a prayer position, he relented. 'OK. I'll get her scooter too, if you're really sure it's OK.' Alfie and Gretchen grinned at each other.

Outside it was a perfect spring day. A spider's web was glistening in the doorframe, as Romy crouched down and made sure that Alfie's safety helmet was done up tightly under his chin. He squirmed, keen to show off in front of Gretchen. Romy warned him not to go too fast, before handing over his scooter, but her request fell on deaf ears. He set off in an elegant wide arc on the pavement, calling for Gretchen, the cherry blossom on the pavement swirling around him. A barge honked as it passed on the sparkling river below the canal bridge.

'I work over in Herengracht. This is my number, if she's any problem,' Lars said, writing on the back of a cab receipt.

Romy didn't tell him that she didn't own a mobile phone. His assumption that she did—that she must have a whole network of friends and family—made her feel nervous. But it was too late to back out now.

'Actually I have a card somewhere.' He patted the pockets of his waterproof jacket and then handed over a card from his wallet.

'European Network and Information Security Agency,' Romy read. 'That sounds important.'

'I fight cybercrime,' Lars said, striking a Superman pose, which made Romy laugh. 'White hat hacking,' he explained. 'Pretty boring in reality. I try and keep banks and council offices safe. But today we have a small crisis and my boss is away on holiday. But don't worry, I won't be long.'

Smiling again, he leant down and kissed Gretchen and talked to her quietly in Dutch. Romy watched as they touched knuckles in some kind of secret pact. For a part-time dad, he sure wasn't bad. Gretchen closed her eyes as she hugged him, pressing her face up against his chest. Would Alfie have been like that with Alfonso? Romy wondered. She felt an ache of sadness. She thought so—yes, he would.

'Thank you again, Susan,' he said.

'Sure,' she said.

She waved to Lars as he set off on his bicycle, pumping his Superman fist into the air once more, much to the children's delight. Then they set off in the other direction to the park, Romy pulling her tatty cardigan around her.

She watched Gretchen and Alfie on their scooters as they weaved in and out of the lamp-posts, amazed that she'd just offered to look after someone else's child. It felt flattering that Lars trusted her enough to hand over his daughter. Perhaps she wasn't quite so socially out of touch as she feared.

Would Lars have done the same thing if he knew who Romy really was? She wondered that too. Would he have reacted to her in the same way if she still looked as she once had? Or would he have been intimidated by her? Would he even have tipped off her whereabouts to one of the tabloids and turned her life into a nightmare again?

In the park, the horse chestnuts were in bloom and the warm air was filled with birdsong. Romy sat on the bench watching Alfie go up the steps to the slide over near the skateboard park with Gretchen. Seeing them together, Romy thought

376

again how she really did need to start socializing Alfie with other kids.

She even had the prospectus for the International School, but hadn't been brave enough to enrol him yet. Not just because she was worried about spending time away from Alfie, but because she'd got used to a life without questions. When she enrolled him, she'd have to answer questions. Lots of them. Not just from the school, but from the other mothers.

Worse, Alfie would have to answer questions too. They'd had so little contact with other people that she hadn't had to tell him yet that she wanted him to keep secrets. About who his father was. And his mother too.

'Watch,' Alfie called to her.

He was waving over from the slide.

'I'm watching,' she called back, as he slid down the slide.

He stood up at the end, grinning. 'Did you see me? Did you?'

'Yes,' she called, clapping her hands. 'You were brilliant.' Sometimes he was so heartbreakingly cute that she wished he would never grow up, or change. Wished that she could hold these precious moments forever.

*　　*　　*

Bella Giordano couldn't wait to leave Amsterdam. She'd been up all night partying and the last thing she needed to do was film a bunch of dumb-arse kids in the park. She'd been working for Italian MTV for three years now, and still no sign of a proper break. Why didn't they ever give her the interviews to direct? Why did she have to do all the donkeywork filler shots, whilst Risso, the so-called real director, got a lie-in on a Saturday?

The worst part was they'd probably cut these shots of the skateboarders anyway. It was a complete waste of her time. She should have listened to her parents and stayed at the newspaper as a reporter. But at the time the job at MTV had been too hip to turn down. If only she'd known then what she knew now. About the lifestyle that went with it. And the terrible pay.

She watched the kids rolling back and forth on the wooden ramp, her head aching from the racket they were making.

'That's good,' she called, forcing a smile onto her face. 'Keep it going. Look like it's fun.' She turned to her cameraman, Kas, next to her. 'You getting all this?' she asked, blowing on her coffee.

'Yep,' he said. 'Hey, look, we've got an audience.'

Two little kids had stopped on their scooters, keen to see what the action was all about.

Wow, he sure was a cutie, Bella thought, looking at the little dark-haired boy. Big brown eyes. He'd look great on camera. Maybe she could do some filming of him and the girl on their scooters. To contrast with the older kids. A kind of next-generation-skater thing. Something to help pad out their slot.

'You want to be on MTV?' Bella asked, first in Dutch, then in English, smiling at the kids, her voice husky from all the cigarettes she'd smoked last night.

The little girl nodded eagerly, her eyes shining excitedly.

'Your mom or dad here?'

'My papa is dead,' the little boy said.

'Oh, I'm sorry,' Bella replied, grimacing, but all the boy did was smile.

'It's OK,' he said, 'he's up in heaven with the angels. And did you know he's very famous too?'

'Is that a fact?' said Bella, playing along, relieved to be off the subject of death.

The little boy puffed out his chest in pride. 'He is Alfonso Scolari. The racing driver.'

Bella stared at the little boy, hardly daring to believe what she'd heard. She wasn't the only one. Kas had lowered his camera to look at the boy direct. He raised his eyebrows at Bella.

Bella stared back at the little boy.

'And your mother? What's her name?' she asked, slowly looking round the park. 'Is she here?'

'Romy,' said the boy. 'Though sometimes she tells people it's Susan.'

Bella felt the adrenaline rushing through her now. She remembered Romy Valentine's wedding to Scolari all right. Who could ever forget those amazing pictures of their honeymoon? They'd been like a dream couple, and Bella—still a student back then—had mourned with everyone else when the handsome Alfonso had died less than a month later after some gangsters had tried robbing him in his own home.

'Why don't you take me and my friend here over to meet her?' Bella said, reaching for her phone and pressing the speed-dial button for Risso. He'd have to get his sorry arse out of bed for this.

'Shall I start filming anyway?' Kas asked, under his breath.

'Hell, yeah,' she replied.

CHAPTER TWENTY-SEVEN

JUNE 2005

If Thea had had the time to study the view from her office at the top of Maddox Tower, she would have noticed the hazy Manhattan late afternoon outside and enjoyed a glimpse of Central Park, shimmering in the distance.

But as always she was too busy working. Inured to the heat of the day by the cool air conditioning, it could have been snowing out there, for all she knew. She swivelled in her chair to look from the latest tax-relief proposals that Legal had put forward to the live feeds of market data flowing across the bank of trading screens on her desk.

Maddox Inc.'s shares were holding steady on the Dow Jones, but Maddox Media, their Internet media spin-off, which was listed on the NASDAQ, was already up three points on yesterday's price, and 30 per cent since its launch. Clear confirmation that the launch of the hip new social-networking service they'd funded had been an undisputed success.

All the more power to Brett, Thea thought grimly. The board had applauded him during last month's meeting when he'd presented his figures.

Yes, there was no doubt that Brett was golden boy of the month, especially after his recent wedding to Bethany Saunders, which had been a lavish affair at Crofters. Thea had had no intention of going, but at the very last minute her father had scooped her out of her office and taken her with

380

him on the company jet. She'd been horrified to discover that Peter Shardlake and Dennis Wisely, two of the Maddox board members and her father's closest allies, had been asked to be ushers at Brett's wedding. It wasn't so much a wedding as a total cementing of Brett's place in the Maddox structure.

Storm had spared no expense for the beachside wedding, and Bethany had invited all her A-list Hollywood acting friends. As the news helicopters swooped overhead, whipping up the sand and rippling the water, the priest had had to shout his blessing. Thea had stood in the front row, marvelling at Storm's extraordinary sequinned kaftan outfit, which was low-cut at the back and had a high collar at the front, which Thea supposed must be to hide yet more plastic-surgery scars. As she posed for the photos afterwards, Storm could barely close her mouth, her rictus grin stretched by her smooth cheeks. She'd certainly gone to every effort to outshine Bethany, but Bethany was more hard-nosed than Storm had bargained for.

The whole event had been so nauseating in its over-the-top ego-massaging and air-kissing that Thea had been sorely tempted to blow the whistle. She'd wanted to take perfect Bethany aside and tell her that she'd married a monster. But the girl was so vain and so utterly self-absorbed that she probably wouldn't care.

Thea had coolly observed the entire proceedings from the sidelines, trying to stay out of the spotlight. She'd been just about to sneak off to stay on Justin Ennestein's yacht, where she knew she'd be safe, when Brett had lurched up to her.

He'd been a little drunk and looked like the cat that had got the cream.

'Aren't you going to congratulate me, Thea?' he'd asked.

'No,' she'd said bluntly, not hiding her hatred.

'It's such a pity you've turned into such a frumpy old maid,' he'd said, enjoying the effect of his words. 'You know, Dad always wanted Maddox Inc. to be a family business. You know—family. Husbands . . . children . . . or,' he paused, as if realizing something, 'maybe you're a lesbian.'

Thea had been furious with him and his words still smarted. It had given her extra reason to work towards tomorrow's quarterly review, when she'd be making her own presentation. Brett was getting too powerful for her liking.

The only problem was that where Brett was excelling, her side of the business had far less headline-grabbing results. Her father had set her the task of getting Maddox Inc. to trade itself out of the recession. He'd ordered Thea to expand their interests, not bury their head in the sand. Yet despite all the successes she'd achieved so smoothly in Germany—where she'd increased Maddox Germany's advertising revenue share by 20 per cent, by snapping up two regional newspaper groups and a popular cable-TV network—her attempts to move into other European countries had stumbled or, in some cases, even ground to a halt.

Scolari, for example, had proved impossible to break. Thea's several overtures to buy it had each been roundly rejected. Even after old man Scolari had been devastated by the death of his son, Alfonso, he'd stood as firm as a rock with regards to his business. Scolari was not—and would never be—open to a takeover. The message had been resoundingly clear.

If Thea had glanced up then at the television playing silently on her office wall, she'd have seen a breaking-news announcement from Reuters featuring Roberto Scolari's daughter-in-law Romy, who'd vanished from the public eye since her husband's death, but had now been found living in obscurity in Amsterdam.

Instead Thea's attention was snagged by the arrival of a new email in her in-box and, seeing the name of the sender, she pounced on it right away.

The moment she read it, she smiled.

It was one of several messages she'd received from Michael since she'd visited him in Germany. He'd still not been discharged from Landstuhl, but was hopeful that he would be soon. His nightmares had been getting less frequent, he'd confided in her during the course of their brief correspondence. And his temper had been getting easier to control. He'd started *feeling more like the old Michael*, he'd written.

Of course she'd wanted to do whatever was possible to help speed his recovery, no matter what it cost. But Michael had been resolute. He'd told her that the Landstuhl doctors were the best in the world. Time was what he needed most of all.

And so she'd decided to be patient. Just like him. But even so, more and more frequently lately, she'd found herself thinking about him, imagining him not in Landstuhl, as she'd last seen him, but here in the States—happier, healthier, somewhere near Little Elms perhaps, walking together with Thea along a cool, deserted country road.

She sighed, catching herself doing exactly that right now. She felt herself blush, embarrassed by the childish romanticism of such a thought. But the fleeting vision of the two of them together had been so vivid that she could almost believe the scent of apple blossom was still lingering in the air. *Would* they end up friends? she wondered. She hoped so. She'd do all that she could to ensure they would.

This email Michael had sent her today wasn't long. Only one line, in fact.

You didn't have to do that, Thea, he'd written. *But thank you.*

She couldn't help but smile once more as she read it again. So he'd found out about her contacting the Brightside Home and paying for his mother's bills and care in perpetuity, as well upgrading Mrs Pryor to the top facilities that the home had to offer.

He'd found out and he'd not stopped her. He'd let her do that much for him, at least. He'd not pushed her away.

'Thea,' her personal assistant, Sarah, chastised her from the doorway, frowning, 'you haven't stopped all day.'

'There's too much to do before the meeting tomorrow,' Thea said, feeling her skin prickle now as she forwarded Michael's message to her laptop at home and deleted the original.

She'd learnt never to leave any trace of anything personal at work. Anything at all that Brett might use against her. There'd been instances—too many to ignore—when Brett had seemed to second-guess her too accurately and she'd been left wondering whether he'd really been guessing at all.

Sarah was wearing a tight red dress that showed off her toned figure and tanned legs, and her dark hair had been curled. Thea remembered then that she was going on a date, which Sarah had kindly suggested she could turn into a double date, although Thea had turned her down.

'You should think about getting changed,' Sarah said, tapping her watch, a Tag Heuer that Thea had given her last Christmas in lieu of her normal bonus, which Brett had blocked for all junior staff in a fit of ostentatious cost-cutting—whilst simultaneously doubling those of senior executives at his level, of course.

'Changed?'

'For Justin's leaving party,' Sarah said, pointedly reminding Thea of her excuse for getting out of the date. 'It's due to start upstairs in about half an hour. You've not forgotten, have you?'

'Shit,' Thea swore.

She *had* forgotten. A whole bunch of eminent New Yorkers had been invited to the head of Legal's final send-off—and the invitation had specified 'Formal'.

She stared at the stack of papers that she was still only halfway through. The top sheet was covered in red marks—her queries. The tax-relief proposals had been instigated by Brett. Meaning that she was going to check through every single damned word.

'I'll have to leave this all until later,' she said, thinking she might be able to come back down here and finish off once the party was over.

But now she needed to get a move-on. She had just enough time to make it home to change out of her suit and into her favourite black dress.

385

Ten floors up, Brett Maddox surveyed himself in the bathroom mirror in his apartment in Maddox Tower and liked what he saw. He took the bottle of Hermes aftershave and sprayed it liberally around his face.

'Which one?' Bethany said from the doorway, holding up a long floaty pink dress and a black sequinned cocktail number.

'Neither. Wear that green one I bought you,' Brett said, smiling at her. She looked so slutty in her black lace underwear. He could feel himself hardening, wishing he could stride across the room and take her roughly over the bed. She said she liked it when he did that. That is, after all, why he'd married her. Because she behaved like a hooker in the bedroom.

Which—he'd discovered to his delight—only made his secret life with his hookers all the more rewarding, and his thirst for kinky thrills even stronger. Not for the first time he wondered whether Bethany would mind if he suggested a threesome. She probably wouldn't. She'd already tearfully admitted how she'd slept with a sixty-year-old Hollywood producer when she was seventeen, to get her first break. A career move that Brett approved of. His wife wasn't stupid.

Which is why she nodded now. She knew tonight was all about playing the perfect corporate wife.

'You're all ready . . .' she put her hand on her hip and giggled, '. . . already.'

'You've got time, don't worry,' he said, winking at her and straightening his bow tie. 'I'm meeting

Peter, Max and Dennis in five minutes.'

'Oh?' Bethany asked, intrigued.

She might be canny, but there was no way Brett was going to share the finer points of his business plan with his wife, he thought as he smiled at her in the mirror.

A few minutes later, however, as he faced his three colleagues in the library room of his apartment, and poured them each a large Scotch from the decanter, he felt slightly nervous. He didn't know how loyal they were to Griffin Maddox, but Brett wanted them to be loyal to him.

'I wanted to discuss something . . . delicate with you,' he said, after the usual banter had died down, and Max had made a rather filthy *Brokeback Mountain* joke after the latest Heath Ledger film. 'Two delicate items, actually.'

Dennis, in his snappy blue suit and trendy haircut, slumped back in the chair, all ears. Peter was more upright. One of Maddox's most trusted financiers, he was grey and starched, with metal-framed glasses that made his beady accountant's eyes even smaller. Max, the marketing guru, wasn't in a suit at all, but in a cashmere jumper and slacks. He'd made no secret of his attraction to Bethany, and Brett liked keeping his philandering enemy close.

'Firstly—and this is strictly confidential between us—I'm sorry to tell you that my father's health isn't great. Mom is very anxious about him. I didn't know this, but he's been for several heart-scans.'

Dennis sat up in his chair, his face concerned, and glanced at the others. 'He hasn't said anything.'

'I played three rounds of golf with him last

week,' Max said. 'He was fine.'

Brett rolled his eyes. 'Well, he's not going to tell any of you, is he? *I'm* not even supposed to know. I just wanted to share the information with you. Just so we're prepared.'

'Well, that's good of you, Brett. I think Justin's handled everything,' Peter said. 'If . . . you know . . .' he trailed off.

Brett nodded and smiled sympathetically, as if they were all thinking the same thing.

Justin Ennestein, that old fool, Brett thought. He had Maddox's ear all right, but Brett had made sure his replacement had the right loyalties. He'd set Storm on the case too.

'It's just made me re-evaluate the future. We can't take things for granted. That's all I'm saying.'

Dennis took a slug of Scotch.

'And the other issue,' Brett said, sighing as if it weighed heavily on his mind, 'is that I've had a sneak preview of Thea's figures. I wasn't snooping or anything—I know she's due to present tomorrow—but,' he sighed heavily again, 'I hate to say it, but I don't think she's carrying her weight. Not when we're so stretched.'

'What are you saying?' Max asked.

'I'm saying that if we're streamlining the company, we should include that to streamlining at the very top.'

It was Max who sat up now. 'You want to get rid of your sister?'

'Hell, no,' Brett said with a laugh, as if that were ridiculous. 'Dad wouldn't want that. But I am concerned that she's out of her depth in certain areas.'

He spired his fingers together and tapped them,

388

as if he'd been thinking long and hard about it. 'I mean, Thea eats, breathes and sleeps Maddox Inc. I felt,' he blew out a breath as if emotionally touched, 'you know, *sorry* for her at our wedding. I mean, when has she got time to live her own life?'

He was gratified to see his father's men nodding understandingly.

'But I'm more concerned that she's just not up to the job. Take Scolari. Now I'm not saying we should do anything sudden, but if, say—hypothetically—I could bring it in as we've wanted—'

'But that's impossible. Thea has made perfectly clear what the situation is there,' Peter chipped in.

'But if it's not impossible for *me*,' Brett clarified, 'then I was hoping for your support in a little top-end restructuring. If—and it's a big if—anything happened to my father, I know he'd distribute everything evenly between Thea and me. But that's him just being a father, being sentimental.'

He paused, looking at them all.

'I'm looking out for Thea's best interests—and the corporation's—here. You know that, right?'

'Sure,' Dennis said, as if Brett's proposal was entirely reasonable.

'I think Thea does a great job,' Peter said. 'I'm not sure what you're getting at.'

'Just blue-sky thinking, that's all. Just sounding you out.' Brett smiled, topping up his glass. 'My sister . . . well, she's incredible. Totally driven. I'm just thinking about everything being fair.'

*   *   *

The party at Maddox Towers was in full swing

when Thea arrived. Griffin Maddox was in a good mood and greeted Thea warmly.

'It's a great party,' he told her now, gazing around the crowded room with a satisfied smile.

The mezzanine floor they all stood on led out onto an open-air terrace and rooftop garden. The Hoover Building was illuminated with green lights tonight, and with the sun fading over the Manhattan skyline, it couldn't have been more perfect a backdrop. Yet Thea sensed a kind of forced atmosphere. She felt as if everyone were deliberately not looking in the direction of where the Twin Towers had stood, so permanently and defiantly. It was as if there was an unspoken tacit agreement between everyone that life would carry on, that no matter what the champagne would flow harder, the laughter would be louder—a deliberate two fingers to those who thought New Yorkers could be cowed.

Thea thought once again of Michael and of his injuries. And she remembered too the missing letters from Mrs Pryor to her that he'd mentioned, and which Thea had never received. Secrets. So many secrets.

'Go and find Storm for me, darling,' Griffin Maddox said discreetly in her ear. 'Justin will be cutting the cake soon.'

But Storm wasn't anywhere to be found. Thea looked all over for her—in her bedroom, the guest rooms, everywhere. She was probably shouting at a member of staff somewhere, or putting on her make-up. But she wasn't in the bathrooms, or with the caterers. Finally only one room remained.

Thea stole herself to go into the private kitchen: the place where Brett had assaulted her all those

390

years ago. The door was stuck, so she pushed it harder with her shoulder.

Storm was inside straddling a man, whose face Thea couldn't see, but whose trousers were bunched around the red socks on his ankles. Storm's head flicked back and she moaned as she rode up and down on him.

Thea froze.

'No . . . no. Jesus!' Thea gasped, backing out.

She slammed the door shut, her heart pounding as she pressed herself against the wall. How could she? Now. Here? How could Storm do that to her father?

A moment later Storm came out, smoothing down her dress over her curves.

Thea stepped towards her. 'How dare you!' she said, her voice shaking. 'How dare you do that to him. In his house.'

Storm flinched. Then her green eyes glittered with menace.

'Don't you dare get on your moral high horse with me,' she snapped. 'My marriage is none of your business. You wouldn't know sex-drive if it hit you in the face. You're just a freaky ice-maiden.'

Thea was astounded. 'But my father? He loves you.'

Storm flicked her head back. 'So what?' she hissed. 'I have needs. And he's never been able to fulfil them.'

Thea shook her head, horrified that Storm was so unrepentant. She'd been caught red-handed with the man in red socks, whoever he was, and yet she didn't give a damn. And Thea realized in that instant that it was doubtful if Storm had ever been faithful. That all along it had only been about the

391

money and the power and the status.

Unable to speak, she turned on her heel.

'Don't you judge me, Thea,' Storm called after her. 'I'm warning you. That would be very foolish indeed.'

Upstairs, Justin was standing by the microphone on a small podium, where a cake had been set out. Thea arrived and stopped next to her father, her knees still trembling. She turned to him and he smiled, but her words faded on her lips.

She felt her chest heaving with all the pent-up words she longed to blurt out. To tell him that his wife was an adulterous liar. But then she remembered that she'd been at a party once before in this room, when that woman had tried to blow the whistle on Brett, and she knew there was no guarantee he'd believe Thea, even if she told him what she'd just seen.

He was blinded by Storm. He always had been. Thea telling him that Storm was a fraud and a liar would do nothing to change that.

He was completely delusional, she realized. So fixated that he'd created the perfect happy family that he'd never see the truth about Brett and Storm.

Well, she wouldn't let them win. Her father's only crime was seeing the best in people, and it was up to Thea to protect him.

Justin banged the microphone, and Griffin Maddox smiled warmly at him. A second later Storm herself came in, ostentatiously adjusting a flower arrangement on her way.

'I have been with Griffin now for most of my working life,' Justin was saying. 'And I have to tell you, ladies and gentlemen, that he has always been so much more than a colleague—a true friend.'

There was a smattering of applause.

'I have been honoured to have been made to feel like I was part of his wonderful family. Thea, Storm, Brett'—he looked around the room, raising his glass to each in turn—'you have looked out for me, put up with me, even listened to me on occasion.' There was laughter in the crowd. 'You are all wonderful people.'

Thea noticed Storm's arm snake around Griffin Maddox's waist and he smiled down at her as the audience applauded. Beyond them, Thea saw that Brett was staring at her. When she made eye contact with him, he winked and a shiver ran down her spine.

'So it was with great care that I chose my successor,' Justin continued. 'I have Brett to thank for all his assistance in helping me do so, but I can honestly say that, in Lance Starling, we have found someone who will truly fit into the Maddox corporation. He comes highly qualified, with an excellent track record, an exemplary legal brain. I trust handing my work over to him entirely.'

Instinctively Thea joined in the applause, hoping to get a glimpse of Justin's successor. She'd heard a lot about him, but she'd yet to meet him herself. Straining to see around the crowd, she saw a good-looking young man walk from the back of the room. He was grinning and shaking hands as he went.

Thea watched Brett's smile widen. Lance Starling was clearly his man. She saw him walking round the crowd so that he too could get a better view. She watched as Lance Starling hopped up onto the podium to shake Justin Ennestein's hand, before hugging him. Which is when Thea saw that Starling was wearing red socks.

CHAPTER TWENTY-EIGHT

SEPTEMBER 2007

In the Rai Uno building in Milan, Romy sat in the small recording studio with her headphones on, trying not to be nervous about the 'on air' light shining above her head and the fact that she was next up to talk on national radio.

She took a sip of water from the glass on the desk, her attention snagged by her own reflection in the window separating her from the team of producers and engineers on the other side.

She looked so serious, she thought. Her hair was long again and today hung loose in soft waves. She was wearing an Alexander McQueen black trouser suit with high red Jimmy Choo shoes. She fought the urge to take one of them off and rub her foot. It had already been a long day.

But she knew she couldn't. Romy checked herself constantly to make sure she maintained her spotless corporate image, and she wondered whether it was on the presenter's sheaf of notes that she'd won a gong for 'Best Dressed Woman' at the *Grazia* awards last week. *Effortless style.* That was the caption they'd used with the photograph in the press, which had made Romy laugh about the irony of it all. Her perfect exterior was far from effortless. Looking natural was the hardest thing in the world.

Her life had changed so much in the past two years. Would she have been happier, she wondered now, if she'd stayed in Amsterdam? But those blissfully empty, carefree days were gone forever. She'd known they were as soon as she'd seen Alfie messing around with the camera crew in the park that day.

It hadn't been Alfie's fault, but Romy had still been upset as she'd hurried back to her flat with him and Gretchen. When Lars had come to collect Gretchen, Alfie had told him about the TV cameras and how angry Romy had been.

Lars . . . Romy remembered his friendly face and easygoing manner. The way he'd made her smile. What might have happened, she wondered, if things hadn't turned out as they had? Might they have become friends, if her life hadn't suddenly spun away from his? He'd been there when she'd needed him, and she'd kept in touch with him by email occasionally, but not as much as she should have. And certainly not recently. Gretchen would be growing up just as quickly as Alfie, she thought.

Romy remembered how calm and kind Lars had been that day, as she'd blurted out the truth about who she was—and who Alfie's father had been. The fact that she'd once been a famous model didn't seem to bother him at all. So much so that Romy wondered now whether he'd known all along. Rather than being surprised, it had been Lars who'd calmed her down. Lars who'd made her think logically. And Lars who'd confirmed what she'd known in her heart: that her time out from her real life was over, and that she had to do the right thing and contact Alfonso's parents and tell them about their grandson. And double-quick, too,

395

before they found out about him anyway on TV, or in the press.

Romy had been terrified during that first telephone conversation she'd had with Roberto. She'd braced herself, expecting his anger and disappointment in her to engulf her like a tide. Instead he'd told her that she didn't have to explain. That he'd be sending his private jet to get her.

*　　*　　*

Two days later Romy had arrived back at the Scolaris' Tuscan farmhouse and Maria had been the first to step forward, wrapping her in a silent hug in the doorway, which had lasted for over a minute. An embrace so profound that Romy hadn't been able to stop the tears coming. All the times she'd ever needed Maria's support, all the times she'd ever been lonely, she'd longed for this hug.

Alfie emerged from where he'd been hiding behind Romy's long dress. He made his grandmother swoon with delight when he spoke to her in Italian and kissed her cheek.

He was his father's son. *Oh yes*, Romy thought, smiling proudly—in spite of her nerves—*there'll never be any escaping that fact. And each day, Alfonso, I see you in him . . .*

The whole family had assembled at the villa to greet her. And Romy soon discovered that the Scolaris were just as kind and gentle and understanding as they had been when she'd been in hospital. They were still ready to accept her as one of their own. Whatever her reasons for staying

396

away, she'd come back. And that was all that had mattered to them.

Without any formality, Flavia and Anna hooked their arms through hers and steered her into the house, where she found herself swamped by a flood of happy memories. This had been the place where Alfonso had taken her the first time to meet his parents, where they'd got engaged by the light of that huge orange moon, and where she'd got ready on the morning of her wedding.

This was the place that had felt like home.

Hours later on that first night Alfie hadn't stopped being the centre of attention amongst all his cousins, as they gathered at the back of the house by the vine-covered terrace.

Romy watched her mother-in-law bring out a plate of her famous dusted cherry biscuits from the kitchen. She sat down in the old wicker chair in the garden, and Flavia's daughter, Marice, lifted up Alfie towards her and started teaching him a rhyme. Looking at Maria surrounded by roses, her lost grandson on her lap, Romy realized how wrong she'd been to stay away.

'I thought it would be less painful if I cut off the past,' Romy tried to explain to Roberto as she walked with him to help him pick herbs in the garden. 'I'm so sorry.'

'You can no sooner cut off your past than cut off your leg,' Roberto said, with a gentle chuckle. 'I know. I have made the same mistake. I thought I would stop being angry with Alfonso if I cut him off.' He shrugged. 'It didn't work. It just made it worse.'

The way his eyes twinkled then as he put his arm around Romy's shoulder reminded her so much of

Alfonso, it made her feel that Alfonso was somewhere near too, watching them. Being here, in the company of his family, was bringing him back to life, in the way that posters and newspaper clippings, she now understood, could never have done.

'Look at her,' Roberto said, his voice soft with love, looking across the garden at Maria, who was playing hide-and-seek with the children. 'She is old now, but just as beautiful as the day I met her. We need to cherish these years whilst we can.'

'Yes.' Is that what she'd done? Romy wondered. Had she made every single second with Alfonso count?

'Which is why I'm thinking of spending more time at home,' Roberto said.

'You mean retiring?' Romy asked, stopping now, surprised. Roberto had always been such an embodiment of his company that it seemed impossible to imagine it existing without him, or indeed he without it.

He nodded slowly. A look of sadness crossed his face. 'Like Maria, I am not as young as I was,' he said.

'So what will you do? Sell up?' The thought seemed abhorrent, for a reason Romy couldn't immediately identify. Maybe because she'd always imagined Alfonso one day giving up his driving and taking over his father's reins. Or perhaps because, deep down inside, it struck her that just selling off something Roberto had worked so hard to build was wrong.

'Sell? Never.' Roberto's voice was fierce and Romy smiled, relieved to see the old fire still burning brightly in his eyes.

He plucked a sprig of mint and put it into the basket she had over her arm, along with the sage, dill and bay. He began walking slowly along the curved brick pathway again.

'This business has been in my family for six generations,' he said. 'I could never sell it. No, I shall do what all the Scolaris have done before me. I shall leave it to the next Scolari in line whom I think most suited.'

And it was only then, as she followed Roberto's steady gaze towards Alfie—who'd cut through the gardens and was waiting for them just up ahead, absently trailing his fingertips through a bed of deep-pink peonies—that Romy realized what Roberto was really talking to her about. In bringing her son here, Romy had made him a Scolari. She'd delivered Roberto his heir.

'But, Roberto . . . you can't mean Alfie? He's only a child.'

'That's why I'm going to teach my business to you,' Roberto told her, gripping her arms firmly now as they walked.

'Me?'

'Yes, you, Romy. Because I'll be too old to ever teach Alfie myself. Meaning that I want you to be in charge after I've gone. Then you can give the business to Alfie when he comes of age.'

Romy panicked. 'What about your daughters? Flavia could run it, surely?'

'I've thought about it, but Flavia has her own life, her own commitments. And Anna is too busy. They have both told me separately that they have no intention of becoming the one in charge. The only one, I think, who ever had enough balls, and business brains to go with them, was Gloria. But she's made her own choices.'

Romy heard the pain in his voice and remembered how Gloria had a boyfriend, supposedly a drug-dealer, of whom Roberto had disapproved, and how she had sided with this man over Roberto in an argument, how she'd crossed her father, and after that there'd been no way back.

Romy remembered now the whole complexity of the Scolari family, its rules and traditions. But most of all she remembered how black and white Roberto was. Any hope she'd had of finally confessing to him about why Alfonso had died—the fleeting fantasy she'd entertained of telling him the truth—vanished.

'And what about Alfie's cousins?' Romy said. 'What if one of the girls . . .'

Roberto sighed. 'Perhaps they will. And, if so, then that is fine. I know it is not fashionable, Romy, perhaps not even legal these days, but I am the sixth male heir to inherit the responsibility of running this business, and I want Alfie to be the seventh. With your help and guidance.' His grip renewed the pressure on her arm. 'I'll need to start training you up straight away.'

Romy's panic only intensified. 'But I'm not a businesswoman, Roberto. I wouldn't know the first thing—'

'You have good instincts, and it's all up here,' he interrupted. The way he tapped his head reminded Romy of Herr Mulcher in the clothing factory in Berlin all those years ago. Was that what this was? Had Roberto too seen something raw in her? Something he felt he could sculpt?

The implications of it all rushed through Romy's

mind. What if he was wrong? Helping to run a business like Scolari was a million miles from suggesting cost-cutting measures for a clothing factory. What if she let him down? And not just him, but Maria and Flavia and Anna, and the other sisters, not to mention all the thousands of employees who relied on Scolari for their livelihoods?

But the biggest question of all she asked out loud. 'But what about Alfie? If I'm working with you, then who's going to be looking after him?'

'You can live with us. Maria can look after him whilst we're at the office. It won't be long before he has to go to school.'

Romy's mind was still reeling. He'd clearly thought all of this through already. Between the time he'd heard he had a grandson and their arrival here, he'd planned their whole future.

'We need Scolari to move forward into the future,' he said. 'We need to expand into future technologies. The Americans and Chinese are taking over. Our competitors are getting stronger and stronger. We need someone at the helm who can be an ambassador for us, who can be the new face of Scolari. Who can get us noticed.'

'And you really think *I* could do that?'

'Just a hunch.' Roberto grinned at her, and that's when the realization really hit her—not only was he looking forward to this, but he genuinely thought it would work. But most of all, he trusted her. Still. After all this time. He saw in her not only the successful international model who'd married his son, but the new face for his company. He hadn't ever thought of her, as she did of herself, as a single mother living in obscurity. Guiltily.

Secretly.

'I think Alfonso would have wanted you and Alfie to be with us,' he said, nodding to where Alfie had now got back to the others and was giggling with delight, as his cousins chased him through the jet of a sprinkler. 'I know it is a lot to think about, but look . . .' Roberto pointed to Maria, clapping her hands with delight. With the sunlight streaming through the vines, it couldn't have looked more idyllic.

Romy had made her decision then. She'd do what Roberto asked. She would honour Alfonso's memory by submitting to his family's wishes. She would work harder than ever. She would do whatever it took to make Roberto and Alfonso and, most of all, Alfie proud.

*   *   *

And, for the last two years, she'd done just that. She'd worked every day and every night, when Alfie had been asleep. She'd learnt everything there was to know about Scolari. In the last three months she'd spearheaded a massive publicity drive, which had brought her even more attention than when she'd been at the height of her modelling career.

It had only been recently, however, that she'd stopped having to answer questions about Alfonso's death. Slowly and surely Romy had managed to switch the media's attention from the past to the future. Which was why this interview on women in business was important, and why she'd juggled her schedule to get here.

And now, here she was. The red light switched

402

to green. They were finally on air.

Romy focused as she listened to Antonella Medici read from her notes about the economic climate and how healthy Scolari was looking, and Romy nodded and smiled. Then Antonella turned her attention to Romy. She had blonde hair, swept high away from her smooth forehead, her deep eyes made up with glittering brown eyeshadow. Her full lips were outlined in dark pencil.

'But there have been many reports,' Antonella continued, 'that the need to raise capital will mean that many Italian private companies will be forced to decide between going public or being acquired by a major international group, which would then of course be diverting many of whatever profits they made out of the domestic Italian market. Would you agree with that? I was reading a piece only last week in the *New York Times*, in which Thea Maddox from the Maddox Corporation was quoted as saying yet again that a company like Scolari would be the icing on the cake for their European expansion plans. Are you a company that would ever—how shall I put this?—sell out?'

Romy let out a sardonic laugh. 'Believe me,' she told Medici. 'The Maddox corporation can only *dream*. Scolari is Italian and will always stay that way. Sure, I can imagine why the Americans would look at us with envy. Our publishing arm goes from strength to strength,' Romy said. 'In the media division too, we have extended our cable and digital channels threefold in the last year, but it is our online development that has been the big success story.'

She went on to recite her carefully rehearsed statistics. She would leave the listeners in no doubt: Scolari was not vulnerable in any way and was able to raise sufficient capital for expansion from private sources.

What she didn't say, for reasons of confidentiality—even though it would have stamped on any speculation over Scolari's future ownership like a bug—was that Scolari's shareholders were so few and so loyal that they'd never be tempted to sell out to any outside aggressor. Roberto had already signed over 5 per cent of his shareholding to Romy, leaving him with 45 per cent. Maria had always had 10 per cent for tax purposes. And the remaining 40 per cent was owned by Roberto's trusted business partner, Franco Moretti.

But even so, she was annoyed. Idle speculation could be damaging, in terms of employee confidence as well as reputation.

She made a mental note to find out everything she could about Thea Maddox. How dare she continue making comments like that about Scolari? Romy knew that Roberto had already pushed her overtures firmly away.

'Yet, despite all this expansion, Scolari has been voted one of the most employee-friendly companies in a recent survey,' Antonella continued, keen to keep the focus on women in business.

Romy smiled, glad that this particular achievement had been picked up.

'I'm doing what I can to create a community-style ethic in our company.'

'It hasn't always been like that at Scolari, though?'

Romy chose her words carefully, knowing that

404

Roberto himself could well be listening in. 'We have moved with the times. In our new main headquarters, here in Milan, we now have a full-time crèche and have actively encouraged successful job-shares. As a working mother myself, I know how important it is to have children nearby.'

But as she continued to talk about the importance of women in the Scolari workforce, Romy knew that she was putting a positive spin on it all. The truth was that she was still operating in a very male world. She didn't understand half of the behind-the-scenes deals that went on at the various functions Roberto attended. The last time he'd been to the Grand Prix, he'd come back having secured a controlling shareholding in a football club. She was beginning to wonder whether Alfonso's rise in the Formula One scene had been entirely to do with his talent, or whether his father had arranged it all for him.

But she would never say a word against Roberto. She would be loyal. No matter what. No matter what the sacrifice. Roberto trusted her. Why else would he have signed those shares over to her? She was family. She would never let him down.

*   *   *

Outside in the corridor Romy's press officer, James, smiled and put his hands up in applause.

'That was great,' he said. He was a young guy— the youngest Romy had interviewed—but he worked hard and was just the kind of dynamic, fresh blood that was making Scolari thrive. She

405

liked his slim-line brown suit and trendy rectangular black-framed glasses. Nico would have adored him, she thought.

'Hey, you know that piece you wanted me to do the other day, for that American magazine?'

'Sure,' James said.

'Call them up,' Romy said. 'We'll do the family piece. You'll have to manage it. Make sure they make us look untouchable.' She knew Roberto and Maria resented intrusion into their lives, but Romy knew that the only way for Scolari to bury these takeover rumours was through a PR offensive—and where better place to launch it than in the country from which the offensive was rumoured to be coming?

Already on the move, James started rattling off a series of new appointments and summaries of phone messages, all the things that needed dealing with just in the short time she'd been in the studio.

'The children's charity have been in touch again,' he added. 'Did you decide whether you'd be their patron?'

Romy sighed. 'I haven't got time, but tell them I'm still thinking about it,' she said, looking at her watch. She was already late to pick up Alfie.

She made five calls and answered three urgent emails as she took the short ride back to the Scolari headquarters to drop off James, and then went on to where Sara, Alfie's teacher, was waiting with him. As usual Romy was the last parent to pick him up and she smiled at Sara and ruffled Alfie's hair, gesturing her apology that she was still on the phone.

'Where were you?' Alfie said as she took his hand. But just as she finished one call, her phone

406

rang again. She growled in frustration. Sometimes she didn't have a second to catch her breath.

It was Franco, Roberto's finance director, and she braced herself. Despite his show of benevolence towards Romy, she'd never forgotten the time she'd first met him and how dismissive he'd been of her modelling career. He'd been jealous, she remembered, that Alfonso had jilted his daughter and had fallen for Romy instead. Roberto had assured her that it was all in the past and that Franco adored her, but Romy wasn't so sure. She knew how men like Franco could hold a grudge, and Roberto appointing her to the board had done nothing to quell Franco's privately held suspicion of her. *How can you be sure*, Franco had once demanded of Roberto—in front of Romy— *that our new director isn't planning on running away again?*

'I've got to take this, darling,' she told Alfie, answering the call and imagining Franco on the company yacht in Sardinia—a perk that Romy had yet to have time to take advantage of.

He explained that he'd been hosting a dinner for the various heads of their media interests. It annoyed her that she'd not even been informed, but she decided to bite her tongue. He wouldn't be calling just to inform her of that.

'We've had approaches again,' he said, finally cutting to the chase. 'From Russia, as well as America this time.'

First Thea Maddox, and now this.

Alfie was scuffing a stone on the pavement. It flicked up and hit a parked car. 'Don't,' she mouthed to him.

'Do you want me to email the details?' Franco

407

asked.

'No. I'm not interested. Don't tell Roberto. You know how worked up he gets about these things.'

'Romy, you're the one who has to look to the future of Scolari. At least consider a merger—'

How dare he. Looking out for the future of Scolari was *exactly* what she did. Every hour of every day. A merger was out of the question. Scolari would go intact, just as it was now, to Alfie. That was Roberto's heart's desire, and Romy was damned sure she was going to deliver on it. 'The answer is no.'

'Do you have to talk on the phone the whole time?' Alfie asked. He scowled petulantly at her as she made her excuses and rang off. She wondered whether he ever thought about how much she had to juggle even to pick him up from school at all.

The sensible thing would be to do as Roberto and Maria had suggested and send him to a good private boarding school. But sending him away wasn't a sacrifice Romy was willing to make. He was still all that was left of Alfonso. She couldn't bear the thought of losing him too.

Romy shut her phone. 'You're right,' she said, crouching down to his level. 'I'm sorry, darling. It's just that I have lots of people waiting for me to make important decisions. But you know what? They can wait. Why don't we go to the cinema? Just you and me.' She knew the new Harry Potter film he'd wanted to see—*The Order of the Phoenix*—was showing at cinemas.

'Right now?' Alfie's face broke into a grin.

'Right now.'

'Is it a premiere?' he asked as she ushered him into the car, but Romy saw in his swagger that he

408

already expected it was. That he'd be once more on the red carpet, as he had been a few times in recent months. That he would stroll in and be the centre of attention.

Alfie had already changed so much, she thought, her conscience pricked. She remembered how he used to be. How just going out on his scooter used to make him happy. But now he was getting used to this privileged life.

Maybe I should get involved in the children's charity, she thought, as the chauffeur opened the door for them and they climbed into the back of the bulletproof limousine. *Maybe it would do Alfie good to realize how little others had.*

Or perhaps this is just how it was—how life always *would* be for her son. After all, both he and she were Scolaris now. And there was no going back.

CHAPTER TWENTY-NINE

NOVEMBER 2007

Thea put on her sunglasses and took a sip of icy water. The late-afternoon sun was beating down. Maybe she should have chosen a table in the shade, she thought, but she'd wanted to be as conspicuous as possible. Besides, she told herself, she shouldn't grumble. After the howling, icy winter days in Manhattan, which she'd temporarily escaped, anywhere warm like this wasn't so bad. Particularly when the view was this fine.

Her gaze moved slowly east from the fixed

billowing sails of the Sydney Opera House towards the Harbour Bridge and the myriad of boats criss-crossing the wide blue bay, thinking how illicit it all felt—and, yes, she admitted, almost enjoyable because of that—to be away, even for just a few days, from the office.

She checked her phone and then put it back in her soft leather tote bag, chastising herself. She had an intermittent signal, but Michael still hadn't replied to her text. But then, it occurred to her, he might actually be fast asleep back home in the States. Even so, she couldn't help wondering what he'd think when he did read her message. Would he be proud of her for taking the plunge and coming to Australia?

Stop it, she told herself. Why was she seeking Michael's approval—or even such regular contact with him—when she knew there was no hope of anything more than a limited friendship ever developing between them? He'd said as much himself a few email exchanges ago: that he doubted he could *ever* be in a profound relationship again.

Damaged goods. That's how he'd described himself.

But not to me, Thea had wanted to reply.

But she knew it wasn't only Michael's lack of faith in his own emotional ability that was keeping them apart. It was her own fear of the barbed tangle of emotions that she'd swallowed deep down inside herself. Because what was the point of even dreaming about one day perhaps being closer to Michael if she could never tell him the truth about herself?

The more he'd told her that he was proud of her

and amazed by her success, the more of a fraud she'd felt. He might think he was weak in comparison, but he wasn't. He was brave. He was strong. He'd faced his demons and found a way to talk about them. When she'd never done anything of the sort.

Even here in the bright sunshine, the thought of it—what Michael would say, what he'd *think* about her, if she ever opened up to him—sent a wave of shivers crawling down her spine.

And yet despite herself, as she took another drink of water and checked her watch and the faces of the people passing by, she couldn't help wondering about Michael. And thinking too that their last meeting, a month ago now, had put a different perspective on their burgeoning relationship. It had left her feeling full of—there was indeed no other word for it—*hope*.

*   *   *

When Michael had called her to say he was back in the States and going to visit his mother, Thea had suggested straight away that she go and spend the day with him at the Brightside Home. Michael had agreed. After all, it had been something they'd touched on during her visit to Landstuhl. Thea had cancelled everything to be there.

She drove way too fast from the airport in her hire car, only slowing as the vehicle's tyres crunched over the last few yards of the rest-home's gravel drive. It was only now that she was here that she realized why Brightside was costing her so much money. The main house, an old sawmill owner's mansion, was an attractive stone building

411

surrounded by dark yew trees. Manicured gardens stretched down towards a glittering lake.

Thea's heart swelled to see that Mrs Pryor was ending her days in such a lovely place. She'd forgotten too how much she loved being in this part of the world. The fresh air and clear blue sky smelt of home. But any joy Thea felt was soon eclipsed by sadness as she remembered how ill the old lady was. Even so, Thea knew Michael must surely approve.

She checked her face in the driver's mirror one more time, feeling her heart thumping. She'd changed five times before she'd come, finally opting for a dressed-down look, with jeans and cowboy boots. She applied a slick of lip-gloss, then grabbed her bag and stepped out on the pathway.

'Thea!' She heard Michael's voice before she saw him.

He was waving at her from the porch at the front of the house and started down the steps to meet her. As Thea approached, she could hardly believe that he was the same man she'd seen at Landstuhl. He'd grown his hair and looked fit and lean in a pair of well-cut designer jeans and a soft blue cashmere jumper. He was tanned and clean-shaven and was no longer trying to hide his scar. But even that no longer seemed nearly so inflamed and had somehow grown to suit him.

He walked quickly towards Thea, smiling, and wrapped her in a tight embrace. When he pulled back, the way his eyes connected with hers made her heart thump hard.

'Hey, look at you,' she said.

He grinned at her. 'It's so good to see you, at last. You know . . . properly. Not in a hospital.' He smiled again, clearly remembering where he was. 'Just outside one instead.'

When their eyes locked again, she realized how long she'd been looking forward to that, to just looking at his face. It was Michael who broke the moment. She saw a blush in his cheeks.

'Mom's inside,' he said, grimacing a little. 'She's . . . er . . . well, come on, you can see for yourself.'

He led Thea inside and she followed him down a long corridor and into a private set of rooms. Across a sweep of clean pink carpet Mrs Pryor was sitting in a chair with a crocheted blanket over her knees. She was looking out at the garden at an empty stone birdbath.

She had become like a tracing of her former self, Thea thought, as she approached, shocked by how much the old housekeeper had aged. Thea's heart ached with chagrin when she thought of what Michael had told her: that Caroline Pryor had written to her every week, and Thea had never replied. Now a thousand memories assaulted her. Of Mrs Pryor brushing her hair before bed; of the fat birthday cakes she'd iced; of hemming her party dress, and teaching her to knit . . .

'You have a visitor, Mom,' Michael said. 'It's Thea. Thea Maddox. She's come all this way to say hello.'

Mrs Pryor slowly turned to face them. Thea thought she saw a glimmer of recognition in her rheumy, near-translucent blue eyes. Thea bent down, touching the downy softness of Mrs Pryor's hand.

'Do you remember me?' she asked her. She leant forward and kissed her cheek. 'It's so nice to see you.'

413

Mrs Pryor's watery eyes searched Thea's. 'She wept so much,' she said.

'Who? Who wept?' Thea asked, sitting down now in the chair that Michael had brought her.

'Her . . .' Mrs Prior answered, before turning sharply to Michael and demanding, 'Who are you?'

'It's Michael, Mom. Remember?' He smiled an exasperated smile at Thea. His eyes were full of regret.

'Michael?' She studied Michael, searching for clues. 'I don't know any Michael. Who are you?' she demanded again, looking panicked now, half-standing up out of her chair. 'Why are you here?'

'Don't get upset. It's OK. We've just come to visit you, that's all,' Michael soothed.

He helped his mother sit back down and she murmured something Thea didn't quite catch, before falling silent again. She stared back out at the birdbath, as if Thea and Michael were no longer—had never been—there.

Michael and Thea tried talking to her, taking turns to remind her of her life, but only twice did she actually look back at them, and not once did Thea see that glimmer of recognition return.

'I'm so sorry,' Thea said. She felt a rush of tenderness as she watched Michael stroke his mother's thin white hair.

'This is a good day. Believe it or not,' he said.

One wall of Mrs Pryor's room had been entirely covered with photographs. Thea walked over and read the Post-it notes stuck to them: names and places and memories. She smiled when she saw a picture of her and Michael as children—she couldn't have been much more than six—sitting on the doorstep of Little Elm's greenhouse, eating a

414

big bowl of strawberries, their grubby knees touching.

'Look at us,' she said, putting her fingertip on the photo. 'And look, there's Johnny.'

'I remember you said you'd seen him,' Michael said. He glanced back at his mother; she was still staring out of the window. 'Let's go and get a coffee,' he said.

'Dr Myerson will come soon,' Mrs Pryor said, shaking her head.

'Sorry, Mom?' Michael said, surprised that his mother had spoken.

But Mrs Pryor didn't answer. Her eyelids started to droop and her head lolled forward. Right before their eyes, she fell asleep.

*   *   *

With their coffee mugs long empty, Thea stared across the polished wooden refectory table at Michael. She really hadn't intended to tell him everything, but as soon as she'd sat down with him in this spacious, silent room overlooking the rolling lawns, she'd found herself confiding in him. She'd told him all about visiting Johnny and finding out about her mother's baby. And then she'd told him about Shelley too. About how her half-sister had been given away.

Sister—sometimes the word still seemed so alien to Thea, but at other times it felt so natural, as if a part of her had always known that a bit of her life was missing and was waiting out there for her.

'My God. I wonder if anyone else knew?' Michael said. 'I wonder if Mom knew. It's a pretty

415

huge secret to keep, huh?'

Thea nodded. 'It puts a weird perspective on everything. On the way I remember Mom. I always thought my father was the love of her life, but now I wonder if it might actually have been Johnny all along. If Mom only stayed with Dad out of loyalty . . .'

'So what are you going to do?' Michael asked.

'I've found her,' she admitted. 'My half-sister. I know where she is.'

Thea thought about all the money she'd spent over the last five years, on private investigators in England and Australia. Her search had been sporadic. As life in Maddox Inc. had become ever more hectic, at times she'd thought of giving up altogether.

And after Tom's death in 2001 she hadn't wanted to hassle Shelley Lawson, suspecting that Thea would be the last person she needed to hear from. But two years ago she'd sent an email reminding Shelley of her promise to help. Six months ago, just when Thea had completely given up hope, Shelley had sent a file of information. Details that Thea had studied again and again.

'But I don't know what to do next, Michael. I mean, do I really have the right to drop such a bombshell into her life?' Thea said. It felt so good to talk about all of this with him.

Michael put his hand on hers. 'It sounds to me like you've already made up your mind. Or why dig up all this information on her at all?'

'But what about her? What about what *she* wants? Of course she has a right to know, but what if she'd be happier just as she is?'

Michael's hand was still on hers. 'Why not just

go see?' he said, smiling at her gently now. 'You're Thea Maddox, after all. What's stopping you jumping on a plane? The Thea Maddox I've known always had a pretty good instinct when it came to other people. So why not just go take a look and judge for yourself if she's the kind of woman who can take it in her stride?'

'You mean spy on her?'

'I mean just go and do what you've got to do.' His face grew more serious as he trailed his fingers along the curved line of his scar. 'Life's too short to play "what if", Thea,' he said. 'Don't end up living with regrets.' He forced a smile. 'The Thea I remember, she never let anything get in her way. Just go and do what you feel is right.'

Thea squeezed his hand tight in hers, his faith in her filling her with confidence. She found herself wishing again for a second, just as she had done in Landstuhl, that he'd never let her go. And as his eyes met hers, despite what he'd just told her, she caught herself thinking: *What if . . .*

*   *   *

And now here she was in Sydney—only all the confidence she'd felt then was gone. She wished she'd asked Michael to come with her. Just like when they'd been kids, with him standing by her side she still felt she could take on the world.

Thea noticed the waitress hovering, waiting to take her order.

'I'm still waiting for someone. Sorry,' Thea said. 'My sister,' she added, testing out the words.

The waitress smiled brightly, as if it were the most natural thing in the world. 'No problem, you

417

just call me over when you're ready,' she said, heading off to where other diners had signalled they wanted their bill.

Thea looked at her watch again. She felt her heart fluttering with nerves. *Would* she come? *Would* she? Would she want to meet Thea as well?

She.

Jenny Mulligan.

Her sister.

In the twenty-four hours since she'd arrived in Sydney, Thea had studied Jenny Mulligan from Balmain in minute detail, sitting outside her house on the street in the hire car, peering through the binoculars she'd bought. She'd watched a seemingly confident woman prepare coffee in the morning, before she'd ushered two boys out of the front door and had driven them to school.

Thea had followed her to a shopping mall, where she'd opened up the grille of a shop and had turned on the lights, before plumping up the soft toys and furnishings in the window. Thea had plucked up the courage to go into the store. She'd browsed for ages, before—her heart pounding at the sheer recklessness of her choice—she'd selected a red heart-shaped cushion embroidered with the words '*Sisters make the best of friends*'. Something about it had reminded her of the embroidered heart Mrs Pryor had helped her make all those years ago for her mother. Her mother, who had kept this secret from her to her grave.

Thea had felt so unconfident and humble as she'd approached the till where Jenny had been standing, as if her secret were written all over her face. But up close, Thea hadn't been able to imagine what genetic traits she might share with

418

this taller, more athletic stranger. Thea had imagined this moment over and over again, thinking it might be like looking in a mirror. But it had been nothing like that. In fact the only trait Thea had recognized in Jenny at all had been their mother's eyes. The rest must have been Johnny's, she'd thought, unable to quell the sense of disappointment that this discovery had stirred up inside her.

'Your sister will love that,' Jenny had said, shocking Thea with her Australian accent. 'I'm assuming it's a gift?' she said.

'Er . . . yes . . .'

'I always wanted a sister,' Jenny had commented conversationally as she'd wrapped the cushion up.

Me too, Thea had wanted to blurt out.

'But instead I just got lumbered with a couple of naughty little brothers,' Jenny had added with a grin, as she'd tied off the bow.

Thea's resolve had wavered then. She had brothers? Thea's file hadn't mentioned that, but of course it was possible. There was no reason why Jenny's adoptive parents shouldn't have had more children? Thea had felt herself starting to panic. What else might she not know?

She'd imagined it would be black and white. She'd thought that, after all this time and money she'd invested, she'd arrive here in Australia and make her grand announcement and have a wonderful sense of: *what?* she wondered. Closure? Elation? But staring at this woman—this *stranger*— Thea had realized that it was all going to be so much more complicated than that.

'I know this is going to sound very strange,' she'd said, plucking up the courage, suddenly knowing that if she didn't do it now, then she'd never come back. 'But I need to talk to you.'

'Me?' Jenny had said, staring at Thea blankly.

'I have something to tell you, Jenny. It's something to do with your family.' Thea had lowered her voice, as other customers had come into the shop.

Jenny had stared at her, dumbfounded, obviously amazed that Thea knew her name. 'But I don't know you. Are you sure you've got the right person?'

'I can explain it all. I've come a very long way to find you.'

'Well, I can't talk here,' Jenny had said.

'Then meet me later. I'll be at the Opera House bar from six.' Thea had put down some cash to cover the cost of the cushion, as well as a business card relating to the bar, so that it would be easy for Jenny to find it. 'Please. It really is vital that you come.'

* * *

And now Thea finally saw her. Jenny Mulligan was wearing the same clothes she'd been wearing at work. She must have come straight here, Thea thought, wondering instinctively who she'd got to look after her kids. Her dark hair was pulled back from her face. She looked around her, as if it was the last place she ever might visit.

Thea stared at Jenny, again waiting for the moment of profound connection she'd been expecting to kick in. But it didn't. Instead she felt an overwhelming urge to run away. She forced herself to smile and wave.

420

She could do this, she told herself, remembering Michael's confidence in her. Jenny might not be what she'd imagined, but she was still *family*. Her family. The only real connection Thea had to her mother. Which is why Thea kept her smile locked in place until Jenny joined her.

Thea offered her some wine, but Jenny Mulligan refused, sitting nervously with her plastic handbag on her lap.

'So what's all this about then?' Jenny asked, startling Thea with her directness. Thea was so used to people being subservient towards her, so used to them treating her like their boss, that it felt weird to be put on the spot. 'Is this to do with Danny's cousin? If he's got into trouble, then we're not bailing him out—'

'No, not at all,' Thea said, startled, and remembering from her notes that Danny was Jenny's husband. She realized that Jenny must have jumped to all sorts of conclusions since their meeting this morning.

'Then who are you?'

'My name is Thea Maddox,' she told Jenny.

'You're American.' The words sounded more like an accusation than a question.

Thea watched Jenny scrutinizing her, her eyes checking out her diamond earrings and Moschino jacket.

She smiled uneasily again. 'There's no easy way to tell you this. But I've recently found out that you and I are sisters. Well . . . half-sisters.'

She looked at Jenny for a reaction—for tears? For denial? for what exactly she didn't know—but all Jenny did was just stare blankly back.

'Your father is Johnny Faraday,' Thea said,

hiding now behind the facts, hoping they'd be enough to convince Jenny that what she was saying was true. 'He lives in South Africa. Your mother— our mother—is . . . *was* . . . Alyssa McAdams.' Thea slid the envelope across the table. The papers she'd spent weeks preparing. 'It's all in here.'

Jenny exhaled. 'You've got to be joking.'

'No.'

'But me? Are you sure? I mean, Mum and Dad—they never said anything . . .'

Mum and Dad. The way she said those words. The way they sounded so solid. So full of history. *Oh, God*, Thea thought, *what have I done?*

'You mean you didn't even know you were adopted?' Thea felt sick.

Jenny's eyes filled with tears and her hard features crumpled. 'I don't know what to say.' She stared at the envelope, not taking it.

And Thea realized that she'd been so utterly wrong to have come here. And Michael had been wrong about her too. Whatever judgement she'd possessed as a child, she'd lost it all now. Jenny already had a caring, loving family. She'd had no need, like Thea, to rake over the past, searching for embers of the truth.

'I don't know what you want from me,' Jenny said.

'I don't want anything,' Thea said.

But she did. She wanted something, she knew for certain now, that Jenny Mulligan would never be able to give her. She wanted the kind of sister who was a mirror-image of herself. The kind of sister who might really be her best friend. The kind of sister that would make the nagging ache about her past go away.

Thea's phone rang. And kept on ringing. She cursed herself for not putting it onto mute.

Jenny was staring fixedly at the envelope.

In frustration Thea snatched up her phone and demanded, 'What?'

Storm's voice crackled down the line. 'Thea, where are you? Nobody has been able to reach you. You've got to come. Thea . . . it's Griff . . .'

CHAPTER THIRTY

OCTOBER 2009

The Nico Rilla Retrospective that Simona Fiore had organized in his memory was being held at the prestigious Belina gallery in Rome. The event had been on Romy's radar for months, but as Saturday night arrived and her driver, Dario, pulled the sleek Mercedes to a halt outside the brightly lit downtown mansion block, Romy suddenly found herself filled with apprehension and dreading the attention and scrutiny she knew she was about to face.

From the shadows of the car she looked at the rain-slicked pavement and the blurred reflection of the gallery lights. Behind the plate-glass windows the venue was already full—a colourful crowd of people laughing and drinking. Even from the car she could hear the hubbub of voices over the beat of the music coming from the open gallery doors. The Black Eyed Peas, Romy recognized. Alfie had this track on his new iPod.

Simona had made Romy the guest of honour

tonight, and in her Dior clutch was a speech she'd spent hours preparing, but still she wondered whether she was strong enough to be around all of Nico's old friends. It would be like travelling back in time. To that night again. The night Alfonso and Nico had died.

Romy had spent so much of the intervening years trying to erase the memory of what had happened—plucking out those shards of shrapnel, those twisted, bloodied remnants of the night her life had blown apart. And mostly she'd managed it. But only by relentlessly and tirelessly focusing on the future—a future, she'd grown to realize, she was lucky to have at all.

And as she'd driven herself forward, Roberto had been only too willing to let her drive his business alongside her. In the last two years he'd given Romy more and more responsibility. So much so that, for the first time ever today, he'd left Romy in sole charge of Scolari while he and Maria set off to enjoy what Romy hoped would be the first of a series of long-overdue holidays.

Romy's only regret was that they'd taken Alfie with them. Romy hadn't been able to refuse their invitation, especially as it had been presented as such a *fait accompli* by all three of them. Alfie had been so excited about going on the yacht. He'd also known, of course, that his grandparents would spoil him rotten, and that Roberto would give him a free rein—far more than his mother ever did at home. And it wouldn't be fair to him, Alfie had argued, if *he* didn't go on holiday, when Romy was going to be at work every day anyway, and had been for most of the time he'd been off school in the summer, he'd added, tightening the

424

thumbscrews of guilt.

But Romy was still full of misgivings. She knew Roberto and Maria would protect Alfie, of course. She knew he'd be safe and would in all probability have a wonderful time, but she had never spent so long away from him before—a whole two weeks. And it had hurt her that he'd wanted to go as much as he had. That he didn't seem to mind being away from her at all.

Does this mean I'm not a good mother? The thought plagued her once again. She'd bent over backwards to do the right thing, whilst still fulfilling her commitments to Roberto's company. Even if it had been for just small parts of each day, she'd tried her best to be there for Alfie whenever she could.

But now she wondered whether that had been enough. Or perhaps whether somehow it might even have made matters worse, and that by seeing him in so many fits and starts, she'd only ever really highlighted how much of the rest of the time she wasn't there.

She remembered how he'd puffed out his little chest as he'd said goodbye this morning. He'd looked so independent, it had made her want to cry. And watching the raindrops snake down the limousine window now, his absence filled her heart with a dull ache. And another sort of fear too. That he was no longer hers. That even though he was only seven and a half, he was already more Roberto's protégé than he was her little boy.

It's only a fortnight, she told herself, reminding herself again what she had come here to do, and telling herself that she too needed to be strong. *In two weeks they'll all be home in time for Alfie's cousin Cesca's eighteenth birthday party in Milan*, she told herself. In the meantime Roberto had told her this morning, before they'd all left, that she should let her hair down and have fun tonight. But Romy wondered whether she even knew how to any more.

Usually she went to events like this with Alfie, or certainly with one of the family. But tonight she was painfully aware of how alone she was, and she regretted not asking Anna or Flavia along. But their lives were busy. She couldn't expect them to drop everything for her. And yet, without Alfie, she suddenly glimpsed the future. Pulling herself together, she took a deep breath and, thanking Dario, who'd opened the limousine door for her, she stepped out onto the red carpet and smiled.

*   *   *

The gallery was crammed with so many people Romy recognized. That model—hadn't they worked together on the Ferragamo campaign? Wasn't that man Pierre, Nico's boyfriend when he'd died? *This would have been Nico's favourite kind of party*, Romy thought, smiling sadly at his self-portrait in the centre of the room.

Simona Fiore burst through the crowd in a purple paisley jacket and greeted her in a perfumed hug. Romy smiled, glad of her warmth, remembering how close she and her former modelling agent had once been.

'You've arrived. Thank God. I was worried you might have changed your mind.'

'I wouldn't have missed it for the world,' Romy said, smiling brightly, as a trio of photographers gathered round her, their cameras' lenses chattering like birds.

'Well, now that you're here,' Simona said, steering Romy away once the photographers had finished, 'you're going to get drunk with me.' She plucked two Martinis from a waiter with a tray. 'To our boy,' she said, clinking glasses with Romy.

Romy laughed at Simona's enthusiasm, but at the same time felt the prickling onset of tears. 'Oh God,' she said. 'I knew this would happen. I spent ages getting made up. And I promised myself I wouldn't cry.'

'Don't worry, you still look sensational, darling,' Simona said, pulling out the skirt of the red Valentino dress Romy was wearing. She'd made an extra-special effort tonight in honour of Nico, calling in a favour from a stylist in Milan. 'Now come, come, before you get whisked away. I want to show you something.'

Simona led Romy through the gallery by the hand, not letting her stop as old acquaintances leant in and tried to engage her in conversation as she passed. She pulled Romy into a darkened room at the back of the gallery and switched on the light.

'Look,' she said, sweeping her arm out dramatically.

On the back wall, in black-and-white, was a blown-up portrait of Romy on the beach of the Hotel Amalfi, her sundress clinging to her wet body, her hair splattered across her face as she'd smiled at Nico behind the camera.

Romy stepped towards it, transported back to that magical, pivotal moment when her life had changed, remembering how she'd just baptized herself in the sea that day, how she'd washed Schwedt and Berlin and London away. She studied her smile and the way the sun shone in her eyes. Had she really ever been that carefree and young?

'I couldn't believe it when I finally found that negative,' Simona said. 'You know, it was the first photograph of you I ever saw?'

Romy remembered how Nico had explained to her how he'd faxed Simona a copy of it, and it had been enough to make the powerful agent sign her on the spot. Romy hadn't ever realized why until now. There was something hungry in the eyes of that young girl, and a look that said she wasn't going to miss one second of what life had to offer.

'He told me he thought you were the future,' Simona continued, 'and you know, that boy was right.' Simona put her arm around Romy and sighed. 'Time moves so fast, eh?'

'Yes,' Romy said, but it was no more than a cracked whisper.

'Which is why I thought I'd remind us all of what fun we've had along the way.' Simona went to a red velvet chair in the corner and lifted up a brown box. 'Nico's mother let me into his flat,' she explained, 'and I spent hours going through all his work to put this exhibition together. But I also found these . . .'

Simona handed the box to Romy. 'Take a look.'

Romy undid the box. Inside were twelve black-and-white, ten-by-eight photos, developed from one negative sheet. But they'd all been taken, Romy worked out straight away, *before* that shot on the back wall. All in order, they'd captured Romy down on the beach, stripping off her clothes and wading into the sea. Then coming back out, her arms thrown up to the sunshine, her scrawny body glistening, her eyes shining with joy.

'He could have made a fortune from them,' Simona said. 'Time and again. If he'd wanted to, he could have changed the whole course of your career.'

Romy nodded, unable to speak. It wasn't the shock of discovering Nico had been spying on her that day, before he'd introduced himself. He was a photographer, after all. Taking opportunistic pictures was part of his stock-in-trade, and *she*'d been the one who'd been naive and foolish enough to strip off on a public beach. No, what left her standing here stunned was that Nico had been loyal to her right from the start, before he'd even known her. He'd chosen to be on her side, from the word go.

She hugged the box of photos close, closing her eyes.

He'd kept her safe, she thought. He'd always tried to keep her safe. He'd *died* trying to keep her safe.

Once again she saw the blossom of red blood on his white shirt. The memory that she'd tried so hard to forget. The memory that was just as real and as permanent as these photographs in her arms. She felt her heart aching as the tears slid from her closed eyelids.

'I can't bear that he's gone, either,' Simona said, touching Romy's arm.

'He's gone because of me,' Romy said.

'It's not your fault.'

'It is,' Romy nodded, opening her raw eyes and looking at Simona. 'It is.'

'He wanted to be with you and Alfonso that

weekend,' Simona said. 'He loved being near you both. You made him feel happy—a part of something great. That's what he always said. Don't blame yourself,' Simona told her, hugging her close now.

Romy buried her face in Simona's neck and sobbed. She felt her chest heave. She knew she should never have come.

'It was just bad luck,' Simona soothed. 'It was just life, that's all.'

Romy bit down the words she so desperately wanted to say. But still she ached to unburden herself. To finally tell the truth about the night Nico had died. About Claudia and Ulrich. About what a naive fool she had been. That she should have trusted her instinct to cut off her past, like she'd always done. That Nico's death was her fault. Would always be her fault.

'Come on,' Simona cajoled her, clasping her by the shoulders and smiling at her bravely, wiping away a tear in her own eye. 'Let's go and join the party. Nico wouldn't have wanted us to be sad. Besides, there are so many people who want to see you.'

Romy faltered for a second, ready to speak, but then she looked into Simona's eyes and saw only trust there. She couldn't unburden herself. Not here. Not now. It would devastate Simona. And tonight was about Nico. She had to remember that. And she knew, too, that unburdening herself wouldn't help. It wouldn't make her feel better. And it wouldn't bring Alfonso or Nico back.

Shut it out, Romy told herself. The past was the past. Nobody need ever know the truth. *Think of Alfie*. Nobody must ever find out.

She remembered Simona telling her once that all she had to do was work hard and then she'd be safe. *Untouchable*. Wasn't that what she'd said? Yes, she would work. She would continue to do what she'd done so well these last two years. She would bury her head in her work and move on.

But as she dried her eyes, fixed her make-up and then went back out, united and smiling with Simona into the crowd, she felt as if she were looking down on herself from the ceiling. She saw herself being greeted and fussed over, complimented and admired. She was Romy Scolari—rich, successful and beautiful. Hadn't she fulfilled every dream she'd had since she'd been the eighteen-year-old in that photograph? Shouldn't she feel, in spite of those she'd lost on the journey here, that she was finally where she belonged? Hadn't all the work she'd put in earnt her that much peace, at least?

It should have done. But it didn't. Instead she felt that she'd escaped nothing. She felt she still belonged nowhere. Inside—beneath the smiles and the carefully cultivated mannerisms and all her projections of cool self-control—Romy Scolari still felt like a frightened little girl who would always be running away.

*   *   *

Brett Maddox was intrigued. No, *more* than intrigued, he thought, he was *excited*. Ever since he'd received the email from this businessman here in Germany, a few weeks ago, he'd been anticipating this meeting. Now he rubbed his hands together as the plain black door in the building on the Munich street opened. He looked quickly round again to check that he hadn't been followed, then stepped inside.

'This way, Mr Maddox,' a suited bouncer said in German-accented English, leading the way up the steep red-carpeted stairs ahead of him. He had a crew-cut and was all muscle beneath his smart black suit.

At the top of the stairs was another black-suited heavy with a crew-cut. An old scar gave the left side of his face an awkward downwards slant. He stared at Brett, who stared right back into his black eyes. He wasn't intimidated for a second. He'd seen plenty of men like this before. Enough to know that guys like this worked for guys like Brett. They asked no questions and did what they were told. Brett watched him reach out and open another door. *Just take me to your boss*, Brett thought.

Behind the door Brett was pleasantly surprised to find what he liked to find behind doors such as these. He walked into a plushly decorated lounge and stopped beneath an ornate chandelier. Along one wall ran a shiny black bar, with a pyramid of glittering bottles rising against an ornate mirror behind it, and a bartender in black-and-whites busy polishing a Martini glass.

A waitress in a short pink leotard, fishnet tights and high heels pouted over her shoulder at Brett as she sat at the bar and lit a cigarette. She was a pro, a hooker. Brett had had enough to know that much for sure.

Oh yeah, Brett thought. This was definitely his kind of place.

There'd been no hint from the street that such

432

. . . facilities . . . might exist inside, and as Brett looked around he felt more and more comfortable. The man who'd asked him here must clearly have known a thing or two about him, to have risked bringing him here at all. Which meant that whatever information they had for him was most likely accurately targeted too.

A few games tables were dotted around the room, and over to the right were two metal poles on a raised stage area. In the evening Brett could imagine this place would be kicking. But now, in the late afternoon, it had a relaxed, sedate atmosphere. In a corner booth he noticed a man with very blond hair fold up a newspaper and stand.

'Mr Maddox,' the man said.

So this must be Heinz-Gerd Solya. Brett had tried researching him online, but had found out little. But from the look of his tailored suit and the expense he'd clearly gone to decking out this club, he was obviously a man of wealth and power.

Brett shook his hand and Solya offered him a seat at his table. As Brett sat down, Solya clicked his fingers. A girl Brett hadn't even spotted jumped up from where she'd been flicking though a magazine in a corner booth.

Brett's eyes nearly popped out of his head. What could she be? Fourteen? Fifteen at the most? She had that vulnerable schoolgirl look that Brett liked. That *frightened, malleable* look. The one that said she'd give no trouble. Not like most of those so-called teenage hookers and lap dancers he'd wasted his money on back home, Brett thought. This little bitch was genuinely fresh. Her young breasts bulged against her waistcoat top.

433

Whatever he was here for, Brett sure hoped she was part of the deal.

'Bring us some champagne,' Solya told her.

The girl hurried off.

'Are all your staff as . . . well trained?' Brett asked.

Solya looked pleased by the compliment. 'If they know what's good for them, they do what they are told.'

The girl returned with a bottle of Krug champagne. The finest, Brett noticed from the label. He watched her stroking the bottle and felt himself harden as she grasped and twisted its cork until it popped. It was all he could do not to delve greedily between her legs as she filled his and Solya's glasses to the brim, a coy smile on her pretty face.

'So . . . I'm intrigued by what you mentioned in your email,' Brett said, watching the girl retreat, eager now to get this business part of this meeting out of the way as quickly as possible. 'That you have information about Romy Scolari . . .'

Solya smiled. 'Oh yes. Romy Scolari.' He ran his tongue across his very white teeth, as if trying out the words for taste. 'For a long time now I've been aware that your company would like to buy Scolari. That is correct?'

The man's confident tone, the way he'd cut straight to the heart of such a potentially huge piece of business, all implied that he could help somehow, that he could make it all come true.

Brett took a sip of champagne to calm his beating heart. Scolari was everything. If he could get Scolari where Thea had failed . . . ? If he could prove to the rest of the Maddox board exactly what he could do, then finally, *finally*, justice might be done and he'd get what was rightfully his.

It had been nearly two years since Griffin Maddox had died. Two years of Thea being Chair of the board, blocking him, stopping him. Two years of humiliation, when he should have been in charge, just like Maddox had promised him. Like Storm had guaranteed he would be. But Lance Starling hadn't been able to sway the old man, or make him change his will in Brett's favour. Though God knows, he'd tried.

'What type of information is it you've got?' he asked.

Solya stared at him and Brett saw a flicker of darkness in his blue eyes that answered all his questions.

You've got dirt on her, that's what, Brett realized, salivating over the thought of whatever dark secrets this man—and very soon Brett himself—had access to. A sex scandal? Drugs? Something even worse? The worse, the better, as far as Brett was concerned. He thought of a recent magazine picture he'd seen of Romy with old man Scolari and his wife and those five ugly sisters. An untouchable Italian family. But apparently not. Romy Scolari was their weak link.

The women always were.

'She is not what everyone thinks she is,' Solya said.

'Go on.'

'Mr Maddox. Speaking frankly, the information I have in my possession is enough to bring Scolari to its knees.'

Brett could barely keep a lid on his excitement. *Fuck me*, he thought. *Is this it? Is this the missing*

435

domino that's going to set my whole plan in motion? Because he'd already done the ground work. Oh, yes. He'd already flattered that fat fool, Franco Moretti, the second most important of Scolari's shareholders after old man Scolari himself. He'd already set doubts in Franco's mind about his own future in the Scolari organization. And secretly promised him double what his shares were currently worth. Was the information he was about to glean here really going to prove the key to bringing the rest of Scolari into the fold?

'And for this information what will you want in return?' Brett asked. Looking once more at the man and his establishment, he sincerely doubted that plain old money would be the answer. This guy clearly had plenty of that already.

'In addition to several clubs like this,' Solya said, lighting a cigarette, 'which cannot in any way be traced back to me, I own a small newspaper group here in Germany, which is in need of . . .' Solya paused and looked at Brett '. . . considerable restructuring and modernization, if it is to be at all competitive in today's market.'

'You mean you'd like me to invest? How much?' Brett didn't care. He'd pay whatever it took.

'It's not the amount that's important,' Solya said. 'Perhaps 5 per cent, certainly no more. It's the connection with Maddox Inc. I'm more interested in. With your name attached, I am sure this small group of mine—of *ours*, perhaps—could go from strength to strength.'

Brett smiled. So not only would he get the dirt on the Scolaris, but he'd get himself a new investment too, and one this Solya guy must truly believe in, if he was only willing to give up 5 per cent.

'You've got yourself a deal,' Brett said.

Solya exhaled a plume of smoke towards the ceiling. 'I'll need it in writing.'

'And you'll get it, just as soon as I've seen the goods. My lawyer's here with me in town. Just like you specified.'

Solya nodded and pushed a thick black dossier across the table towards him. Another flash of those sharp white teeth.

'Romy Scolari is an orphan from East Germany,' he said. 'I have testimonies that will back up the other evidence you see here. She killed a boy and burnt down an orphanage. She's a murderer who has lied all her life. She also knew the people who killed her husband and attacked the Scolari household. She let them in, to steal all that priceless art.'

It was all Brett could do not to punch his fist in the air in triumph. He slowly turned the pages of the dossier over, feeling an emotion akin to desire.

He'd done it. He'd done it. He'd got exactly what he wanted.

How Solya knew all this—or why—well, who cared? Brett thought. Maybe he had some personal vendetta against the Scolaris, or even against Romy herself. Who knew? Maybe that slut had even worked for him in a place like this once upon a time.

'This newspaper group of yours,' Brett said a few minutes later, finally putting the dossier down, 'tell me more about it.' He finally allowed himself a satisfied smile. Because you and me, Solya, I think we're going to have a lot of fun doing business together, he thought. Oh yeah, I can feel

437

it in my guts.

They talked for a while about Solya's business proposal, with Brett quickly outlining how to bring Solya's legitimate operation under the Maddox umbrella. Solya ordered more champagne, until soon Brett could no longer tell if he was still feeling euphoric or merely drunk.

There were several more scantily dressed girls and three other men now chatting away in the lounge. Brett noticed that first girl again—the dirty little slut who'd brought their drinks—chatting animatedly to a grey-haired suited man over at the bar. It irritated Brett that she was flirting with him. After all, Brett *had* seen her first.

'I see you have an eye for her,' Solya said.

His white teeth gleamed, his cold blue eyes making Brett feel as if he'd read his thoughts. He might not have found out very much about Solya, but what had Solya found out about him? Brett suddenly had a sense that this man knew him. And not just his tastes in business, but in his personal life too.

'I guess,' he said.

'And do you like them all young, like her?' Solya asked, staring at Brett. 'Or perhaps you're feeling in the mood for something even more . . . extreme?'

Extreme . . . Oh yes, Brett thought, I've always liked a bit of *that*.

Brett nodded and a slow smile spread across Solya's face.

'Then why don't we take our drinks upstairs,' he said. 'I keep a few special *playthings* of interest up there, some of whom I think you might like to meet.'

438

party here, Romy knew that she'd have to come to
the Villa Gasperi again.

*   *   *

Alfie held up the screen on the back of his digital
camera to show Romy.

'And this is me waterskiing,' he said, flicking
through the photos on the tiny screen. 'Look, look,
Mom. Check out my wipe-out. Talk about
awesome!'

Romy laughed, enjoying sitting next to him,
loving the way his hair touched her face. She
stroked her hand along his tanned wrist. Her boy
was home and he was safe. By the look of it, his
holiday with Roberto and Maria had been
amazing.

They were in the garden at the back of the Villa
Gasperi in Milan, sitting on a low wall beneath the
cloistered walk. For a long time after the night of
the crash Romy had avoided coming here at all.
Roberto had understood, of course, and the
Scolaris made a point of socializing elsewhere, or
coming to Romy and Alfie's apartment on the
other side of the city.

But after the robbery on the night of Alfonso's
death when the house and wine cellar had been
wrecked, Roberto and Maria had stripped back
and refurbished the whole place, replacing many of
the artworks. It had been important to Roberto to
restore Gasperi to its former glory. To erase all
trace of the vandals who'd defiled his home. To
make it once more the home that Alfonso had
always loved.

So when Anna, Alfonso's sister and one of
Alfie's favourite aunts, had rung Romy to tell her
that they were holding Cesca's eighteenth birthday

439

party here, Romy knew that she'd have to come to the Villa Gasperi again.

She remembered now when she'd first met Cesca in Tuscany and how she'd given her that sparkly hairclip. She'd always liked Anna's fun-loving daughter and wasn't surprised when she'd insisted on a fancy-dress party. She saw Cesca and three of her friends laughing now, sitting on a bench on the far side of the garden as they tried on their ornate opera masks.

The garden itself had been transformed. Fire-flares were dotted all around, and costumed waiters were carrying cases of wine and stacks of plates into a marquee that had been decorated to look like an opera house. It was where the dancing would be later on.

Romy noticed that the first of the guests had already begun to arrive. She wondered where Roberto and Maria were and whether they'd changed into the costumes Anna had hired for them. Personally she couldn't wait to see Roberto in his eighteenth-century get-up and white wig.

'I'm going inside to check Papa is OK,' Romy told Alfie, kissing him on the head. He was dressed in a purple velvet doublet and hose, which Romy thought he'd refuse to wear, but Alfie thought was hilarious. She knew he fully intended to enter into the spirit of the party with his cousins. 'Don't drink too many fizzy drinks.'

Romy gathered the skirt of her long blue silk dress and walked inside the house and past the kitchen. Even though she didn't want them to, her eyes flicked automatically towards the corner of the room where Nico had slumped. But the kitchen was full of staff, busy preparing food. She was grateful for how different it all looked.

Roberto was in the den, his embroidered coat only half-fastened up, his wig ignored on the floor. He was standing, wearing his reading glasses, leafing furiously through a sheaf of papers with a look of disbelief on his face.

'What's wrong?' she asked.

Roberto's eyes were dark as they met hers over the top of his glasses. Wordlessly he handed the papers across.

Romy saw the logo at the top and scanned down the covering letter. They were offer documents from Maddox Inc., stating clearly why they should take over Scolari. They were formal papers for a takeover bid.

'Did you know about this?' Roberto asked her.

'No, of course not.'

'I had an email from Franco earlier. He has sold his shares to Maddox. All of them.'

'What?' Romy couldn't believe Franco was still talking about that. She'd already made it clear to him that it could never happen, that Roberto would never let it happen and *neither would she*.

'But now I can't find Franco or get hold of him to discuss it,' Roberto said.

Romy's mind raced. She hadn't seen Franco either, for more than a week.

'And, worse, the media have got hold of it.' Roberto flicked on the TV. The rolling news channel had a breaking-news banner shouting out the imminent takeover of Scolari by Maddox Inc., a bid that Franco Moretti had now publicly accepted.

Romy felt fury boiling up inside her.

'But it doesn't matter what he says,' she said.

441

'Even if he has sold his shares to Maddox Inc., we still have enough—between you, me and Maria—to maintain control of the company.'

'So what *is* Franco's game then?' Roberto demanded, throwing his arms up in frustration. 'To publicly pressure me into selling? Does he think I will be intimidated? What does he take me for—a fool? Is this what's been going on whilst I've been away?'

'I'll find him,' Romy said, smarting. 'I'll get to the bottom of this, Roberto. Right now.'

*   *   *

Romy hurried upstairs to the room she and Alfie would be staying in tonight—a staff room at the opposite end of the property from the one where she and Alfonso had spent their last night together.

The helium balloon Alfie had brought home from his holiday, of a red racing car, bobbed against the ceiling. She unclasped her dress and stepped out of it and back into her jeans, her phone clamped to her shoulder as she called James. She'd need him to meet her at the office.

Then she saw Maria standing in the doorway. She came in and closed the door. She was wearing a deep-red long dress embellished with sequins. She slowly pulled the white wig from her head. Her short dark hair underneath made her make-up look garish.

'I've never seen Roberto worried like this, Romy,' Maria said. 'You need to calm him down and tell him everything is going to be OK.'

Romy pulled on her jumper. 'There's nothing

442

Maddox or Franco can say or do to hurt us, or the company. Roberto is still in charge. I just need to get that message across to the media and then find out what the hell Franco is playing at.' She stepped into her boots and jerked the zips up tight. 'But just tell him not to worry, OK, Maria? And try to enjoy tonight.'

Maria's voice was no more than a whisper when she spoke. 'There's something you've got to know.' She looked down at the wig in her hands. Romy stopped still, realizing they were trembling.

'What is it?'

'I've been selling Franco my shares.'

'What?' A shiver ran down Romy's spine.

'Just temporarily. It was a private arrangement between us.'

Romy couldn't believe what she was hearing. 'You mean you did this without Roberto's say-so? Oh *no*, Maria. Why?'

'For Gloria. To clear hers and Marc's debts—enormous debts, gambling debts, debts that might have got them both killed—and to set them up with their own apartment. I knew Roberto would never give her his blessing. I had no choice but to do it myself . . .'

Romy wanted to shout at Maria. How *could* she? How could she have done such a thing. But shouting would solve nothing, and the poor woman was clearly heartbroken over what she'd done.

Think, Romy told herself. *This still doesn't have to be a disaster.* Even with Maria's shares, Franco didn't have a majority shareholding. He still only had 50 per cent. To sell the company from under Roberto's nose, he'd need to own Romy's shares too.

443

And she'd die rather than ever betray Roberto like that.

* * *

Romy's mind was whirring as Dario drove her across town back to Scolari's HQ. She still couldn't get over what a fool Maria had been. Or how blindly trusting Roberto had been. But then Roberto had always trusted Franco. The two of them had been like brothers. They'd been friends since they were kids.

So what the hell was Franco playing at? How could he possibly condone a Maddox takeover? When things were going so well for Scolari? Her mind raced. How much had Maddox offered him for his shares? What had they told him would happen if he didn't sell up?

Stepping out of the lift on the top floor of the Scolari building, she saw the lights in her glass-fronted office were on. And right there—she couldn't believe it at first—was the man she was looking for, the man with all the answers. Franco was right there waiting for her. Even stranger, he was sitting behind her desk.

'What the hell's going on?' she demanded as she stormed in. 'What the hell have you been saying to the press?'

Franco didn't reply. He didn't even get up. She saw that he wasn't alone. Another man stepped from the shadows to join him. Another man stayed back, against the dark window.

'Have you met Brett Maddox?' Franco asked. 'And this is Lance Starling, his attorney.'

Romy stared at Maddox, a distant memory

444

sparking. But a memory that made no sense. Of a night on board the ship *Norway*. One of the men who'd been playing the tables. Could she really have seen him before?

'Mr Maddox has made a very generous offer, given the circumstances,' Franco said.

She noticed the trace of a smile beginning to spread across Brett Maddox's unpleasant fleshy lips.

'What circumstances?' Why was Franco talking like this? Why couldn't he meet her eyes? But now she saw what he was looking at. A plain black dossier on the desk.

Romy grabbed it and opened it, but as she looked inside, she felt as if she'd been plunged into icy water. There were pictures of Ulrich, of Claudia. A picture of the orphanage. A newspaper report of the fire . . .

'You lied to us all,' Franco said. 'About who you are. Your past. The boy you killed in the orphanage. The fact that you knew who killed Alfonso. And it would be terrible—for everyone, not least your son—if this ever got into the press . . .'

'You can't,' Romy gasped. 'You can't do this. You can't blackmail me—' she began, but as she stared at Franco and then at Brett Maddox, she knew that was exactly what they were doing.

'It's really very simple,' Maddox, said. 'We have all the papers ready for you to sign.'

445

CHAPTER THIRTY-ONE

NOVEMBER 2009

The cold wind blew sheets of fine rain across the grey Hudson and up the grassy slope of the cemetery in Manhattan, where the rows of headstones faced into the bleak grey sky like hardy seagulls.

This was considered the finest resting place in New York, and even to get on the waiting list for one of the few remaining plots here with a view of the Statue of Liberty was next to impossible. The headstones, ancient and new, read like a *Who's Who* of New York society.

Thea stood by Griffin Maddox's granite headstone, adjusting the white roses in the simple pewter vase. He'd died two years ago today and she remembered thinking then, as they'd lowered his coffin into the cold ground, that she'd get something special to stand here beside his grave.

She looked up at the grey marble statue she'd commissioned—an abstract piece from an artist her father had admired. It looked so new, the autumn rain only adding to its lustre, but Thea wondered now how long it would last. Fifty years? A hundred? Longer than Griffin Maddox's legacy—the one she'd always hoped he'd have left her to manage alone?

She closed her eyes, remembering the last time she'd seen him alive, regrets overwhelming her about all the questions she'd never been able to ask.

*   *   *

The moment Thea's plane had touched down at JFK, after her journey back from Australia, she'd rushed straight to the Cedars Private Hospital, delirious from shock and lack of sleep.

She'd found Griffin Maddox prostrate and barely conscious beneath a green sheet in the intensive-care unit, hooked up to drip-feeds and eerily lit by the banks of monitoring machines around his bed.

He'd been brought here to recover after the emergency operation he'd undergone following his aortic aneurism. But he hadn't recovered. Instead he'd suffered a stroke and two further seizures since.

Thea had already spoken to the consultant cardiologist before coming in. Further invasive surgery would kill her father, the consultant had said. There was nothing more they could do except hope.

'Daddy.' Thea gently took his hand in hers. 'I'm here.'

Griffin Maddox's watery eyes opened. She felt his fingers contracting faintly around hers. His hands looked wrinkled and old and, as Thea stared at his face, she saw how much the stroke had transformed him. The right side of his face appeared frozen, while the corner of his mouth hung down.

'Thea.' Her name sounded more like a cough than a word. His speech was slurred and hard to understand. 'There are things . . . I should have . . .'

A rattling sound came from his chest. She wiped

away the spit from his chin. Thea wanted to cry. Her poor daddy. How could this have happened to him?

'Don't. It's OK,' she said, staring at him, willing him to get better, to be all right. *What if this consultant isn't the best?* she was already thinking, her initial shock being replaced by her determination to make this right somehow. *As soon as I leave here I'm going to sort this out, find someone new. We can't just give up on you. There has to be someone who can make you well again.*

'I want you to know . . .' He was struggling even harder now just to get the words out, his eyes searching hers, as the tendons in his neck tightened like wires. 'I always loved you—like you were my own. You were always her . . . gift . . . from . . . God . . . But you became mine too, Thea—you became mine . . .'

What was he talking about? Thea's forehead creased in confusion. None of this made any sense. Was he delirious? she wondered. Did he even realize any more that it was Thea who was here?

'Daddy,' she said, tears running down her face. 'It's me. It's Thea. Of course I'm yours. I've always been yours.'

He gripped her hand then. The sudden show of strength shocked her. He gripped her hand tightly and didn't let go. She tried to pull way, but she couldn't.

'No, listen . . .' he hissed, still not letting her go. He was hurting her now. His ashen skin—she watched it darken and swell with blood. 'You need to understand . . .'

He groaned in pain and twisted his head to one side. One of the machines he'd been hooked up to began to beep. It didn't stop. It rose in volume. What did it mean? Thea was panicking now. It had to be some kind of alarm.

Griffin's face was turning purple now. His eyes bulged. A hissing sound came from his mouth, from deep down inside him, as he desperately tried to force his mouth to form the words and speak.

'What?' Thea begged, fear coursing through her now. 'What is it, Daddy? Please, just tell me—what?'

His eyes rolled back. He started to shudder. She realized the beeping sound was no longer intermittent. It had become one long continuous wail.

'Help!' she shouted. 'Someone. Please. Help.'

Griffin Maddox's whole body was jerking now. He was having some kind of a fit.

A thunder of footsteps. Two nurses rushed into the room.

'Move,' one of them told her.

Thea pulled herself free. She scrambled out of the way. The nurses crowded round her father. Like curtains being drawn, they blocked him from her sight. They shut her out. She watched in horror as one of them punched the panic button on his bedside table. Another, louder alarm began to wail.

Thea stumbled back towards the doorway, right into someone. She turned, expecting to see a doctor—the consultant, she hoped. But it was Brett who was standing there. And even then, tumbling in the vortex of her terror and despair, from the spark of dark triumph in his eyes she knew that he'd been standing there all along, coldly observing and listening in.

449

Thea stared across the Hudson and delved deep into the pocket of her black woollen coat, her fingertips worrying once more at the sharp edge of the letter she'd received this morning.

It could only have been sent by Brett, she'd decided. He'd finally found proof of what Griffin Maddox's dying words had implied. And now he'd shared it with her. And Thea still felt numb from the shock.

With the death of her father—or 'our' father, as Brett still insisted on calling him—Thea had hoped she'd be able to sever her own and Brett's relationship entirely. But Griffin Maddox had had other ideas.

In his will he'd shown no favouritism between Thea and Brett, in spite of the fact that Thea had already been practically a teenager by the time Brett became a part of their lives. If anything, it was Thea who'd been sidelined. Because Storm, too, had been a major beneficiary of Griffin's will. Meaning that together she and Brett had inherited the lion's share of Griffin's personal wealth.

Griffin had also enshrined both Thea and Brett's roles in Maddox Inc., by carefully balancing the board members during his last few months in charge to contain an equal amount of support for them both. Thea might be Chairwoman now, but her position was a precarious one. If she didn't perform, or if the other board members thought Brett would do a better job, then Thea knew she'd be out.

Healthy competition—that's probably what

450

Griffin had envisaged. The two of them competing, thereby driving the business forward twice as fast. But this wasn't competition. It was war.

Brett had even moved himself and Bethany from his apartment into Griffin and Storm's apartment right at the top of Maddox Tower, while Storm herself now divided her time between there and Crofters.

Thea had asked Brett several times if she could sort through her father's personal belongings and go through his private paperwork, but his reply had always been the same: she could come up any time she wanted. The way he'd said it had left her in no doubt of the danger she'd be in if she did.

Feeling the letter in her pocket now, she knew she should have braved a visit anyway. The self-mace she always carried on her would, surely, have made a match for him now? She should have been stronger. She shouldn't have given Brett open access like that to her father's papers and her family's past.

And I should have told you, Thea thought again, looking back at her father's grave. *I should have told you what he did to me. I should have told you the truth*, she thought, feeling the letter as she gripped it in her cold hand, *just the same as you should have told me . . .*

Thea felt Michael put his arm out to steady her. It had been Michael she'd called that day her father had died. Michael who'd stood beside her here at the funeral, supporting her so that she didn't collapse. And Michael who'd been the only person she wanted to be here with her today.

'Are you all right?' he asked, worry etched across his face. 'You looked like you were about to

451

faint.'

She felt as if she were unravelling and had no way of stopping herself. She felt weak, insubstantial. Everything she thought she'd ever known—it had all become a lie.

He looked up at the marble statue. 'You did a good thing here today,' he assured her, misreading her expression, assuming it was being here and remembering Griffin that was making her look so upset.

'If only the rest of my life was that solid,' she heard herself say.

'What do you mean?' he said.

'Nothing.' The letter in her pocket—she didn't want to talk about it. She didn't know *how* she could even begin. But Michael was still staring at her. 'It's just . . . I was always so sure of everything,' she said.

A bitter smile crossed her face as she remembered what he'd told her before she'd gone to Australia, about how *she never let anything get in her way*. Thea no longer felt like that. She no longer recognized that woman at all.

'But now,' she said, 'every time I try and reach for the truth—about who I am . . . what I am— everything just seems to crumble into dust.'

Michael was still looking confused. 'What is it you're trying to say?'

'It doesn't matter . . .' Thea said dismissively, shaking her head in frustration.

But Michael stayed exactly where he was. 'You know you can tell me anything, Thea,' he said. 'Anything at all.'

She turned once more to face him and saw only kindness and concern reflected back in his eyes.

He was the strong one now, not her. She realized he was also probably the only true friend she had.

She took her hand out of her pocket. She did it quickly, surprising even herself. She handed him the letter before she had time to change her mind. She knew she could no longer handle this alone.

He read her name and address on the envelope, 'What is it?' he said.

'Just read it. Then tell me what you think.'

Quickly, she thought. *Do it quickly, before I snatch it back.*

Michael took the creased typed letter out of the crisp new envelope. It was dated June 1970. Thea watched his face as he read the kind but firm words of Dr Myerson telling his patient, Griffin Maddox, that he was sorry to inform him, but this new set of fertility tests was conclusive. Griffin's active sperm count was zero. And due to the complications of his wife Alyssa's previous pregnancy and the extreme unlikelihood of her ever being able to conceive again, they were not going to be able to have children.

'So you see,' Thea said, as Michael finally looked up, 'they weren't my parents.'

'But . . .' Michael started to object, but his words ran out.

'That's what he meant when he died,' she continued, as Michael stared unblinking at the letter again. 'When he said, "I always loved you like you were my own," that's just what he meant. *Like* his own. Because I never actually was.'

'Oh God, Thea.' Michael looked up at her, ashen-faced. 'I'm so sorry . . .'

'All my life,' Thea said, trying to keep the anger and resentment from her voice, 'my mother called

453

me her "gift from God". My name—Theadora—even means that. But it's only now that it makes sense. Because I was a gift—a present. Someone else's baby that they took as their own.'

Michael was nothing but a silhouette now, blurred by her tears.

'All I keep thinking is that, if he really loved me, then why didn't he tell me the truth? If you love someone, you tell them the truth, no matter how much it hurts.'

'I don't know,' Michael said. 'Maybe he didn't think you needed to know. Maybe he didn't think it made any difference.'

'No,' Thea said, and this time she couldn't hide her anger any more, 'it wouldn't have made any difference if he *had* told me. Not telling me—lying to me—*that* makes all the difference in the world.' She rubbed furiously at her tears. 'And not just him. Mom. *Her*. I don't even know what to call her any more. Both of them lied to me every day of my life.'

'They still loved you, Thea.' Michael reached out to touch her shoulder. 'Isn't that the most important thing of all?'

Thea shook him off. All of it made sense now. All of it. Why Griffin Maddox had favoured neither her nor Brett in his will. Because they'd both been adopted, so of course he'd treat them the same. And it explained why Jenny in Australia had looked nothing like her. Because she *was* nothing like her, because neither of their parents were the same.

'You're still you, Thea,' Michael said. 'This . . .' he waved the paper at her, '. . . this might change where you came from, but it can't change who you

454

are.'

'No.' Thea was shaking now. Her voice began cracking as fresh tears welled up in her eyes. 'This could have changed *everything*. Everything I've ever done—every day I've ever worked—I did it for him, for the man I thought was my father . . . To make him proud. To prove that I could be just as much of a Maddox as him.' Thea's tears wouldn't stop. 'And all the time I kept smiling, I kept smiling for him . . .' She hauled in a great shuddering breath, her words rushing out in a torrent now, a torrent she just couldn't stop. 'And I bit down on them—on all those disgusting, dirty secrets . . . on everything Brett did, everything Brett did to me—I did all that to protect him. And for what?'

It all came out then. Everything. She told Michael everything that had happened. About Brett. About how he'd abused her as a child and raped her as an adult. And about Tom and how she'd broken his heart. And about the abortion too. She held nothing back. And about everything else Brett had ruined for her since, and how he'd protected himself by marrying Bethany, and how Storm had fucked her father's most trusted lawyer. How she'd had to lie and lie, and uphold the hideous Maddox family myth, for her father. She told Michael all this, as he held her tight in his unwavering arms.

But when her breathing slowed and she finally stepped away from him, she saw cold fury burning in his eyes.

'You've done nothing wrong,' he told her. 'None of this. None of what's happened is your fault.'

He turned his back on her. He marched away.

'Where are you going?' she called after him. She couldn't believe he was just going to leave her like this.

'To find him,' he shouted, his words echoing furiously across the graveyard. 'To find him and make him pay.'

'No.' Thea ran after him. She grabbed at his coat sleeve. 'Please, Michael, you can't.'

He shook her off. He didn't break his stride.

'But I've got no proof,' she said. 'Nothing.'

'I don't need proof.' He spun round to face her. The scar on his face had turned livid. His fingers had curled into fists. 'I believe you. I've always believed in you.'

She knew it then. She knew he was telling her the truth. Panic rose up inside her. 'But if you do anything to him, you'll end up in prison,' she said.

'It'll be worth it.'

'It won't be for me.' She meant it. No matter what had happened, she wouldn't let Michael get caught up in this too. 'Because don't you see?' she said. 'Hurting you—that would be giving Brett what he wants.' She suddenly saw the full truth of this now. 'Because hurting you would be hurting me.'

'Then leave,' he finally said. 'Quit today. Walk out of there and never go back.'

'Oh God, Michael, you don't think I've thought of that?' So many long nights, for so many months now, she had thought of that—the easy way out; she'd thought of that and nothing else.

'Just do it. Cut him. Cut all of them out of your life.'

And Thea could see it, the kind of future he meant, where she could draw a line under her past

456

and move on, away from the company. And Michael was right. This was within her power. All she needed to do to make it so was say 'Yes'.

But instead she answered, 'No.'

Michael threw up his arms, but she slowly shook her head. 'Because if I walked away,' she said, 'then everything would be . . .'

'Would be . . . ?' he prompted.

'Would be Brett's. And that can't happen,' she said. 'Not after what he's done to me. What he's still trying to do to me.' She felt the determination rising up inside her. 'The only way I can beat him,' she said, 'the only way I can punish him for everything he's done, is to take it. All of it. To stay and fight for that company, and one day take it back. To snatch everything he's ever wanted from out of his hands.'

Michael's whole body seemed to sag then. A look of resignation and distress replaced the anger on his face. He knew he couldn't change her mind. And he knew he shouldn't try. He knew he'd support her no matter what she did. And Thea knew it too now.

She remembered then what she'd said about her father: *If he really loved me, then why didn't he tell me the truth? If you love someone, you tell them the truth, no matter how much it hurts.*

Was that what she felt right now? she wondered, as she stepped towards Michael and let him gather her into his arms. Was this something like love? Was that what this strength was that she now felt pouring into her, filling her and raising her up?

'If he ever lays a finger on you again, you tell me,' Michael said. 'You promise me now, Thea. You swear that you will.'

'Yes,' she answered. 'I swear it, Michael, I will.'

'No one's ever going to hurt you again.'

Standing there with him, as the cold wind blew around them, whipping up spirals of autumnal leaves in its wake, Thea knew for certain that she would not be cowed by this letter. She would not let Brett win.

She turned and stared one final time at Griffin Maddox's grave. She thought of her mother and the wonderful times they'd once had. And she thought of Griffin, too, and how he'd always had one eye on the future, as Thea did now. And as she turned and slipped her hand into Michael's and the two of them walked away, towards the storm gathering on the horizon, she wondered if maybe Michael had been right. Maybe she really was much more Griffin Maddox's daughter than she thought.

*　　　*　　　*

It was late afternoon and Thea was riding in the lift up to her office in Maddox Tower. She checked her reflection in the mirror. Thank God for make-up, she thought. Her tear-stained face was nothing but a memory. She looked on top of her game and felt it too.

She thought of all the floors the lift was rising up through, and of all the people there whose lives Maddox Inc. controlled. She was going to be watching Brett's every move from now on. With whatever means it took. In his business life and his private life too. She was going to get the proof she needed to finish him off. The phoney war between them was over. The real war had now begun.

458

She thought too about Michael. She could still feel a 'ghost' impression of his hand, of his fingers intertwined with hers.

She'd told him everything and he hadn't judged her. Or been disgusted by her. *He doesn't hate me because of what happened*, as she'd always thought he might.

Tonight she was going straight from the office to the small apartment he'd rented over in Queens. He'd been offered a job last week, bossing for a private corporate-security firm. He was going to cook for her, he'd said. Just one of his mother's old recipes. A favourite from both their childhoods, he'd teased her, refusing to tell her just what it was.

Thea hadn't even known that he could cook. In fact, she knew so little about all the small details and quirks that made up the grown-up person he'd become. But it didn't seem to matter, because in another way she felt she knew him completely. Who Michael was at his core. Who he'd always been, and always would be.

No one's ever going to hurt you again. That's what he'd told her. And she believed him.

Brett couldn't hurt her. Ever again.

Thea stepped out of the elevator and glanced at the bank of TVs on the reception wall. One of them was switched to CNN. As she took a sip of the takeaway coffee she'd picked up at her favourite deli on the way over, she read the news banner line and slowed to a stop.

She turned, rereading what she'd just seen. Which is when her assistant, Sarah, came hurrying over.

'I've been trying to get hold of you,' Sarah said,

459

not hiding the panic in her voice.

Thea realized that since she'd gone to the graveyard, she must have left her phone switched off.

'Brett's called a board meeting. They've all been waiting in there for over half an hour.' It was obvious from her flushed cheeks that poor Sarah had been bearing the brunt of the fallout from Thea's absence.

'Tell them I'm coming,' Thea said, her eyes being drawn back to the TV screen, still disbelieving what she saw.

It was impossible. The news banner line said that Maddox Inc. had just taken over Scolari. But how could that be possible? Thea had tried everything. Only last week, in fact, she'd informed the board—much to their disappointment—that she'd failed to secure a deal and believed that one could never be made. Her mind was whirring. She dumped her coffee on the receptionist's desk and marched towards the boardroom.

'Why didn't I know about this?' she barked as she saw Peter and Dennis, two of the other directors and her father's most trusted allies, standing in the corridor outside the boardroom door.

'Brett said he had your full authorization,' Peter said, but she noticed something sheepish in his tone.

'Brett?' Thea didn't understand. 'What's Brett got to do with any of this?'

'Brett closed the deal,' Dennis said, clearly puzzled by Thea's reaction. 'He said you'd asked him to take over negotiations after you'd failed. That you didn't think he'd get anywhere, but he was certainly welcome to try.

Failed . . .

Thea suddenly saw the danger she was in. Brett had done this to show the board what he was capable of. He'd done this to show them that, where Thea failed, he'd succeed.

'He said you'd be pleased, that he'd turned one of your dreams into reality.'

The liar, Thea thought. And Peter and Dennis too. *More liars.* Thea could see it in their eyes. They'd all known what Brett was up to with Scolari, and had deliberately kept it from her. They'd sided with him. How many other directors had done the same?

She could see the answer written on their faces the moment she stepped into the boardroom. None of the men seated around the table would look at her.

'Ah, there you are at last,' Brett said.

He was standing at the head of the boardroom table in a smart new suit. His smile was wide, his eyes as cold as a shark's, as he pulled at his pristine white cuffs beneath his sleeves.

Thea walked towards him, towards where she normally sat to chair these meetings, but Brett didn't move. Because of the way he'd positioned himself she found it impossible to get to her seat.

'You've heard the wonderful news then?' he said.

'I don't know how you could have—' The words were out of Thea's mouth before she could stop them, her surprise and incomprehension clear for everyone to see.

'Convinced old man Scolari?' Brett said with a grin.

461

Thea felt her pulse quicken as she saw that all the other board members were seated around the table. One or two of them were even smiling.

'The truth is, I didn't have to,' Brett said. 'I decided to think laterally instead. To get the other shareholders on-side. To bring them round to my way of thinking.'

'But that's not possible,' Thea said. 'Roberto Scolari and his wife and daughter-in-law—they had a majority shareholding. None of them would ever have sold to you.'

Lance Starling cleared his throat.

'Er, that's where you're wrong,' he said, getting quickly to his feet. 'If I may?'

'Absolutely,' Brett said, and he and several other directors all turned—in a clearly rehearsed show of unity, obviously designed to sideline Thea—to watch Lance Starling as he switched on a projector and began to explain quickly how the deal worked.

Thea sank down into a chair as Lance continued to speak and several other of Brett's closest allies began to chip in, congratulating him, mentioning other acquisitions he had in the pipeline. Brett didn't even look at her. As if she was no longer significant. As if she was no longer even there.

'As you all know,' Brett said then, as soon as Lance Starling had finished, 'I've called a press conference, which will begin in less than'—he checked his Rolex, her *father*'s Rolex, Thea saw, with horror—'half an hour. Which,' he added, would also seem an opportune moment to announce, Thea, your resignation as Chairwoman of the board.'

Thea sprang to her feet.

'Resignation? But I'm not resigning.'

'It's too late,' Brett said. 'We've been having an emergency board meeting, which I note you failed to be here for, during which we cast a vote of no confidence in our Chairwoman.'

'No confidence? But—'

'Frankly, Thea, this has been on the cards for quite some time. And your personal failure with Scolari'—Brett took a moment to smile at his colleagues—'well, it's only served to highlight your shortcomings, both as a leader and a businesswoman.'

Thea couldn't believe this was happening. The speed at which he'd moved had taken her completely by surprise. 'But . . .'

'That's all, gentlemen,' Brett said, ignoring Thea's protests and gesturing for the others to leave the room. 'I'll see you at the press conference.'

'You're just going to let him do this? Sit here and take this bullshit?' Thea cried out, but everyone stood up and started to file quickly past her. But this was wrong. She'd done all she could to close the Scolari deal, all that anyone could. Brett couldn't be *allowed* to do this . . . . Only it seemed that he could.

'Good luck,' Peter said under his breath as he left.

'Wait,' Thea implored, wanting them all to come back, but in a moment she faced Brett alone.

'I will not let you get away with this,' she cried. 'I will fight you.'

'Interesting,' Brett said. 'But I doubt you will.'

He opened his laptop and hit a few keys. The screen loomed into life. 'There are plenty of reasons why you had to go,' Brett said.

'Professional, of course, but personal too. The fact that you aren't really Griffin and Alyssa Maddox's daughter being one. And I've checked. He didn't legally adopt you, whereas he did legally adopt me. Which means that I have much more right to this company than you. Now unfortunately, because your mother is dead, I can't take steps to prove with a DNA test that she didn't by fluke manage to have you with somebody else. Which means I can't get you disinherited.' His fury about this blazed in his eyes. 'God only knows where they got you from, Thea,' he said, as if she was dirt on his shoe. 'But there's another personal reason too. What I would term . . . professional misconduct.'

Now a grainy but clear image of Thea and Reicke in the hot-tub in Vienna came up on the large screen at the far end of the table.

'Turn it off,' Thea said. She slammed the lid shut.

'Oh, that's a shame,' Brett chastised her, grinning widely—triumphantly—at her now. 'Because this really is one of my favourite films. I like the bit where you let him fuck you over the tub.' There was a malevolent glint in his eye. 'Now, then. You could accept your resignation and go quietly in a dignified way, or I could easily email this file to, say, your good friend Michael?'

Chapter Thirty-Two

NOVEMBER 2009

Lars Artman jolted awake. Careful not to disturb his daughter, Gretchen, who had once again slipped into his bed, he rolled back the heavy duvet and got up. He picked up Gretchen's worn and much-loved teddy bear and placed it in her arms, before tenderly smoothing her blonde hair from her face.

Lars shivered in the pre-dawn cold, treading as quietly as he could across the bare floorboards into the sitting room.

Pale-yellow lamplight from the Amsterdam street below spilled through a crack in the curtains. Beyond the kitchen table, which Lars had dragged through here and which was now crowded with laptops and papers—as well as the remains of last night's Indonesian takeaway—the sofa bed was pulled out.

Beneath a twist of white sheets Lars saw the long, angular shape of Romy Scolari. Her brow was wet with sweat.

This wasn't the first time she'd woken him in the night. She hardly ever slept, but when she did . . . this happened. It wouldn't have mattered so much, he supposed, if she hadn't already been so exhausted. But as it was, she hardly ever ate, and only remembered to drink water when he told her to. He was scared she would burn herself out.

She'd arrived here unannounced three days ago, on Thursday morning, just after he'd got back from

465

a two-week business trip to India and had been about to go to the office.

When the doorbell had sounded, but no one had spoken into the intercom, Lars had assumed it was a delivery. He'd gone down to open the front door, only to be confronted by his old neighbour, Susan, standing there, trembling visibly, wearing dark sunglasses and a hat pulled down low on her head.

Except that she wasn't Susan any more, he'd remembered. She was Romy Scolari.

Lars had become the subject of much ribbing at the agency since his neighbour's true identity had been splashed all over the Dutch and international media. His colleagues had thought it typical of his ignorance of celebrity gossip that he'd had a supermodel living upstairs and hadn't even realized. *What kind of an investigator was he*, they'd all joked, *if he couldn't even see what was going on right under his nose?*

But why should I have guessed her real identity? That's what Lars thought now, staring down at Romy's dark hair, streaked in damp fronds across her face, resisting the urge to tidy them as he'd just done for Gretchen. *Wasn't being a model just the name of her old job, not the actual person she was at all?*

All Lars had known right from the start was that his new English neighbour had been disarmingly attractive. So much so, in fact, that he hadn't even been able to look her properly in the face those first few times they'd spoken, for fear he might actually gawp.

Even dressing down the way she'd done, without make-up or any other obvious signs of care for her appearance, her striking natural beauty had been impossible to miss.

But not only had she not dressed like a model, she hadn't conducted herself like one, either. Lars had witnessed none of the prima-donna behaviour that the press so often associated with such types.

In fact, after he'd got over his initial nerves about speaking to her, she'd just become Susan—his shy, but charming neighbour, and a good and loving mother to her son, Alfie. He'd got to know her a little then, but certainly not as much as he'd have liked. And certainly not enough to have ever expected to see her sleeping here in his apartment.

After she'd gone back to Italy, from time to time he'd tapped her name into Google and had read the news-bites covering her re-emergence into society and her blossoming into a successful businesswoman.

She'd emailed him a few times when she'd first left, just some personal details, such as how Alfie had been getting on and how much she still missed her husband, but also what a wonderful extended family she now had. But then her emails had fizzled out.

Lars had tried to imagine what it must have been like for her, living such a glamorous lifestyle with Alfie, and had concluded that she probably felt much more at home there than she had ever done here.

He'd been happy for her, but he'd missed her all the same, and had sometimes even regretted his shyness with her while she'd been living here. But he'd come to accept, too, that they were now from different worlds and he'd probably never see her again.

Only now here she was.

It had been a big enough shock to see her back here in Amsterdam. Without an entourage, or even a chauffeur. An even greater shock to discover that she'd come without her son.

But what had shocked Lars most had been that, beneath her dark glasses, Romy's dark-blue eyes had been red-rimmed from crying and her lips dry from dehydration. She'd looked like some kind of hunted creature, as if at any second she might collapse.

He'd taken her in and up to his apartment—glad, so glad, that Gretchen had been with her mother until Saturday and therefore had not been here—and had listened as Romy's whole story had poured out.

She'd told him about how horrendous the last month of her life had been and how she'd had to flee Italy because she'd been blackmailed by a man called Brett Maddox into signing over her Scolari shares, thereby allowing the media giant, Maddox Inc., to take control of her family's firm.

More terrifying still, she'd confessed to Lars about all the information they'd used to blackmail her. About her husband's killers coming from Germany, from her past. A past that involved her horrible escape from an abusive orphanage, and how she'd had to kill a boy to protect her best friend, she'd claimed, and Lars had believed her.

She'd begged Lars then to forgive her for coming to him. But this had been the only place she'd been able to think of where she might find sanctuary, and Lars had been the only person in the world she'd known who might have the skills to help her make amends for what she'd done, and—most important of all—get her precious Alfie back.

And it was this, even more than the affection and pity Lars had felt for Romy, that had clinched his support. The thought of having Gretchen taken from him. The thought that anyone could stoop so low as this man Brett Maddox. The thought that anyone could ever put money and power above a mother and her child.

Romy Scolari was in trouble all right. But Lars would do all he could to protect her. Using every skill and contact he had, he would try and win back her boy for her.

She let out a shuddering groan. He crouched down and gently squeezed her arm. He couldn't stand it any more, seeing her look so scared. 'Hey,' he whispered as she twisted in her sleep.

*   *   *

Romy woke with a start from her nightmare: Ulrich, the dogs, Claudia on the ground. The same nightmare she'd had all her life. Only this time it had been worse. This time they'd been adults and she'd been running, with sirens at her back . . . police and fire engines had hurtled, somersaulting, past her, bouncing off the tarmac, exploding into flames . . . Then she'd heard Alfonso screaming . . . and then their son—and she'd known that they were all about to die.

'I wanted to leave you to sleep,' Lars said, his face swimming into focus, 'but I worried you might wake Gretchen up again.'

Romy sat up on the sofa bed. 'I'm sorry,' she gasped. 'I'm so sorry.'

She looked up at Lars in the dim light. He was wearing stripy pyjama bottoms and a tatty grey

469

T-shirt. He smiled at her gently. As he yawned and stretched, she saw the lean curve of his hips. His hair was messed up and his jaw was thick with stubble.

Romy looked at her watch on the small coffee table by the sofa. It was five in the morning.

'Do you want some tea?' Lars asked. 'I'm awake now. I thought I might as well stay up.'

'Sure. Thanks,' Romy said, suddenly aware that she was wearing only her knickers and bra.

As Lars padded into the kitchen, she pulled the sheet tighter around her, lay back down on the bed and felt herself slipping back into a darkness. A moment later, when she opened her eyes, she found herself disorientated, as if she'd just been dredged up from the bottom of the sea.

It was this apartment. It had the same layout as the one she'd had upstairs. For a fleeting second, hope soared through her, as she imagined Alfie might be sleeping safely behind the door just over there. It was all she could do not to leap out of bed and push it open, but she knew it was only Lars's storeroom and was filled with coats and skis.

And not her precious son.

She swung her legs off the side of the sofa bed and pulled on one of Lars's old sweatshirts that he'd lent her, then buried her face in her hands. Even though she was awake, the nightmare of her real life persisted.

Because that bastard Maddox had done it anyway. After he'd blackmailed her into signing over Scolari, he'd leaked the information he had on her to the press. To ensure that she'd never come back. To blacken the Scolari family name. To break Roberto by breaking his heart.

470

The first television report about how Romy Scolari
had covered up her connection to Alfonso's
murderers—and how she herself was still wanted
for questioning in Germany in connection with a
young cadet's murder—had appeared less than an
hour after the conclusion of her meeting with Brett
Maddox, Franco Moretti and their lawyer, during
which she'd signed over her Scolari shares to
Maddox Inc.

Afterwards Romy had gone to her office to clear
out her personal possessions, under the watchful
eyes of two security guards who only two hours
before had owed their loyalty to her. Brett's first
move as acting Managing Director of Scolari had
been to fire Romy. But even in her fury over the
unjust way in which she'd been manipulated and
usurped, all she'd been able to think about was
how she was ever going to break the news to poor
Roberto.

Now, she decided, shutting her desk drawer for
what would be the final time. She'd have to do it
now. She'd have to tell him the truth: that she'd
sold the shares to protect his family from a public
scandal that would have consumed them all like a
fire. She'd have to tell Roberto about Fox, she
decided. About what she'd done. And why. She'd
have to tell him and pray he'd forgive her. *But not
the fact that she knew Ulrich and Claudia. He didn't
need to know that. He didn't need to know what her
secret past had done to his son.*

One of the security guard's intercoms crackled.
A static-laced voice hissed a garbled message into

the guard's ear. He walked to Romy's old desk, picked up the control and switched on the wall TV.

'Mr Maddox said there's something you should see,' he told Romy impassively, as the screen flickered into life.

A photograph of Romy's face stood alongside an excited newscaster.

That's when Romy discovered that Maddox had betrayed her and had gone public with everything he knew—*everything*, including her prior knowledge of Ulrich and Claudia. He might have given Romy the dossier in exchange for her selling her shares, but he'd kept a copy. And he'd given that copy to the press.

Romy reached Villa Gasperi less than twenty minutes later. But as she drove in through the new steel gates, she was greeted by silence. Cesca's party was over. The guests had all gone. Glasses were still half-full, plates of food left half-eaten, the flares in the marquee still alight, the record on the DJ turntable hissing with static.

As Romy hurried through the courtyard, a movement caught her eye and she looked up at one of the second-floor windows. A curtain there snapped shut. But before it did, Romy was certain she saw Maria's face.

'In here,' Roberto's voice boomed out, as she closed the front door behind her.

There were no staff in sight. As Romy passed the kitchen, she saw it was still in a mess. Dirty dishes and wine bottles lay stacked in piles on the floor. As if in the middle of their job, the entire staff had walked out. *Or were dismissed*, Romy realized, nausea rising up inside her now. *Or were dismissed when Roberto cancelled the party and sent everybody home.*

'Maria has told me of her stupidity,' Roberto said as she walked into his study. 'And about how Franco took advantage of her and went behind my back.'

He was sitting behind his desk, a half-drunk bottle of whisky gripped in his fist. He gazed at her flatly. His face was a mask of indifference. It frightened her more than if he'd been angry. This was his boardroom face, the one that already had all the answers, which had already made all the decisions.

'And now I learn that you have signed over your own shareholding too,' he said.

'They blackmailed me. Brett Maddox—'

'Yes.' He cut her off. 'I imagined as much. From that.' He gestured with his bottle towards the television news channel, showing his own face, playing silently on the wall. 'They lied to you, and told you they would keep all that quiet. And you agreed because you thought you had no choice.'

Relief burst inside Romy. So he *did* understand. Even though she'd known Ulrich and Claudia, Roberto was still on her side.

'But you *did* have a choice not to lie to *us*,' he said. 'Not to lie about your past. For all this time.' The betrayal that he felt was clear in his voice.

'Roberto, please. I'm sorry. Let me explain. I—'

'Explain why you've let us keep you so close, when you've done all these terrible things? Things that you knew would undo our family if they ever came to light?'

The scorn in his voice made panic swell inside her. 'I didn't want to hurt you. Any of you. Ever,' she said.

473

Roberto didn't seem to hear. 'You knew. You knew those people who killed Alfonso. You knew them and let them into my home and let them destroy all my art and all my wine, and then kill my son, and you never said.'

It was an accusation and a judgement all rolled into one. She understood then, with fear in her heart, that he did not forgive her at all and that he was only just controlling his fury.

'I'm sorry.'

'How could you have lied so to the police? And how could you have lied to us all, Romy? After everything we've done for you.'

'I didn't want to. I didn't mean to. I told Alfonso everything. He knew before he died. He forgave me,' she said.

'He forgave you?' Roberto said incredulously. 'I don't believe you. I don't believe anything you say.'

'It's true,' Romy pleaded.

'No. What's true is that Scolari is gone. I have lost control of everything my family ever worked for.' Without warning he thumped his fist onto his chest. A rage of blood rushed to his face. 'And I have lost my only son, because of you.'

'The company,' she said weakly. She could no longer look him in the eyes. 'I'll find a way. I'll get it back . . .' She could never make up for losing Alfonso, but she could at least attempt this.

'No,' he snapped. 'Even if I wanted to regain control of Scolari, our family name, our good reputation has gone now. You've made people believe that everything we've done is all based on corruption and lies. And you've made me look like a fool.'

'No . . . no,' Romy cried. 'Roberto, you have to

474

listen to me—'

He stood, leaning furiously over his desk. 'Now you will do as I say. You will leave this house right now and never, *ever* come back.'

Romy stared into his eyes and saw then what she'd always known. Roberto was black and white. You were either in or out, and now there was no way of appealing to the man she'd grown to love like her own father. His eyes were cold.

She forced herself to stop her chin trembling. 'If that's what you really want, I will get Alfie.'

'I don't think you understood me. *You* should leave. Now.'

And that's when she realized the true meaning of what he was saying.

'No,' she said. 'No. Alfie is mine.'

'And what happens when the police come for you? These claims of murder . . .'

He was right. They *would* be coming. She'd been so busy thinking about Roberto and the company that she'd forgotten to think of herself. She had to get away. She had to get herself and Alfie out of here now.

'Where is he?' she demanded. 'Is he upstairs?'

'No. He's my grandson. My heir. I will do whatever I have to do to protect him.'

Protect him? The force of the words hit her like a hammer blow. He meant from her.

She ran out into the corridor and up the ancient stone steps to Alfie's room. But as she threw open the door, she saw it was empty. His helium balloon-car hung limply in the air, buckled and crumpled, as if it had crashed. Their bags were gone.

She heard a footstep behind her. She spun

round, hoping to see her son.

But it was Roberto who was standing there.

'What have you done? Tell me where he is?' she cried, shaking with rage now, seeing him for what he had become—an enemy, not a friend—someone who wanted to take away her son.

'He's where you will never find him,' he said.

In the distance, she heard sirens.

'It's time you faced up to who you really are,' Roberto said.

The sirens were getting louder.

'My God.' She stared at Roberto. 'You've called them already, haven't you? You've just called the police.'

*　　　*　　　*

Romy wrapped the long arms of the sweatshirt around her as she walked through to where Lars was standing with a steaming mug in his hands, gazing out of the kitchen window at the first glow of sunlight spreading out across the city's roofs and spires.

'Was it the same nightmare as before?' he asked.

Romy nodded, feeling the tears that were always so close these days rising to the surface again.

'I deserve it. I'm a bad person. I've lied to everyone.'

'You haven't lied to me. Well, not during your latest visit to Amsterdam anyway,' he smiled.

Romy still couldn't believe that he'd forgiven her. Not just for how she'd deceived him while she'd been living in this building, but for all the terrible baggage she'd brought to his door.

'It's all such a mess.'

476

'Trust me,' he said, putting his mug down. 'It'll all turn out OK.'

He smiled gently and punched her playfully, reassuringly, on the shoulder. But Romy let out a sob. Because as much as he wanted to be kind, he couldn't protect her. She wasn't safe. She would never be safe. The police would find her sooner or later. And if they didn't believe her about what had happened with Fox—if she was convicted—then she doubted she'd ever see Alfie again.

'I just want my son back,' she said.

She felt a fat tear rolling down her cheek. If only she could talk to Alfie. Just once. Just to hear his voice. But he, like everyone else, probably hated her by now. The mood Roberto was in, he'd probably have told Alfie everything. About how she'd known his father's killers. She imagined Roberto telling him his mother was a liar. She pictured Alfie's confused face as Roberto shattered his innocence. How would her poor baby react?

Lars hugged her. 'We'll find a way to get through this,' he said.

She pressed her cheek against his T-shirt, sinking gratefully into his hug. She should never have left Amsterdam, she thought. She should never have gone back to Italy. Lars was the only person left in the world who hadn't judged her. Who hadn't demanded anything from her.

She could hear the steady thump of his heartbeat and, suddenly, she was aware of his hard, lean body against hers. She felt his hands on her waist and, out of nowhere, she felt desire rushing through her. She stared up at him, into his soft grey eyes. And there was a moment when she felt as if he were looking right inside her soul. Before she could stop herself, she kissed him. She heard him moan as he kissed her back. But just as suddenly as they'd started, Lars stopped. He pulled away.

'No, Romy, I can't. I won't,' he said, as if he'd just come to his senses.

Romy closed her eyes. She tried to recover her breath. If Lars hadn't stopped, then she knew she wouldn't have been able to, either. What had she been thinking? She was stunned that she'd acted on such an impulse. She hadn't kissed anyone since Alfonso. And Gretchen was here . . .

'I'm sorry,' she said.

'Don't be. I'd be a liar if I didn't tell you how much I want to do this. But you're vulnerable and you're exhausted. I'm not going to take advantage of you.'

'Oh God, I'm so embarrassed,' she said, putting her hand on her head.

Lars looked embarrassed too. Gone was the confident information security guy. He now looked as awkward and bashful as a teenage boy, which if anything drew her to him even more. He smiled.

'Hey, you're only human,' he said, stretching his hands out wide, and Romy laughed.

'That's better. It's good to see you smile,' he told her, adjusting his glasses squarely onto his face, suddenly all business again. 'Now, let's get some more caffeine inside us and work out how we're going to get Alfie back.'

*   *   *

After he'd fixed them a coffee, Lars pulled Romy's

478

duvet from the sofa bed and they went out together onto his small balcony. They sat on the cast-iron bench out there and shared a cigarette, even though, as Romy admitted, she hadn't smoked since she was a kid.

'Since we seem to be breaking all kinds of laws together, then we might as well have a little fun while we're about it,' he joked, as she sat huddled against him, watching the cold dawn light creep over the rooftops and spires.

The last few days Lars had pulled up all the newspaper articles he'd been able to find about Schwedt, cross-checking them against Romy's real name. Sure enough, he'd found the original details of the fire and Fox's death, and the fact that Romy had been listed as a suspect in both the arson and the murder—something that four other orphans (the three boys Pieter, Monk and Heinrich) had confirmed she'd been guilty of, as well as Claudia Baumann.

So Claudia had given Romy's name up to the police. No doubt to save her own skin. In spite of what Claudia had done to her since, Romy did not blame the little girl she'd once been. Claudia would have had no other choice. Just as she hadn't had a choice to do anything other than accept Ulrich's protection. And the consequences that Romy knew must have been involved.

Lars had also got an old student friend—a lawyer from The Hague—to check out whether crimes from East Germany were even kept open, let alone ever investigated, by the German police.

The bad news had come back that they still sometimes were. Meaning that the media reports should be believed: Romy Scolari was a fugitive from justice, who could theoretically be arrested anywhere within the EU. Regardless of the fact that she'd been a minor at the time of the murder, the fact that she'd used arson to cover it up and then flee made her unstable in the eyes of the law. The lawyer had also said that, should a suspect like Romy—Lars had been careful, of course, not to give her real name—be convicted, then in the worst-case scenario she would lose custody of her son, possibly for good.

The good news was that two of the orphan boys, Monk and Heinrich, who had confirmed that Romy was guilty of the murder had latterly been convicted of several offences—including rape— which would add credence to Romy's version of events.

Now that Lars and Romy had established what level of trouble Romy was in—and had some hope that she at least might be able to mount some kind of defence—they'd both decided to use whatever liberty she had left trying to right a different wrong. Namely, to win back Roberto's company for him somehow. And in time, she hoped, his trust.

Which is what Lars was clearly thinking about as he turned to Romy now.

'This Brett Maddox,' he said, 'if he was prepared to blackmail you, then he might have done it to other people too.'

'Or worse,' Romy agreed. 'I'm telling you, Lars, the way he looked at me, I don't think he's right. The malice in his eyes, the *enjoyment*—it wasn't business, it was pleasure. He's some kind of sadist, some kind of psycho, I'm sure. He'll certainly stop at nothing to get what he wants.'

480

'A guy like that, operating the way that he does, *will* have left a trail of what he's done,' Lars reassured her. 'No matter how smart he thinks he is, there'll be a chink in the Maddox armour somewhere. There always is. There's no such thing as a clean corporation.'

'But where? Where would we even start looking? Maddox is so big. God knows how many accountants and lawyers it's got working for it. It might take us months, even years, to find a paper trail worth following. And then even that might peter out.'

'We'll just have to look for any irregularities. The same tricks that I see companies pulling all the time. Shell corporations. Dummy accounts. Fake employees. Anywhere cash vanishes, that's where the corruption generally starts. But I'm also thinking that maybe we shouldn't just go after Maddox Inc.'

'You mean we should go after Brett Maddox himself as well?'

'Why not? Everyone has their own personal paper trail these days. Emails, laptop files, personal records of meetings and business transactions—it's all out there. It's just getting access to it that's hard.'

'And illegal.'

'Right.'

'And something you could get into trouble for if you got caught?' she said, worry rising up inside her. She'd hurt enough people already. She couldn't risk Lars too. She said, 'No—'

'But I won't get caught,' he said. He pressed his finger to her lips as she began to protest again. 'I'm the good guy, remember? The white hat hacker.

481

Well, what's the point in being all that if I can't actually try and bring a bad motherfucker like this down?'

*　　*　　*

Romy tipped the pancake from the frying pan onto the plate for Gretchen, amazed that the little girl could eat so many. She smiled, squirting the honey bottle in circles over it.

'Do you like my daddy?' Gretchen asked.

Romy blushed. She hadn't seen them in the kitchen, had she? Romy still couldn't believe what had happened this morning. She felt shame swamping her—even though Lars had been so nice about it.

'Yes, I do,' she said. 'He's been very kind to me.'

'He likes you.' The way Gretchen raised her eyebrows reminded Romy of Lars. She tucked a strand of hair behind her ear.

'Is that a fact?' she said.

'He doesn't have girlfriends. He thinks I'll mind, but I wouldn't. All I want is for him to be happy.'

Gretchen shovelled another mouthful of pancake into her mouth as Romy thought about Lars. He'd gone early to work this morning after he'd spoken to her, even thought it was a Sunday— or *because* it was a Sunday, in fact. Because it would be safer to do the kind of work he needed to do without anybody else there, leaving Romy to have a day with Gretchen, which, she realized, was just what she needed.

'Do you miss Alfie?' Gretchen asked.

'All the time. Especially days like today. He loves pancakes,' she said. How long had it been

482

since she'd found time to make them for her son? What if she never got to make them for him again? She fought down the panic that had lessened since this morning with Lars, but was now back again.

'Why don't you just call him?' she asked.

Romy sighed. 'It's complicated.'

'Why?'

'I did something bad once,' Romy told her. She realized now that she wouldn't have been that much older than Gretchen when she'd run away from the orphanage. Only a few years older. Now it amazed her that she'd been so resourceful and brave.

'Did it make you feel horrible?'

Romy nodded slowly. 'Really horrible. And I thought I could forget all about it.'

'But you can't?'

'No. No, I can't.'

'I stole something once,' Gretchen said. 'I felt so bad about it.'

'What did you do?'

'What you're meant to.'

'And what's that?'

'I gave it back and said sorry. I felt so much better when I'd owned up.'

*　　　*　　　*

Gretchen's words were still on Romy's mind as she sat side-by-side with Lars later that night. They were both looking at the screen of his laptop where the files he'd mailed on from work were coming through.

'Lars, I've made up my mind about what I'm going to do,' Romy said.

'What?'

'I'm going to stop running. I've been running away from this all my life. And the only way I can fix it is if I stop and go back. To Germany. Back to Schwedt.'

She expected him to be shocked, but he didn't object. And the look in his eyes gave her all the confirmation that her decision was the right one.

'I'm going to go to the police and own up— about the fire and the orphanage and Fox.'

Lars let out a soft whistle. 'I think that's a very brave thing to do.'

'It's the only thing to do,' her confidence was expanding. 'I have to tell them what really happened. I have to make them believe that I'm telling the truth.'

Lars nodded slowly and Romy smiled, amazed that he'd accepted her decision, that he respected her enough to do that, and that he clearly believed in her sufficiently too, that she could convince the police of her case. But then a frown appeared across his brow.

'Do you want me to come with you?' he asked.

Romy shook her head, smiling gently at this man who'd done so much for her, touched that he'd offered. 'You've done enough. You have Gretchen. You're needed here. Anyway, I think this is something I need to do alone.'

'You do realize they'll probably arrest you?' he said.

She shrugged and sighed. 'Maybe, but they'll catch up with me sooner or later. It'll look better if I hand myself in.'

'When are you going to go?'

'Well, now, I suppose. The sooner, the better.

Living like this is torture. I have to do this thing. The longer they have Alfie, the worse it'll be.'

'Then I'll contact my friend Tegen Londrom. She's the best lawyer there is. She'll help.'

Romy nodded, her head spinning that the plan was already taking shape.

'How will you get there?' Lars asked, clearly on the same wavelength.

'I'm not sure. I don't think I can fly. I don't want to risk getting arrested at the airport. And the same goes for train stations too. They're too public, the press would be all over them—and I want to actually get there, to the place where it all began.'

'Take my car.'

'You have a car?' she asked.

'It's a camper van, but it's reliable and you can sleep in it, if you need to. Although it might be a bit cold. We'll get it working, and get you a cheap mobile in the morning.'

They stared at each other for a moment and Romy realized that her plan had been sealed. She really was going to do it. She was going back to Germany.

Then Lars's laptop chimed out a tune. 'OK, now listen, what I've got here are comprehensive details of all of Maddox Inc.'s recent transactions, including those of all its subsidiaries. I'll start with Italy and everything connected with Scolari, and if we strike out there, I'll branch out into the rest of their European operations,' Lars said. 'It's going to take time, but I promise you this now, Romy, I'll ring you the second I get something. And I won't stop until I've nailed these bastards to the wall.'

CHAPTER THIRTY-THREE

NOVEMBER 2009

Michael's finger pressed against Thea's, no doubt meaning to reassure her, as he handed her a bone-china cup and saucer in Mrs Myerson's front parlour.

But Thea didn't feel reassured. She felt sick with nerves. She tried to still her trembling hands before she spilt scalding tea all over her lap. She still couldn't believe Michael had cajoled her into coming here, although she also had to admit that it had initially felt good to get out of New York. To get away from her house, where she'd been holed up since that awful day she'd announced her resignation just over a month ago.

She wasn't as raw as she had been, but her fury had distilled into a dull ache of injustice. Brett had humiliated her in front of her staff and colleagues. He'd taken away her power in the most public way.

Scolari—it was as simple as that. The word seemed to be seared into Thea's brain. Because no matter how much she tried to tell herself that Brett had acted despicably, the truth was that he'd also succeeded where she'd failed. How he'd done it, how he'd managed to persuade the Scolaris to do what they'd always sworn they wouldn't, Thea guessed she'd never know. But everything she'd been terrified might happen had now happened.

She'd lost.

And Brett had won.

In the devastation that had followed, Michael

had been the only person she'd let in. She'd had so little pride left that she'd no longer cared if he saw her at rock bottom. When she hadn't shown up for dinner on the night she'd confessed everything to him, he'd come to find her, fighting through the press camped out on her stoop. As she'd sobbed, pacing back and forth in her kitchen, impotent with fury that she'd been ousted from her position and from the company, he'd listened.

'I don't know what to do,' she'd ended up railing at him, her face raw and puffy from crying. 'I don't know what I'm meant to do, or even who I am any more.'

'That's not true.'

'He's taken everything,' she'd sobbed.

Michael had been patient, talking her round.

'You always said you could beat him at his own game,' he had reminded her.

'Yeah, well I lost.'

'Only because he knows more than you. It's information, Thea, that's the key.'

'I have no access to information. They've shut me out of Maddox Inc. I've been fired. I can't even access any of my computer files.'

Michael had rubbed his brow, taking a different tack. 'That letter Brett sent you and what he then told you—about the fact that your parents hadn't even adopted you—maybe now's the time to get to the bottom of it . . .'

Thea had stared at him. Did he think a distraction like that mattered. Now? When *this* had happened?

'I wouldn't even know where to start,' she'd cried.

But Michael had been patient. 'I'm only

487

bringing it up because I called Mom earlier. Whenever I mention you, she always says that Dr Myerson will come.'

Thea had remembered, then, that she'd heard Michael's mother saying that exact same thing herself.

'She says it over and over,' Michael had continued. 'I think that's where we should start. Maybe he knew something about where you really came from.'

'Even if he did,' Thea said, 'he died years ago. It's hopeless.'

But Michael hadn't given up. And that was how Thea came to be sitting here in Dr Myerson's widow's front room today, with its polished French windows overlooking a perfectly manicured garden and white picket fence.

'Herbie adored your father, Thea,' Mrs Myerson said, glancing at the black-and-white photograph of Dr Myerson on the mantelpiece as she poured herself a cup of tea from a blue and white Dalton pot.

Thea remembered the gentle doctor who'd daubed calamine lotion on her and Michael when they'd both got chickenpox as kids. And how he'd always stopped in for tea and cake with Michael's mother in the kitchen at Little Elms.

'I'd like to ask you some questions about my parents,' Thea said. Again she glanced at Michael. His soft eyes beamed encouragement and resolution. And he was right: it was too late to back out now.

'Ah, yes. Poor Alyssa. She was so fragile,' Mrs Myerson said, pouring the last cup of tea for herself. The clock on the wall ticked loudly. She shooed her little dog from her armchair and sat down.

'I know that she . . . well'—Thea spat the words out—'probably wouldn't have been able to have children of her own. Not after the baby she had in England.'

Adelaide Myerson looked up at Thea, surprised. 'You do?' she slowly said, her pale cheeks colouring with a fresh influx of blood.

'And I know that my father couldn't have children, either. And we've also checked . . .' Thea's voice faltered. She felt suddenly ashamed, as if she'd somehow betrayed Griffin Maddox's memory by speaking his secret out loud.

'What Thea's trying to say,' Michael said, 'is that we've checked the official adoption records. And as well as knowing that Thea's parents couldn't have had children together—'

'We know that I wasn't adopted, either,' Thea said, regaining her voice, determined once more to see this through.

What she'd said was true. She'd checked with the National Adoption Agency. With Michael at her side, prepared to support her, no matter what she'd found. Except that she'd found nothing. There'd been no record of Thea on any of their files. Or any of the international databases that the agency had gone on to cross-reference on her behalf.

Brett had been right. Thea had never been officially adopted by the Maddoxes at all. Which had made for an even grimmer revelation. Because if Thea hadn't been adopted, then how had she come into their lives? *God only knows where they got you from, Thea.* Brett's words echoed in her mind.

Mrs Myerson shook her head and blew a stream of air out through her thin, painted lips. Her hands had clenched into fists. As she looked back at Thea, Thea felt her whole body tense. The old woman's eyes were heavy with fear and regret.

'They *couldn't* adopt,' she said. 'Not legally. Not with Alyssa's mental-health record. She'd tried to commit suicide, you see.'

Suicide? Alyssa Maddox had tried to kill herself. That wonderful, positive woman who'd been Thea's mother. Who *still* felt like her mother, she realized, in spite of all that she'd learnt.

'She went into a dark depression early on in her marriage. The drugs they had to correct such problems, they were much less effective in those days. And so when she and Griffin dis covered they couldn't conceive together, they were left with no hope,' Mrs Myerson explained. 'The adoption authorities wouldn't even let them register.'

'So what happened?' Thea's voice sounded empty, distant, as if it was playing on a radio in another room.

'Herbie knew the situation was desperate. He offered to help. And he knew how to. He had a second cousin, Walchez, in East Germany. One who could find abandoned babies. Babies who needed a good home. No questions asked.'

No questions asked. The phrase sounded so casual, so normal—the kind of phrase you'd use about an item of commerce. A nothing. Something that was traded. Thea stared at Mrs Myerson, aghast. Was that what she'd been?

'Herbie made the arrangements. His cousin's wife, Rena, turned up here one day with you in a

490

little yellow blanket. You were so tiny. You'd lost weight on the boat on the journey over here. You know . . . I think I've still got that blanket somewhere. Herbie insisted in taking you to Alyssa in a clean one, but it felt wrong to throw it away.'

Thea could barely take in what she was saying. 'But what about my real parents? Do you know who they were?'

My real parents.

In East Germany.

The country I was born in.

A country that no longer exists.

Mrs Myerson smiled desperately at Thea. 'You have to understand—where you came from . . . you were not wanted. But here . . . never had a baby been wanted so much. Your parents were overjoyed, Thea. You must know that. They wanted you so desperately. They gave you love, Thea. They gave you everything.'

Except the truth.

There were tears in the old lady's eyes now, but all Thea felt was anger.

'Please,' Mrs Myerson implored, 'don't judge me. My husband thought he was doing the right thing—he only wanted to help . . .'

But Thea couldn't look at her. Not any more. She couldn't look at this woman who knew what her own husband had done. This woman whose husband had moved babies from the East to the West, from the poor to the rich. This woman whose husband had stolen away Thea's life.

*　　*　　*

Thea watched Michael walking down the street

491

towards her. She was waiting for him in the old-fashioned diner on the corner. She'd not been able to stay in Mrs Myerson's perfect home a second longer. She couldn't have trusted herself. She'd wanted to smash her china teacup across the pristine primrose wall. She'd wanted to tear that photo of Dr Myerson in two. She'd wanted to destroy everything he'd ever cared for, the way he'd once destroyed her.

Michael slid onto the red leather banquette beside her in the booth. She saw that he had a plastic bag in his hand.

'Still livid?' he asked.

She didn't answer. If she opened her mouth she'd just scream.

'I don't think what they did was right, Thea. But I don't know if that makes them bad.'

'He was a child-trafficker.'

'The way she sees it, her husband was doing the right thing by saving an unwanted baby. By giving you a new life.'

'But what if I wasn't unwanted? Thea said. That was at the heart of it. Whose word did she have for that? Some cousin of Herbie Myerson? Some East German guy called Walchez? For all she knew, he might have kidnapped her. Her real mother and father might have spent the last thirty-eight years wondering where she was and praying that she'd come back.

Michael stared at her. 'What are you saying?'

'No past, no paperwork? There has to be a reason I was smuggled out in such an underhand way.'

'You heard what she said. It was a "no questions asked" kind of deal.'

There it is again, she thought. That handy, catch-all phrase. That broom with which to sweep dirt nicely out of sight.

'Yeah, well, now I'm asking the questions,' Thea said. 'And I'm going to damn well find out. We can't give up, Michael, you've got to promise me that,' she said, grabbing onto his hands.

He nodded and stared out of the window, back down the street towards the Myerson house.

'OK,' he said. 'Listen, I've been planning on going back to Germany to see some of my colleagues at Landstuhl. I could look up this Walchez guy—see if there are any records on him. I have a few contacts in the military police who might have access to some old East German records. I'm not promising anything, but I'll try.'

'I'm never going to give up,' Thea told him, meaning it with all her heart. 'Not until I've uncovered the truth.'

Michael handed it to her then. The bag he was holding.

'What is it?' Thea said.

'Take a look.'

She opened it up and took out the yellow knitted blanket. She held it in her hands, then buried her face into it, smelling it. It was the only thing that she'd ever truly owned.

*   *   *

A week later Thea was on a plane to Germany to meet Michael. True to his word, he'd called in the favour from his colleague, who had run Walchez's name through some old databases. On Tuesday Michael had found Rena, Walchez's wife.

According to Rena, Thea had been delivered to them in the dead of night, by a huge bear of a man called Udo. Udo hadn't been hard to find, Michael had told Thea on the phone. He'd been a permanent fixture at the small town's main bar. Part-bouncer, part-furniture. He hadn't wanted to talk, but money had lubricated his tongue, although the only thing Michael had got out of him was that he remembered a man called Volkmar and his driver, Sebastian Trost.

The records that Michael's military police contacts had got showed that Volkmar had died in jail years ago. He'd tried to bury his past after the Wall had come down, but his illegitimate business practices had caught up with him. Michael had then turned his research to the driver. When he'd told Thea on the phone how much he'd found out, she'd come over straight away.

Now, as they drove from Berlin airport, where Michael had picked her up, deep into the heart of the former East Germany, Thea stared out of the car window, the windscreen wipers batting away slushy snow. She tied her light-blue cashmere scarf tighter around her neck.

Along the forest road the shadows were lengthening. She'd never seen pine trees so dense. On the right was an old burnt-out building—two ten-foot-high rusting gates propped up askew against its hinges. It was like the set for a ghost movie.

Shouldn't she feel some sort of affinity for this place? she wondered. This, after all, was where she'd come from.

'I think we should stop at the next village,' Michael said. 'We won't be able to do anything until the morning. We'll find somewhere to stay the night.'

'OK,' Thea said, straightening up in her seat.

The lights of a lorry on the other side of the road briefly illuminated Michael's face, and Thea felt a momentary dart of desire—even here, amongst all the apprehension that she otherwise felt—but she pushed it away.

They would stay in separate rooms tonight. She knew that. They were friends, she reminded herself. Just friends. Nothing more. Michael had never indicated that he wanted more. Or was ready for more.

She remembered again how he'd once described himself as damaged goods. But she'd proved herself to be more scarred than he'd ever be. And after the way she'd been these past few weeks, she couldn't imagine that Michael would ever desire her.

A resigned half-smile crept to her lips. What a mess of a couple they'd make.

But there was no point, either, in denying that all the time he'd been away this time in Germany, she'd missed him like crazy. She hadn't been able to stop thinking about how much he'd done for her. Or how dejected she felt without him by her side.

He'd been there for her when she'd most needed him. He'd started this whole search, which had given her something to focus on other than losing control of Maddox Inc. She wondered how she could ever repay him. But even as she thought it, she knew the answer. She had to repay him with the truth. The truth about what Brett had done to her. And about the film of her that Brett had in his

495

possession—the one he'd threatened to use against her. Even if it meant losing Michael for good.

She shivered now as they drove towards the centre of Schwedt, with its ugly, uniform buildings all covered in snow, and the weak yellow light of its intermittently lit street lamps illuminating flashes of grey concrete in their sickly glow. A 'Vacancies' sign hung outside a hotel, and Michael pulled up on the potholed road outside.

'It's not exactly George Cinq,' he said, 'but it might do. We can check in in a little while. I don't know about you, but I could do with a beer.'

Everyone stopped talking as Thea and Michael entered the local bar. It was probably as much their clothes, she thought, as the fact that they were strangers. Or her clothes, at least. She was wearing a DKNY leather coat with fur trim, while Michael had dressed more appropriately in an old Barbour-style coat and jeans.

She sat down at a small wooden table in the corner of the bar, beneath a pair of antlers on the brick wall, and took a menu out from behind a green bottle encrusted with layers of dried candle wax. That Lady Gaga song, 'Bad Romance', was playing and Thea suddenly remembered the compilation tapes Michael had made for her all those years ago. She wondered if he remembered them too.

She looked down the printed list of schnitzels and steaks on offer and thought about her sessions in the gym and the pool in the basement of Maddox Tower, and how religiously she'd used to watch her figure. That Thea—that New York version of herself—seemed so distant now. So unreal and absurd somehow.

A waitress in jeans and a scruffy jumper arrived with a basket of bread. Michael ordered and started chatting easily to her in German. Thea knew enough to know that he was asking her if she knew of Sebastian Trost.

'Are you American?' the waitress asked, suddenly switching to English.

'Yes,' Michael said.

'When I was little the Trosts ran the bakery,' she said, clearly charmed by him. 'You could try there.'

Thea smiled, watching her go. She saw the waitress look back over her shoulder at Michael, but she caught Thea's eye and blushed. Did the waitress find Michael attractive too? What if he got whisked away from her by someone like that? Thea remembered the woman soldier at Landstuhl and how much she'd flirted with Michael. She felt her own inadequacy swamping her.

'You know, I never knew you had such good German,' Thea said. 'You'll have to teach me.'

'You end up with a lot of spare time in hospital.'

Thea remembered when she'd first met him at Landstuhl and how she'd been afraid of all the things he'd seen. How she'd been afraid of asking, in case she'd upset him with her questions, and in case he'd upset her with her answers too. But now she found herself longing for him to confide in her. Longing to know everything about him. Longing for him to trust her.

And so—as they ate their food—she did ask him. About his army training and how it had been when he'd first gone out to Iraq. And she listened to what he had to say as he told her everything. About his men and what they'd gone through, and about how scary it had been to be the one making

497

decisions on the front line.

As he opened up more and more, she asked him all the questions she'd never asked—about the car bomb and what had happened. And he told her what he remembered of the explosion. The pain. About his friends who'd been killed. How he'd shut down after that. How he'd wanted to be dead. About how frightened he'd been, but how the doctors and nurses at Landstuhl had somehow given him strength. And how Thea had helped him too. How seeing her had made him realize more than ever that there was still a world out there that he could be a part of. He'd told her all this. He'd held nothing back. And as she'd listened she'd felt humbled by his bravery, by his honesty, and touched that in a small way she'd helped him to recover.

And later, as they'd trudged through the frozen snow towards the dim, distant lights of the hotel, she'd known that the time had finally come for her to do the same.

'Michael, there's something I want you to know,' she said.

'What?' His voice sounded buoyant, maybe as a result of the beers they'd drunk with the meal, or maybe because of everything he'd just got off his chest. Because it had been good, he'd told her, to talk about it all like that, after all this time.

She almost said nothing then, hating the fact that she was about to bring him down. But still she pressed on. *Now or never. Say nothing to him now and you know you never will.*

'That day,' she said. 'That day Brett fired me. It wasn't just Scolari that made me go,' she said.

Michael's eyes grew dark. Every time she'd

mentioned Brett it was the same. Thea knew he was still furious with her for not letting him go and confront Brett himself.

She took a breath, bracing herself. 'He has a film of me and . . . well . . . a colleague.'

She squeezed her lips together, remembering those shaming images of her and Reicke. Reicke, who'd avoided talking to her ever since, who'd hurt her feelings and who, she realized now, had probably been blackmailed by Brett into trapping her.

'It was something I never should have done, but Brett had our encounter, our . . .' she swallowed hard '. . . our sexual encounter recorded somehow. He told me he was going to send a copy—to you and the board—unless I went, straight away.'

Michael stopped under a lamp-post. 'He threatened you with that?'

Thea nodded. Her chin trembled. This was the one secret she'd held on to. It was the one thing left that Brett had on her, which he could use against her. And now that it was out, she had no idea how Michael might react.

'You promised me. You promised me that you'd tell me if he hurt you again.'

'I didn't want to tell you,' she said, tears suddenly choking her. 'I was too ashamed. And too terrified about what you'd think, if Brett sent you the film.'

Michael let out a growl of frustration and put his head in his hands.

'I've been so scared. So scared he'd do it anyway. So scared he'd try and destroy us. You and me.'

'So you walked away from everything, because

499

of that?' Michael said. 'Because of what you thought I might think?'

She nodded, tears tumbling from her eyes.

'Do you think I'd let him come between us?' Michael asked her.

'I don't know,' Thea said. 'All I know is that I don't want to lose you. I can't lose you.' The words came then. She couldn't stop them. They came from the deepest place inside her, where she'd refused to look, where she'd kept them buried for so long—not understanding them, refusing to accept them, because she'd always been too busy focusing outwards on the rest of her life. 'Because I love you, Michael. Because I think I always have.'

'Oh, Thea,' he said, stepping towards her and folding her into his arms.

Then his lips were on hers. His kiss felt so right, so powerful, like a charge running right through her. They stayed there together, as the cold snow swirled around them, locked tight and kissing more passionately, until she thought that she might faint.

* * *

The next morning Thea couldn't stop smiling as they left the small hotel and stepped into the sunshine. The snow had frozen overnight into twinkling crystals and the sky was a clear, endless blue.

Michael joined Thea on the steps and put his hand in hers, taking a deep breath of fresh air. It felt as if they were honeymooners. They'd certainly behaved like honeymooners. The sex last night had been incredible, and although neither of them had slept, Thea felt bright and wide awake.

500

'Why don't we stay?' she asked, smiling across at him.

'Here?'

'Why not? Oh, Michael. I think this is the first time I've felt'—she grinned like a little girl—'well, *happy*, for as long as I can remember.'

He lifted her hand and kissed her knuckles. And as she stared into his eyes, all the other terrible things that had happened to her lately, and all the frightening revelations she'd undergone, seemed to loosen their grip and their power over her. She and Michael had each other. And they had a future together, she just knew it; but right now she had this moment and she knew she didn't need anything else.

'Me too,' he said, putting his arm around her shoulder. 'But come on. Let's go and check out the bakery.'

The bell above the door chimed as Thea and Michael walked in, and Thea felt the rush of hot air and the smell of freshly baked bread. Shiny brown plaits of strudel were laid out neatly behind the counter. Loaves were stacked high on shelves behind the old-fashioned till.

'We are looking for a man called Sebastian Trost,' Michael explained in German to the burly man dressed in a white apron who was standing there waiting to serve them.

The man looked immediately suspicious. He glanced towards an old woman who was standing over by a heater in the corner of the shop. Thea noticed how she pulled the knitted shawl around her shoulders, clearly wary of strangers.

But Michael was charm itself, and soon Thea and Michael were ushered upstairs, where the

501

woman—Thea's heart was pounding, she could hardly believe their luck—Martina Trost, lit the small gas fire in the cramped apartment. Embroidered headrests covered the brown utilitarian furniture. Michael chatted the whole time, offering compliments and encouragement, some of which Thea picked up in her rudimentary German, but all of which seemed to soften Martina.

An old man sat in a chair in the corner. His eyes had an opaque kind of look, but they turned towards Thea and Michael as Martina showed them in.

'Who's there?' he asked gruffly in German.

Martina answered, equally irritably, walking briskly over to him. She whispered something harshly in his ear, which made him sit up straight. She then began neatening him up. She brushed biscuit crumbs from the grey stubble on his beard and took off the bib he was wearing. Underneath was a neat shirt and jacket. These people may be poor, Thea thought, but they certainly didn't lack pride.

'*This* is Sebastian Trost, my husband,' the woman said. 'So what is this news you have brought for us from America?' she asked.

From the look on her face, and the sudden look of concentration on her husband's brow, Michael had done more than suggest they were bringing news, Thea deduced. He'd clearly implied there might be something—such as money—in it for them too.

'We are looking for information,' Michael explained, leaning close to Sebastian now. He delivered the bullet then. 'We know you were

Volkmar's driver.'

Martina hovered. 'Volkmar?' Her voice was shrill. Thea noticed her backing into the corner, scared now of Michael, eyeing the door, no doubt thinking of her own son downstairs. Sebastian said nothing. But Thea noticed his grip tightening on the brown wooden arm of his chair.

'We want to know about a baby that Volkmar once came into possession of somehow. In 1971. A baby he gave to a man called Walchez. A baby he probably *sold*.' Michael let the word echo through the air like a curse. 'Were you there?' he then asked. 'Do you remember?'

Martina's shrill voice interrupted again. She talked quickly and urgently to her husband. She was scared, Thea could tell that much. She might have even decided they must be the police.

Sebastian held up his hand. '*Nein,*' he told her.

It was the first time Thea had heard him speak and his voice was surprisingly strong.

He rolled his hand for Michael to continue talking. Martina stayed frozen in shock.

Michael nodded at Thea. It was her turn to speak.

'I think I might have been that baby,' she said, nodding to Michael to translate as she pulled the yellow blanket from her shoulder bag.

Martina gasped. In two steps she crossed the room and snatched the blanket away from Thea, her voice rising as she started gabbling at her husband, inspecting the blanket, turning it over in her hands. She shouted at Sebastian.

Alarmed, Thea tried to follow what she was saying, but Sebastian's hands were reaching for Thea. He leant forward in his chair, grabbing her desperately.

'You . . .' he whispered, in English. 'You're alive . . . You're here?'

Martina started talking again, but suddenly she was stopped dead in her tracks by Sebastian, whose bony hand stretched out and touched Thea's cheek.

'You know me?' Thea asked.

'You were going to America, with Walchez. I thought . . . I thought . . .' Sebastian said. He let out a long sigh and sat back in his chair.

'Do you know where I came from?' Thea asked.

Sebastian shook his head, turning it towards her voice. 'Volkmar.'

Michael spoke to him rapidly—forcefully— again.

Thea listened as the old man began to speak in German once more. This time his eyes welled up with tears. Thea could only follow some of it, but she sensed the emotion he was describing as he recalled a night in the forest long ago. And the men there. Volkmar. Solya. Udo. Their names clear in his description. And his fear of them.

Michael frowned at Thea.

'What's he saying?' she asked.

'He's saying . . . "But what about the other one?" He's adamant there was another one.'

'What does he mean? Another what?' Thea asked, confused.

Michael turned to Thea as Sebastian continued to talk. 'Another baby,' Michael said. 'There was another baby there that night with you. In a green blanket. Your sister.'

504

CHAPTER THIRTY-FOUR

NOVEMBER 2009

A feeling of dread rose up inside Romy Scolari as she gripped the steering wheel of Lars's camper van and turned north onto the potholed road towards Schwedt.

She remembered her childhood as being cold and grim. But the bright sunlight today made the snow dusting the high pine trees on either side of the road sparkle and glare. Romy snatched her sunglasses from the dashboard, feeling a fleeting sense of relief and security from the anonymity they gave her as she hurriedly put them on.

A beeping sound jolted her. She delved through the wreckage of fast-food containers and Coke cans on the passenger seat for the little yellow mobile phone that had been her lifeline since she'd left Amsterdam. But there were no new texts, she saw. Just a message informing her that she'd run out of credit.

It was hardly surprising. She and Lars had talked on it so much since she'd left, even though he'd said it was only for emergencies. But the further she'd driven from him and the closer she'd got to here, the more her confidence that she'd been doing the right thing had wavered, and the more she'd needed to hear the reassuring sound of his voice.

She hadn't used her own phone since she'd fled from Villa Gasperi. Or indeed any of her credit cards since she'd withdrawn a large amount of cash before leaving Milan. She'd been worried—correctly, Lars had confirmed—that through one of them her whereabouts could easily have been traced by the police, or even the media.

And Romy was still determined to control her own destiny for as long as she could. Which meant handing herself in. Here, in Schwedt. As her 'first declarative statement of innocence'—a phrase that Tegen Londrom, Lars's lawyer friend, had used when she'd spoken to Romy and had agreed to take on her case, as well as agreeing to fly to Germany to be with Romy when she gave herself up.

'Nearly there,' Romy said, watching the shadow of the van flickering anarchically over the utilitarian grey buildings that she passed.

It was Lars who'd suggested that she talk out loud to his camper van. He'd said that he'd gone on a road trip when his wife had left him, running off with his best friend. He'd meandered through Europe as he'd tried to come to terms with it all, talking to himself, first to relieve the boredom and the loneliness he'd felt, but then because he'd known it was helping him too. He was now convinced that it had been the safe haven of the van that had helped him deal with his despair and his feelings of resentment and rejection.

Romy liked the fact that this crazy vehicle, with its bright-yellow flower in a vase on its dashboard, and its collection of old Eighties record sleeves pinned to its tiny dining area's walls, held a special place in Lars's heart. And that in spite of this—or perhaps even because of it, she hoped—he'd become fond enough of her now to let her use it too.

506

She thought back, by no means for the first time, to that kiss they'd shared in his kitchen, before they'd both remembered themselves and had broken apart. She thought, *If this all ends well—*

'*When* this all ends well,' she told herself, knowing that she had to truly believe that it would end well, or she might as well turn back now.

Once this had all ended well—what she was doing now, putting her faith in justice and the law, setting out to clear her name of any guilt, once and for all—once that was all done with, she *would* see Lars again.

She would see him, and the first thing she would do was kiss him. And not just on the cheek as a friend. But on the lips. As more than a friend. As a man she wanted to be with. To be happy with. One day perhaps even to build a life with. As someone with whom she could move on.

She wished so much that all the difficulties—the police, the lawyers—were already behind her. And that this road trip had a different purpose. She added another flourish to the fantasy that had developed and sustained her over the last few days. She pictured herself on holiday in the van, with Lars and Gretchen and Alfie. The four of them together, watching the sun rise over the ocean somewhere. She wondered whether Alfie would fall in love with the van's furry green seats and 1970s appliances as much as she had. She wondered whether he'd still like Lars.

She prayed that one day she'd know.

She turned on the radio, fiddling with the dial. She'd listened to a brilliant station all the way to Berlin, singing along to their 'golden oldies' hour, amazed that she still remembered all the words to the Bowie, Queen and Eurythmics songs. But then it had switched into modern dance music and she'd turned it off.

Now, apart from a news channel, there was only static on the radio. She remembered the old guy in the laundry who'd taught her to read. Karl, wasn't that it? He'd had a small battery-operated radio, but could never pick up any stations. Romy had thought it had been because Lemcke had somehow blocked the airwaves to stop them from hearing about the outside world, but perhaps the poor reception had just been a matter of geography after all.

Only another mile to go. Another road sign flashed by.

SCHWEDT.

Even seeing the name instilled fear in her. It made it impossible to pretend, as she'd tried so often, that this place had never really existed, that she'd never really been here.

She fumbled for a cigarette and lit it, remembering as she did so sitting with Lars on the balcony, but remembering the fire in the orphanage too.

This is your past. And this is why you've come back, she told herself. *To confront it. To admit it. To stop running from it and pretending it never happened. To become yourself. For the first time in your life.*

Such sights as the road sign—the memories they induced—Romy had already begun facing up to them throughout her journey here. Outside Berlin she'd stopped by the high wire fence surrounding the airport and had leant against the side of the van as she'd looked at the undercarriages of all the aeroplanes, remembering how she'd once been a stowaway taking off from this very runway.

In the city centre she'd parked the van and had walked through the Brandenburg Gate, remembering Ursula and how they'd used to ride their bikes there on Sunday mornings. She remembered, too, the clothing factory, and playing poker with the guards, and the bag full of Lemcke's cash that she'd kept hidden in her mattress.

She now started reclaiming her earliest memories too, letting them live and breathe again inside her mind. She'd shut them away for so long, buried them so deep, but now she pictured herself playing make-believe games in the yard with Marieke and Tomas, and how little Tara and the other small kids in the dormitory had snuggled up to her at night, pressing their cold feet against her back and her legs.

As she drove through the swathe of forest on the outskirts of Schwedt, more memories sprang to life. The enormous height and shape of the trees left her feeling dwarfed. And the sky—that same vast grey expanse that she'd gazed at from the orphanage roof, which had seemed so solid, so much a part of her imprisonment, so ready to fall and crush her if she'd ever tried to escape—made her feel now as if she'd just travelled back in time. That she was a child again. That she was in danger. Every cell in her body screamed at her to turn back.

She shook her head. She was a grown-up. An adult. A mother. With so much to live for that she would not allow herself to give up.

509

As she entered the town's outskirts and the forest diminished to nothing but a blur in the rear-view mirror, she felt the power of the past relinquishing its grip on her. Streets and houses blurred by.

Schwedt. A town she'd heard plenty of—with its church bells and traffic—but had never actually seen.

Anger rose up inside her as she drove along the main street, past a bakery where two people chatted in the sun. That *this* had always been so close. All these people. Their shops and their school. Hadn't they ever wondered about the orphanage and the abandoned children imprisoned there?

Even now, twenty-six years after she'd left, the fact that they hadn't done anything—had turned a blind eye and carried on their lives as if nothing sinister were happening on their very doorstep—made her want to spit.

She followed the signs to the municipal car park in the town square. She drove the van into an empty bay and sat for a long time with her forehead on the steering wheel. She waited until she felt calm enough to get out.

She locked the van and patted its door. She felt suddenly, helplessly, alone. But this was it. This was real. She was no longer in her own private road-trip movie. She was here, and the time had come to do what she'd come to do. To confess. To present her side of what had really happened. To win back her freedom. To clear her name. And then get her son back.

She walked towards the police station. A granite building, tall and bleak. She imagined the police who'd have staffed it when she'd lived here as a child—those men who'd hunted her mercilessly through the wood.

She stopped at a phone booth halfway there. She scuffed another cigarette out on the floor as she dialled Lars's number. In the leafless tree in the middle of the square a robin landed on a branch. She hoped it was a good omen.

'Please,' she whispered. 'Please be there.'

And please, God, let him have dug up something. Something to help her win back Alfie. Something they could take to the Italian and American authorities to prove that Brett Maddox had gained control of Scolari through some illegal means. Something to get Roberto his company back.

But as the phone continued to ring unanswered, Romy dreaded what she might hear. Because, even though Lars had worked through that last night she'd been in his apartment in Amsterdam, he'd found nothing—not a single example of any irregularities, nothing at all they could use.

A click, then: 'Yes,' Lars said.

She felt absurdly relieved just to hear his voice. 'It's me.'

'Oh, Romy. Thank God. Where've you been? I've been worried sick.'

'I'm here. In Schwedt. I'm calling from a phone-box,' she said, feeding more change into the booth's slot. 'The phone you gave me, it ran out of juice.'

'But you're OK?'

'Yes.'

'You'd still better brace yourself,' he said.

She felt a flare of hope rise up inside her then. It was impossible to miss the excitement in his voice.

511

'What?'

'I think I've finally found something.'

Romy gripped the receiver with both hands. 'What?'

'Six weeks ago Maddox Inc.'s new media division bought into CYZ Holdings, a small German media company.'

'I've never heard of it,' Romy said, confused.

'Me neither. But it's not the name of the company that's interesting; it's where it was originally registered.'

'Go on . . .'

'Schwedt.'

As Romy stared out through the grimy phone-box window across the town square towards the brooding police station and the long, thin spire of the church, she felt her heart pounding hard against her ribs.

Brett Maddox—the man who'd just uncovered all the carefully hidden secrets of her past, all the secrets that had begun right here in this town—he'd recently invested in a company from this town as well.

'Who owns CYZ?' Romy asked, desperate to hear more now, the implications of what Lars had just told her already multiplying exponentially in her head.

'I thought you'd ask that. So I took the liberty of compiling a list of the directors' names,' Lars said. 'So let's just see if any of them might in any way have known something about your past.' Lars began to read out the names: 'There's a T. Twigner,' he said, 'and an H.G. Solya and a R. Beluzzi—'

'Wait. Hang on. Back up,' Romy said.

'Twigner?' Romy said.

'No.'

'Solya? H.G. Solya?'

Solya . . .

Somewhere in the far reaches of Romy's memory a dusty, forgotten light switched on. The boys in the orphanage—the bullies she'd tried to forget—rose up clearly in her mind. All those boys who'd always tried to frighten her, but who had always been frightened themselves by something else.

By *someone* else. A phantom. A bogeyman. *Solya . . .* She remembered the whispers in the darkness of the dormitory. *Solya's gonna get you. Solya's in charge of everything. If you make Solya angry, he'll crush you like a fly. Solya's got Lemcke in his pocket. Solya calls all the shots. Those girls are for Solya. You wait and see, one day he'll get you too.*

The laundry. The orphanage. Solya had controlled both. The children who'd been photographed; the kids who'd disappeared.

It must have been Solya who'd known about her all along. Who'd pointed Ulrich in her direction. Who'd told Brett Maddox all about her past. In return for Brett investing in his business, Romy guessed.

Romy felt adrenaline rush through her.

Solya was now Director of a Maddox Inc. company. Solya and Brett Maddox were publicly—undeniably—linked.

Solya was once a gangster.

She'd found her weapon at last.

'What else have you got on him?' she said.

'Nothing yet . . . but that's not to say I can't find something.'

513

'Then do it,' Romy said. 'Dig up anything—everything you can. 'Solya's an animal. A criminal. Tie any of that to Brett Maddox and we'll be able to bring that bastard down too.'

* * *

Romy pushed through the door of the old police station. Inside, the grubby grey floor led to a high grey reception desk. Posters curled on the wall. A clock ticked loudly in the silence.

'I'm here to talk to a police officer,' she told the female guard, in German, the words feeling awkward in this once-familiar tongue, even though she'd rehearsed them a thousand times on the journey here. 'I want to talk to someone about Heinz-Gerd Solya and his connection with the Bolkav State Orphanage. And I want to give a statement about the fire that burnt the orphanage down. My lawyer will be here to join me soon.'

She'd expected more of a reaction to her grand announcement, but the woman behind the desk continued writing. A long moment later she looked up at Romy. She was wearing a grey uniform and a shade of pink lipstick that didn't suit her. Romy saw her checking her out—looking at Romy's stained jeans and roll-neck jumper. Her hair was greasy and tied up in an elastic band.

'I'm afraid we're short-staffed. The officer you need to speak to is out on a call.' She looked at her watch. 'He'll be back in the hour. Would you like to wait?'

Romy nodded. 'Please.'

'It's warmer in here,' the woman said. She unlocked the door next to the reception desk and

514

Romy walked into a small glass-sided interview room.

She stared at the coffee stain on the desk. Every impulse in her body told her to run once more—to get out of here. But she forced herself to stay. She had to do this.

The clock ticked. Romy shuffled nervously in her seat. This was excruciating. She'd come here to confess. She didn't want to wait. She'd been waiting all her life.

'Are you OK in here?' Another police officer stuck his head around the door. He was young, Romy saw, barely old enough to shave. 'Can I get you a coffee?'

Romy nodded mutely, wondering how well they'd treat her once they knew the truth.

'What's your name?' the female officer asked, finally looking as if she meant business, walking in armed now with a clipboard and a pen.

'My name is Romy Scolari, but originally I was from here. From the orphanage.'

Now the attention of both of them was caught by the outside door opening and a man and woman coming into the reception area. The man had short hair and when he pushed his sunglasses up into his hair, Romy saw that he had a scar across the left side of his face. But its effect wasn't sinister, Romy thought.

The woman, who, from the way she looked at the man, was clearly his girlfriend, had long blonde hair tied in a plait. She was wearing an expensive leather coat with smart trousers and a cashmere jumper and matching blue scarf. Together they approached the reception desk.

Romy stood up and walked to the glass window.

And as she watched as the woman on the other side of the glass started talking to the officer, she felt a jolt right in the pit of her stomach. That wasn't any woman. That was . . . that was Thea Maddox. She was sure of it.

She wouldn't forget a face like that. James had dug out loads of press clippings of her in Milan. When Thea Maddox had tried to take over Scolari.

Thea Maddox. What the hell was she doing here? Was she involved with Solya too, like her brother Brett? Because there was no way, surely, she could know that Romy was here.

Then the strangest thing happened. Even though Romy hadn't moved—hadn't done *anything* to catch the other woman's attention—Thea Maddox turned and stared right at her. *Through* her, it felt.

And in that moment it was like looking into a mirror. Romy saw a flicker of recognition in Thea Maddox's eyes, which quickly turned to shock. She was clearly just as surprised to see Romy.

She pointed at Romy and then the officer looked at the small office where Romy was. In a moment Thea Maddox and the man had marched into the small meeting room too.

Romy hadn't expected Thea Maddox to be so beautiful in the flesh. Or so strangely familiar. Her blonde hair and radiant skin seemed to light up the dull grey room.

'You're Romy Scolari,' Thea Maddox said, as if she could hardly believe it. 'I'm—'

'I know who you are.' Romy couldn't keep the bitterness from her voice. She didn't want to, either. She wanted to scream.

Why was Thea Maddox here? Why now? Why

516

here in the police station? Did that mean the police here were corrupt as well? By coming here had Romy just made the biggest mistake of her life?

'I—' Thea Maddox started to speak again, but Romy refused to listen.

'Don't,' she said. 'I don't want to hear it. I don't want to hear anything you have to say. When your company bought Scolari—*stole* Scolari—when *your brother* blackmailed me, I lost *everything*. Including my son.'

Thea Maddox's blue eyes locked with Romy's. 'Brett Maddox is *not* my brother,' she said. 'He's a liar and a cheat. And he blackmailed me too. And when *you* sold him Scolari, he used it against me to make *me* resign. Now, I don't know why you sold to him, but let me tell you, it cost me everything too.'

The policewoman interrupted then. Romy had almost forgotten she was there.

'Excuse me,' she said to Romy. 'Your lawyer is here.'

A smartly dressed woman in her late thirties walked into the office.

'I'm Tegen Londrom,' she said. She flashed a neat business card and shook hands with Romy. She shrugged off the camel coat that was slung around her shoulders. 'And you are the police?' she asked Thea Maddox and the man she was with.

'No,' Thea said.

'Friends?'

'Never,' said Romy.

'Then why are you here at all?' Tegen Londrom demanded of Thea and the man, before turning angrily to the policewoman. 'My client is here to make a statement about the burning-down of the

517

Bolkav State Orphanage in December 1983, and also to discuss'—she checked her iPad—'a certain Heinz-Gerd Solya, who may once have had connections here.'

'Wait,' Thea Maddox said, 'did you just say Solya?' She didn't even wait for Tegen Londrom to reply. 'But, Michael,' she said, her eyes blazing now as she turned to her male companion, 'that's him. Solya was the man in the woods with Volkmar. He was the one . . .'

Romy looked between the two of them.

Then Thea Maddox spun back round to face her and said, 'What's Solya to you?'

Romy was so shocked, not only by the question, but by who was asking it, that before she could stop herself, the words she'd meant the policewoman to hear began pouring out of her.

'Solya was connected to the orphanage where I grew up. He did terrible things to the girls there. He—'

'*You* grew up in Schwedt?' Thea said, incredulously.

'Yes. In the orphanage. That's why I'm here. It's because of me that it burnt down.'

Something extraordinary was happening to Thea Maddox's expression. It had started blazing with what Romy could only imagine was some kind of triumph, some kind of hope.

'Your age . . .' Thea said, stepping closer to her now. 'Your eyes . . . Do you have any idea who your parents are? Where you came from?'

'Nothing,' Romy said. 'I never found anything in the orphanage files.'

'Nothing at all?'

'No, I tried to find out once. But there was no

paperwork. Only an old green blanket.'

Thea Maddox let out a gasp. Her hand flew to her chest. 'It's you,' she breathed. 'It's you. Oh my God . . .'

'What do you mean?' Romy asked.

'That's why I'm here. To find the baby in the green blanket. And if that's you . . .' she said, her eyes brimming with tears.

'What?' Romy asked.

'Then that means . . . that means that you're my sister.'

CHAPTER THIRTY-FIVE

FEBRUARY 2010

In the cold morning light at Berlin airport Romy stood on the tarmac outside the arrivals area where the private planes landed. She stamped her feet against the bitter cold, looking up again at the white cloud, waiting for Roberto's private plane to land.

She took her phone out of her pocket and looked again at the text Thea had sent her from America, knowing that she must have got up in the middle of the night to send it at the right time.

'Good luck,' it said, 'I'm thinking of you xxx.'

And I am thinking of you, Romy thought. *Dear Thea. My sister.*

After everything that had happened in the past few months, it seemed unimaginable now to Romy that she'd never known that she'd had a sister. Romy would never forget Thea's revelation in the

519

police station in Schwedt, and how she'd told Sebastian Trost's story about the babies being sold in the woods, and the feeling Romy had had—even before Tegen had suggested blood tests—that Thea was right. It had been an indescribable feeling of certainty.

The fact that she'd actually discovered family— real family—for the first time in her life had made Romy feel as if all her childhood dreams had come true. But it hadn't been the homely German *Hausfrau* that Romy had always fantasized she might one day meet. No. Her sister was Thea Maddox. *The* Thea Maddox, whom everybody knew. The Thea Maddox who was wealthy, influential and smart.

But she was an altogether different kind of Thea, too, Romy had discovered. A kind, sweet, wonderful, generous and beautiful Thea. A Thea whom Romy was still getting to know. But a Thea whom Romy truly thought of as her own gift from God. Because she'd been there. Just when Romy had thought everything was lost, Thea had saved her.

It had been Thea who'd stayed right by Romy's side in those horrible weeks as the police had launched their investigation into the Bolkav State Orphanage fire. And Thea who'd held Romy's hand as they'd gone back to the site of what had once been the orphanage, and had encouraged her to step through the gap in the white police tent to where the police had dug down through the ruins and rubble. It had been Thea who'd walked first down into the interconnecting basements of the orphanage and laundry, where the police had unearthed rusted cages and cameras, manacles and

520

fragments of human bone. And Thea who'd held Romy as she'd wept.

It had been impossible not to. As the policeman's torch beam had swept through the dusty air, the ghostly screams of Lemcke's victims had rung out in Romy's ears, and she'd remembered once again the names of those lost children whom the rest of the world had forgotten all about. But she'd vowed to Thea, right at that moment, that she would start remembering them.

Afterwards it had taken hours and hours of police interviews, but eventually, Romy hadn't been charged either with the murder or manslaughter of Fox or with starting the orphanage fire. Of the four witnesses—the boys who'd raped Claudia, and Claudia herself—who'd originally made the accusations against Romy, the only two left alive were now serving sentences for various crimes, including rape, in a maximum-security jail. The German State Prosecution Service did not believe that any testimony these men gave could be considered reliable enough to lead to Romy's conviction.

And her description of Ulrich and the boy who'd been there the night Alfonso had died in the Villa Gasperi had been enough to link them both to several unsolved murders and brutal assaults in the region.

Furthermore, as the investigation into the orphanage had become more public, other witnesses—other children who'd been there—had begun coming forward and telling their stories; and in each case Lemcke's and Solya's names had become more prominent. To the point where Solya himself had been arrested at the airport en route for South America and had been taken in for questioning.

Thea had flown immediately back to the States with Michael, hoping to make public the association of Maddox Inc. and Solya's company, but Brett had been careful to distance himself. As usual, she said, allegations weren't sticking, but Thea was determined to find a way to make them.

More importantly—in part thanks to Tegen, in part to Thea's authority in managing the proceedings and in part to the integrity of Romy's version of events—the police had come to believe that Romy had indeed acted in self-defence. They'd decided not to press charges. For the first time in her life Romy found herself truly free.

And there, waiting for her when she'd been released, had been Lars. She remembered how they'd got back to the camper van, still in the car park—weeks after Romy had left it there—and had hugged each other close. And then they'd kissed. Properly this time, neither one of them pulling back. It had just seemed like the right thing to do. Then Lars had done two more amazing things.

He'd driven her straight to The Regent hotel in Berlin, where he'd booked a suite. Then he'd given her his laptop and let her write a long-overdue email to Roberto Scolari.

The reply that had come back had been curt. Alfie was booked to go skiing at Christmas with Cesca's family. Their reunion could wait, certainly until Romy had dealt with all the press in Germany, and until Roberto had had time to clear her name with the authorities in Italy and remove the charges against her.

Overjoyed to hear anything from Roberto, Romy had called Flavia, who'd filled her in on what had been happening in Italy since she'd left. Maria had been in hospital, the stress of losing Scolari having caused a heart attack. They'd all been worried they'd lose her, but she was getting better now. And the good thing to come out of it had been that Roberto and his estranged daughter Gloria had been reconciled.

And Alfie? Romy had pressed her. Flavia had assured Romy that he was safe. Roberto and Maria had sent him to a wonderful prep school in Paris, which he'd been loving, having been selected for the football and skiing teams. The news had hurt. Romy knew that sending Alfie away had always been what Roberto had wanted for him. It had been Romy who'd fought to keep him with her in Milan.

But best of all was that Alfie remained innocent of everything that had happened, Flavia assured her. Romy had slumped with relief then. Roberto had protected her son. Alfie might not hate her after all.

And that had been when Lars had handed her a glass of champagne and kissed her again. Then they'd fallen into bed together and had stayed there for a whole week over Christmas, ordering room service and only remembering the outside world when they'd called Gretchen at her mother's to wish her a happy Christmas.

It had felt like a whole new beginning, Romy thought, And now, finally, here was the day she was going to see Alfie. She knew that Roberto planned to take Romy home with them, but she wondered whether home really was in Italy now, especially with Alfie away at school in Paris. Especially since she didn't have a job.

She pictured Lars in his apartment in Amsterdam. She'd Skyped him and Gretchen this morning, and they were just as excited as she was that she was going to see Alfie. Lars was still working all hours to find a tangible connection between Solya and Brett Maddox, although it was difficult since Solya had covered his tracks so carefully.

But Romy had no time to think about it any longer because there it was—a small black dot coming closer and closer—and Romy felt as if her heart might burst as the small plane landed and rolled towards her along the tarmac.

She raced forward as the truck with the steps approached the plane. Then the doors were opening.

'Mamma,' Alfie called, racing down the steps, waving. He was taller than Romy remembered, as if he'd grown a foot since she'd last seen him, and he was tanned from skiing. His hair was different too. It was scruffy—just like Alfonso's had been when she'd first met him. The likeness between them both took her breath away.

And then he was in her arms, her cheek against the top of his head.

'I missed you,' she breathed, a sob in her chest. 'Oh, how I missed you. My darling.' She held his face, drinking in his features, kissing his cheeks and forehead.

'How was the campaign?' Alfie asked, his nose wrinkling at her over-the-top affection. 'Flavia said you'd probably be so tired. Did you really have to go to Africa and all those places?'

'Uh-huh,' Romy lied. Flavia had explained how the family had told Alfie that Romy had been called away to do an important top-secret charity campaign and wouldn't be able to be in touch with him for a while—a lie they'd all stuck to and one that Alfie hadn't once questioned. Especially since he'd been sent away to school so fast, to a country where he wouldn't understand the press.

Romy didn't want to spoil this reunion with the actual truth. Not now. But as soon as they were alone she'd tell him everything. Of that she was sure. But for now she was so grateful to Flavia for the lies she'd told. 'I'm sorry I didn't call. It's been impossible.'

'I know,' Alfie said. 'It's OK. I knew it wouldn't be that long. Anyway, I'm proud of you. And *so* much has been happening. The Elysée is amazing. Thank you so much for getting me in there.' Again she realized the lies the family had told to protect him.

'You like it?' she asked.

'I love it. Did you know I've been selected for the skiing team?'

She nodded, trying not to cry. She saw that, as always, he was racing forward, just like his father had been. If he'd been hurt by her absence and lack of communication, there were no visible scars. The Scolaris had made that possible.

And she knew then that, no matter how much she'd hurt them, Roberto and Maria had loved her son enough to protect him. Just as Flavia had said.

As Alfie carried on, asking her permission to go on a skiing trip in the Alps, she saw Roberto at the top of the steps to the plane.

He looked older—the trauma of what had

525

happened to Maria and the loss of his company clearly having eaten away his vitality. Romy hugged Alfie close again as Roberto walked down the steps towards her. Then, as he reached her, she saw that his eyes were full of tears, and she opened her arms and let him join in their hug too.

'Can you ever forgive me, Romy?' he asked.

'Oh, Roberto, how can you even ask that?' she cried, repeating what he'd told her on her wedding day. 'You gave me back my son.'

*   *   *

Thea smoothed down her lipstick, then the skirt of her simple cream silk suit. She felt her heart pounding with excitement as she looked at Michael. He was wearing a blue pinstriped jacket with a cream rose in his buttonhole, and Thea thought he'd never looked more handsome. He was being much calmer about today than she was, she thought, as she brushed his hair to one side.

'You ready?' Michael asked her, taking her hand.

She recognized the beautiful strains of Bach's Double Violin Concerto—the music they'd both agreed on—coming from the other side of the frosted-glass windows.

In fact, they'd agreed on nearly everything, Thea thought, wondering how many other brides ever felt the same. Michael had proposed on Christmas Day, making her pull a Christmas cracker that he'd selected from the huge tree they'd put up in her house. Inside had been a simple diamond engagement ring.

Every decision since then had been easy.

There'd been no announcement and no press. They'd wanted the ceremony to be a small private affair that they could enjoy together. Thea had made it totally clear to Marie, their celebrant, that the press were not to get so much as the slightest hint that she and Michael were getting married.

Yes, Thea was pretty sure she'd done everything in her power to make sure that Brett would not be able to ruin her day. Although he had more pressing issues on his mind, Thea thought—like running Maddox Inc. without her.

From the few inside sources she still had, as well as reports in the newspapers, Brett hadn't fared well since he'd fired her—he hadn't banked on the fact that such a board reshuffle would rock the share prices. He wasn't quite as universally popular as he'd assumed, it seemed. It hadn't helped that Bethany had appeared in public last month with a black eye, her quiet 'No comment' sparking huge press speculation about affairs at the top of Maddox Tower and whether her celebrity marriage was on the rocks.

For once in her life Thea was glad to be out of it. Since finding Romy she hadn't had time to think about work. Or the life she used to lead. Everything was different now. She had the future to think about, not the past.

She smiled at Michael now as he pushed open the door. Inside, the room was flooded with spring sunshine. A large vase of daffodils was on the table at the front next to the marriage register. Marie was standing close by, with a huge smile on her face.

They had been going to have the ceremony all alone, but had both agreed on a few witnesses, and now Thea was glad they were here as they walked hand-in-hand up the soft green carpet to the front. Sandy, Thea's trusted housekeeper—who, Thea noted, had made a big effort to be smart for the occasion—smiled, and Thea waved to her.

Sarah, her old assistant from Maddox Inc., and her new husband Tony were also at the front. Sarah beamed at her.

'You look beautiful,' Sarah mouthed. Then she flicked her eyes to the man in the row behind her, clearly impressed that Ollie Mountefort—Thea's old friend from college, fresh from his latest filmset—had made it, just as he promised he would. He winked at Thea as she passed.

She wished that Romy and Alfie could have been here, but Romy had been unable to secure a visa to get into the States, despite Thea's protests about her sister's criminal record having been cleared. But she hoped they'd be together again soon, and Romy had sent over a blue lace handkerchief that she'd had on her own wedding day, which Thea had tucked firmly up her sleeve.

They'd both invited Johnny too, but at such short notice he hadn't been able to leave South Africa, although he couldn't have been more happy for them both. Thea and Michael planned to go over there for a week of their honeymoon to see him, and Johnny had told Thea on the phone that Gaynor and Marcel Leveaux were thrilled that they were visiting, and were insisting on them staying in their new luxury guesthouse at the Leveaux vineyard.

On Michael's side there were five soldiers, who were all smiling at their old captain. Thea knew them all, having met them when they'd arrived to take Michael out on a stag night that it had taken him a week to recover from. But today she hardly recognized them in their uniforms, they looked so smart, especially Bud, Michael's closest colleague, who saluted him.

At the front, Michael's mother's wheelchair was being turned by Rudy, her helper. It had been touch-and-go whether Caroline Pryor would make it from the Brightside home, but Rudy had driven her the whole way and would take her back later. Michael didn't want his mom to miss today, even if she didn't remember it.

Thea bent down to kiss her cheek as she arrived at the front of the room. 'You made it,' she said. 'I'm so glad.'

Then to her surprise Mrs Pryor smiled. 'Thea,' she said, speaking like she always used to, her voice full of joy, 'I knew you and Michael should be together. God bless you both.'

Thea turned to Michael, her eyes wide with shock, hoping he'd heard his mom say something so lucid. She saw tears in his eyes as he hugged his mother and kissed her, knowing that this moment would vanish and he'd lose her again. But it had happened nonetheless. His mom knew how happy they both were.

Then Michael stood and took both of Thea's hands, and she felt as if they were kids, embarking on a daring new adventure, as Marie started the ceremony to make them man and wife.

*　　*　　*

It was exactly two months after Thea and Michael's wedding that the Solya scandal hit the States. Thea would think afterwards how ironic it was that it should happen at the very moment when she felt so peaceful.

It was a perfect spring day. Thea was out jogging in Central Park, going over the conversation she'd had with Michael before he'd left for work this morning about getting a puppy, when Romy's name flashed up on her iPhone. She and Romy had spoken for an hour on Friday, so she was surprised that she was calling again, especially since Romy was in Amsterdam for the weekend with Lars.

Thea slowed down, switched off her running playlist and answered the call, still out of breath.

'Lars has done it,' Romy said, and Thea could hear the excitement in her voice.

Thea walked down towards the lake, trying to take in the magnitude of what Romy was telling her—her heart beating hard now, not from her run, but from what Romy was telling her. Because after months of careful and meticulous searching (and not a little of his 'dark arts', hacking into certain seemingly impregnably fire-walled personal email accounts), Lars had finally uncovered a trail of video files sent between Brett Maddox and Heinz-Gerd Solya.

'What kind of files?' Thea asked, but she already knew the answer.

She closed her eyes, feeling a mixture of relief and disgust as Romy told her about the underage girls and how it looked as if the files led to a huge Europe-wide network of pornography-sharing. Lars couldn't believe what he'd uncovered, and the more he looked, the more he found.

'Late last night Lars called Tegen, and then he

sent the files to the German and American anti-child-pornography police and the paedophilia task forces. All hell broke loose this morning. And now Tegen's just called. She's just heard . . .'

'Heard what?' Thea asked.

'The police are on their way to Maddox Tower. They're going to arrest him,' Romy said. 'They're going to get Brett. We've done it, Thea. We've got him.'

*　　*　　*

The TV cameras were already blocking the sidewalk as Thea arrived in a cab with Michael outside Maddox Tower half an hour later.

'Miss Maddox, how do you feel about your brother's arrest?' a reporter asked her as she stepped onto the kerb.

She saw the cameras turning towards her. She glanced at Michael as he got out of the other side of the car. He nodded, telling her to go for it.

It had been Michael who'd come straight back from work and forced Thea to have a shower and change into her smartest suit, then get down here to Maddox Tower. He for one, he said, was not going to miss a moment of Brett's public humiliation. And neither was his wife.

'Glad,' Thea replied.

She pushed her way through the reporters in time to see Brett being escorted out of the front doors of Maddox Tower, both arms held by two officers. He looked furious as the camera flashes strobed. There was no sign of Bethany.

Lance Starling followed close behind, shouting over the media, as the journalists clamoured to picture Brett. Thea watched as the officers led Brett into the back of an armoured police van. He didn't look in her direction as the doors slammed shut. Lance Starling got into a Maddox car behind the police van. Thea watched as the van pulled away, the siren blaring, cameras snapping.

More police vans got into position now. Thea saw the giant glass revolving door of Maddox Tower swinging round as several officers came out carrying computers. In the foyer Thea could see a crowd of Maddox employees, their hands to their mouths in shock and disgust.

Then Storm was coming out of the building too. She looked like a painted clown, she was wearing so much make-up.

'My son is innocent,' she declared, dramatically stopping in a pose as if she were at the end of a catwalk. She was wearing a low-cut silk blouse and high heels with a tight pencil skirt. She looked ridiculous. 'Whoever has instigated this slander has made a huge mistake. And they will pay.' She stood defiantly in front of the cameras. 'He's innocent, totally innocent,' Thea heard her reiterate as the cameras closed in on her.

'Miss Maddox, Miss Maddox,' Thea heard a reporter say to her, as she pushed through the crowd towards Storm. 'What do you make of these allegations against your brother?'

'I'm sure they're all true,' Thea said.

She could sense the frenzied atmosphere amongst the journalists. She knew what she was saying was truly sensational—that this was news-breaking gold—and yet she felt strangely calm.

But Storm was far from calm.

'You! *You!*' Storm said, turning to Thea. 'Don't

532

you dare! Don't you dare say anything. He's family.'

'He's not my family,' Thea said. 'And neither are you. Brett Maddox has been arrested today on utterly justifiable charges. I hope this is the start of a thorough investigation into the despicable practices in his personal life. I also urge anyone who has any evidence, or has been affected by Brett Maddox in any way, to come forward and help the police.'

'She's a liar!' Storm screamed, pointing at Thea. 'She'd do anything to get where my son has got. This is all her fault.'

Thea—along with the rest of the world—watched in horror as Storm launched herself at Thea, trying to scratch and hit her. She was immediately restrained by two officers, but that drove Storm even wilder. She kicked and bucked, as the reporters stared at the spectacle. Then she turned and punched an officer in the face.

In the pandemonium that followed, more officers bustled into the throng to grab Storm, her blouse unhitching from her skirt as she screamed at Thea. Michael was by Thea's side.

'Are you OK?' he asked, holding her elbow. 'Did she get you?'

'No, she didn't,' Thea replied as Storm was dragged away by the police. Thea watched as the policeman Storm had hit pushed her head down to make her sit in the back of the patrol car.

'Thank God for that,' Michael said. 'You're going to have to do some serious damage-limitation after that little spectacle.'

'Ms Maddox,' one reporter shouted. 'What are you going to do now?'

533

Thea stared up at the skyscraper and the huge M at the top. Then she smiled at Michael and squeezed his hand, knowing that he would support her.

'I'm going to try and save my company,' she said, walking towards the revolving door.

CHAPTER THIRTY-SIX

SEPTEMBER 2011

Romy moved the room-service tray out of the way, then kicked off her shoes and joined Thea on the cover of the double bed in Thea's bedroom in the Presidential Suite of the Ritz Hotel in London. She smiled at her, glad that they were alone; that they had this last night to discuss everything that had happened.

Sitting barefoot on the bed in comfortable tracksuit bottoms and a T-shirt now, Thea Maddox looked as far away from her corporate image as it was possible to get. But Romy had come to learn never to underestimate her little sister. She was a formidable businesswoman—one who had completely turned around Maddox Inc. in the last year. And one of her first decisions as newly instated Chairwoman of Maddox Inc. had been to sell Scolari back to Roberto and put him back in control of his company—a favour Romy knew she could never repay, and one that had delighted Roberto.

'What time will Lars be here tomorrow?' Thea asked.

'His train's not in until eleven. So we'll get a lie-in.'

'That's if we ever get any sleep.'

'True,' Romy said, with a sigh.

'Although you should get some beauty sleep before you see him,' Thea teased, knowing how much Romy was looking forward to her first proper holiday with Lars.

'You're the one who needs sleep,' Romy reminded her. 'When are you going to finish work?'

'Soon,' Thea said. 'But I can't sit around waiting. Anyway, I've already gone down to four days a week, and when the baby's born I'll take a full nine months off. Hey, feel this,' Thea said, rolling onto her back, grabbing Romy's hand and putting it under neath her own on her swollen stomach. 'It's kicking.'

'I felt it,' Romy gasped. And—there—she felt it again: the tiny jab of Thea and Michael's baby.

'It never does that for Michael, although he puts his hand on it for hours,' Thea said, smiling gently as she stroked her bump. 'It must like its Aunty Romy already.'

'You promised Michael you'd call,' Romy reminded her.

'I know. And I will, when it's a more sociable hour for him over there. Anyway I still feel too shell-shocked after today, don't you?'

Romy nodded. 'Come on,' she said, forcing a brave smile. She'd escaped the past once. She would not let it drag her down again. 'Shall we look at the photos again? Let's focus on the good and not the bad.'

Thea nodded, pulling the album towards them.

They sat up on the bed, side by side against the headboard, turning over the crinkled pages.

*   *   *

In all the press furore that had surrounded the high-profile arrests of Brett Maddox and Heinz-Gerd Solya, even more people had come forward, on both sides of the Atlantic, to accuse the two men of other criminal actions.

A total of three American women so far had accused Brett Maddox of rape and sexual assault, amongst them a Senate researcher named Ally Monroe, the daughter of the woman Thea had once let into the party in Maddox Tower. Bethany had made a fortune from a book auction to sell the salacious inside story of her abusive marriage to Brett. Thea had heard she'd even sold the film rights.

In Europe, more and more people had come forward in connection with Solya and his past crimes, but the one that stood out was Petra Bletford from England, who had claimed to be the girls' aunt.

After a blood test had confirmed this to be true, Thea had met Romy here in London this morning and earlier they'd visited Petra in her home in Kingston-upon-Thames. They'd sat in her large conservatory, overlooking a well-kept garden, as Petra had told them the story they'd both been longing to hear.

Petra herself had come over to England when the Berlin Wall had fallen and had married an Englishman, Geoffrey, with whom she'd had two sons—now grown-up. Her children's photographs

536

were on the wall. She had been a teacher for most of her working life and she didn't sound German at all, but as she started speaking, Thea got the impression that memories were flooding back.

'This was your mother,' Petra had said, opening the pages of an old photo album, the yellowing tissue paper crackling.

Thea leant in close to Romy, who had the album on her lap, looking at the black-and-white image of the woman. She was wearing a headband in her long hair, which swished out as she danced and laughed in the sunshine. That was their mother? That pretty woman with blonde hair, just like hers, but a smile just like Romy's?

'Ana was always the one taking photos. It's rare to have one of her,' Petra said.

'She was pretty,' Romy said, sadly.

'Yes, a real beauty.' Petra turned to Romy and Thea. She put her hand on her chest. 'If only she could have seen this day. If only she could have seen you two. I can hardly believe it myself.'

Romy smiled softly at Thea and put down the photo album on the table. 'Can you tell us, now we're here, what happened? I know from your emails that it's hard . . . that you wanted to tell us in person what happened . . .'

Petra sighed, clearly having prepared herself for this conversation. She sat, her hands crossed in her lap, as she told Romy and Thea about her childhood in East Germany and her little sister, Anaka.

Thea listened, feeling ashamed. She'd had so much, when her real mother had had so little.

'What was she like?' Romy asked.

'Romantic. Headstrong,' Petra said. 'It was no

surprise when she fell for Niklas. He worked at the factory and was young and handsome. When she saw something she wanted, she went after it and didn't stop. And she was determined to marry him, right from the start.'

Thea glanced at Romy. From what she'd learnt already of her sister, it sounded as if she took after their mother. But Romy had already turned to stare at her, and Thea knew she'd just thought the same thing.

'So what happened to Niklas?' Thea asked. 'Was he our father?'

Petra shook her head. 'Niklas worked at the steel factory, but one day he didn't come home. Ana was frantic. She went to the factory and confronted the guy Niklas had worked for—Hans Volkmar.'

Volkmar. *The man who'd taken the babies to the wood.* Thea would never forget his name.

'He laughed at her, but she was determined not to give up. She started making a fuss to the boss, which is when Volkmar and another man—a scarier man—visited her at home. Our home.'

'A scarier man?' Romy asked.

'Solya,' Petra said.

Romy stared wide-eyed at Thea, who gripped her hand, horrified that this monster she'd heard so much about had touched their mother's life.

'Solya took one look at Ana and wanted her for himself. He told her that Niklas was dead. When she fought him, he . . . well, he hit back. And . . .'

Petra looked away from them then. She pulled out a handkerchief from the sleeve of her blue cardigan and wiped the corner of her eye. She took a breath to steady herself.

'A month later Ana discovered she was pregnant. With you.' Petra's eyes locked with Romy's.

'You can't mean . . .' Thea gasped.

'That Solya's *my father*?' Romy said.

Thea felt her heart hammering. She could see the shock on Romy's face. But Petra didn't stop talking. There was clearly more to come.

'Even so, she loved you when you were born,' she told Romy, staring unwaveringly into her eyes. 'God, she loved you. But word got out that she'd had a baby, and Solya came to see her.' Petra took a deep breath. 'This time he was calm. He offered Ana money, and then new furniture arrived and clothes for you. He said he'd look after her. He told her she was the most beautiful girl he'd ever seen. But she told him that her heart would always be Niklas's and that she wanted nothing from him. He was furious. Then, the same thing—he raped her again . . . And he kept coming back, and she would try to fight it off, but always it ended the same . . .'

Romy's hand was over her mouth, her eyes bulging with tears. Thea clasped her other hand tightly.

Petra looked over at Thea sadly now. 'And then eight months later you were born.'

Thea felt bile rising in her throat. That animal—that *monster*—he'd done the same thing to their mother that Brett had done to her.

'When she had you,' Petra continued, 'so soon after her first baby, she was ill. I thought we'd lose her, she was so weak. She wouldn't let you out of her arms, though—either of you. And for a while we thought it was all over.'

539

'But what about Solya?' Romy asked.

'Ana planned to run away from him, when she was strong enough. But then he came back. He gave Ana one last chance. To submit to him, to love him properly. He told her that he would forgive her and they could start all over again together.'

'But she said no?' Thea guessed.

Petra nodded. 'Of course she did. She could never have submitted to that monster.'

'What happened?' Thea asked, her voice catching.

'He did not ask her again. He beat her worse than he'd ever done before. He washed his hands of her and then he took his revenge.' Petra blanched. 'I will never forget the sound she made when Volkmar took you both from her. I tried to fight him. Our father did too. But Volkmar was too strong. He said he would kill us if we went to the police.' Petra shook her head, wiping tears from her eyes. 'Our neighbour had a gun, which he kept in his woodshed. That's where we found Ana the next morning. She'd shot herself in the head.'

*　　　*　　　*

Now, sitting here next to Romy on the hotel bed, Thea put her finger on the picture of their mother and her bright, lovely smile.

'I'm so glad we were together today. I don't think I'd have been able to cope if I'd been on my own,' Romy said.

'I can't imagine how it must have been for her,' Thea said. 'Even living through everything Brett did—I can't imagine being that scared.'

540

The thought of having her baby taken away from her terrified Thea, and her baby hadn't even been born yet. The thought of her mother loving Niklas, and then losing him—Thea couldn't bear that, either. Because she couldn't imagine losing Michael, and what that might do to her.

Now, once again, Thea imagined Solya in the woods forty years ago, playing God with two precious babies, the whole image so much viler now that Thea knew he'd known all along that they were his own children. She thought of him deciding which one to give to Walchez, and the twist of fate that had sent Thea to America.

Thea couldn't begin to imagine what it would be like to confront Solya. Their father was in jail now, awaiting trial in Berlin. Romy and Thea would have to go there to face him eventually. But that was something to worry about another day.

The most important thing was that she and Romy were together. And that, more than everything else, made Thea feel that evil had not triumphed. Not Solya. Not Brett.

The way things were shaping up—even though Storm was using every last cent of her wealth, in an attempt to clear Brett's name—Brett would be spending a long time in prison. Behind bars, physically and mentally. Michael had told Thea what they did to rapists and child molesters in jail. As far as Thea was concerned, Brett deserved everything that was coming his way.

Which meant that Maddox Inc. was now truly hers—with the board firmly behind her, and Brett's previous supporters already gone. Somehow though, with Brett gone, her own commitment to running the company had waned.

As a result she'd dramatically cut back her hours and had learnt to delegate far more. And when the baby was born, she meant what she'd told Romy: she was going to take at least nine months, maybe even a year, off. She wasn't going to miss a second of it. Romy had convinced her of that already.

Thea stretched and got off the bed, pressing her hand to the small of her back for support, as she padded over to her suitcase on the rack in the hall. She delved inside it, remembering the present she'd brought. She picked out the wrapped package and dusted it off.

And as she did, she thought of Jenny in Australia and her visit out there. They'd been in touch last year, and Thea had asked the company lawyers to see if they could find a settlement that would allow Jenny compensation for the inheritance she'd never received from her mother. It seemed only fair, since it had been Alyssa McAdams's fortunes that had founded Maddox Inc.

But Jenny had astonished Thea by refusing the money. She hadn't wanted to become a part of the Maddox empire. She hadn't wanted her life to change. What was much more important to Jenny than any money Thea could give her, she'd told her, was what she'd already given her. She'd found her father, Johnny Faraday. And Johnny couldn't have been more delighted that he had two strapping grandsons, when Thea and Michael had seen him on their honeymoon last summer.

'Here,' Thea said, coming back to where Romy was carefully putting the album away. 'I've got a present for you. I've been meaning to give it to you, but now feels like the right time.'

'What's this?' Romy asked. She took it and opened the bow, then pulled out the cushion embroidered with the words 'Sisters make the best of friends'. Thea felt a rush of emotion as Romy held it tight against her chest. And as Romy opened her arms to embrace her, Thea knew that everything she'd once dreamt a sister might be had come true.

*   *   *

The next morning Romy woke up in the bed next to Thea. As she opened her eyes and looked at Thea's sleeping face, Romy realized she hadn't dreamt. Of anything. Of being chased. Of Lemcke. Of losing Alfonso. In fact, she thought, as she stretched, it had probably been the best night's sleep of her life.

She got up and washed her face and looked at herself in the bathroom mirror.

She'd talked late into the night with Thea, as the idea for the Anaka Foundation had taken shape. And now, in the cold light of day, Romy felt more certain than ever that it was the right thing to do.

Thea would help Romy finance it, but together they were going to find a way to help all those girls Solya had abused. Even ones like Claudia. It was a huge idea, but a challenge that Romy was already relishing—how she'd track them all down, and how she'd help other girls too, girls who were out there right now, lost and alone. Romy knew in her heart it was what she had to do. What she'd always known she must do.

She wondered what Lars would say when she told him. Now it was Thea's words she

543

remembered—the last thing she'd said before they'd fallen asleep just before dawn, 'Go for it with Lars. You have nothing to be afraid of.'

Romy smiled at herself in the mirror, feeling butterflies in her stomach. She couldn't wait to see Lars and Alfie and Gretchen walk off that train. They were going to see the sights in London, and then take the camper van on a long holiday through Europe. Romy only wished Thea could come too. But she needed to get back to America and Michael. Still, they'd be together again soon. Of that Romy had no doubt.

Romy and Thea had breakfast together, laughing at the small quirks they delighted in noticing about each other—how they were both left-handed, how they both took their coffee black with half a teaspoon of sugar. Romy couldn't get enough of her sister and her stories. She wanted to know everything. They were still talking as they both took a black cab to Waterloo Station.

'How are we doing for time?' Thea asked, as she paid the cab driver.

Romy looked at her watch. 'Any minute now.'

Thea smiled. 'You're excited, aren't you? I am too. I spoke to Michael earlier. He sends his love. He says he wishes he was here.'

They walked together into the cavernous arrivals hall.

'Wow. I haven't been here for years,' Thea said. 'It's certainly changed.'

Romy stared up at the high glass ceiling. 'I came here once. One night.' *One of the worst of my life*, Romy now remembered. 'I'd just arrived in London, and I was so desperate. I had nothing and I was completely alone.'

'The last time I came,' Thea said with a rueful smile, 'I was going on a school trip to the theatre. I was fat and lonely, and had had my head screwed up by Brett. I remember coming out of the Tube and giving a girl some money, and that's how I got talking to Bridget Lawson. You remember I told you about Bridget, Tom's sister? And Shelley, their mom?'

Romy stared at Thea as she continued talking, remembering how the girl in the red coat had appeared like an angel. And as the sun shone down today through the terminal roof, catching Thea's blonde hair, Romy experienced a sudden moment of perfect stillness. As if life had been paused, suspended—and all the commuters, all the travellers and the coffee-vendors, had become freeze-framed.

And she knew in that moment, with absolute certainty, that the girl in the red coat had been Thea. That their sacred, golden thread of sisterhood had connected them across the years— their fates bound together, unbroken by continents and time.

'Here they come,' Thea said, pointing to the arrivals board. She smiled at Romy. 'What?' she asked, noticing her strange expression.

'Nothing . . . just . . . thank you,' Romy said. Then, linking arms together, they walked into the crowd.